Praise for *The Last Debutantes* and Georgie Blalock

"Storm clouds hover over high society on the brink of war, tarnishing the glamour of the Season in this wonderfully told story of love, war, and friendship."

—Bryn Turnbull, author of *The Woman Before Wallis*

"As the world teeters on the precipice of war, a glittering group of debutantes try to hold on to life as they know it, even as they know everything is about to change. A perfect *Downton Abbey*-esque story to get swept away in!"

—Stephanie Marie Thornton, *USA Today* bestselling author of *And They Called It Camelot*

"A fascinating portrayal of London high society overshadowed by the threat of World War II, Georgie Blalock's *The Last Debutantes* follows Valerie de Vere Cole, niece of British prime minister Neville Chamberlain, as she navigates the perilous waters of the London Season, guarding a dreadful secret that will surely spell ruin if it gets out. Beneath society's sparkle lurks pain and betrayal, and Valerie's courage and empathy bring nuanced understanding to these privileged but damaged souls. Atmospheric, moving, and compelling, *The Last Debutantes* is a must-read!"

—Christine Wells, author of *Sisters of the Resistance*

"An exciting and compelling view inside the glamorous lives of debutantes coming out in the 1930s before World War II put a hold on society soirees. Georgie Blalock brings to life not only the glitz of the aristocracy but the sometimes ugly gossip behind the scenes in this fascinating tale of family, friendship, betrayal, and survival."

—Eliza Knight, *USA Today* bestselling
author of *The Mayfair Bookshop*

"Rich with historical detail, *The Last Debutantes* is an immersive read about the final season of house parties and champagne fountains before the war. Young, headstrong Valerie de Vere Cole must navigate a labyrinth of political and domestic dangers as she struggles to define herself in a society about to change forever. A must for fans of *Downton Abbey* and *The Crown*!"

—Kerri Maher, author of *The Girl in White Gloves*

"*The Last Debutantes* by Georgie Blalock gives us a glimpse into a social season that will be unlike all of the others that came before it. Valerie de Vere Cole may be the prime minister's daughter, but she has family secrets to hide—will her fellow debutantes prove themselves to be friend or foe? A story about friendship and finding yourself in a world that is about to change irrevocably, *The Last Debutantes* will appeal to historical fiction lovers."

—Brenda Janowitz, author of *The Grace Kelly Dress*

The LAST DEBUTANTES

Also by Georgie Blalock

The Other Windsor Girl

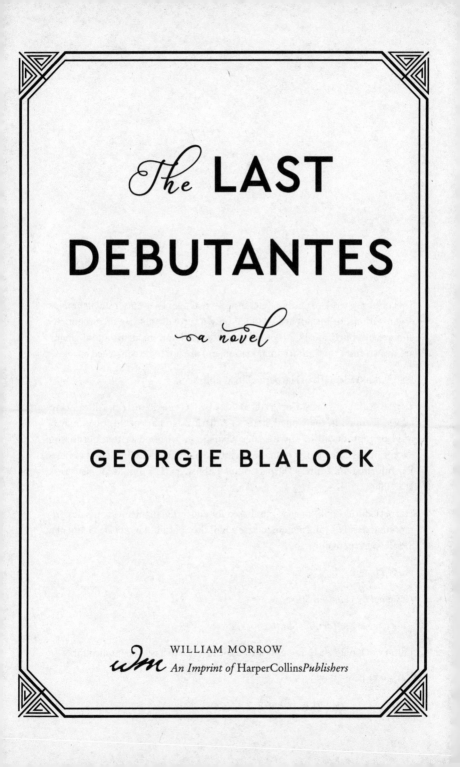

The LAST DEBUTANTES

a novel

GEORGIE BLALOCK

WILLIAM MORROW
An Imprint of HarperCollins*Publishers*

P.S.™ is a trademark of HarperCollins Publishers.

HarperCollins books may be purchased for educational, business, or sales promotional use. For information, please email the Special Markets Department at SPsales@harpercollins.com.

FIRST EDITION

Designed by Diahann Sturge

Title page art © Tartila / Shutterstock, Inc.

Library of Congress Cataloging-in-Publication Data has been applied for.

ISBN 978-0-06-300929-5

21 22 23 24 25   BRR   10 9 8 7 6 5 4 3 2 1

To my Anne. I love you to the moon and back.

The LAST DEBUTANTES

Chapter One

M iss Valerie de Vere Cole presented by Mrs. Neville Chamberlain," Lord Clarendon, the Lord Chamberlain, announced in his baritone voice. The Life Guards Band continued playing in the Buckingham Palace ballroom but the conversation beneath the music stilled. Hundreds of debutantes in their white court dresses with the required eighteen-inch train watched from the red velvet benches against the gilded walls. Their matron sponsors were perched beside them in a cluster of family tiaras and Molyneux dresses waiting for Prime Minister Neville Chamberlain's niece to curtsey to the monarchs.

After four weeks of curtsey lessons and dress fittings, the moment was finally here, and Valerie couldn't move.

Lord Clarendon cleared his throat, the gold oak leaf embroidery on his blue coat as crisp as his glare when Valerie didn't step forward. Gentlemen in military uniforms mingled behind the line of Gentlemen at Arms standing guard in the center of the room and whispered to one another about the pause. Valerie had interrupted the seamless procession of debutantes and everyone had noticed. She still couldn't make her feet move.

Why the devil did I decide to do this? I don't belong here. She wore the required Prince of Wales ostrich-feather headdress and a demure strand of pearls like the other girls but she wasn't one of them. Her late father, Horace de Vere Cole, had seen to that. If she stepped in front of this crowd someone was sure to announce that she didn't belong. Behind her, the court page in his red and gold Buckingham Palace livery fussed with Valerie's train, kind enough to pretend it was the dress, and not Valerie's nerves, failing her. She gave the page a wan smile of appreciation. This was no time to fall to pieces, but still she couldn't do anything except wonder how fast she could run from this deep in the palace to the car. She'd be the talk of the town then. The debutante who fled. Good heavens.

The flick of a green-feathered fan on the far side of the red carpet caught her attention. Her aunt, Anne Chamberlain, stood beside a gaudy Victorian candelabra, the light from it shimmering in the gold brocade of her gown and the facets of her emerald necklace. Even while Mary, Princess Royal, in her fringe tiara scowled to shriveled old Princess Louise, Queen Victoria's aged daughter, Aunt Anne remained as unruffled by the hiccup as she had been by the long wait in the Rolls-Royce in the Mall. She simply smiled and with a serene nod motioned Valerie forward.

Valerie eased her tight grip on her rose bouquet. She couldn't embarrass the one person who'd done so much for her, not in front of all these titled ladies and cabinet ministers' wives.

Valerie took a deep breath and, with the graceful stride she'd practiced in the corridors of No. 10 Downing Street, glided toward the monarchs. If anyone booed or hissed, she'd endure it as she had every insult and depredation flung at her during her eighteen years. She had no choice.

The satin skirt beneath her white tulle-and-silver-trimmed dress swayed with her stride as she crossed the red carpet. Above her, the crystal chandeliers illuminated the massive tapestries set into the walls and the statues in the arch above the royal canopy. The carpet seemed to go on forever until Valerie finally reached the gold crown embroidered in it, her cue to stop and face the sovereigns.

King George VI and Queen Elizabeth sat on high-backed thrones set out from the crimson canopy of state. They were surrounded by the Duke and Duchess of Gloucester, the Duke and Duchess of Kent, and various other royals and court officials in military uniforms and court dress. The King wore a gray-blue RAF uniform with a large gold braid across one side of his slender chest and a line of medals on the other that barely moved when he nodded for Valerie to continue. She imagined his neck would be quite stiff tomorrow from so much motioning. It didn't matter. Reaching Their Majesties was the first part of the ritual. The most difficult maneuver was yet to come.

With the subtle flourish instilled in her during curtsey lessons at Miss Vacani's dance school, Valerie swept one leg behind her and lowered herself into the required pose. She held it for three beats, back straight, head down, legs shaking with the strain of staying steady. She'd thought bobbing up and down with an old curtain for a train ridiculous but she thanked heaven tonight for the tutoring. Stumbling through dance steps at a ball was one thing. Falling on her face in front of the throne was quite another. She had enough to contend with without having to recover from that sort of humiliation.

She straightened and raised her face to meet the King's. He smiled warmly, making the shadows beneath his sharp cheeks and the lines at the corners of his tired blue eyes deepen. Valerie's chest tightened. His Majesty resembled her father the last time she'd seen him.

I can't think of that now. Her moment before the throne was only halfway through.

Valerie gracefully kicked her train out of the way and took three steps sideways to place herself in front of the Queen. Queen Elizabeth sat resplendent in a white duchess satin gown dusted with diamantés that sparkled as bright as her diamond-and-ruby parure. A massive red train trimmed in ermine cascaded from her shoulders and pooled at her feet. Her presence was as magical as the King's was regal, and when she smiled, her expression softened the way Aunt Anne's did whenever the two of them sat for a good chat.

Down Valerie went again, legs bent, head tilted, before she rose and took three careful steps backward to avoid catching her heel on the hem. She turned and walked to Aunt Anne while the Lord Chamberlain called out, "Lady Harlech presenting the Honorable Katherine Ormsby-Gore."

"Well done, my dear." Aunt Anne enveloped her in a congratu-latory hug, surrounding her with the heady scent of Shocking by Schiaparelli. The perfume was the single shocking thing about Aunt Anne, and Valerie inhaled the bracing notes of jasmine and clove before they faded.

THE MASS OF debutantes and their sponsors crowded down the long Picture Gallery toward the State Rooms, passing the stern-faced Yeomen of the Guard stationed along the walls. The second court presentation of 1939 was over, and the girls would spend the first hours of their debutante Season enjoying a champagne supper.

"It's all so grand," Valerie gushed as she and Aunt Anne passed the massive Van Dyck portrait of King Charles I astride his white horse. Most of the girls walked together in small groups, their os-trich feathers fluttering as they turned to take in the palace. They'd met during the many preseason winter teas and lunches, renew-ing acquaintanceships and forging friendships as the matrons had compared calendars and claimed dates for balls, cocktail parties, and dinners. A nasty bout of flu had kept Valerie from participat-ing in those social events, leaving Aunt Anne the only person she knew here.

"It is impressive." Aunt Anne didn't seem quite as awed by their surroundings, perhaps because she'd been to the palace many times with Uncle Neville.

They followed the flow of guests into the State Rooms, where large tables were laid out with sandwiches and tarts from Lyon's Tea Shop. Beneath paintings of King George IV and other Hanoverians, Valerie stepped into line behind Aunt Anne and selected one of the gold-rimmed plates emblazoned with the King's coat of arms. It'd been hours since she'd last eaten, too distracted by the manicurist, the hairdresser, and the makeup woman to think about food. She helped herself to the treats arranged on elaborate Victorian silver platters and sighed at the rich butter and fresh cucumbers between the fine white bread. It was hard to believe the girl who'd once endured stale baguettes at a French convent school was eating off of Buckingham Palace china.

When they'd had their fill, Aunt Anne handed their plates to a footman and surveyed the room. "Are you ready to make some new acquaintances?"

No, but she couldn't very well slip home either. She was the Prime Minister's niece, not some obscure country girl, and she was expected to do the rounds. It was what she anticipated from others that made her hesitate, but she had to trust Aunt Anne. If she thought Valerie would be a dismal social failure, she'd have left her at West Woodhay House with Great-Aunt Lillian instead of spending hours and pounds training her up in London. Heaven help her, if she wanted to make friends and have a successful Season, she must meet people. "I'm ready."

"Come along, then."

Valerie followed Aunt Anne into the adjoining Blue Drawing Room, careful not to collide with anyone while marveling at the tall pillars reaching up to the gilded ceiling. Large pier glasses caught the light of the crystal chandeliers and made the gold-framed portraits and wall fixtures shine. She couldn't see the sides of the room through the crush and she wasn't about to jump up and down like a rabbit to get a better view. She'd made enough of a spectacle of herself in the throne room without bouncing around like a country rube.

She nearly bumped into her aunt when she stopped before a stout matron and her dark-haired daughter. They stood at one of the massive windows overlooking the dark palace garden, the lights of London visible beyond the thick line of trees at the far end.

"Good evening, Lady Ashcombe," Aunt Anne greeted. "May I introduce my niece, Miss Valerie de Vere Cole?"

Valerie smiled, determined to make a go of her first introduction.

"Your brother's daughter, I presume?" Lady Ashcombe looked down over her prominent cheekbones at Valerie. "I hope you don't intend to follow in his outlandish footsteps."

Valerie wanted to melt into the floor, but all she could do was keep smiling like a brainless china doll. She'd hoped that after all these years no one would remember Father and all his ridiculous hoaxes. She was wrong. "No, Lady Ashcombe, I don't."

"Good. A young woman must guard herself and her future from the more disreputable aspects of her family tree." She glared at her dark-haired daughter, who turned away to roll her eyes. Then Lady Ashcombe fixed on Aunt Anne. "How is your dear brother these days? Still up to his old antics?"

"Horace died a year ago in France. He's buried at West Woodhay House," Aunt Anne stated with more grace than Valerie could've mustered after that thoughtless comment.

"My condolences, of course." Lady Ashcombe had the good sense to blush beneath her makeup, laying one hand on her crystal-beaded blue silk bust. "After everything he'd done, I thought his obituary another of his practical jokes."

"It was quite serious, especially to him."

"Of course." Her tiara, in desperate need of a polish, struggled to catch the light as she motioned to her daughter. "Allow me to present the Honorable Miss Rosalind Cubitt."

"A pleasure, I'm sure." Rosalind was more engrossed in the doings of the other debutantes than in Valerie. She was thin but not slender and shared her mother's high cheekbones and soft, rounded chin. She wore a full-skirted dress with a wide neckline that displayed her shoulders, which slumped in boredom. Then something caught her eye and she jerked up straight. "Mother, there's Priscilla and the others. Let's do go visit them."

"Of course. I must cajole Lady Esher into sharing her list of gentlemen. It's so hard to come by suitable young men these days, especially with all this nasty business in Europe, but we must do our best. Can't have our protégés sitting out dances, can we?"

"Not at all. Good evening to you both." Aunt Anne drew the dyed green feathers of her fan through her fingers as the ladies left to join the birdlike Lady Esher and her rail-thin daughter.

"Perhaps that explains why so few people attended Horace's funeral."

"They'd given up on him long before that." Valerie sighed. His stories of digging up Piccadilly, dumping manure in the Piazza San Marco in Venice, or posing with his Bloomsbury Circle friends as the Emperor of Abyssinia to receive honors aboard the HMS *Dreadnought* had once made her laugh. They hadn't been so amusing when the bills had outgrown his dwindling income and he'd fled to France. Not one of his old friends, not even Virginia Woolf, who'd been involved in many of the pranks along with her brother Adrian, had bothered to write. They'd distanced themselves from Father. With Father's last name firmly affixed to her, Valerie didn't enjoy that luxury.

"There's Lady Fallington and her daughter, Lady Windon." Aunt Anne waved to two women, who offered limp waves in return. "Her daughter married the Earl of Windon last winter and was presented to announce her new title. Lady Fallington's son is a few years older than you and someone you'd do well to know. You're sure to see him at dances."

Valerie doubted the ladies were interested in making her acquaintance but she dutifully followed Aunt Anne to the tall woman with the curving tiara artfully set in her blond curls. Lady Fallington wore a slimming dress of rose silk with voile sleeves, a blush to her daughter's white silk court dress. A stunning set of pink tourmalines encircled her wrist and neck, their color perfectly complementing her gown.

"Lady Fallington, Lady Windon, what a pleasure to see you tonight," Aunt Anne greeted, then introduced Valerie.

"A pleasure," Lady Fallington drawled, as stiff as a Greek marble statue in her draping silk gown. "Your father was the one who humiliated my cousin, the mayor of Cambridge, by pretending to be the Emperor of something or other and tricking him into very publicly feting him, wasn't he?"

Father had pretended to be the Sultan of Zanzibar's uncle and his friends his official retinue, but that little detail hardly mattered. "Yes, that was my father." *The thoughtless fool.*

"I see. Congratulations on your presentation. If you'll excuse us." Lady Fallington turned to reveal the scooped back of her dress as she and the newly minted Countess of Windon strolled away.

If every introduction went like the last two, it was going to be a long and lonely Season. "Perhaps it's time to go home."

"A bit of a stumble at the start, but that's no reason to give up. There are many others to meet."

"Most of whom think I shouldn't be here."

"Nonsense, you have more reason to be in society than any of those jumped-up girls Lady Clancarty is paid to sponsor. You're the granddaughter of a baronet, the great-grandniece of the Earl of Oxford. It's an Irish title but an old and impressive one all the same. That's no shabby pedigree."

"I'm also the daughter of the Sultan of Zanzibar and the Emperor of Abyssinia." Curse Father for those two ridiculous hoaxes and their awful legacy. They'd been fodder for the newspapers and society back before the Great War but they'd left a taint on her, and a few out-of-joint noses. Even after he was gone, it was still her having to pay for his failings. "That's nothing to brag about, as Lady Aschombe and Lady Fallington were polite enough to remind me."

"Chin up, my dear. Lineage trumps everything. Lady Ashcombe and Miss Cubitt are proof of that." Aunt Anne straightened Valerie's pearl necklace. "If the daughter and granddaughter of Mrs. Keppell can find a place in society, then so can you."

"Mrs. Keppell? King Edward VII's mistress!" People turned to look at Valerie as if she'd broken one of the royal plates. Her cheeks burned at having been so indelicate, and in Buckingham Palace, of all places.

"The very one. There's Lady Astor and her niece. I'm sure they'll adore you."

Valerie had her doubts but once again followed her aunt, bracing for another scolding about Father, followed by a view of a peeress's backside.

"Anne, I hope you don't intend to barrage me with your husband's plans for handling this latest debacle in Europe." Lady Astor's English accent was tainted by the faint twang of her Virginia roots. She stood erect, twisting the long strand of pearls draping the front of her pale peach gown around her slender fingers. She was tall, with a long face made more pronounced by the high peaks of the Astor tiara with the large Sancy diamond set in the center. Beside her stood a dark-blond-haired girl with a sleek pageboy that curled in toward her similarly long face.

"That's not for me to say, but I'm sure you'll hear about it after the cabinet meeting tomorrow. I'd like to introduce you to my niece, and for her to meet yours. Miss Valerie de Vere Cole."

"My niece, the Honorable Dinah Brand."

Valerie waited for one of them to mention her father. *Fish it. I'll do it for them.* "I'm the Emperor of Abyssinia's daughter."

She waited for the pearl-clutching to commence. Dinah's eyes lit up instead. "Smashing! I absolutely must introduce you to the others."

That was certainly a change from the last two introductions.

"How good of you to amuse her. Anne, we must discuss this cabinet meeting. I hate to walk into a room cold." Lady Astor drew Aunt Anne aside, barely pausing between words as she told Aunt Anne exactly what she thought Uncle Neville should do about the German invasion of Czechoslovakia that had dominated every newspaper headline this morning.

"So you're the debutante in Downing Street. Awfully grand to be in the middle of things, isn't it?" Dinah took Valerie by the elbow and pulled her through the throng of women. "Aunt Nancy's house is always full of government types but the papers can be so beastly, writing all sorts of nasty things about them. The palace is marvelous, it makes you really want something special to remember it by, doesn't it?"

"We're visiting Lenare's Photography Studio afterward to take my picture." All the fashionable portrait studios remained open late on presentation nights to accommodate the extra demand for photographs. "There wasn't time for a sitting this afternoon."

"I'm having mine done at Wrightson's later, but I want something more than a boring old photo." She stopped near a Georgian table loaded with discarded plates and slid a dessert fork off the top one. A wicked smile turned up the corners of her lips, which were tinted with a faint sweep of pale pink lipstick. "A more unique souvenir."

"You can't!"

"Why not? Unity Mitford stole a heap of palace stationery at her presentation and then sent letters on it to everyone."

"Before she ran off to worship Herr Hitler."

"My point exactly. A fork is far more patriotic." She opened the bodice of her dress, ready to drop the fork down it, when Valerie grabbed her hand.

"You can't. The Yeomen of the Guard are watching." They stood around the perimeter of the room, their scarlet coats a stark contrast to the pale evening gowns and pastel palace decor.

"They're so bored they're practically asleep. They won't notice a thing."

They probably wouldn't. Their eyes were glazed over and it was a wonder they hadn't slumped to the floor to nap. Valerie let go of Dinah's hand and Dinah shoved the fork down the front of her bodice so fast, Valerie might have blinked and missed it. She hoped no one else had seen it. She didn't want to be escorted out of the palace for abetting a thief. People would certainly comment then that the apple hadn't fallen far from her father's tree.

"You should get one too," Dinah said.

"No."

"Come off it, with a father like yours you can't be against a touch of harmless fun."

"You'd be surprised."

"My cousin Phyllis says the only way to truly enjoy the Season is to be a little daring. Otherwise it's simply dancing and teas and no chance to stand out at all. Go on. I won't tell a soul."

Dinah pushed her toward the pile of abandoned plates and forks and Valerie stared at the mound of half-eaten tarts and scattered cutlery. She shouldn't risk her already precarious reputation for a bit of royal tat, but Dinah hadn't turned up her nose at Valerie. She wasn't about to thank her by landing her in a heap of trouble or acting the prude. She'd had enough of being snubbed. If the cost of acceptance was a dessert fork, then so be it.

Glancing around to make sure no one was watching, Valerie snatched up a fork and stuffed it in her purse. Dinah's smile of triumph was worth the weight of the flatware sitting on her conscience.

"Did you do it? Did you get some paper?" A dark-haired girl with round cheeks and a slight Scottish burr rushed up to Dinah's side.

"We nicked something better. Show them, Valerie."

"I thought you weren't going to tell a soul."

"This is Christian Grant, you can trust her, and I'd show her mine but I can hardly reach it." Dinah patted the silk bodice of her dress. "Go on. She won't rat us out."

"I won't." Anticipation brightened Christian's dark brown eyes.

Oh well, in for a penny, in for a pound. Valerie opened her purse wide enough to give Christian a peek inside.

"How marvelous. I wish I'd thought of that. Where's Katherine?"

"Here I am." A girl with round cheeks and prominent teeth pushed in between Dinah and Christian. "What did I miss?"

"Dinah and the PM's niece stole some dessert forks," Christian whispered.

"Well done. Katherine Ormsby-Gore." The new girl held out a gloved hand to Valerie, her throaty voice muted by a very proper accent that pulled down the end of every word. "What else do you think we can get?"

"My purse is big enough to fit a teacup." Christian held up a drawstring bag made from the same embroidered brocade as her gown.

"Then let's try for one of those." Katherine adjusted the ostrich feathers set at a tilt in her caramel-colored hair.

"What do you say, Valerie? Should we do it?" Dinah asked.

The girls turned to Valerie as if this escapade were her idea. How she'd become the ringleader she didn't know, but it was preferable to being an outcast. "Definitely, and by the end of tonight maybe we'll have an entire tea set."

This was the most fun she'd had since coming to London.

Chapter Two

Aunt Anne peered over her spectacles as Valerie stumbled into No. 10's small dining room. She sat at the head of the oval table, the red dispatch box with *Prince Arthur* engraved in gold on the top in front of her. She'd inherited the box from her father, and inside, her correspondence was as neatly organized as her graying dark blond hair was perfectly waved. Her father had been the Duke of Connaught's, Queen Victoria's third son's, comptroller, and the box was one of the many gifts he'd received for his faithful service. "You're up early this morning."

"The Horse Guards woke me." It'd been well after midnight when they'd left Buckingham Palace, and past two before they'd finally arrived home from Lenare's Photography Studio. She wished she looked as well put together as her aunt did this morning. Her aunt wore a tailored morning dress of red roses set off by a strand of milky pearls. Valerie's yellow polka-dot day dress with the hastily tied sash was wrinkled and her black curls had been forced into a loose chignon after a good fight with the hairbrush.

"What news of the Premier, Miss Leaf?" Aunt Anne motioned for Mr. Dobson, the barrel-chested butler, to pour more coffee while she flipped through the *Daily Mirror*.

"The *Observer* supports Mr. Eden's calls to form a new government," Miss Leaf, Aunt Anne's willowy social secretary, said. She sat at a narrow side table in an impeccable gray suit, her tight blond curls pinned up high on her head. She read aloud the many harsh comments from Mr. Eden about Uncle Neville, making them wince.

"After everything Uncle Neville did for Mr. Eden, to have him turn on him like that is perfectly dreadful." Valerie scooped eggs and ham from the silver chafing dishes on the sideboard onto her plate. The tart scent of both mingled with the beeswax wood polish used to make the oak-paneled walls gleam. In the window alcove above the fireplace, the bust of Sir Isaac Newton watched the ladies with an impassive marble air. "Why does Lord Astor allow something so awful to be printed in his paper? I thought he supported Uncle Neville."

She sat at the table, thanking Mr. Dobson for the cup of coffee he set beside her.

"He does, but he's afraid people won't trust the *Times* or the *Observer* if he puts undue pressure on his editors. It allows his reporters to run amok. At least the articles on the presentation are marvelous. Add these to the book, please, Miss Leaf." Aunt Anne handed the *Daily Mirror* to Miss Leaf, who, besides reading out the horrors of the editorial page, had been tasked with clipping and pasting articles into the large scrapbook of Valerie's Season.

My Season. Despite the auspicious start, last night had been jolly good fun. She expected more of the same at today's Queen Charlotte's Birthday Ball luncheon, especially with Dinah and the others there. No eating alone for her, not this time, maybe not ever again.

Aunt Anne selected the *Times* from the newspapers fanned out on the table in front of her, including the society ones such as *Bystander* and the *Tatler*.

"I'm surprised they printed anything at all about it, considering the news from Europe." Valerie tugged the *West London Observer* out of the pile and read the large advertisement at the bottom calling for women to join the London Volunteer Ambulance Service, warning that if the bombs began to fall, their driving skills would be needed. What a dreadful thought.

"People enjoy a little distraction from their troubles." Aunt Anne leisurely thumbed through the *Times*. "It makes life bearable."

Didn't Valerie know it? She'd lost count of how many books in the Saint-Jean-de-Luz library she'd escaped into during her six years with Father in France.

"Besides, if the papers didn't print the presentation, they'd have the matrons of Mayfair to contend with, as the *Times* will soon discover. Not a word in here about last night, only stories about the German invasion of Czechoslovakia. Poor Lord Astor, this simply isn't his morning." Aunt Anne flipped the offending paper closed and laid it off to one side, choosing the *Sketch* next.

Valerie sipped her coffee, the charred taste of burnt beans making her blanch. "Mrs. Bell over-roasted the coffee again."

"Nonsense, her preparation adds robustness. I've had a number of compliments on it."

Valerie bit her tongue about the *compliment* she'd overheard downstairs when Mr. Colville had grumbled that Uncle Neville never invited the staff to dine with him. The newly hired second secretary had been told by Mr. Rucker and Mr. Seyer, the senior private secretaries, to be thankful. Aunt Anne was a fine hostess who could employ the government chef to distinction, but she wasn't known for keeping a capable family cook.

"Here's a lovely picture of you and some of the other debutantes." Aunt Anne handed Valerie the *Sketch*.

Across the page were arranged portraits of Eunice Kennedy, the daughter of the American Ambassador; the Honorable Vivien Mosley; the Honorable Rosalind Cubitt; Lady Margaret Boyle, daughter of the Earl of Suffolk; and Lady Anne Fitzroy, the Duke of Grafton's daughter. In the center of the layout was Valerie in the green satin dress she'd worn for her official debutante portrait taken at the beginning of the month. Beneath each picture was a glowing description of each girl and her family. Valerie read it, expecting another mention of Father's ridiculous old pranks, as if people needed reminding, but it wasn't there. They simply stated her lineage, her relation to the Chamberlains, naming her Aunt Anne's protégée and praising her as "a beauty who does the Prime Minister proud."

"What utter tosh," she said with a laugh. "It's worse than Father's old poetry."

"Don't dismiss it, my dear. You deserve the compliment." Pride brightened Aunt Anne's blue eyes and sobered Valerie. This was more than she'd ever seen in Father's similarly hooded eyes or the Mother Superior's haggard face. "You've already received an impressive number of invitations."

She motioned to Miss Leaf, who handed Valerie a thick stack of envelopes.

Valerie sifted through them, boggled by the many names written in fine calligraphy. She recognized most of them from the hours spent studying *Debrett's Peerage* with Great-Aunt Lillian at West Woodhay House during the last six months. She'd been sent there to recover her health after France. With everything happening in Germany and the Munich Agreement, Aunt Anne had been forced to remain with Uncle Neville in London. Great-Aunt Lillian had been more Victorian-stern than Mother Superior–hard, and had been quite dismayed by Valerie's lack of a proper English education. Having dismissed Valerie's experiences in France as something best forgotten, she'd launched into a rigorous training program, her pursed lips and exasperated sighs when Valerie had said Leveson-Gower instead of properly pronouncing it *Looson-Gore* as cutting as the Mother Superior's switch. Valerie's father had once rubbed elbows with these families but she'd certainly never met them. That was going to change this Season. After years of social exile, she'd find a proper place in society, make friends, and build a new life in London, even if she had no idea what that life might eventually look like. "What encouraged all of these?"

"The articles in the society pages and your current residence. People are curious. That's to your advantage."

One of the few she enjoyed, but even that hadn't made a difference to Lady Ashcombe or Lady Windon last night. Whether it would change enough minds over the next four months to secure Valerie some sort of respectable station remained to be seen.

Aunt Anne slid the stack out of Valerie's hands. "We'll decide which ones to accept and decline later. You'll have a full calendar this Season."

"Good morning, Mother, Valerie." Cousin Dorothy swept into the room and enveloped Valerie in a flowery, Mille Fleurs–perfumed hug before taking the chair across the table. Her nose was long and sharp like Uncle Neville's, and she had his dark eyes, but the soft shape of her face was Aunt Anne. She was ten years older than Valerie but her dour hairstyle and clothes made her appear older. A better hairdresser and seamstress would do her a world of good, but, unlike Dorothy during the court dress fittings, Valerie kept her opinion about people's fashion choices to herself. "I saw your picture in the *Daily Herald*. You looked marvelous."

"I haven't seen that one yet." Aunt Anne riffled through the papers.

Dorothy found it first, opening it to the center and folding it back before handing it to her mother. "That wasn't the only item of interest. Did you know about this?"

Aunt Anne's perfectly arched eyebrows rose. "I did not."

"It isn't about my hesitation, is it?" Most newspapers could be counted on to flatter society, but some were more cutting. One usually had to read between the lines to find the insults, but they were there.

"What hesitation?" Dorothy demanded, as if Valerie had spit on the royal carpet.

"Valerie's train caught on her heel, it was nothing," Aunt Anne dismissed.

"This isn't nothing." Dorothy took the paper from her mother and handed it to Valerie.

Neither of them needed to point out what'd caught their notice. At the bottom of the page was a black-and-white photo of Valerie's twenty-eight-year-old stepmother, Mavis, hanging on the arm of her new husband, Mr. R. E. Mortimer Wheeler. The caption identified him as the Honorary Director of the London Museum, and, given his picture, he was as old as his antiquities. The tart certainly appeared young and spry. Her hair was better curled and much lighter than the last time Valerie had seen her storming out of the Hotel Etchola in Ascain with her ratty suitcase.

"What will people say when they see that?" Dorothy pulled off her gloves with quick jerks and laid them on the table. "Mr. Wheeler is hardly a persona non grata."

"He's a distinguished archaeologist charged with evacuating the London Museum should German bombing become a threat," Aunt Anne explained to Valerie.

"How does that scheming witch always find some notable old man to make her respectable?" Valerie flung the paper on the table. "I wonder if she'll foist her lover's bastard off on him the way she tried to do with Father."

"Valerie!" Dorothy tugged at the knot of her scarf while Mr. Dobson set down her coffee. "Didn't you hear anything I told you about minding your tongue?"

"I did. I also heard Father wailing at Mavis's feet to not leave him. He was so thrilled when she returned, you'd think Mary of

Lourdes had appeared instead of that knocked-up tart." He hadn't been that excited when he'd met Valerie at the train station after summoning her from the drafty Cambridge dame school to join him and Mavis in France. She'd been banished to that scholarly inept Cambridge boarding school at five, Father only visiting once or twice in all those years before summoning her to live with him and Mavis in France when she was twelve. She thought he'd finally wanted her. All he'd wanted was to save money on her Cambridge school fees, another outstanding bill Uncle Neville had been obliged to settle after he'd died. Valerie had begged to be allowed to live with Aunt Anne, but Father had refused, unable to admit to yet another failure in a lifetime full of them. He'd rather Valerie suffer with him in poverty than swallow his pride and ask for help. *The bastard.* "Besides, it's only us, and we all know Mavis was involved with that painter. At least Augustus John had the good sense not to marry her. Why, even Miss Leaf has heard the story."

Miss Leaf glanced up, about to agree, then thought better of it and returned to clipping articles.

"Whatever people may or may not know, if you don't mind what you say in front of us you'll forget yourself with others," Dorothy huffed. "We've worked very hard to give you the advantages your father wasted. Don't ruin it by acting the fishwife. No one wants to associate with crass young ladies and they certainly don't want their daughters or sons befriending them either. You'll find yourself quite the outcast if you carry on like this."

She thought of the Buckingham Palace fork hidden in her desk upstairs. The girls hadn't given a fig about Valerie's past, thinking

Father a riot and Valerie a good sport. How long after their parents read about Mavis would they warn their daughters off her? She didn't relish walking into the Queen Charlotte's Birthday Ball luncheon and having them snub her the way Rosalind Cubitt had. Everything was on the verge of changing for Valerie, and Mavis was going to bitch it up.

"You must be careful. Wouldn't you agree, Mother?"

Aunt Anne watched them with her usual unshakable poise. Valerie didn't give two pence about Dorothy's opinion but she very much minded Aunt Anne's. It's why she hadn't told her everything about France. She couldn't bear to have her look at Valerie with the same horror Dorothy flung at her.

"I trust Valerie knows how to conduct herself in proper company."

Valerie let out a long breath. At least someone believed in her, even if she wasn't certain she deserved it.

"Of course. You know best." Dorothy dropped a sugar cube into her coffee and stirred it with a fury. "What are we to say when people ask about Valerie's time in France? The Hotel Etchola is hardly a finishing school, and someone is sure to mention it once they see this wedding announcement."

"We'll say what we've always said, that Valerie lived with my brother in Ascain, where she perfected her French while he recovered his health. With so many young ladies venturing to France or Germany for a continental polish, I doubt anyone will think twice about it."

"But what happens if Valerie reveals the true depths of her French *polish* by forgetting herself?"

Valerie was about to forget her polish by telling Dorothy that her double-breasted coat made her look fat, but she bit her tongue, refusing to prove she couldn't mind her words in polite company. She also hated to admit, even to herself, that Dorothy's low opinion wasn't too far off the mark. It wasn't her fault. It was Father's and Mavis's. *The bitch.* Why couldn't her stepmother have stayed under whatever rock she'd crawled beneath after Valerie's supposed half brother Tristan's birth? Instead she'd chosen now of all times to flaunt her new marriage, as if the last one hadn't been a disaster and an endless source of drawing room tittle-tattle. The reporter hadn't failed to mention Mavis's connection to the Chamberlains and Valerie. She was surprised people hadn't brought that up last night along with all their fond memories of Father's pranks.

"If Vivien Mosley can come out with little more than a sideways glance or two, then we have nothing to fear." Aunt Anne banged the stack of invitations against the table and handed them to Miss Leaf.

Dorothy flicked drops of coffee off her spoon and laid it in the saucer. "A few old hoaxes do pale in comparison to Vivien's father and his British Union of Fascists starting a riot in the East End."

At least Valerie didn't have to live that down on top of her many other real and imagined sins. "May I be excused?" She'd had enough of her cousin's fretting for one day.

"Of course. Try and get some rest before the luncheon," Aunt Anne encouraged.

Valerie slid the *Daily Herald* off the table and left, but Dorothy's voice made her pause outside the door.

"Extra etiquette lessons might be in order, especially before the

King and Queen come to dine. We don't want Valerie to embarrass us in front of such esteemed guests."

"Don't be too hard on her. She's doing her best and still has a great deal to learn, far more than you did at her age. She hasn't enjoyed your advantages."

Valerie didn't wait for Dorothy's response but stormed into the Pillared Drawing Room, pausing in the center to look at the photograph of Mavis. What Father had seen in that scullery maid's daughter she didn't know, but if her picture could send Dorothy into a tizzy about Valerie's past, she could imagine what Lady Ashcombe and Lady Elmswood were mumbling into their teas about it.

Valerie crushed the paper between her palms and tossed it in the wastebasket beside the writing desk, the portrait of Sir Robert Walpole above the fireplace watching her. She stormed into the Blue Drawing Room. On state occasions, it and the adjoining drawing rooms served as a ballroom. This morning it was quiet, the cushions on the gilded chairs and sofas still fluffed from the maid's diligent work. By the end of the day they'd be flattened by Aunt Anne and Dorothy chatting together before Aunt Anne hosted one of her regular At Homes. Valerie and Mavis had never been so cordial with one another. Valerie's mother hadn't been in her life long enough to leave her with such warm memories, vanishing shortly after Valerie's birth for reasons no one cared to explain. Father used to go red in the face whenever she'd asked him about it, demanding she forget the woman. Aunt Anne had been more polite but vague with her answers and quick to change the subject. What little Valerie knew came from overheard whispers about a new husband, a house in Ireland, and the wild spending of a trust Valerie might one day enjoy a share in. Valerie's mother was as taboo a subject as Tristan's true paternity, but it didn't matter. She hadn't been there for her when she'd needed her the most. Few people had.

She fingered the porcelain Chelsea shepherdess figurine on the mantel, one of the many from Great-Grandmother's collection spread throughout No. 10. Cousin Frank had broken the matching shepherd years ago, leaving the shepherdess alone between the carriage clock and a set of bronze candlesticks. Aunt Anne had never matched her with any of the other companionless figurines. Valerie wondered what about this one in her pink-flowered dress and bare feet made her unworthy of a companion.

Like me. Father, Mavis, the girls at the French convent school, the Mother Superior, and Mr. Shoedelin had scorned her, and she'd never done anything to deserve it, except one thing, but that wasn't her fault. She prayed Aunt Anne would never notice whatever it was about her that had driven everyone who ever should have loved or cared about her away. Aunt Anne's derision would crush her.

Tears stung her eyes as she walked into the White Drawing Room. She jerked to a halt when Mary rose from where she'd been kneeling to clean the fireplace.

"Good morning, Miss de Vere Cole," the maid greeted in her thick northern accent. She, like all the upstairs staff, had come with Valerie's aunt and uncle from their house in Edgbaston near Birmingham. The government paid for everything on the ground floor that involved official business, but the family maintained the upper spaces, including the first-floor drawing and dining rooms and the second-floor bedrooms. Aunt Anne and Uncle Neville could afford the household expected of a prime minister. Father hadn't been able to afford a house with proper floors in the end, having died of a heart attack in a derelict cottage in Honfleur.

"Good morning, Mary," Valerie forced through a smile before hurrying out of the room and up the stairs to her bedroom. Usually she'd chat with the woman, keen to hear the society gossip the servants loved to collect. They relished a jolly good scandal more than Madame Freville, the landlady in Ascain, had. It'd turn Dorothy's hair gray if she ever discovered how much Valerie had learned about English and Parisian society from that old woman and the servants. Valerie didn't have the stomach for it today, afraid to inadvertently hear something about herself.

The family's private rooms on the second floor were quiet except for the low rumble of buses driving down Whitehall that made the crystals in the wall sconces rattle. It was a far cry from the hotel in Ascain, where she used to hear the bawdy calls of prostitutes on the street outside. The walls were painted pale blue, and the plush red carpet made visiting the loo in the middle of the night far more pleasant than it'd been at the convent school. Aunt Anne had insisted on the second-floor remodel after Uncle Neville had taken office two years ago. The White Drawing Room had been converted from a boudoir into a public room, Aunt Anne having no desire for Uncle Neville's secretaries, who thought nothing of interrupting dinners and lunches, catching her in a dressing gown.

In Valerie's room, a small desk and a stuffed chair were situated in front of the window overlooking the No. 10 garden and the Horse Guards parade grounds over the back wall. A narrow bed stood against the far side of the room and was draped with a fine down comforter in Aunt Anne's favorite shade of pale pink. The furnishings were simple but the best she'd ever enjoyed, and a far cry from the sagging bed in the Hotel Etchola where she used to read *Alice in Wonderland* while Father and Mavis screamed at one another in the sitting room.

Valerie opened the scratched and battered dispatch box on the desk. Uncle Neville had given her the cast-off red and brass box to keep her copies of *Alice in Wonderland* and *Alice Through the Looking-Glass* in. Both books had been a rare gift from Father during her time in Cambridge, and two of the few items he hadn't hocked when things had turned dire. She lifted *Alice in Wonderland* out and traced the fancifully wrought title with one manicured finger before flipping it open to Sir John Tenniel's fine illustrations. The one of Alice in her sweet dress and clean pinafore having tea with the Mad Hatter and his friends was her favorite. Valerie used to wish for pretty clothes and a fine house like Alice's. Except Alice wasn't home in this illustration but sitting at a table and as exhausted by the stupidity around her as Valerie used to be by Father and Mavis's endless fights.

We're all mad here.

She snapped the book closed, about to set it in the box when the stack of letters bound in string at the bottom made her pause. They'd been among Father's few sad possessions at the time of his death. Mr. Shoedelin had sent them to Valerie at the convent, then forwarded the rest of his effects to Aunt Anne. She laid the book on the leather blotter and lifted out the envelopes, turning the cheap and stiff paper over in her hands. The flaps were wrinkled and curled from having been opened too many times, and Father's last address in Honfleur had faded, almost illegible, but it didn't matter. The sheer number of them had committed the address to her memory, along with the pleading and desperation dripping from every word.

Tout passe, tout lasse, tout casse, her father used to drunkenly slur through his graying mustache whenever Valerie had begged him to do something to earn money to pay Madame Freville and the other creditors or to buy food and clothes. *Nothing lasts, everything breaks, everything fades.*

Useless pessimist. She tossed the letters and the book inside the box and slammed the lid closed, itching to knock the red thing off the desk. The entire first floor would come rushing up to see what was wrong if she did. As far as they were concerned everything was fine, nothing had ever been wrong. Even if it wasn't, she couldn't tell anyone the full truth about France, not if she expected to stay here.

She opened the desk drawer and pushed aside the fine stationery, embossed with her name, that Great-Aunt Lillian had given her for Christmas. She fished out the Buckingham Palace fork hidden underneath and rubbed her thumb over the cool metal tines, gently warming them. Some footman had polished it to perfection before Dinah had convinced her to pinch it.

No one wants to associate with crass young ladies and they certainly don't want their daughters or sons befriending them either. You'll find yourself quite the outcast if you carry on like this. Dor-

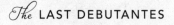

othy's warning echoed through the quiet room before the calls of the Horse Guards galloping in formation caught her attention. The riders in their red uniforms sitting atop their various-colored mounts were a stark contrast to the packed dirt of the parade grounds just over the Downing Street back wall.

Mavis and Father were why Dorothy and people like Lady Ashcombe looked down on her.

That's going to change this Season. She'd come to London to put France behind her and to prove to everyone she was a proper young lady worthy of the respect due the Premier's niece. She wouldn't allow anyone, not Father's ghost or her awful stepmother, to ruin this chance to claim the life she would've had if Father hadn't frittered it away. She'd hesitated last night at Buckingham Palace. She refused to do it again and see herself sunk before the Season truly began.

Chapter Three

Valerie crept down the curving Grand Staircase of No. 10, past the portraits of the previous Prime Ministers arranged on the cream wall in order of their terms. The ground floor was a flurry of activity, the clerks and secretaries who normally greeted her with cheerful smiles passing with curt nods, heels banging against the carpet covering the corridor outside the offices and Cabinet Room. Even Mr. Rucker and Mr. Seyer's usual laughter from the Senior Private Secretaries' Office was replaced by low murmurs and the tinny ring of phones. The dreadful seriousness was a stark contrast to last night's pomp and ceremony. Aunt Anne had assured her there was nothing about the German invasion of Czechoslovakia for her to worry about, but the grave faces down here made her wonder.

At least with all this activity, the government staff wasn't likely to notice her leaving. No one upstairs would miss her either, so long as she was back in time to dress for the luncheon. If Dorothy knew where Valerie was off to, she'd have another panicky fit about Valerie's behavior. One would think a married woman with two children wouldn't be so easily shocked, but one would be wrong. Valerie had no desire to discover what Aunt Anne thought of this, and if she were sensible she'd march back upstairs and take her time preparing for the luncheon, but she couldn't. There was little she could do about people associating her with Father, but she could darn well stop Mavis from besmirching her already fragile reputation or reminding them about France. The last thing she needed was anyone asking too many questions or discovering details about her life in Ascain that were better left buried there.

"Good morning, Miss de Vere Cole," Miss Marian Holmes, one of the No. 10 typists, greeted. She wore a simple brown dress with buttons on the front and a sensible green sweater that complemented her businesslike manner. "What brings you down here this morning?"

So much for slipping out unnoticed. Valerie should've known better, the young woman never missed anything. She was one of the Garden Room Girls who worked under the watchful eye of Mrs. Margaret Stenhouse. When the house was quiet, Valerie could sometimes hear the bells ringing to summon the typists upstairs to take dictation for the Prime Minister and his staff.

"I wanted to see how Uncle Neville is holding up." It was partly the truth. His gout had been bad enough before the trouble with Germany had forced him into early morning cabinet meetings and late-night question sessions in the Commons. It must be torturing him now.

"He's as you might imagine, with the state of things in Europe.

We were here past eleven last night and will be again before this is settled." Miss Holmes shifted the stack of files in the crook of her arm and pushed her curled hair behind her ear, revealing the dark circles beneath her eyes. "Mrs. Stenhouse is already preparing beds for us and the secretaries in case we miss the last buses. Even the Premier accepted phone calls well after dinner last night."

"Are things in Europe really so bad?" Uncle Neville had spent most of his life serving the people of England, first as a Member of Parliament for Birmingham, then as Minister of Health and Chancellor of the Exchequer, but his dedication rarely extended past seven P.M.

Miss Holmes's eyes went wide in surprise. "Don't you know?"

Valerie cursed not having slipped out of the house and through the garden. It'd be a great deal less embarrassing to climb the Horse Guards wall than admit she knew so little about world events. "I didn't have a chance to properly read the newspapers this morning."

Not exactly the truth. The *Times* hadn't been as tempting as the *Tatler*, and Aunt Anne hardly encouraged her to read beyond the married, birthed, and buried sections.

"I see." Miss Holmes nodded with the same understanding Madame Freville had shown when Valerie had innocently asked about the women lingering outside the Hotel Etchola in Ascain. The landlady had matter-of-factly broadened Valerie's education the same way Miss Holmes was about to do. "Herr Hitler invading Czechoslovakia crushed the peace Mr. Chamberlain worked so hard to secure in Munich last September, and Mr. Churchill is blustering on in the Commons about the Premier being naïve

enough to trust the Germans and demanding that something be done, as if the Premier is hunting at Chequers instead of working himself to the bone to find a solution, which is more than that old bulldog has done."

"Good morning, Miss de Vere Cole." Sir John Simon, Chancellor of the Exchequer, approached. "Miss Holmes."

"Good morning, sir." Miss Holmes's pale cheeks went red at being caught voicing her opinion. Garden Room Girls took dictation. They didn't share their thoughts.

"Congratulations on your presentation, Miss de Vere Cole. It's quite an honor and an achievement," Sir John offered, his chin stiff above his starched collar and the lapels of his immaculate suit. Valerie imagined his attire would be a great deal more disheveled by the end of the long day. "Everything is open to you, or it soon will be. You must enjoy it while you can."

"While I can?" What did he know about Germany that Miss Holmes didn't?

"Before the heavy responsibilities of marriage and motherhood, of course." He ran his hand over his bald head bounded by white hair and offered a tight smile. "If you'll excuse me."

He strode off to the Cabinet Anteroom, sidestepping Mr. Rucker hurrying out of it.

Marriage and motherhood. What a thought. Valerie could barely keep the constant stream of government and society people straight, much less contemplate managing a household and children. Maybe someday, but not this Season. If she ever hoped to attract a man worth his salt, her reputation must be solid, and not undermined by Father's and Mavis's pasts, or her own.

"Congratulations on your presentation. What an honor to curtsey before the King and Queen." Miss Holmes clutched the files to her chest with a dreamy sigh, looking more like a girl Valerie's age than the talented typist much in demand by the ministers and secretaries. The winsome expression lasted for a second before she faced Valerie with the usual directness the men appreciated, eyeing her yellow dress covered with a fine blue overcoat. "Where are you off to today?"

Valerie adjusted her felt hat and hoped her hair didn't frizz while she was out. There wouldn't be time to redo it when she returned. "To visit an old friend."

My, the lies were piling up this morning.

"Really?" Miss Holmes leaned back to peer down the long central corridor to the black-lacquered front door and the sidelights with a view of the street. "The car and driver aren't out front."

The woman didn't miss anything. "I didn't call them. I'm going to take the bus."

Miss Holmes drew back in horror, like Dorothy after Valerie's candid assessment of Mavis. "The Premier's niece can't ride the bus. What will people say?"

That Dorothy was right about my ignorance of social graces.

"I'll call the car for you." Miss Holmes set the files on the second secretary's desk and picked up the black phone, tapping the receiver to alert the switchboard operator. "Please tell Mr. May to bring the car around for Miss de Vere Cole."

"Miss Holmes, we need those files," Mr. Colville snapped, leaning out of the Cabinet Anteroom door, his small round face drawn into a tighter scowl than usual.

"Yes, sir. Good day, Miss de Vere Cole." Miss Holmes snatched up the files and scurried off as fast as her sensible brown shoes could carry her.

A cadre of secretaries smelling of cigarettes and hair pomade hurried past Valerie on ministerial errands. She stepped aside to allow them to pass and bumped into the chair behind her, dislodging Uncle Neville's black silk umbrella from where it rested across the arms. She caught it before it tumbled to the floor, the initialed gold band fixed to the Malacca wood handle glinting in the morning light. Her aunt had given it to him years ago and it'd been recovered by Thomas Brigg and Sons many times since. He never left No. 10 without it, not even when he'd flown to Munich to negotiate with Herr Hitler last September. Once, she'd asked him why he carried it. He'd rested it on his shoulder and told her it reminded him to always be grateful to Annie. Without her he wouldn't have become Prime Minister, a position his father and half brother had aspired to but had never reached.

No one had ever thought so highly of Valerie. That would change this Season. She'd see to it.

She set the umbrella back across the chair's arms and hurried down the long corridor to the entrance hall, thankful Miss Holmes had stopped her from taking the bus. Arriving on Mavis's front walk in a Rolls-Royce instead of red-faced from hoofing it down the street would be far more impressive. The car would show the jumped-up tart that Valerie wasn't the unwanted stepdaughter she'd looked down on in France. What she wouldn't give for all those tormenting snots from the convent school to see it too, but Mavis would have to do for today.

"A fine morning, Miss de Vere Cole, isn't it?" Henry, the guard, rose from the black leather porter's chair in the entrance hall, his medals bright against his dark wool uniform. A cheerful fire burned in the fireplace and the grandfather clock ticked quietly against the wall.

"It is." At least it had been when she'd awakened this morning still alight from last night. It'd grown progressively more vexing since, and it wasn't even noon. Heaven knows what the rest of the day would bring.

"Mr. May hasn't brought the car around yet. Would you like to wait inside?"

Even Henry expected her to take the Rolls and not the bus. Maybe she was as ignorant as Dorothy feared. "No, I'll wait out front."

"Very well, miss." He opened the black-lacquered door and she stepped onto the pavement beneath the wrought-iron lamp.

Valerie's appearance sent a ripple through the small crowd standing at the entrance to Downing Street from Whitehall. They were held back by a line of policemen, and it left her as exposed as a mannequin in the window of Selfridges. It was a minuscule gathering compared to the one that had greeted Uncle Neville after his meeting with Herr Hitler in Munich last September. She hadn't been here to watch his triumphant wave from the upper floor but she'd seen the pictures in the newspapers and sat with Great-Aunt Lillian in front of the wireless to listen to him speak. The crowds in the background had drowned him out so many times with their cheers that it'd been difficult to hear his speech. He'd come home a hero, having secured peace in our time.

"Miss de Vere Cole, ya 'ave any news for us?" one man shouted. "We've been waiting to 'ear somethin'."

"Will he give us peace again?" an old woman in a squirrel stole shouted.

"I don't know. I'm sorry." She wished she could assure them that they wouldn't be bombed to rubble the way Mr. Churchill thundered on about, but for all the prestige of her new address, she knew little more than they did. Aunt Anne rarely discussed the goings-on downstairs, and even if she did she couldn't tell them anything. Valerie was simply the Prime Minister's niece, not the Foreign Secretary.

The guards ushered the people aside to allow Uncle Neville's Rolls-Royce to drive through. It stopped at the curb and Valerie started for the door before she caught herself and waited patiently for Mr. May to come around and open it for her. She settled in against the leather seat, resting her purse on her lap while Mr. May slipped behind the wheel.

"Where to, Miss de Vere Cole?" he asked.

"Here, please." She handed the paper with Mr. R. E. Mortimer Wheeler's address written on it over the seat. The London Museum assistant had been kind enough to provide it after the No. 10 switchboard operator had informed him that someone from Downing Street had requested it. That was certainly a perk of living in No. 10.

The car slid past the crowd, and the old woman in her squirrel stole peered in enviously at Valerie. Valerie didn't blame her. She used to be jealous of Dorothy every time she and Aunt Anne had left her at the train station to return to boarding school, or at the port to sail to that god-awful hellhole in France.

She took a deep breath. Those days were behind her, thank heavens, but it wasn't hard to imagine her present good fortune meeting the same inglorious fate. This time it might be Herr Hitler who ruined it instead of Father's or Mavis's reputations or her own rotten luck.

The car glided past the Palace of Westminster with its Gothic spires and sandstone façade. Big Ben tolled ten o'clock and men streamed in and out of the two Houses of Parliament past the mounds of sandbags piled there after the Anschluss, the German invasion of Austria last year. Uncle Neville's success with the Munich Agreement had staved off the threat of war but the sandbags had been left in place, the situation in Europe still too precarious for anyone to breathe easy.

The driver guided the car down Millbank to Grosvenor Road. The streets followed the curve of the River Thames, where ships cruised the murky water. The tone of the neighborhood changed from the government buildings of Westminster to the houses and squares of Pimlico. Across the river, the tall smokestacks of Battersea Power Station came into view before another bend in the embankment brought them into Chelsea. Mr. May guided the Rolls to the curb of tree-lined Chelsea Embankment, stopping at No. 10, with its black front door and iron railings.

How ironic that Mavis should also end up in a No. 10 in a respectable neighborhood. It was too good for the whore.

The click of the car door as Mr. May stepped out made Valerie jump, and she wished he weren't so efficient about coming around to hand her out. This idea had been all well and good at Downing Street, but it seemed a terrible mistake in front of the red-brick town house with a view of the Thames from its bow front windows.

The damp of the river across the street filled the air when Mr. May opened her door. She hesitated, debating whether or not to get out. She could change her mind and let it alone, but of all the things and people that might rise up to ruin her Season, she wasn't about to allow Mavis to be one of them. She had no control over Herr Hitler or Father's old pranks, but she could tell her stepmother a thing or two and show her she wasn't someone to be derided and scorned.

"Please wait for me, Mr. May." She wouldn't stay longer than necessary but she had no idea how long that might be.

"Yes, Miss de Vere Cole."

He stood beside the car while Valerie approached the house, the brisk wind off the river cutting through her fine wool coat. A boat on the Thames sounded its horn and she flexed her fingers to shake out the tremors before reaching up to ring the front bell.

The chill deepened while she waited for someone to answer but no one hurried to the door. Mavis was probably out spending her new husband's money. He must have some means, if she married him. She'd probably investigated his finances this time instead of trusting his word like she had with Father.

Valerie glanced at Mr. May, who remained plain-faced in his forest-green livery. She was about to leave when the lock clicked and the door swung open.

"Yes?" a battle-ax of a day maid growled, put out at having left whatever she'd been doing to answer the bell.

"I'm here to see Mrs. Wheeler."

"Who's asking for her?"

"Miss Valerie de Vere Cole." She stepped aside to give the impertinent woman a good look at the Rolls-Royce. The sight of it wiped the sneer off her bulldog face.

"Come in."

That's more like it. Valerie entered the narrow front hall cluttered with old statues and curiosities. Despite the spattering of antiquities on the entryway side table and the coats and umbrellas hanging on the coatrack, the entrance was tidy except for the small pair of white leather boots tossed in the corner.

Tristan's.

She didn't see or hear the little boy. He was probably upstairs with his nursemaid, tucked out of sight up under the eaves. Mavis wasn't likely to lift a finger to raise him. She hadn't done much for Valerie in Ascain, tossing magazines and run stockings about without a care for whether Valerie had spent the entire afternoon tidying up. Neither of them had ever thanked her, but she'd still done it. Pride hadn't allowed her to live in filth, but poverty had nearly beat that pride out of her.

The memory of Mr. Shoedelin, the British Consul in Bayonne's disbelief when she'd told him how awful things with Father were in that last miserable hotel, made her dig her nails into her palms. She'd begged for his help and he'd scoffed at her, accusing her of exaggerating how little food and how many rats there were until she'd put her pleas into terms he could no longer ignore. It'd wiped the doubt off his bored expression and replaced it with a repulsion that still made her cringe in shame.

I can't think of that now. There was a more immediate demon to face.

"I'll tell her you're here," the maid said.

"No need, Mrs. Parker," a familiar voice called from the top of the stairs. Valerie winced at the sound. Father's efforts to erase Mavis's low-class accent had worked, and she must have taken more elocution lessons since. Valerie could hardly hear the peasant in her pronunciation.

Mavis descended the stairs, eyeing Valerie with the same disdain she used to fling at the Ascain creditors. "Well, look who decided to pay me a call."

The nerve of this tart, sneering at her and making her wait like a tradesman. She'd probably been upstairs watching from one of the windows while deciding when to come down. Valerie was about to tell her what she thought of this little ploy but she bit it back, forcing a pleasant smile to her lips. Civil. She had to be civil. "I saw your marriage announcement in the newspaper."

"So you decided to rush over here and wish me good luck." Mavis marched into the sitting room, not asking Valerie to join her but expecting it.

Valerie grudgingly followed, noticing the numerous curiosities crowding every table in the surprisingly tidy room. The bulldog must see to the dust. Valerie couldn't imagine Mavis getting off her back long enough to maintain her husband's home. "I've come to have a chat."

Mavis didn't invite Valerie to sit but remained standing across the large and faded Persian carpet, the two of them eyeing one another like fighting dogs, each waiting for the other to lunge first. It wouldn't be her, but she'd certainly snap back if provoked. "I'm sure you've heard, Aunt Anne is bringing me out this Season from Number Ten."

"I heard. What's it to me?"

Valerie trilled her gloved fingers on her purse handle, trying to think of a polite way to tell Mavis to bugger off, quite proud of her control over her tongue. "Since we're both in London, I thought it best if, for the duration of the Season, we're civil to one another and forget our time in France. We wouldn't want anything to arise that might cause us or the Chamberlains any embarrassment."

Mavis crossed her arms, trilling her red nails on her forearms. "You think I give a fig about the Chamberlains, who never did anything for me except lie about Horace's money and lands in Canada, both of which were a fraud?"

"If you two hadn't frittered away what little he had, we might've lived better." Her hold on graciousness was slipping as fast as Mavis's pretension to a posh accent.

"I kept us from starving while your father played the gentleman, never doing anything except wasting money on wine, books, and you."

"Father gave you more than you deserved, and you betrayed him with that painter, and half the men in the village." So much for civility. "You did everything you could in France to pull us down. Don't you dare do anything here to embarrass me or my aunt and uncle."

Mavis opened the pewter cigarette box on the table beside her and plucked one out. She selected a match from the attached holder and struck it on the brick fireplace. The smell of sulfur filled the air before she touched it to the tip of the cigarette, then flicked it out and tossed it in an ashtray. "How surprised you'll be when you discover that everything you're hungering after is as common as what you left behind."

"You're the only one who's common."

Mavis sauntered up to Valerie, who stepped back, her cheek stinging with the memory of the sharp slap Mavis had meted out after Valerie had stumbled in on her and the grocer's son and threatened to tell Father. Now Mavis didn't do more than blow a long line of smoke out of the side of her mouth. "The only difference between me and those hoity-toity types you're so desperate to impress is their money. Ancestry, fancy clothes, and jewels cover up so much coarseness. You hope it'll conceal yours, but it won't. The second you walk into a ballroom, those society biddies will sniff you out for the poor country cousin you are. Then that high-and-mighty aunt of yours who didn't get off her perch to come to my and Horace's wedding because I wasn't good enough for her dear brother won't want anything more to do with you than your father or mother did. I don't suppose your mother has rushed to congratulate you on your grand Season, has she? No, she never wanted you. She still doesn't, and I don't blame her. Who'd want such a pathetic creature?"

Valerie gripped the straps of her purse so tight she risked tearing them off in an effort not to wrap the patent leather across Mavis's smug face. Calling on every ounce of poise Great-Aunt Lillian had drilled into her at West Woodhay House, and the patience she'd seen Aunt Anne exercise at No. 10, Valerie tucked her purse beneath her arm. "You're the only one who'll out yourself as the trash you are once you're up the duff with some other man's child. Mr. Wheeler won't put up with it the way Father did, and you'll find yourself back in the gutter where you belong."

Valerie turned, head high, back straight, and marched to the front door. The bulldog maid leapt up from the stairs where she'd sat listening and pulled it open. The cold outside air cut against the tears welling at the corners of Valerie's eyes.

"Tell yourself whatever you like to help you sleep through the night," Mavis cackled before the bulldog closed the door and cut off the grating sound.

Valerie jerked up short on the pavement, nearly colliding with the nurse and the chubby, curly-haired boy clinging to her hand. She stared down at him, the resemblance between Augustus John and Tristan striking. Of course he wasn't her brother, no matter how much Father had tried to cheer her with the promise of a sibling. She'd been too old to be fooled by that lie, but not his others. At sixteen, she'd believed him when he'd left her at the French convent school door, Mr. Shoedelin impatiently checking his watch while Father had promised to collect her as soon as possible or to send Aunt Anne to fetch her. She'd held on to that lie until the stretching months with no word from him or Aunt Anne had revealed the truth. Even in the end he hadn't cared enough about her to help her.

She stepped around the old nurse and hurried to the car, refusing to wipe away a single tear in sight of the entire embankment and whatever window Mavis watched from. She wouldn't give

Mavis the satisfaction of seeing how deep her nasty comments had cut.

Mr. May ushered Valerie into the Rolls before taking his place behind the wheel. He said nothing as he guided the car away from the house.

In the quiet of the backseat, the tears fell fast, soaking the handkerchief she tugged out of her purse. She let out a very unladylike snort as she tried to hold in the sobs. *I shouldn't have gone to see her.* It hadn't settled anything, but dredged up the ugly awfulness of Ascain and every belittling she'd ever endured because of Mavis and Father.

The car stopped at a traffic signal and Mr. May handed a dry handkerchief over the seat.

"Thank you." She took a ragged, steadying breath, but the tears continued to slide down her cheeks and stain her dress. Outside the window, the Thames flowed in dark ripples between the banks, not caring about her troubles any more than her father or mother ever had.

She never wanted you. She still doesn't, and I don't blame her. Who'd want such a pathetic creature? Mavis's ugly words made Valerie want to retch.

It's not true. It can't be. Father had refused to discuss his first wife with Valerie, and he wasn't likely to have told Mavis much . . . unless he had. There'd never been a rhyme or reason to anything he'd done with that slut.

Then I should be glad my mother bolted. She would've been more trouble than she was worth. A divorced woman couldn't present a debutante at court, but she could've been there afterward to congratulate her or cherish her when no one else had, protected her, loved her, and kept her from falling into the near-ruin she'd skirted so close to in France. Instead, it'd been left to others and they'd done a rotten job of it, except for Aunt Anne. She'd been there for Valerie during every school holiday, and would've done more if Father hadn't interfered, insisting he knew what was best for his daughter and certain this time he'd be the superb parent he longed to be. Selfishness and the bottle had quickly ruined that fantasy.

The spires of Parliament came into view. She slipped a compact out of her purse and tried to blot away the red streaking her cheeks. No one could see her like this, but even if she could stop the tears, she wasn't likely to fool anyone at No. 10 any more than she was fooling society about who she really was. Mavis was right, they'd realize at once she was a sow's ear parading as a silk purse and they'd scorn her for trying to push into their ranks. Last night, some of them already had. They would again if Mavis decided to smear her. After that little visit, Valerie wouldn't put it past her to find some way to humiliate her, Aunt Anne, or Uncle Neville. Hopefully, Mr. Wheeler would force Mavis to show some restraint, but she doubted it, and Valerie would have yet another bad apple on the family tree to live down.

Chapter Four

"How is the new Mrs. Wheeler?" Aunt Anne asked from beside Valerie as they rode past St. James's Park toward the Dorchester Hotel.

Valerie caught Mr. May's eyes in the rearview mirror before he focused on the road. Hers were still puffy from the last car ride that everyone in Downing Street must have heard about by now. No wonder Aunt Anne knew about her visit to Mavis. It was impossible to flee to a bedroom when one had to walk through the chaos downstairs simply to reach the staircase. Thankfully, Aunt Anne was straightforward about Valerie's little escapade. She couldn't bear more hysterics today. "Exactly as you'd expect."

"Well, tigers and stripes and all that." Aunt Anne brushed the wrinkles out of her pleated, calf-length mauve skirt, her gold bracelet clinking against the buttons of her long sleeves. She wore a coat of fine wool trimmed with mink. Everything about her spoke of grace and social position, all the things Dorothy and

Mavis had been kind enough to remind Valerie she didn't possess. "You mustn't think about her. She's too common to merit your notice."

"It doesn't mean she isn't right." The thought of walking into the luncheon to find a hundred Lady Ashcombes waiting to prove Mavis's prediction true shook her resolve. She adjusted the bow on the hip of her forest-green tea dress, wondering how she'd get through this luncheon without hiding in the ladies' room. She'd never imagined being *that* debutante.

"What did Mavis say to you?"

"Nothing that isn't true."

"I very much doubt that. You must learn to ignore most of what others say. It's usually nonsense."

"Is it? Lady Ashcombe reprimanded me for having the audacity to be Horace de Vere Cole's daughter, as if I had a choice. Then there was Lady Fallington, who barely spared me the time of day, and Dorothy panicking into her coffee that I might pick my teeth in front of Their Majesties." She didn't mention Mavis's remarks about her mother, unable to endure another dodged discussion or to discover that it was true.

"You must especially learn to ignore Dorothy, she tends toward the prim and dogmatic like her grandmother. She certainly didn't inherit that from me or Neville." Aunt Anne adjusted her peaked hat, unruffled as always, even by Valerie's outburst. "As for the rest, that's to be expected from certain members of society who revel in looking down their noses at everyone. It's as much a custom with some as afternoon tea, and eventually you'll become accustomed to it. I promise, all the world isn't Lady Ashcombes or Lady Fallingtons. Dinah, Christian, and Katherine were quite taken with you."

They were the brightest spot of the last two days, but they'd spent their whole lives in this world. They understood the rules and habits and probably how to ignore a jibe better than she did. They also recognized who did and didn't belong and how to close ranks on undesirables. She didn't want them to recoil from her when they realized she wasn't the well-bred young lady she pretended to be or that her time in France had been more Charles Dickens suffering than grand Paris shopping tour.

"Did you know, Lady Curzon once called me a powder puff, and that's one of the nicest insults I've endured? I've developed the hide of a rhinoceros, thanks to Neville's position. Eventually, you will too."

That she'd have to endure more days like today to develop a thick skin made her want to crawl back into bed and not come out until August. She'd been presented; that was all some girls aspired to before they slipped off to their country estates or wherever they'd come from. No one thought any worse of them because they weren't feted at every dinner and ball. They simply vanished. Valerie could do the same. Returning to the Victorian rigidity of Great-Aunt Lillian wasn't the glittering, life-changing Season she'd dreamed of but it would be a great deal less insulting. "Perhaps I should spend the summer at West Woodhay House instead of London."

"Nonsense. I have no intention of allowing you to give up the moment things turn thorny. Cowardice is an awful trait I refuse to encourage."

"I am hardly giving up." Her being in London instead of rotting away in that horrid convent school was proof of that. If Valerie hadn't stolen the stamps and written to Aunt Anne, she'd still be with the nuns or cast out on the streets once she turned eighteen. She might have been forced to marry some doddery old Englishman as Mavis had done to survive, or ventured irrevocably down the road that'd landed her in the convent to begin with. If Aunt Anne and Uncle Neville ever learned why Mr. Shoedelin had locked her away, their faith in her would vanish and she'd be as alone in England as she'd been in France.

They'll never know.

Aunt Anne shifted to face her, the tenderness softening her cheeks and the lines at the corners of her eyes making it easy to see why Lady Curzon had called her a powder puff. She was greatly mistaken. That languid expression hid a strength few people outside the family ever saw, one Valerie wished she possessed. "The purpose of the Season isn't to curtsey to the monarchs or wear fashionable clothes and impress everyone with witty conversation. It isn't even to find a husband, although a number of girls will, but not you. Instead, you must learn the most important lesson—to handle difficult people and situations with grace and poise, to discover your strengths and weaknesses, and hone one and build up the other. When it's all said and done and you've run the gauntlet of balls and sporting events, met people of all personalities, you'll be well prepared for whatever life you choose to make for yourself."

"The life I choose? I've never had a choice in anything. It's always been up to others, Mother, Father, Mavis." *Mr. Shoedelin, the bastard.* "I've never had a say in anything, I've simply been left to lump it."

"Not anymore." Aunt Anne grasped her hand and gave it a squeeze. "You've been forced to endure a great many difficulties in your short life but you've handled them with bravery and wisdom beyond your age. The Season will be no different. Once you find your footing, you'll be a success. I'm certain of it. You have the spirit for it, more so than many others you'll meet."

Valerie stared at her aunt's hand in hers. She wasn't sure she could stomach more insults, cuts, and snubs, but she must. She'd been at No. 10 for a month and this rare opportunity might disappear if the opposition ousted Uncle Neville. She couldn't throw it away by fleeing and proving to Mavis and everyone that their poor opinion of her was correct. Father had been a coward, running from debts, heartbreak, and anything that'd ever demanded more of him. She refused to be like him and watch the pride in her aunt's eyes fade to disappointment. She must face the next four months and whatever they threw at her. "I promise to make the best of the Season."

"Good, because we're nearly there." Aunt Anne patted her hand, then slid her Yardley compact out of her purse and handed it to Valerie. "Freshen up. One must look one's best when entering the arena to face tigresses."

While Valerie powdered away the redness in her cheeks, the car glided past the Wellington Arch and the brown sandstone and columned front of Apsley House at the corner of Piccadilly and Park Lane. The Dorchester Hotel with its stone walls, iron balconies, and three Union Jacks flying from the rooftop masts came into view. The white spires of the hotel stood out from the mass of green trees surrounding it, their lushness echoed in the plantings in the circle outside the main door. Mr. May didn't stop there, but continued around to the hotel's ballroom entrance. When the car came to a halt, the doorman in the Dorchester's green tailcoat and black and gold top hat stepped forward to hand them out. Valerie followed Aunt Anne in through the revolving door and with the turn of it the noise of London settled to the quiet tinkling of a piano and the high buzz of feminine voices.

The debutantes gathered in small groups around the brass-embellished entrance hall, many faces familiar from the morning papers and last night's presentation. Dinah, Katherine, and Christian weren't among them, but Rosalind Cubitt stood chatting with Priscilla Brett on the stairs leading to the gilded Crush Room. Valerie smiled at her, hoping for at least a tepid greeting after their introduction, but Rosalind's gaze merely floated over her before settling back on her friend.

All the world isn't Rosalind Cubitts, she reminded herself as she followed Aunt Anne past them to the seating chart outside the main ballroom.

"Anne, at last. We're near the patronesses' table," Caroline, Lady Bridgeman, Aunt Anne's dearest friend, greeted with a continental kiss. She was thicker in the middle than Aunt Anne and taller, with graying dark hair drawn back into a low chignon. "You look lovely today, Valerie. You're at table twenty-two with Miss Betty Dunn and Lady Margaret Boyle."

Valerie peered through the open ballroom doors. Those girls

not standing with friends sat by themselves at the large round tables covered in pale blue linens and flowered centerpieces. They either pretended not to notice that they were alone or silently willed anyone passing by to stop and sit with them the same way Valerie used to do during the sparse meals at the convent. She didn't relish joining their ranks if Dinah and the others had changed their minds about her.

"Talk to the girls at your table about volunteering for the Personal Service League," Lady Bridgeman pressed. "Since we've shifted our focus from collecting clothes for the unemployed to gathering supplies for hospitals, we need more volunteers than ever. As the vice chairman, I'm tasked with bringing some young blood into the organization."

Valerie doubted a tableful of ladies and honorables would be of much use to Lady Bridgeman but she'd find a way to broach the socially acceptable subject. It would at least give her something besides the weather to discuss. "I'll do what I can."

"Think about it for yourself too. You could set the trend for joining. Shall we go in?"

It wasn't a question so much as an invitation Valerie wasn't quick to accept.

"Steady on." Aunt Anne patted her encouragingly on the arm. "Remember, many of these girls haven't had the advantages of school like their brothers. They're fresh from the country or the schoolroom and as nervous as you. Be kind and friendly and you'll do well."

Aunt Anne followed Lady Bridgeman to the patroness table at

the front of the room, welcoming and receiving greetings from the regal matrons in their inherited jewels and custom Schiaparelli dresses.

Valerie wasn't likely to get that effusive a welcome from anyone seated with her, but she refused to stand there like some ignored Lady Clancarty protégée either. She followed the table numbers deeper into the room, passing under the intricately carved ceiling with its curving chandelier. Pale pink drapes hung from every wall, the line of them broken by pier glasses set with large crystal sconces. She passed many girls as she wove through the well-laid tables. Some smiled at her, while others paused in their conversations to eye her the way they had last night. She ignored them and committed the friendly faces to mind, determined to strike up a conversation with them when she had the chance. She reached table twenty-two and was about to set her purse at one of the last open places when a dark-haired girl approached her.

"I don't believe we've had the pleasure of meeting." Her smile was more stalking cat than innocent beguiling.

"Valerie de Vere—"

"I know who you are. You're the debutante in Downing Street, fresh from finishing school in France."

Valerie didn't correct her about where she'd come from or ask what newspaper had given her that ridiculous sobriquet. "And you are?"

"The Honorable Vivien Mosley." She clasped her hands in front of her, eyeing Valerie with the same superior smirk that Antoinette and her beastly friends used to sport at the convent whenever they'd decided to pester *une jeune Anglaise*. "Rosalind, have you had the pleasure of meeting Miss de Vere Cole?"

"I have." Rosalind stepped up beside her friend, giving Valerie more consideration than in the entrance hall. "Allow me to introduce Priscilla Brett."

She motioned to the petite, brown-haired girl in the blue-flowered dress with a Peter Pan collar. "A pleasure, I'm sure," Priscilla greeted with more graciousness than her friends. "I like your frock."

There was a genuine and surprising compliment. "Thank you."

"I simply adore following politics, and there you are, right in the heart of things," Vivien said, stepping in before they became too chummy. She wore her black hair parted to one side with large, draping curls that brushed the shoulder of her pale pink cotton dress. "I bet you know ever so much, such as what your uncle has in store. To read the papers one would think he was trying to work out how much more of Europe to give to the Germans."

Rosalind and Priscilla giggled behind her like the French schoolgirls used to do during Antoinette's daily torments. The sinking sense that Mavis might be right about ancestry covering coarseness made her stomach drop, but heaven help her if she was going to allow Vivien Mosley to be the one to try to sniff her out. There were black sheep all over her family's fields.

"You shouldn't disrespect the Prime Minister. He kept Britain out of another awful war and saved a good many Englishmen's lives," Valerie reminded the chit.

"He humiliated us in front of the entire world. My friend in

America sent me this." Vivien tapped the white enamel umbrella pin on her chest. Valerie recognized the pin. It stood for Uncle Neville's umbrella and the cowardice many thought he'd shown by giving part of Czechoslovakia to Germany in exchange for Herr Hitler's guarantee of peace. "They're all the rage there. The Yanks think less of your uncle than we do."

"What do the Yanks think of your father cozying up to Herr Hitler?"

"My father is no admirer of his."

"No admirer," Valerie snorted as Dinah and Katherine joined the growing group of girls surrounding them to witness what was fast becoming Valerie's second spat of the day. She had to stand up to Vivien or the girl would bully her for the rest of the Season. It was a hard lesson she'd learned from Antoinette. "Herr Hitler was the witness at your father's marriage. I'm surprised your father finally married Diana Guinness after all those years she spent as his mistress."

A sharp intake of breath from everyone around them nearly sucked the air out of the ballroom.

Vivien's face went pale beneath her dark hair. "How dare you?"

"Why? I haven't said anything that isn't true," Valerie mocked. "I think you and your father are still bitter because he lost a Parliament seat to Uncle Neville all those years ago. What a grudge."

"My father is more of a politician than your uncle could ever hope to be. If the government had listened to him, we wouldn't be in this mess now."

"We'd be in a bigger one with more Englishmen beaten senseless by your father's awful Blackshirt thugs."

"Stop it, you two," Betty Dunn scolded from across the table. "No one wants to hear about all that."

"Yes, give it a rest," Lady Margaret Boyle insisted from where she sat beside Betty. "Don't spoil our lunch with politics."

Valerie almost said she hadn't started it, but they didn't care. She doubted the patronesses would care either once news of this unladylike tiff reached them. It was sure to, with this many people watching and having heard what she'd said about Lady Mosley. As ignorant as she could be of how things were done in society, even she knew it wasn't polite to air other families' dirty secrets in public. They were supposed to be whispered around private tea tables, not bandied about like the morning headlines, especially not by a properly bred debutante who shouldn't even know about mistresses.

Vivien marched off with Rosalind and Priscilla in tow. The girls still crowded around Valerie cast sideways looks at the uncouth deb in their midst. She wanted to kick herself for not having been more dignified. She could've shown everyone that she was too re-fined to be drawn into a petty squabble. Instead, she'd sunk to Vivien's level, outdoing the chit in an effort to best her. It was a hollow victory and was likely to hurt more than help her. There were thousands of debs this Season and only three hundred had been invited to participate in the Queen Charlotte's Birthday Ball. She imagined it wouldn't be long before a cadre of patronesses marched over to order her out of the room. Vivien would gloat then and there'd be another hand-wringing lecture from Dorothy and a one-way train ticket to West Woodhay House. Mavis would cackle into her coffee when she read between the lines about this in the *Tatler*. She should've walked away from Vivien and kept her mouth shut.

She was about to visit the ladies' loo and become better acquainted with the attendant when Dinah grasped her arm. "Is it true what you said about Lady Mosley?"

"I shouldn't have mentioned that."

"Of course you should've. The nerve of Vivien, attacking you for no reason, but don't let her ruin the day. Let's find our seats."

"Mine's here." She glanced across the table at the girls shooting daggers at her. She supposed this wasn't the best time to mention joining the Personal Service League. The number of people she was disappointing today was quickly racking up.

"Not anymore. You'll sit with us."

"We want to hear everything," Katherine said.

"I don't think that's a good idea. I'm sure to get in trouble for this. I don't want either of you to suffer too." The story was probably flying around the room.

Dinah batted her hand at Valerie. "If I had a shilling for every time someone did that to me because of my aunt, I'd be richer than Uncle John Jacob. Come on." She tugged Valerie off, Katherine hanging on to her other arm as they shifted to a table closer to the front of the room.

"That's my seat," a redhead in a brown dress complained when Dinah laid Valerie's purse at the place next to hers.

"There's an open one at table twenty-two. It's over there." Dinah dismissed the redhead with an imperial flick of her wrist and the redhead sulked away to take Valerie's empty seat and probably get an earful from her new tablemates about the juicy row she'd missed.

"Valerie, did you really tell off Vivien Mosley?" Christian demanded, dropping into the chair beside her. "Everyone in the ladies' is talking about it."

Valerie wanted to groan. The story was spreading faster than she'd anticipated.

"I'll bet there are twice as many pictures of you in the newspaper tomorrow than there were today," Dinah mused. "I need something like that to happen to me."

"Don't wish for that. It isn't as grand as you think."

"Neither is obscurity."

"Who's this girl I heard about who told the Mosley one where to go?" an American voice asked from behind her.

Valerie wanted to crawl under the table and die. Nothing about today was going as expected and it was getting worse by the moment.

"Here she is." Dinah pointed to Valerie, introducing her before naming their new tablemate. "This is Eunice Kennedy. She's the American Ambassador's daughter."

"Well done. It's about time someone put that pompous brat in her place." Eunice drew out her words with the same Boston accent as her father's. Valerie had met the bespectacled and balding American ambassador during one of his many visits to Downing Street. Eunice had a toothy smile in a broad face made more pronounced by the large curls arranged at the side of her head. "I saw your picture in the paper from last night. I won't be presented until the diplomatic presentations in July, and there are a lot this year. Daddy made sure there weren't many last year so my sisters Kick and Rosemary could hog the spotlight. No one cares if I have to share it, but that's what happens when you're in the middle of nine kids."

"Nine children?" Valerie couldn't think of a family in England that was so prolific, at least not with their spouses.

"To the number. And you're the PM's niece. Look at us all, so distinguished. They should seat us closer to the front."

"No," Christian balked. "Then we'd never have a chance for a real chat, and I want to hear all about Vivien's stepmother."

"Me too," Eunice insisted. "I need something delicious to throw at Kick when she's crowing about visiting Blenheim with Debo Mitford and all her aristocratic friends. Wait until she hears Debo's sister Diana was Sir Oswald Mosley's mistress. She won't be so hoity-toity about her new chums then."

Valerie stared at the girls seated on either side of her waiting for her to launch into an entirely inappropriate subject for a ladies' luncheon. She hated to disappoint them, especially when they were risking their reputations to sit beside her, but she refused to give their chaperones another reason to demand they have nothing to do with her. She'd made enough mistakes today. She didn't need any more.

A sharp whine from the speakers made everyone shudder and saved Valerie from being pressured into sharing salacious gossip.

"Ladies, your attention, please." An older woman with a square face and a mouth tucked in behind round cheeks stood at the front of the room. She tapped the microphone a few times before clearing her throat. "Good afternoon. I'm Lady Howard de Walden, President of the Queen Charlotte's Birthday Ball Committee."

She welcomed everyone and introduced the women at the long rectangular head table. Each held a title grander than the next. Then Lady de Walden launched into a description of the night itself, of the gorgeous white gowns they'd wear accentuated by the keepsake necklaces designed by Schiaparelli. She held up one of the bright red hearts hanging on a red satin ribbon and a wave of excitement swept the room. The heart was so large they had no trouble seeing it from where they sat.

"They look like overdone Christmas ornaments," Dinah whispered.

"We'll fall ankles-over-head curtseying to a cake with those things around our necks," Christian said.

"Curtseying to a cake," Eunice scoffed. "Who ever heard of such a silly thing?"

"It's more than a grand cake you'll curtsey to, ladies, but a representation of a long tradition of service both of the monarchs to the country and of society to the mothers of England through the Queen Charlotte Maternity Hospital," Lady de Walden announced, as if she'd heard Eunice's question.

Christian, Eunice, and Dinah giggled. Even Valerie had to work to hold back a laugh.

"Quiet, you lot," Katherine scolded with a sly smile. "We don't want to tweak the wrong noses."

"But it is ridiculous." Dinah wriggled her fingers at one of the scowling debs at the next table and the girl screwed up her face tighter before returning her attention to Lady de Walden.

Valerie sobered, thoroughly chastised. She was on thin enough ice already. She didn't need to make it worse by acting the trouble-maker.

"Despite any differences between you ladies, be it home coun-try or politics, during this event you'll be and act as one, a grace-ful parade of youth, beauty, and innocence to inspire the girls of England," Lady de Walden said, waxing poetic.

"What utter nonsense," Dinah whispered to Valerie. "Vivien couldn't put her differences aside over a salad. She and her friends aren't likely to do it in front of a cake."

Valerie dared to look at Vivien, who sat rigidly between Pris-cilla and Rosalind at a table near the mirrored wall. She narrowed her eyes at Valerie before turning and raising her chin to listen to the speaker. "I'll have to. I can't let her goad me into forgetting myself again."

"Nonsense. You stood up to her and gave her exactly what she deserved. That's more than most girls would do." She raised her water glass to Valerie. "Well done."

Her slip in etiquette hadn't driven Dinah and the others away. It was certainly promising.

The patronesses continued to speak while the waiters slid sal-ads in front of them and later replaced the dishes with chicken in a thick cream sauce. Lady de Walden thrilled at the unusual number of duchesses attending and how tiaras would be worn be-cause of it.

"At least with this ball we don't have to wait around for a chap to ask us to it, we can ask them," Dinah whispered to Valerie. "Who's your escort?"

"I have no idea. I don't know any chaps."

"We'll have to change that."

"Shhh," the blonde across the table hissed.

"Shh yourself," Dinah shot back and leaned closer to Valerie. "These cats are never going to let us have a good chat. Come to tea with us at Aunt Nancy's tomorrow, then you can spill all the gossip without everyone hissing at us like flattening tires."

"My cousin's hair will go gray if she hears I've been discussing adultery at the home of a viscountess."

"Then don't tell her. It's none of her business what we say. I'm sure she doesn't tell you everything she and her married friends chat about."

"She doesn't tell me anything except what to do or say. It's terribly exhausting."

"What a bore. Never mind her, you have my permission to speak with us however you like. Promise me you'll come."

Valerie picked at her chicken, thrilled and terrified by the invitation. She'd made a right royal mess of things with Vivien, but Dinah and the others didn't care. They wanted to spend more time with her, and the pile of invitations at home couldn't compare to this personal one. Like living in No. 10, this was an opportunity she couldn't miss. Hopefully, she wouldn't ruin it either, but she'd never make friends by staying home and she very much wanted friends. "I'll be there."

Chapter Five

ood afternoon, Valerie." Dorothy came in from outside, removing her coat and handing it to the No. 10 footman while Henry closed the black-lacquered door. "Is Mummy here? I popped by to see her on my way to the dressmaker's."

"She's reviewing arrangements for the King and Queen's dinner." It wasn't until the second week of April but the endless details and royal protocol constantly demanded Aunt Anne's attention. Valerie eyed Dorothy, wondering what she was really about. With her milliner in Knightsbridge, Downing Street was hardly on the way.

"Where are you off to?" Dorothy scrutinized Valerie's gray floral day dress with the shirred top and the gray wool overcoat.

"Lady Astor's house in St. James's Square. Dinah Brand and some other girls and I are having tea together." Valerie waited for her cousin to be impressed. She wasn't.

"What other girls?"

Valerie tried not to sigh as she listed their names. Dorothy nodded her approval the way the Mother Superior used to do when Valerie successfully listed the cardinal sins. "A notable group of girls worth knowing, but I'd be remiss if I didn't warn you to be careful. Some women, even those who claim to be your friends, don't have your best interests at heart. You might innocently mention something about Mavis or that dreadful school of yours in France thinking you have their confidence, only to find they're all too eager to tell everyone."

"If they were going to be cruel they would've done it already." Vivien was proof of that, and it was no wonder, given the stock she came from, but it made Valerie wonder why Dinah and the others were so quick to befriend her.

"Perhaps, but lady friends can be very catty and such jealous beasts, wrecking your chances with a man because they don't have one." Dorothy brushed a bit of fluff off Valerie's coat the way she often did with her daughter when they went for walks. "A little caution may save you a great deal of regret later."

As sick as it made Valerie to admit it, Dorothy was right. During Valerie's first days in the convent school, she'd befriended Nanette, a new girl who'd been skinnier and shier than her. At night they used to whisper across the space between their beds, telling each other about their lives before the convent. She thought she'd finally found a true friend until Nanette had told Antoinette everything. The taunting had grown more vicious after that. They'd been jealous of the English girl who still had family and the chance to leave. It was a hope they hadn't enjoyed. "I'll be cautious."

"Good." Dorothy laced her hands in front of her like the nuns used to do during inspections. "Who's your chaperone for the ride to Lady Astor's?"

"No one. I'm going alone."

"You can't."

"Good heavens, this isn't Queen Victoria's reign. Unless Mr. May suddenly has some amorous ideas about me, I'm perfectly safe in the back of Uncle Neville's car."

"That isn't the point." Dorothy puckered her lips in the same lemon-sucking scowl the Mother Superior used to flash every time Valerie had begged for more stamps and writing paper. "There are rules that must be followed, no matter how ridiculous you think they are. One is that respectable young ladies must be chaperoned. Mummy should send Miss Leaf with you."

"Miss Leaf has too much to do to babysit me about London."

"Then we'll find someone else. You, there." Dorothy snapped her fingers at Miss Holmes, who had the unfortunate luck to happen by with her notepad and pencil. "Miss de Vere Cole needs someone to accompany her to Lady Astor's. You'll ride with her and then return with the car."

Miss Holmes glanced from Valerie to Dorothy before she lowered her notepad. "With all due respect, Mrs. Lloyd, it isn't the typists' place to serve as chaperones for the Premier's family."

"Nonsense, I'm sure you can be spared. Who do I speak with to arrange it?"

Valerie threw Miss Holmes an apologetic smile, but the Garden Room Girl remained as composed as before. There was a skill Valerie hoped the Season would instill in her. "Mrs. Stenhouse."

"Take me to her at once."

Miss Holmes escorted Dorothy downstairs with the same efficiency she employed with ministers and secretaries entering the Cabinet Room. Maybe Mr. May would bring the car around and Valerie could slip away before Dorothy turned the entire government upside down in her propriety crusade. She wasn't that fortunate, and Dorothy and Miss Holmes returned before he pulled up to the curb.

If the smile brightening Dorothy's face hadn't announced her triumph, then Miss Holmes in her camel-colored coat and carrying a large envelope was a dead giveaway.

"It took some maneuvering with that stubborn woman in the Garden Room. Does she not understand the importance of propriety?" Dorothy complained.

"She understands the real work you're pulling Miss Holmes away from."

"Nonsense. I doubt Miss Holmes has anything important to do. There's Mr. May. Off you go. We don't want to keep Miss Brand and the others waiting."

Henry opened the door and Miss Holmes made for the car. Valerie was about to follow when Dorothy stepped in front of her. "Be friendly but not too friendly with Miss Holmes. You didn't grow up with servants, so you don't understand the delicate relationship between them and us. Remember your place and hers and you'll be fine. Now run along. Tardiness is bad manners."

Valerie didn't bother to point out that Dorothy's fussing was making her late. Instead she marched outside and stepped in the car. "I'm sorry about Mrs. Lloyd. She can be a touch overbearing at times."

"It's all right, I'm quite used to it." Miss Holmes settled the envelope on her lap. "My sisters are like that, always at me for sounding posh and accusing me of reaching above my station. They're jealous, but if they'd studied harder they might work somewhere more important than shops in Clapham. It's easier to tear people down than it is to praise them."

Didn't Valerie know it? "I hope this doesn't put you too far behind in your work."

"If it does, it can't be helped, and I don't mind getting out for a little while, even if it's just to the War Office." She motioned to the envelope.

"Miss Holmes, shall I drop you there now or on the return?" Mr. May asked.

"On the way back, please. I'd like a little time away from the typewriter, my next half day isn't until Sunday." She settled against the seat with a tired sigh, watching London pass outside the window.

Mr. May drove the car down Whitehall and past the white-brick War Office building with its columns and domes. Piles of sandbags blocked the view of the ground floor and men in army uniforms came and went from the maze inside. The War Office appeared a great deal busier today than it had the many other times she'd passed it.

"Is Uncle Neville any closer to a solution?" Valerie asked, hating to intrude on Miss Holmes's moment of peace but wondering if there was more to worry about than possibly wicked female friends.

Miss Holmes appeared more surprised by this than by Dorothy's demand for a chaperone. "Has he not told you anything?"

"I haven't seen him enough for him to tell me anything, and Aunt Anne doesn't discuss it. Politics isn't considered an essential part of a debutante's education." Valerie had taken the evening papers upstairs after supper yesterday, determined to read the political and international news, but after the late court night and the stress of the luncheon, she'd collapsed into bed exhausted. Mary had collected the papers when she'd come in that morning to light the fire. Valerie hadn't been any more diligent about world affairs during breakfast, poring over the *Tatler* and *Bystander* without a thought for the *Times*. She'd searched the society pages for any mention of yesterday's tiff with Vivien but there'd been nothing except glowing praise for more debutantes.

"Politics isn't part of any young woman's education. If it weren't for my position, I'd be as ignorant as my sisters, but there's no reason why you should be." She faced Valerie with the seriousness of a headmistress but with far more humor and warmth than any teacher Valerie had ever endured. "The Premier isn't any closer to a solution than he was the other day, and there are rumors that Herr Hitler will widen his aggression to Lithuania. He has his eye on the Memel, a crucial port on the Baltic Sea."

"What'll happen if he invades it?"

"I don't know, but most ministers aren't willing to start another war over a small slice of Lithuania, and there's still hope that once Germany reclaims everything it lost in the Treaty of Versailles they'll be satisfied."

"Grasping people are never satisfied." She'd spent enough time with Mavis to know.

"Keep faith in the Premier. He'll do all he can to protect England."

"I'm sure he will." No one wanted war, not after the last one.

The car continued down Whitehall to Cockspur Street, passing beneath the shadow of the high statue of Admiral Nelson in Trafalgar Square. Miss Holmes continued to take in the passing streets, her position and knowledge making her seem very mature but she couldn't be more than a year or two older than Valerie. She probably thought Valerie a silly deb who looked down on working girls, but Valerie didn't dismiss them like Dorothy did. How could she? If Valerie could've earned a living in Ascain, she wouldn't have fallen as far as she had. "How did you become a typist?"

"My father encouraged me to take the Civil Service exam after secretarial school. He said I'd get further there than anywhere else. He's a conductor at the Victoria Palace Theatre and wanted at least one of us to do better." She said it with as much pride as if her father were an earl. Her refined accent might trick one into thinking that was the case, but she was simply a young woman trying to improve her life.

Not so different from me. Except Father had squandered her opportunities instead of encouraging them. If it weren't for Aunt Anne, Miss Holmes would be a great deal better off than Valerie. "You've done very well for yourself."

"I think so, and now I get to rub my sisters' noses in having ridden in the Premier's private car." She laughed like Valerie had yesterday with Dinah. Valerie offered a matching smile, relaxing for the first time since Dorothy had dragged Miss Holmes into this drive.

They turned onto Pall Mall, and the lush green trees of St. James's Square surrounding the bronze statue of William III in the center came into view. The car glided to a stop at a small pillared entrance stuffed in the corner of the square of cheek-by-jowl houses. With its dark brick facing, Palladian front, and white-trimmed windows, it seemed too small for Lord and Lady Astor's notoriously large personalities and soirees. How they fit the hundreds of guests who regularly attended their parties in there she didn't know, but she was about to find out, along with how much of Dorothy's unwelcome warning about female friends was true.

Curse Dorothy. Why does she have to spoil everything?

Mr. May came around to open the door. Valerie gathered up her purse and prepared to step out.

"Shall I walk you to the door so no ruffians attack you?" Miss Holmes asked with an impish smile.

"I think I'm quite safe here." She wished she could invite Miss Holmes to join her, to bring in an ally to help her face whatever waited for her inside, but it was impossible. Miss Holmes had her work to do and Valerie had hers, even if society didn't seem quite so important as government business. Except it was. Valerie's future depended on making friends and forming connections. Without them, she'd be as alone and overlooked in England as she'd been in France. "Thank you for accompanying me."

"It was my pleasure."

Valerie approached the Astors' front door, where the butler, a lanky man in black tails and a white waistcoat, greeted her. "Miss Brand is expecting you."

He ushered her inside and helped her off with her coat. Valerie barely felt him removing it from her shoulders, too in awe of the house. To say the plain entrance expertly concealed the space and grandeur of the inside was a misstatement. Everything on the walls that wasn't a work of art was either covered in ornate molding or gilded. The high ceilings supported by the plaster Corinthian columns with gold tops gave the foyer an airiness anchored by the marble and bronze statues tucked in the alcoves.

"If you'll follow me." The butler led her up the staircase.

She trailed her hand over the polished dark wood banister, grasping it every so often to lean back and take in the intricate friezes set in the high walls. Large windows filled the marble staircase with light that sparkled off the gilded-columned spindles that matched the ones holding up the ceiling. The sheer opulence was breathtaking and far more lavish than No. 10, the Astors' wealth and status echoing in every detail. None of it was weighed down by the practical needs of civil servants and the government. She couldn't help but wonder how different things might've been if her father hadn't lost his town house in Cadogan Square to creditors. She would've been raised in London, and Dinah and this house might have been a part of her childhood, familiar from years of birthday parties and children's teas. Instead, she'd been exiled to boarding school and France.

She paused at the top of the stairs and drew in a steadying

breath. That was all behind her. She was the debutante in Downing Street with friends to visit, and unless Dorothy's doom-and-gloom predictions came true, this house would become a regular part of her life.

They walked down the wide upstairs hallway, passing the antiques, paintings, and fine rugs filling the space. Various footmen and secretaries hustled by, their activity similar to the bustle of Downing Street. With Lord Astor in the House of Lords and Lady Astor in the Commons, she wasn't surprised by the flurry of people.

"We must support those Germans who are willing to stand up to Herr Hitler. They could foment a revolution within Germany that will oust him and end this menace once and for all," Lady Astor's refined but commanding voice rang out. Valerie paused at the open door of a study with red-silk-covered walls and a painting of a manor house hung between the windows. Lady Astor sat behind a large burled-wood desk with a black telephone receiver pressed to one ear. She signed the paper on the blotter with a flourish and handed it to the secretary on her left, while the man on the right slid another in front of her. "Yes, thank you for calling."

Lady Astor dropped the phone on the base and looked over her shoulder to the older social secretary who sat at a Louis XV French writing desk near the window. "Mrs. Wendell, place Sir Vansittart on the list for dinner. He'll offer valuable insight into the German situation."

"Yes, Lady Astor."

"If some of these ignorant men, such as Sir Arnold Wilson, can't see who Herr Hitler really is after the last two days, then a dose of truth about what it's like to live under that awful man might open their eyes."

"I doubt it." Lord Astor brushed his hand over his graying dark hair, his round face accented by a bushy mustache. He lounged in a wing chair by the large fireplace, his feet propped up on a footstool. "Meeting the Führer didn't open the Duke of Windsor's eyes. It only made that gullible fool more enamored of him. If he were still King he'd be cozying up to that German menace instead of trying to thwart him."

"The Duke of Windsor supports Herr Hitler?" Valerie exclaimed, then clapped her hand over her mouth. She shouldn't eavesdrop on a private conversation, and she expected them to sternly say so. She was surprised when Lord Astor rose, smiling instead of scowling.

"The Duke of Windsor isn't known for good judgment."

"If he were, he'd still be King, not the husband of that fourth-rate divorcée." Lady Astor swept out from behind her desk, the wide collar of her teal blouse fluttering with her movements. A tight strand of pearls encircled her wrinkled neck and a pair of pearl earrings dangled from her earlobes. "Good day, Miss de Vere Cole. It's a pleasure to see you."

"I'm sorry to interrupt."

"No need to apologize. Treat our house as if it were your own and come whenever you like. It does Dinah good to have friends about, and you can plot your conquests. Now, if you'll excuse us. World affairs are pressing."

"Of course." Valerie left them to their work and followed the butler, stunned by what she'd overheard. She'd thought German admirers all extremists like Sir Oswald, not the former monarch and who knows what other members of society Lady Astor intended to convince. She hoped Lady Astor succeeded. Uncle Neville needed England's full support to maintain the peace. At least Lady Astor hadn't pounced on Valerie for interrupting them. They'd welcomed her despite her slip, which was more than Lady Ashcombe and her ilk had done. Whether Dinah and the others would continue to be welcoming after another go at her remained to be seen, but there was no backing out of it, not with the butler opening the sitting room door.

"Valerie, at last!" Dinah jumped up from the table where she and the other girls sat and clasped Valerie by the arm, dragging her into the white-paneled room accented with Wedgwood blue, and past the two marble Greek philosophers holding up the fireplace mantel. "We were afraid you wouldn't make it."

"I had some trouble with the car at Number Ten." Valerie took the empty seat between Christian and Katherine, sitting back to allow the butler to lay a napkin across her lap and pour a cup of tea. The airy brightness of the room was a far cry from the dark wood and plain plaster walls of the convent dining room or the drafty and cluttered Victorian sitting room of the Cambridge dame school. Conversation during meals at both places had been forbidden, leaving plenty of time to concentrate on the poor food that'd never quelled her hunger.

"Are you excited about the *Midnight* film premiere?" Christian asked. "I think it'll be divine."

"I can't wait to meet Ronnie Howard," Katherine gushed. "I heard he'll be there. Maybe his father will join him. Imagine seeing Leslie Howard in person. I wonder how he'll be in *Gone with the Wind*."

"He's sure to be marvelous, as he is in everything," Eunice assured. "I've read all the film magazines about it. Mother thinks they're perfectly dreadful rags but I adore them. It's my one vice."

"Then you aren't a nun after all." Dinah dismissed the butler, who bowed and left.

"I would be if Mother let me, but it'd ruin her plans for me to marry an important Catholic man who'll bring more grandeur to the Kennedy name. Mother's only devotion besides Catholicism is to never be looked down on."

"A tall order for an ambassador's wife. Speaking of chaps." Dinah turned to Valerie. "Will you be at Lindsey Furneaux's coming-out ball tomorrow night?"

"I will." Valerie accepted the plate of scones from Katherine.

"Good, I've decided that none of us will allow the others to stand alone if we don't have a dance partner."

"Then you'll be standing out a great deal with me. I barely know a soul," Eunice complained.

"I thought your sister knew everyone."

"To hear her tell it she does, but heaven forbid her little sister tag along and meet them."

"All the more reason for a pledge. We'll make sure we introduce one another to the chaps we know."

"I don't know any." Christian poured cream into her tea.

"Neither do I, except for government secretaries. With everything happening in Europe, they aren't likely to attend balls. Even if they did, you wouldn't be interested in them, they're terribly droll." Valerie popped a piece of warm scone in her mouth, enjoying the tang of lemon curd to keep from blurting out anything else to make her appear more socially inept.

"Then you must meet my cousins, their friends, and Katherine's brother. They're all great pals." Dinah wasn't nearly as concerned with Valerie's nonexistent circle of male friends as Valerie was.

"They aren't very good dancers, so don't wear any shoes you mind getting stepped on," Katherine suggested with a rumbling chuckle.

"I'm more worried about the conversation than the dancing," Eunice complained. "What are we supposed to talk about?"

"If you can't think of anything, then use the alphabet game," Katherine suggested. "My sister taught it to me. You begin with a topic that starts with an *A*, and if that doesn't do it, then keep going through the letters until you find something that sparks his interest. Hopefully, you won't have to resort to that, but there you have it in case you need it."

"Heaven forbid." Eunice sighed. "Given the sheer number of invitations I've already received, I'm sure I'll have to use it once or twice. They won't all be great conversationalists. How are we ever to get through all of the dances?"

"By sticking together. We can make it a sort of club similar to Aunt Nancy's Ark Club but without the intellectual conversation or naming everyone after animals and such," Dinah continued in a rush of words.

"What was it they named my father?" Katherine looked to the ceiling as if the answer were written beside the chandelier medallion. "Gore the Gorilla."

"Aunt Nancy was the Gnat."

"Quite fitting, since she's always moving." Lady Astor hadn't been still the entire three minutes Valerie had watched her work.

"What shall we call ourselves, then?" Christian asked. "A club must have a name. All the good ones do."

"Hmm." Dinah touched her finger to her chin while everyone mulled over something worth suggesting.

A couple of ideas came to Valerie but she kept them to herself, thinking them too silly. She didn't wish to be laughed out of their circle before the end of the first tea.

"I've got it." Dinah clapped her hands together and sat up straight. "We'll call ourselves the Excellencies because we're all related to politicians."

"My father was merely the Deputy Lieutenant of Aberdeenshire," Christian lamented. "Hardly notable, considering he never did anything."

"That's good enough. What do you say, Your Excellencies?"

"It's a grand idea," Katherine seconded, and Eunice and Christian both agreed.

"What about you, Valerie? Are you in? Please say you are. It'll be ever so fun."

Valerie paused in dishing out a dollop of lemon curd. For girls waiting to pounce, they were certainly going to a great deal of trouble to look out for one another, and her. *Fish Dorothy's fearmongering*, she wasn't about to risk standing out alone at dances. She set down her spoon and picked up her tea. "I am, Your Excellencies."

"Your Excellencies." Dinah clinked her teacup against Valerie's, the others joining in to make the Astor china ring to the corniced ceiling.

"Wait, before we drink, I have something more bracing." Dinah dashed to a walnut bombé chest to fetch a dark glass bottle from inside. She hurried back to the table, pulled the cork, and tipped a sherry-like liquid into each girl's cup.

"What is this?" Katherine sniffed, wincing at the petrol smell.

"I thought your aunt was a teetotaler." Uncle Neville and Aunt Anne had grumbled more than once after a dinner at Lady Astor's about the lack of libations to smooth out the more argumentative guests.

"She is, but the gamekeeper at Cliveden has a hidden still. I slip him a few bob to keep me in regular supply. I'm quite popular at dinners when guests need something more bracing than witty conversation to get them through the evening. Cheers, girls."

They took a sip, most of them coughing and sputtering at the aperitif.

"A charming recipe." Katherine cleared her throat.

Christian coughed, her cheeks bright red. "It'd pop the pennies off a dead Scotsman's eyes."

"I quite like it." Eunice licked her lips and held out her cup for more.

Valerie could almost see Dinah refilling it through her watering eyes. "Well, Your Excellencies, what's our first order of business?"

"To widen your circle of chaps." Dinah tapped the cork into the liquor bottle. "Aunt Nancy told me Elm is going to be at Lady Dunford's coming-out dance."

"A tree?" Valerie didn't think floral decorations were anything to get riled up about.

"Lord Elmswood, the Marquess of Fallington's son, a very eligible bachelor with a family pile that's still flush," Katherine matter-of-factly explained. "He's a friend of my brother David's and of Dinah's cousins, Jakie and Michael. They were all at Eton and Oxford together."

While Katherine continued to detail the young lord's lineage, Eunice whispered to Valerie, "I can't keep track of all these titled people and I'm tired of looking the fool for asking."

"Me too." Most of the society families were so intertwined, one needed a chart to keep it all straight. Her lineage was mixed in there somewhere, but instead of having been raised with these names and titles tossed about like dinner dishes, Valerie struggled to keep them and their social idiosyncrasies straight. "At least they're kind about explaining it."

"Tell me about it. I made the mistake of asking Lady Meade about a title once and she looked at me as if I'd spit on her scone." She stuck her nose in the air in what Valerie thought was a perfect impression of a snotty dowager.

"Elm's father is in government and banking like mine and Dinah's," Katherine explained. "And a vocal member of the House of Lords. He's one of the many men being considered for First Lord of the Admiralty."

"Elm's a real deb's delight." Dinah returned her contraband to its hiding place. "A bit broody but quite the charmer."

"Heathcliff-broody or Mr. Rochester–broody?" Valerie pushed away her unfinished tea.

"I don't know either of those chaps, but get to know Elm and you'll always have at least one dance partner."

"No, thanks. I've already had the pleasure of being snubbed by his mother and sister. I don't need the son and heir looking down his aristocratic nose at me."

"Don't take it personally, Lady Fallington does that to everyone, but Elm isn't like that. I've spent loads of time with him at Cliveden. He's can be a touch serious and self-involved but not at all nasty."

"Then why haven't you made a rush for him?" Christian asked.

"I don't care for him like that. Although I must admit he'd be tolerable enough to stare at across a breakfast table and when it comes to other things." Dinah rolled her spoon in the air, then set it in the saucer with a clink.

"What other things?" Eunice innocently asked, and the girls burst out laughing.

"Didn't they teach you anything at Catholic school?"

"The sisters don't talk about such things, and don't act so worldly," Eunice chided. "I've seen how the young marrieds clam up whenever us unmarrieds are around."

"You don't need to eavesdrop like a scullery maid, simply ask your friends. That's how I learned everything. It certainly wasn't from my mother. She won't discuss it even when I ask," Katherine said with a sigh.

"My stepmother never held back even when I wanted her to keep her mouth shut." And her legs. It would've spared Valerie and Father a lot of trouble in Ascain if Mavis hadn't been so free with her favors.

"Is that where you heard all those delightful stories about Mrs. Guinness, I mean *Lady Mosley*?" Christian asked.

Valerie gripped her fork so hard, the pattern imprinted on her palm before she set it down. She should've held her tongue instead of advertising her worldliness, which, according to Dorothy, was a cardinal sin. If it was, Their Excellencies didn't think so, practically perched on the edge of their chairs to hear more gossip. "I don't know anything more than anyone else."

"Liar," Dinah challenged. "Tell us everything about Lady Mosley and her awful sisters. We're desperate for the delicious details."

Valerie shouldn't say anything, but she could hardly pretend to ignorance, not after the licking she'd given Vivien at the luncheon. There was nothing to do but spill what she knew and sing for her supper; after all, this was why she'd been invited here. She glanced around to see if the butler had slipped into the room. She'd never be allowed out of No. 10 again if Dorothy caught wind of this.

"Don't worry, there's no one to overhear. Even if there was, Aunt Nancy pays her servants well enough to keep the gossip flowing into the house and not out of it."

Given some of the things Valerie had heard from Mary, stories were slipping out of the Astors' back entrance, but this room seemed safe enough, assuming none of them walked out of here and told their parents or siblings what they'd heard and from whom. Valerie didn't need that kind of reputation, assuming their families were easily offended. Valerie doubted they were. She'd sat through enough debates in the House of Commons to know Lady Astor didn't suffer from delicate sensibilities and Ambassador Kennedy was rarely shy with his opinions. As for the other girls, she couldn't say what their mothers might think, but at least she'd come out of this with one or two friends. That was better than none and worth the risk of getting in trouble for appearing a touch too worldly.

"Debo Mitford is the best of the sisters," Valerie began, her voice trembling as the girls perched their elbows on the table to listen with rapt attention. "The rest are simply awful, especially Vivien's stepmother, Diana. She left her husband, the Guinness heir, to live in sin with Sir Oswald. If it hadn't been for the baby, he never would've married her. Jessica Mitford is no better. She ran off with Esmond Rommilly, an avowed Communist and nearly as bad as Sir Oswald. They only married after Nancy, the eldest sister, cornered them in Spain. Even then it took some maneuvering to get them to the altar and keep Jessica from complete ruin."

"Where did you hear so much, Valerie?"

"Our French landlady in Ascain shared more gossip than a lady's maid."

"What were you doing there?" Dinah asked, more curious than perplexed.

"The weather there was better for my father's health than in Paris." She was repeating the story Dorothy and Aunt Anne had concocted like a well-trained parrot. "He had heart troubles."

His constant drinking had exacerbated them, along with the biting cold and lack of food during their last few weeks together before Mr. Shoedelin had stepped in and made things worse.

"Pneumonia did my mother in." Dinah frowned and turned her teacup in its saucer, staring into the dark liquid before she looked up, her expression bright as ever. "Hard to believe there are so many bad eggs in the Mitford family."

"Unity was in Germany while I was there studying last year." Katherine set her napkin beside her empty plate. "I don't understand her beastly fixation with Herr Hitler. I heard what he said about the Jews and saw what they're doing to them, taking their shops and stripping them of their rights. That she and Lord and Lady Mosley want it to happen here is perfectly dreadful."

"I'll say," Christian agreed. "Anne Schuster, the girl I'm sharing my coming-out ball with, her family is Jewish, and I heard her mother talking to mine. She's in an awful state about it."

"It won't happen here," Eunice assured them. "Not after those East Enders stood up to the Blackshirts and gave them a taste of their own medicine."

"Or when Valerie made Vivien think twice about spouting such nonsense in polite society," Dinah added. "But enough of that nasty business. Who wants to host our next tea?"

"Valerie must do it," Christian insisted. "Assuming, of course, you're allowed. I don't want to seem pushy or impose, but I so want to see Downing Street."

"Go on and impose," Katherine encouraged. "You won't see me sticking my nose up at an invitation to Number Ten."

"It isn't as posh as you think. The house is drafty, even after all of Aunt Anne's improvements."

"Sounds like every house in England," Eunice replied. "But I don't care. Kick will be green with envy that her sister is chummy with the Prime Minister's niece. To hear her talk you'd think she was the Queen of England's best friend."

"If she and Billy Harrington continue on, she might very well become the next Duchess of Devonshire," Katherine said.

"The saints in heaven forbid!" Eunice made the sign of the cross over her white and blue sprig-patterned dress. "She can't marry a Protestant. She won't. That's a mortal sin."

"It's a sin I'd commit." Christian dreamily stirred her tea.

"It's a sin we'd all commit, but we'll settle for tea at Number Ten," Dinah proclaimed. "Valerie, old girl, you're the next to host."

"Is that why you invited me here today, to cajole me into giving you a peek inside the Prime Minister's residence?" It was a half-serious question. She wanted to know why they were so quick to accept her when everyone else practically sprinted away.

"Yes, and you're smashing fun to be around."

"That's not what the girls at my French finishing school thought." *Finishing school.* What a lark, to call the convent that simply to save face. Oliver Twist's workhouse would have been a paradise in comparison, but its real name was too dreary to contemplate. Valerie's knees still ached whenever she heard Latin, the memory of kneeling on the cold stone during the endless masses while light-headed with hunger making her shudder. "They were ugly little snots."

"I'm not surprised. You know how the French are," Dinah said, as if this were enough to explain the hard-hearted nuns or the nasty students. But of course they knew nothing of what it'd really been like there. They assumed Valerie had lived in genteel luxury with some poor aristocrat paid to teach French and expose them to art. She couldn't tell the truth and have them regard her with the same horror as Mr. Shoedelin.

"Oh, I know how the French are," Eunice concurred. "Mother takes us there every year to buy clothes. Even the shopgirls are arrogant. It must be something in the water."

"Or the wine."

"The Swiss aren't any different, at least the French-speaking ones. The girls at my boarding school in Fetan were beastly." Dinah finished her tea and dropped the cup in its saucer with a clank.

Valerie's heart went out to her, hating to think anyone else had been locked away in one of those awful schools. "Then you must come to Downing Street. I'll send a note around with the date once it's fixed. It won't be nearly as interesting as Buckingham Palace but it'll be fun."

They fell into conversation, discussing this girl or that chap. Valerie listened, soaking it all in. If this was sitting in a pit of vipers, then they were the most charming and fun she'd ever met, which would make it all the more deadly and disheartening if they did decide to strike. Oh, it was too ridiculous to think that every woman in society was filing her nails into points and waiting to scratch some other's eyes out. If that were true, then Aunt Anne wouldn't have friends, and she and Lady Bridgeman were as thick as thieves. Unless, of course, there was something Dorothy knew about these girls that Valerie didn't, a trait she wouldn't discover until it was too late. She hoped that wasn't the case.

UNCLE NEVILLE AND Valerie strode through St. James's Park early the next morning. Wisps of fog clung to the edges of the trenches dug through the green grass after the Anschluss last year. Men in uniform tromped along their tops, inspecting the crumbling sides and shooing away boys trying to play in them. The lines of the earthworks weren't neat or tidy, having been left to the London winter instead of the army after the Munich Agreement.

"How are you finding the Season?" Uncle Neville swung his umbrella in time with his gait, his detective remaining a respectable distance behind to give them privacy.

"Exhausting. I don't know how I'll manage three and a half more months of this." After tea with Their Excellencies and then the late dinner party last night at Lady Londonderry's, she'd craved a long lie-in this morning, but the Horse Guards had been particularly vigorous with their drills. She was glad she'd come downstairs instead of trying to fall back asleep, catching Uncle Neville as he'd set off for a quick jaunt around the park before the cabinet meeting. It was a rare treat to have him all to herself.

"You'll find a way, and it's good training for the rigors of life, a chance to build your stamina. I was your age when I ran my family's plantation in the Bahamas. It was grueling work, but it taught me to overcome mistakes and setbacks instead of allowing them to defeat me. I wouldn't be where I am today if I hadn't learned those lessons. This Season, you'll do the same. Never dwell on failure or the past. Take what lessons you can from them and then carry on."

"I'll do my best." Ignoring the past was not her strong suit. It wasn't as long ago as she'd like.

He raised his umbrella in greeting to an old couple sitting on a bench by the lake feeding the ducks. They offered a cheerful wave in return. "How are you getting on with the other debutantes?"

"Well enough, I suppose." Despite the splendid afternoon at Dinah's, she still couldn't shake Dorothy's fearmongering.

"You suppose?" Uncle Neville pressed.

"You don't want to hear it, not when you have more important things to manage." There was no mistaking the dark circles beneath his eyes or the slight bend in his shoulders from his responsibilities. He didn't need her concerns added to the pile.

"Nonsense, it'll give me something to consider besides Germany." He slid her a sideways smile that softened the deep lines around his eyes.

"All right." If anyone could see things clearly, it was Uncle Neville. "I've become friendly with a few girls, I like them very much and I'm sure they like me, but Dorothy says they're simply lying in wait to hear something delicious about me to tell everyone. Do you think they are?"

He rested his umbrella on his shoulder, pausing as he often did after a difficult question from the Commons. "Annie's told me about some of the girls. I think it's splendid you getting to know Lady Astor's niece, and the Ormsby girl, her father is well regarded in government circles and the House of Lords. They're fine connections that could serve you well in the future."

A very practical way to view things. "But is Dorothy right? Should I be wary of them?"

"If you tell your secrets to every flibbertigibbet who flutters around thinking they have your best interests in mind, you will regret it. However, if you're cautious, you'll eventually learn whom to trust or avoid. You might also discover that some of those girls need your friendship as much as you need theirs."

"How can that be, when they've always been here and have known one another for ages?"

He stopped, hooked the umbrella handle over his arm, and faced her. He was tall and thin, his top hat adding to his impressive height and shading his eyes. He studied her with genuine care and concern, the way she wished Father would've done. "No matter what it appears from the outside, not everyone has it easy. Given everything you've endured, you might be in a better position to understand and help them with their difficulties than the people they've grown up with."

"I hadn't thought of it that way."

"They may not either, they may simply be drawn to something in you that you have yet to see in yourself."

"Mr. Chamberlain, Mr. Chamberlain!" Mr. Colville's high voice carried across the grass as the lanky second secretary hurried toward them, nearly out of breath once he reached them. "Sir John must speak to you at once about the latest draft of your speech condemning Germany's hostile actions. He and some cabinet members believe it should be stronger."

"I'll condemn the invasion and suggest reprisals if Germany refuses to halt their aggression, but I won't risk outright war by threatening them. We must be careful, Mr. Colville. The situation is too precarious to be careless."

Mr. Colville glanced uneasily from Uncle Neville to Valerie and back again. "Perhaps it's better if we discussed this alone, sir."

Uncle Neville offered Valerie a regretful smile and took hold of the umbrella handle. "It appears our walk is at an end."

"Thank you, Uncle Neville, you've given me a great deal to consider."

"I'm glad I could be of assistance." With a tip of his hat, he and Mr. Colville walked back to No. 10, the affairs of state as pressing for him as the requirements of the Season were for her, except his domain was world affairs. Hers was balls and dresses and her new friends.

Chapter Six

Lord and Lady Dunford

Request the pleasure of your company
at a dance in honor of their daughter
The Honorable Guinevere Brodrick
On Wednesday the twenty-second of
March at half after ten o'clock

---

44 Cadogan Place, Belgravia

The pillared entrance to the house in Cadogan Place was identical to the ones on either side of it, the wrought-iron fences as uniform as the front façades. The line of cars waiting to reach No. 44 had been so long that Valerie and Aunt Anne had abandoned the Rolls in favor of a walk and joined the stream of guests eager to arrive before the party ended. The house stood across from a leafy green square where men and women in silk evening dresses and white-tie mingled under the stars, taking advantage of the rare warm late March evening to steal a moment of private conversation away from the chaperones' watchful eyes.

At the front gate of every house they'd passed, Valerie wondered if that was the one her father had owned. *I could've lived next to a lord instead of that bottom-pinching Major Bolton.* Ascain and nearby Saint-Jean-de-Luz had been infested with lecherous old army men desperate to live on the cheap. It's too bad one of them hadn't snapped up Mavis instead of her father doing so, but his judgment had never been sharp, unlike Mavis's talons. Valerie followed Aunt Anne into the house, turning to allow the footman to remove her black velvet coat and reveal the light blue satin dress with the flowing ruche skirt and puff sleeves. *No bitterness, not tonight. Leave the past and learn from it.* She'd be better than Father, and become a respected member of society despite all his efforts to ruin her.

They stepped into the long receiving line snaking up the wide staircase. Below them was the square entrance hall flanked by sitting rooms, and an abundance of gentlemen, more so than two nights ago when every grandfather or younger brother up from Eton had been pressed into service. It simply wasn't done, for a man who could dance to shirk his duties and risk a girl sitting out for lack of a partner. A haze of cigarette smoke hung in the air and mixed with the bright scent of the lemon trees arranged in grand pots around the room. Tarps of faux–painted brick meant to resemble a medieval Spanish castle were draped over the walls and multicolored Spanish garlands hung between the high chandeliers and the heavy, black wrought-iron candelabras filled with dripping candles. It was the most extravagantly decorated ball Valerie had attended so far, outdoing the German-beer-hall-themed one from last night that many had thought in bad taste given the tension between Britain and Germany.

"Good evening, ladies." Lady Astor slid up to Aunt Anne, her ruby necklace and red dress complementing the Spanish theme. "Anne, can you believe we're putting up with this charade?"

"It isn't Miss Dunford's fault her mother is who she is, and I'm not one to visit the sins of the mother or the father on any child." Aunt Anne leaned closer to Valerie. "Lady Dunsford was a showgirl in America before her two advantageous matches. Her first husband was an American millionaire with a taste for actresses."

"They all have a taste for actresses, but they usually don't marry them. Lord Dunsford did, and we've been saddled with her progeny ever since. I'm not one to poo-poo any American woman with an eye for a title, but to foist her prior children off on society as if they were His Lordship's, forcing everyone to call them honorable when they're about as honorable as I am retiring is beyond the pale. If I'd tried that, Waldorf would've shipped us back to America. Look smart, ladies, Prince George and Princess Maria are approaching," Lady Astor warned.

They straightened out of their gossip circle to watch Prince George, the King's younger brother, and his slender wife, Princess Maria of Greece, descend the stairs and leave a ripple of curtseys and bows in their wake. The Princess wore a Grecian-style black silk gown that draped over one shoulder and across a bosom Valerie tried not to stare at to see if she was wearing a brassiere. If she had to bet with Their Excellencies, she'd insist the Princess was quite nude beneath her gown, but it was bad manners to stare at a royal's bust. She kept her eyes on the Prince instead, the dark-haired young man by far the most attractive of the royal sons.

"Mrs. Chamberlain, Lady Astor." Prince George stopped to bow to the ladies. "I'm glad politics doesn't prevent you from enjoying the delights of the Season. It wouldn't be as glittering if it did."

"You're too kind, Your Highness," Aunt Anne said.

"As are you, for hosting the King and Queen. We're sorry to miss it," Princess Marie offered.

"We're sorry you aren't able to join us."

With a parting nod, the Prince and Princess moved on to chat with other guests.

"The scandal following him is as strong as his cologne," Lady Astor remarked to his back as he disappeared with his wife's exposed shoulder into the crowd. "Born with a silver spoon. Exchanged it for a silver syringe."

"No wonder he smiles so much."

Valerie gaped at the women, afraid to breathe for fear they'd remember she was listening and stop talking. Whatever it was that'd made Aunt Anne remark on a member of the royal family, it must be bad. She'd have to ask Dinah about it later.

"I'm off to do my chaperonely duty," Lady Astor announced, not elaborating on their comments. "Valerie, I'll be sure to have Dinah find you."

Lady Astor wound her way up the crowded staircase, stopping here and there to chat with more people. She spoke with a group of elderly dowagers with diadems tucked into their gray hair, her words punctuated by large sweeps of her hands before she bade them adieu. The moment she left, the women tugged small notebooks out of their handbags and furiously wrote in them.

"What are they doing?" Valerie asked.

"Writing down Nancy's quips for their memoirs. It's all the rage with the elder set even if the old dears rarely get the details right."

Valerie suppressed a wide laugh and looked out over the railing at the guests mingling in the entrance hall below, hoping to catch sight of at least one of Their Excellencies. Last night, it'd been two hours before she'd spied Christian, and then it'd been off to dance before they'd had a chance to talk. Valerie had enjoyed the company of Mr. R. M. Chaplin, a lanky young man with more chin than some but far less than most and an obsession with horses.

Now she didn't see any of her friends in the sea of debutantes in their pastel gowns and simple pearl necklaces that paled beside the older women's ostentatious diamonds. Pearls were the only jewelry besides a touch of gold here and there that debutantes were permitted to wear. It was one of the many rules that governed the debutantes' Season and a great deal less tedious than the strict adherence to writing thank-you notes to every hostess, wearing very little makeup, not going to nightclubs, and never riding alone with a gentleman in a taxi. Not that Valerie had been alone at any event since the tea. Their Excellencies had held up their end of the pact over the last few nights of debutante dances. Valerie had yet to stand out by herself when at least one of them was around, and she'd done the same for them. Thank heaven. Without them, she'd be as alone as the girls Lady Clancarty was hired to bring out. Valerie had overheard more than one mother comment on the pointlessness of making friends with a nobody who'd disappear the moment the Season ended.

Speaking of commenters. She locked eyes with Vivien, who stood with Rosalind and Priscilla near a heavy bronze statue of some ancient Roman. Vivien sucked on a cigarette, the end of it burning as hot as her eyes. In a smoky breath, she said something to her friends, who turned to stare Valerie down, but she didn't flinch. She held the high ground and she used it to rain as much venom on them as they flung at her. *How typical.* Dinah's cousins and friends had yet to turn up for a dance, but Vivien and her lot were at every event.

Vivien stubbed out her cigarette on the foot of the bronze Roman statue on the pedestal beside her.

"Mr. Baxter, fetch that young lady an ashtray." Lady Dunsford's voice with its garbled American and English accents rang out from the top of the stairs. "She's there by Caesar."

The entire entrance hall and receiving line followed the line of Lady Dunsford's raised finger to Vivien, who turned as pale as her satin dress.

She swept the cigarette butt and ash off the bronze and deposited it in the footman's silver ashtray. She glared at Valerie as if it were her fault she'd been caught being rude, then trounced off with Rosalind. Priscilla lagged behind, shrugging helplessly at Valerie before following her friends.

"I don't know what's come over young girls these days," Lady

Dunsford exclaimed to Lady Boyle and her daughter as they approached for their introduction, moving Valerie and Aunt Anne to the front of the receiving line.

Lady Dunsford greeted her guests with effusive gestures that made the line of blue ribbons on the front of her Edwardian-style gown bounce against the silk. Her daughter Guinevere stood beside her, the deb's demure graciousness a stark contrast to the black velvet evening dress cut tight to her envious figure. Valerie was torn between giving her the same shocked glance she saw on a number of dowagers' faces and admiring her with the wide-eyed amazement of the chaps across the way. Valerie brushed her hands over the fitted bodice of her dress, wishing it were a touch more daring. What she wouldn't give for a little more sophistication and little less country mouse.

Aunt Anne whispered their names to the butler, who announced them to the hostess.

"Mrs. Chamberlain, it's a pleasure to have you here." Lady Dunsford beamed and Valerie could practically see her writing in her memoirs about the Premier's wife honoring her party.

She wasn't as charmed by Valerie, her smile stiffening about the corners as she greeted her. "Miss de Vere Cole. I believe my husband knew your father."

"Did he?" This could very well end with a great deal of finger-pointing and a footman escorting her out. She hoped Aunt Anne's presence would keep the woman in check, but after what she'd seen with Vivien she doubted it.

"I was involved in Irish politics when your father was living there," the slender Lord Dunsford harrumphed from under his bushy mustache. "I assisted in the selling of his Irish assets in Midleton after his divorce."

"You mean when he went broke after the divorce," Lady Dunsford was kind enough to clarify for Valerie and everyone nearby.

The second you walk into a ballroom, those society biddies will sniff you out for the poor country cousin you are. Valerie took a deep breath, her girdle tight under her dress, struggling to maintain her composure in the face of their insults. She'd have the hide of an elephant by the end of the Season. "Thank you, Lord Dunsford, for helping my father. I'm sure he appreciated it."

Lord Dunsford arched one eyebrow in doubt but it was Aunt Anne who spoke first, all manners and polish in the face of vulgarity. "Congratulations to you both, and to you, Miss Dunsford."

"Thank you. It's a pleasure to have you here, and you as well, Miss de Vere Cole." Guinevere had better manners than her mother, but before she could say more, Lady Dunsford flapped a silencing hand, flashing an overly wide smile when Valerie and Aunt Anne noticed.

Aunt Anne drew Valerie away but not before they heard Lady Dunsford warn her daughter, "She may be the Prime Minister's niece, but there are better, more lucrative friends you can make."

"Ignore her. A social climber isn't worth the bother," Aunt Anne advised.

"How many others are saying the same thing about me out of my hearing?" The quiet of the last week had lulled her into a sense of peace. This had broken that bubble.

"I'm sure there's a few, especially those not enamored with

Neville. It happens to everyone and you have to learn to let the comments roll off your back. Come along, your friends and dance partners are waiting."

My friends. None of their mothers or aunts had warned them off of Valerie. Still, Lady Dunsford's comment smarted as she and Aunt Anne entered the ballroom. She wasn't looking to be proclaimed Debutante of the Year, but she could do without another round of unwarranted criticism or dredged-up memories of Father.

Despite the Spanish colors and decorations in the ballroom, the very American "Stairway to the Stars" put Jack Harris's orchestra's horn section on display. They played at the far end of the room surrounding a large piano and Mr. Harris's smooth voice carried over the swish of taffeta and silk gowns. Dinah waved to Valerie before her stiff-legged partner turned her around with more of a shuffling motion than a dance step.

Mr. R. M. Chaplin approached when they settled on the outskirts of the dance floor. "Miss de Vere Cole, might I have a dance with you?"

"Of course." She handed Mr. Chaplin her dance card, thankful to have at least one line filled in. Every gentleman at the dinner party beforehand had been well over sixty and rubbish for partners. With this dance already under way, Mr. Chaplin signed up for a dance, then handed the card and pencil back to her, bowed, and left. Valerie glanced at his name, hoping he might have written out what R.M. stood for, but no luck. She'd have to ask and give him something besides horses to talk about for a few stanzas.

Three more young men approached Valerie to add their names to her card. They were taken for the next few dances but willingly signed up for later ones, leaving a number of blank spaces between their names and Mr. Chaplin's. Hopefully, at least one of Their Excellencies would be free during those numbers to stand and chat with her. She'd thought the cards silly when Aunt Anne had tied one to her wrist before Miss Furneaux's ball. She was glad for them now. It made the monumental task of remembering names much easier, except for Lord Fulton, or was it Fultmore? Valerie couldn't tell from his handwriting. "I'm going to learn a great deal about horses, cricket, and rowing by the end of the Season."

"An amusing way to round out one's education."

"Isn't it just?"

The song ended and the dancers shifted on and off the dance floor.

"Valerie, at last." Dinah grabbed her arm and read the card. "Good, you have time to chat before the next number."

"I'll leave you to it, then." Aunt Anne made for one of the empty gilt chairs along the edge of the room where the chaperone mothers, aunts, and cousins sat chatting or engrossed in knitting. One or two of the grandmothers dozed, their diamond necklaces rising and falling with the steady movement of their chests. The few fathers braving the ballroom were surrounded by a horde of mothers who giggled more than a debutante dancing with her favorite delight.

"Where are Their Excellencies?" Valerie asked.

"All taken for the next dance. I begged off mine. I'm simply knackered. I want to introduce you to someone." She pulled Valerie through the crowd and up to a group of gentlemen near one of the open windows. "Elm."

"Shhh, we're waiting for Lord Herbert's monocle to fall off." The tall chap with light blond hair and a square jaw pointed across the room at a rotund and balding man chatting with a girl half his age. "He's had it on for the last hour and he hasn't lost it yet."

"Wait a moment," one of the men urged.

Lord Herbert threw back his head and laughed at something his companion said and the monocle slipped off his cheek, sending the Baron and the young woman scurrying to the floor to retrieve it.

The gentlemen groaned or clapped one another on the back. "That's five quid you owe me, Elm."

"Here you are, David." Elm slid a five-pound note out of the slender billfold tucked inside his evening jacket, pulling it back before David could take it. "Another fiver says he goes the next three hours without losing it."

"You're on."

"If you're done having a flutter on a blind old baron, I have someone for you to meet." Dinah stepped in the middle of the gentlemen, pulling Valerie in with her. "Miss Valerie de Vere Cole, may I introduce the Honorable David Ormsby-Gore, Katherine's brother?"

"A pleasure, I'm sure," the dark-blond-haired chap said in the same mumbling accent as his sister's. He had a sharp nose and his sister's long and rounded chin.

"These two rabble-rousers are my cousins, the Honorable Mr. Jakie Astor and the Honorable Mr. Michael Astor."

"I say, you're Mr. Chamberlain's niece," Michael said.

"The debutante in Downing Street." Jakie flashed a broad smile that resembled his brother's. The two of them were close in looks and height with the same dusty brown hair and their mother's slanting nose that pointed decidedly downward. The only notable difference between them was the round scar-like indent on Jakie's forehead above his right eye. "Isn't that what the *Sketch* called you?"

"It is." She didn't mention what it'd labeled him, especially after the wild car accident that'd left him with that unfortunate scar. It'd been in all the papers that winter.

"The winner of the wager is Lord Elmswood." Dinah turned Valerie to face the square-jawed blond with hooded eyes above strong cheekbones who studied her so intensely, it made her cheeks burn with a blush.

"Call me Elm. Everyone else does, even if I detest it." He winked at her. How he could spare her a look when Guinevere moved through the room with more wiggle than considered proper for a debutante, she didn't know.

"Richard, meet the Premier's niece." Elm grabbed his friend by the arm and pulled him over. "The Honorable Dr. Richard Cranston, son of Lord Lansdown."

"A pleasure." The dark-haired man, nearly as tall as Elm but with a broader chest and fuller shoulders, bowed to Valerie, then straightened. "We were just discussing your uncle."

"In favorable terms, I hope."

Dr. Cranston flashed a lopsided grin. "Mostly."

"Then I'll have to make it entirely." She glanced at her dance card.

"I think you must." Dr. Cranston, taking her none-too-subtle hint, slid a pen from his coat pocket and reached for the card, but Elm took her hand before he could get it.

"Precedent and all that, old chap." Elm removed the small pencil from its elastic holder on the side and wrote his name, his fingers curling around hers. His lithe chest gave him a grace that his height might have stolen if he'd been gangly and clumsy, but he wasn't. He was all smooth motions and charm. "Here you are."

He passed Valerie's hand to Dr. Cranston. The doctor's grip was firm where Elm's had been more subtle. He glanced up at her from time to time while he wrote, his brown eyes as startling in their darkness as Elm's had been in their blue intensity.

Two gentlemen flirting with her in one night. This was a first.

"What about us?" Jakie said.

"We're the sons of a viscount, after all," Michael said, completing his brother's thought.

"The younger ones," Dinah reminded with a smirk. "They're hardly worth anything."

Dr. Cranston paused in writing his name on Valerie's dance card and she inwardly cringed. Some debutantes were renowned for refusing to dance with any chap without a title or the possibility of one. Dinah rarely turned down a gentleman but clearly she didn't think too highly of the aristocratic equivalent of leftovers.

"Don't be formal with them, Michael and Jakie will do," Dinah insisted when Dr. Cranston passed her hand to the younger Astor.

"How presumptuous of you, dear cousin," Jakie playfully scolded as he added his name to Valerie's card for a later dance, leaving the one after Dr. Cranston's open as he offered her hand to his brother.

"Ah, let her alone. You know we hate all that stuffy business anyway." Michael claimed the dance after his brother's instead of filling the gap between Dr. Cranston and Jakie. "What's it like to be in the middle of things in Number Ten?"

"It must be exciting," Jackie pressed as Michael released her hand.

Valerie rubbed the feeling back into her fingers. "It'd be more exciting if they let me into the Cabinet Room, but they don't."

"Good, the government is no place for a woman," Elm drawled.

Valerie exchanged a look with Dinah, each waiting for the other to berate him for his comment, but neither of them said anything. She shouldn't be so shy, but after Lady Dunsford's snub, she'd didn't relish another.

"Better not let Mummy hear you say so," Jakie chided for them.

"She'll take you to task for sure," Michael added, but Elm shrugged, unruffled by the rebuke.

"It's all well and good for old married types, but the rest hardly need to bother."

"I imagine politics is far duller than we'd like to believe anyway," Dr. Cranston said, making the peace.

"I'll say." Jakie rolled his eyes. "Especially when Mum is going on about it but we can't help it . . ."

". . . we're fascinated," Michael finished. "Tell us what your uncle is going to do about Germany. Mum either doesn't know or won't say."

"I don't want to be hanged for revealing state secrets." Miss Holmes had told her this morning about Uncle Neville's attempts to bring Britain, France, Russia, and Poland together in a pledge of unity against Germany but she wasn't certain how much of that she could discuss in public.

"Stop trying to worm state secrets out of Miss de Vere Cole," Dr. Cranston warned in a voice as smooth as the circle of dancers moving in the center of the room. "Her neck is too pretty to risk the noose."

"Thank you."

"My pleasure."

The song came to an end, igniting a massive shift of people on and off the dance floor. Mr. R. M. Chaplin appeared beside Valerie.

"I believe this is our dance." He held out his arm, his wide smile making his small chin sink deeper into his neck.

Valerie was about to take his arm, regretting leaving Dinah's cousins and friends so soon, when Elm stepped in between her and Mr. Chaplin. "Be a good sport and give me this one. You can have another."

Mr. Chaplin's smile dropped and he lowered her arm. "Of course, Lord Elmswood."

Valerie should insist on dancing with him now but she didn't, too shocked and flattered by Elm cutting in to do more than offer Mr. Chaplin an apologetic smile. "I'm sorry, Mr. Chaplin. Dr. Cranston is next on my list but the dance after his is open and it'd be smashing to partner with you for it."

Mr. Chaplin's smile returned but it wasn't quite as wide as before. "All right. Until then." He left to ask a young woman without a partner to dance. Valerie was glad the girl accepted him. He might be dull but he was awfully nice and she knew what it was to be rejected.

"That wasn't very sporting," she dared with Elm, needing to say something. It was the most she could muster with his sturdy arm beneath her palm as he led her out onto the dance floor, whirling her around to face him, one hand on hers, the other solid against her back.

"It was dreadful of me to pull rank like that but I couldn't bear to let our conversation end."

"It wasn't much of a conversation."

"Only because there wasn't enough of it." He drew her a little closer, swaying them back and forth with fluid grace.

"If you hope to get any state secrets out of me, you'll fail." But she wouldn't mind him trying.

"I'm not interested in state secrets but whether or not there'll be war. Some papers say there won't be but Lord Beaverbrook and his rag are certain of it. Are they right?"

My, he's a good dancer. He swung her about, the skirt of her gown swishing back and forth between their legs. With anyone else leading her she would've looked like a swaying curtain, but with him it was all elegance and sophistication. They were cutting quite the figure, and more than one head turned to admire them. "I can't say, but Uncle Neville is doing all he can to make sure there isn't."

"While Herr Hitler is doing all he can to make sure there is." He sighed as if he believed war was inevitable. Did all the chaps think so? If they did, they were certainly enjoying themselves in the midst of a crisis. Everyone around them smiled and laughed except for Vivien, who scowled at Valerie over the very short shoulder of her partner. Valerie jutted out her chin, pretending not to care while silently gloating. She was dancing with the son of a marquess while Vivien was with a mere knight's son. Around the room, the mothers continued to chat and knit while some sagged in their chairs, anxiously waiting for the band to play "God Save the King" so they could go home and crawl into bed. Even the few fathers weren't any more grave-faced than normal, enjoying hearty laughs along with their champagne. Everyone carried on as if things were as they'd always been and would continue to be. No one behaved as if bombs were about to fall through the arched ceiling.

"We avoided war before. We'll avoid it again," Valerie insisted.

"I hope so." That sigh again, and the far-off look in his eyes as he peered over her head. It cast a gloom over the silver ribbon hung between the pillars. Dinah said he was a touch serious, and he was, fretting about a war that wasn't certain to happen. Maybe Elm was simply a pessimist like Mr. Churchill. She'd met more than her fair share of those sort at No. 10.

"Will you fight if there is a war?"

"I have no choice. I'm a Second Lieutenant in the Coldstream Guards. I must report for duty at Windsor tomorrow morning after tonight's fun." He turned them in an elegant step, the serious man replaced by the knave who'd stolen her from Mr. Chaplin. "There are recruits to whip into shape."

"With such a schedule, when will you sleep?"

"When I'm dead." He threw back his head and laughed, the sound more grating than amusing. "I intend to enjoy myself to the fullest until then."

Her father had done the same in his youth, chasing fame and

notoriety through his outlandish pranks. He'd enjoyed it until it'd cost him his fortune, his place in society, and eventually his dignity. She had no desire to ever be like him. Fun was all well and good, but nothing came of trying to forget problems in heady excitement. "I hope it doesn't come to that."

"It might." The last strains of the waltz faded away and everyone stopped and clapped before Elm escorted her off the dance floor. "Thank you for a very reassuring dance."

"Was it?"

"As much as it can be in times like these." He bowed and relinquished her to Dr. Cranston, the only chap who hadn't invited her to call him by his first name.

"I hope I'm as interesting a partner as Elm." Dr. Cranston led her back onto the dance floor, where most of the girls who'd been there before were around her again. Some appeared a great deal happier with their new partners, while others were quite bored.

"Be different. I'm not interested in serious discussion." The band played a quick foxtrot, the two of them keeping time to the livelier pace. "But don't be droll either."

"I'm only droll with patients."

"Then I won't get sick." She breathed hard, the dance keeping her on her toes as much as the conversation. "What hospital are you at?"

"St. Thomas's."

Like the other chaps, he was older than her by a few years, but not so many that he came off as an old fogy but more mature than her usual partners. No wonder he hadn't insisted she use his first name. She supposed maturity was the price one paid for being a doctor instead of a viscount. "Do you enjoy it?"

"It'd be bad luck if I didn't. I'm the fourth son. By the time my father got to me, my elder brothers had taken all the places in the army, navy, or law. It was either the church or medicine, and I'm not particularly religious."

"A noble calling. Will you be back on duty in the morning?"

"Me and half the room. I'll let you in on a little secret." He lowered his lips close to her ear, his breath whispering across her exposed neck as he spoke and raising a line of goose bumps along her back. She wasn't sure if he was a cad eager to touch flesh or more friendly than Elm. Either way, he was a swell of a good time and he could get a little closer if it meant enjoying the dance as much as she did. "When mothers need men to round out their guest list, they post notices at the hospitals. Any resident who owns an evening suit is invited to come, no questions asked. That's how most of us chaps ended up here."

She jerked back to look at him. His eyes were as stunning as the defined cut of his chin. "They aren't."

"They are. You'd be surprised what us poor residents will do for a free dinner and breakfast."

She was tempted to tell him what it was really like to be poor with no food and the *propriétaire d'hôtel* threatening to toss their flea-infested things into the street, but she kept her mouth shut. That wasn't appropriate ballroom conversation. Besides, he wasn't the first person to cry poverty at a party. There were always girls in the ladies' complaining about buying their wardrobe at

Harrods instead of having it custom-made. The horror. "You're lying."

"I'll prove it." He turned her around in the dance, his moves smooth and coordinated but not nearly as natural as Elm's. "The man dancing with Lady Margaret Boyle works with me at St. Thomas's, and that bloke over there with Miss Joan Debenham is at St. Bart's. The short man with Lady Anne Fitzroy is at Guy's. We've quite overrun the place tonight. Lady Dunsford must've been hard up for gentlemen."

Yet she'd had the nerve to sneer down her nose at Valerie. "I suppose hosting a few doctors is better than risking too many girls standing out." Especially given the money spent on most dances. Everyone wanted to be seen as a success, and a room full of wallflowers wouldn't accomplish that.

"Solicitors too. Half the Inns of Court are here."

Their Excellencies would die of laughter when they heard this.

Sadly, Jack Harris waved his baton to silence the orchestra and brought their dance to an end. Valerie and Dr. Cranston clapped with the rest of the crush before he escorted her off the dance floor.

If it wouldn't horrify Dorothy to hear that Valerie had danced with the same gentleman twice in one night, she'd have demanded every dance from him and Elm, but she couldn't, especially not with Mr. R. M. Chaplin approaching. "Thank you for an interesting turn about the room."

"It was my pleasure. Until the next dance."

"Until then."

He handed her off to Mr. Chaplin, who escorted her out. To

her shame, she glanced over her shoulder at the doctor, pleased to catch him looking at her. He raised a gloved hand, then returned to David, Jakie, and Michael, falling back into conversation with them.

At least there's still Jakie and Michael to look forward to. She'd do all she could when they danced to pique their interest. It wasn't like her to pursue gentlemen, but the wider her circle of acquaintances, the more successful the Season. Nearby, Christian danced with a tall chap with dark hair who bounced up and down more than he swayed. Valerie had no idea where Dinah and Eunice had gone off to, but they were sure to catch up later.

"What have you been doing with yourself since we last danced?" she asked Mr. Chaplin.

"Discussing adjustments to the training schedule with my groom."

Her aunt was certainly right about one aspect of the Season. By the end of it, Valerie was going to master conversing with almost anyone on nearly any subject.

Chapter Seven

"I'll have to be more thorough in vetting dance partners." Katherine plucked another sandwich from the hamper resting on the car's hood. The girls sat on the runners of Dinah's and Katherine's cars parked close together to offer some protection from the steady breeze. Despite the sunshine brightening the green fields and white fences of Hawthorn Hill racecourse, the air hinted at the coming rain that would dampen tomorrow's races and the second day of the Household Brigade Steeplechase Meeting. "A barrister or doctor is passable for a husband. Their wives can be presented at court. But a solicitor . . . one would have to be out a few Seasons and still on the shelf to be quite so desperate."

"What if you fell in love with one of those doctors?" Christian tucked the edges of her houndstooth tweed skirt under her legs. There were no toppers and fancy dresses at Hawthorn Hill, but a sea of sensible country tweed for racing enthusiasts and those like Valerie who were here for society rather than a rousing flat race.

"Heaven forbid." Katherine rolled her eyes. "Who was that chap you were waltzing with at Cecily Berry's ball?"

This was their first proper chat since Lady Dunsford's dance three days ago, each of their social diaries so full, they'd been pulled this way and that. If it weren't for Miss Leaf's meticulous calendar, Valerie wouldn't know where to be when.

"John Miller. We've known each other for ages. He lived near us in Scotland and was ever so sweet to brave the bohemians of Chelsea to call on us when he arrived in London."

Valerie wondered at Christian's Chelsea address. It didn't seem fashionable enough for the debutante daughter of a Scottish baronet, not that Valerie was one to throw stones at other people's neighborhoods, not after some of the horrid places she'd lived in at Ascain.

"Does Mr. Miller have money, a title, lands?" Dinah asked, as direct as Lady Astor. "Aunt Nancy says a woman shouldn't marry for money but should always look for love where money is. It makes life a great deal easier."

Valerie drew her fitted tan coat a little closer around her neck, surprised at the turn in the conversation. Their Excellencies weren't usually snobs and she wondered if they'd be more discerning about spending time with her if they knew how low Valerie had been forced to sink in France for lack of money. None of them was ever going to find out because she had no intention of telling anyone that secret. She was here to build herself up, not let her past tear her down. As for the rest, she'd shared a number of things with them over the last week during teas at Claridge's or while sitting out dances. It was everything from the silly advice

Dorothy gave her to whatever gossip she could get out of Mary, but she'd been cautious about revealing too much, taking Uncle Neville's advice to wait and see. With the exception of this conversation, Their Excellencies had yet to disappoint her.

"Is this where you've gone off to?" Jakie peeked over the Daimler's black curved hood, making the girls jump.

"Where have you been?" Dinah swatted at her cousin, catching the sleeve of his herringbone jacket. "Half the day is over."

"We had a devil of a time getting here." Michael helped himself to a sandwich and sat down on the runner between Dinah and Christian. "Elm's Bentley ran out of petrol."

"I thought my man had filled it. I'll have a word with him when I return." Elm leaned against the Lagonda saloon's deep green hood and traced the sleek chrome ornament. "Were you disappointed we weren't here?"

He eyed Valerie from beneath his snap-brim fedora and she nearly choked on the last of her biscuit, wanting to shift closer to Christian but not about to admit how easily he flattered and unnerved her. Instead, she'd give as good as she got. She crossed her arms over her chest and pinned him with a teasingly reprimanding look, her voice far more velvety than jovial. "We were terribly disappointed, you're such good fun."

"Luckily, there's still the afternoon races." He arched one eyebrow at her and she couldn't tell if he was intrigued or about to laugh. Either way, she'd caught his attention, and that was never a bad thing.

"Where's David?" Katherine glanced around for her brother,

oblivious to the little tête-à-tête between Valerie and Elm. "And Richard?"

"David was summoned by your parents and Richard is walking the wards," Jakie replied.

"No rest for the weary doctor." Michael plucked a biscuit out of the hamper and popped it in his mouth. "At least he has something worthwhile to do, that's more than I can say."

"Still banging on about working?" Elm asked, examining his fingernails.

Michael narrowed his eyes at his friend. "Thanks to Mum, I haven't got anything to do but bang on about it. She wants to dictate my life, but I won't let her. I'll find something instead of waiting for her to tell me what to do."

"Where's that American friend of yours?" Jakie poured a cup of coffee from the thermos, changing the conversation before it could escalate into who knows what. "Ambassador Kennedy's daughter."

"Eunice is at a luncheon for the French President and his wife." Katherine exchanged a curious look with Christian. "Why do you ask?"

"We want to know if it's true what they say about her father."

"What do they say?" Valerie and the girls perked up, ready to rush to their absent friend's defense.

"He thinks Britain is sunk if there's a war and we should do everything we can to stay out of one."

"Especially since it's bad for business, his specifically," Michael said.

"We heard he commandeers cargo space on government ships for his private liquor import." Jakie finished his coffee and poured another cup. "He doesn't care about anyone except himself and his interests. Certainly not ours."

"How nasty of you both," Dinah scolded. "Especially when Eunice isn't here to defend her father."

"We didn't say we believed it."

"We simply want to know if it's true. Is it?" Michael and Jakie looked at Valerie as if she had the answer.

She didn't know anything about Ambassador Kennedy's private thoughts on Britain, but Uncle Neville didn't care for the balding and bespectacled ambassador. He'd said so a few times during their morning walks in St. James's Park before all the business in Europe had made him scarce. Of course, she wasn't going to breathe a word about this to the chaps, but she had to give them something. They were looking to her for insight and if she offered a reasonably intelligent reply they'd do it again.

"He's not wrong about war being bad for business. Your families are in banking and must've seen that during the Great War. Even horse racing faltered back then. With Newmarket the only track allowed to run, all those trainers and stables went off to America and never came back." She silently thanked Mr. Chaplin for this little bit of horse information. "Ambassador Kennedy wants to avoid war as much as Uncle Neville and so many others do. He has sons who'll have to fight and I'm sure he doesn't want them on the battlefield any more than your fathers want you in harm's way."

"Our fathers may not have a say in the end, and neither will we." Elm flicked the end of the chrome hood ornament, making it ring. "We'll be shipped off with no idea who'll return and who won't."

Laughter from a nearby group of young marrieds and their husbands carried on the breeze along with the neighing horses and the crush of gravel beneath a passing car's wheels.

"Don't be so frightfully dull." Dinah stood and brushed the crumbs off her skirt as the bugle sounded for the first afternoon race. "There isn't a war today and no one is in danger of dying from anything but a chill. Don't let Europe's troubles ruin our fun."

"I agree." Elm pushed off the hood, his mood shifting as fast as it had on the dance floor at Lady Dunsford's. "We're here to enjoy ourselves."

"Come on, then," Dinah urged. "I'm rooting for Discretion and I want to see him win."

"Are we going to stalk the whole thing?" Jakie asked.

"We didn't come all this way to sit with the nonsporting folk, by Jove."

"What about you, Elm?" Katherine asked, adjusting her felt jockey hat.

"If I had my horse I would, but I couldn't bring him. I have to report to the barracks this evening."

"What a pity. I wish I had mine. I'd love to follow the race." Katherine fell in with Dinah, Elm, Jakie, and Michael as they made for a prime viewing place at the fence. The chaps would ride out together like many spectators did to watch the race from the track.

"What's got your interest?" Valerie asked Christian, who dallied beside her reading the day's racing program. "I didn't think you mad for horses."

"I was before Father died and Mummy moved us to London."

"I'm very sorry about your father." It was something she didn't wish to have in common with anyone.

"It's all right. Riding was the only thing we had in common. I'm lucky I learned to read, what with the way he ignored me and my siblings, but I suppose I should be glad. When he did notice me, all he could say was how plain I was and that no man would ever want me. He didn't get to see his ugly duckling turn into the swan before you." She held out her arms and twirled around as if his insults had never mattered; but they had, it was in the heaviness of her eyes before she returned to reading her program.

"My father wasn't much better." Valerie's heart thudded in her ears. Dorothy claimed the world would stop spinning if she so much as uttered a word about her past, but she wasn't one to allow a person to believe they were alone. "Literature was the only thing we had in common. If it hadn't been for his love of books and drilling quotes into me, I'd be quite illiterate too."

"It's a wonder any of us English girls know how to read, what with the awful governesses and dame schools."

"The Cambridge one I attended was dreadful. The headmistress made Miss Minchin from *A Little Princess* look like a doting mother. The lessons, when she bothered to glance up from her novels long enough to teach, were as rubbish as the meals." Father had been horrified by how little she'd learned after seven years there. He might've noticed sooner if he'd paid her any mind, but she doubted he'd have done anything about it. There wasn't a single mistake he'd made that he'd ever worked to correct. "If it hadn't been for the library in Saint-Jean-de-Luz, I'd be a complete fool."

"Eunice says Americans actually educate their daughters and Mrs. Kennedy expects her to go to university when they return home. Can you imagine our mothers thinking that?"

"Not a one." Not even hers if she'd remained in her life. It simply wasn't done in England, but it felt good to commiserate, even over something as small as their pathetic schooling. "Who are you going to bet on?"

"I haven't decided." She handed the program to Valerie. "What do you think?"

Little more than the names of the owners and the horses made any sense to her. Before arriving at West Woodhay House she'd never been on a horse, and her efforts to become a competent horsewoman had been a dismal failure. The grizzled head groom who'd smelled of hay and oiled leather had done his best to teach her confidence in the saddle but even the most docile geldings had refused to obey her. After the fifth pointless lesson, and despite Great-Aunt Lillian's insistence that proper English girls must know how to ride, they'd abandoned the effort. "I haven't a clue."

"Me neither, but it's still fun, isn't it?"

"It is." She returned the program to Christian, relishing the fresh air and freedom of the races. She waved to Lord Astor, Dinah's uncle, who passed by with Lady Margaret Ogilvy. Even the farmers milling about while waiting for the Farmers' Steeplechase were treated like equals, the love of horses a great leveler, at least for today. She wasn't naïve enough to think it would last past the final race, but it hinted that true acceptance was at least possible, or so she hoped. All the talk of who was and wasn't suitable for a partner wasn't rolling off her back nearly as fast as she'd like.

"I'll ask Jakie to place a pound on Schubert for me." Christian tucked the program into her coat pocket and straightened her silver Scottish thistle brooch. "I feel lucky, especially since Schubert is Mummy's favorite composer."

"Ask Jakie to place a quid on Schubert for me too." She fished a sovereign out of her purse and gave it to Christian. "Maybe we'll both win."

"Wouldn't that be grand, especially since the odds on him are ten-to-one." She hurried to catch up with Jakie, giving him the coins and her instructions before he and Michael set off for the paddock to place their bets and collect their horses from the stables.

Valerie joined Katherine, Dinah, and Elm at the fence to watch the horses assemble at the starting post. A robust crowd stood around them sending up cheers and murmurs of appreciation about flanks and withers and fine-looking animals.

It wasn't long before Christian returned. "Jakie is placing our bets on Schubert."

"You're going to lose," Elm said from beside Valerie, the woodsy scent of his aftershave carrying over the tangy aroma of wet mud and horses.

"We have as good a chance of winning as you do. Who'd you bet on?"

"Mixed Fouresome." He slid her a sideways glance that made her silk scarf seem tighter around her neck.

Tilting her head so the brim of her Robin Hood hat covered one eye, she glanced at him, hoping she didn't look too much like a little girl playing at sophistication. "A daring choice for a bet."

He arched an amused eyebrow. "I enjoy a little thrill with my wagers."

"Does that only apply to horses?"

"It applies to cars too. You should see me driving back to the barracks after a night in London."

"You handle the wheel well, then?"

"I handle everything well." He shifted a little closer, his fingers on the railing resting enticingly close to hers. "It's expected of me."

"What else is expected of you?" *Careful, girl, you don't want to come off sounding as cheap as Mavis.*

"That I return to the barracks before roll call or I'll have to resign my commission." He straightened, the teasing chap suddenly replaced by a quite serious one. "We can't have that."

"No, w-we can't." His sharp change sent her reeling before she got hold of herself. "I'm sure you appear quite dashing in your uniform."

"So I've been told." He admired the line of horses on the track instead of her, his interest in their conversation waning.

She dropped the coquette act as fast as she'd put it on, failing to wind him up. He'd been ribbing her and she'd fallen for it like a convent school simpleton. Of course, she was one—well, not the simpleton part, at least she didn't think so. A touch too worldly when it came to some things, but far from silly. "If I ever see you in it, I'll tell you how dreadful you look, like an overdone peacock, so you don't get conceited."

"I'll rely on your levelheaded judgment to keep me humble." He swept off his fedora and bent himself into a bow before rising and tapping it down over his blond hair. "If you'll excuse me, there's Captain Petre, Mixed Foursesome's owner."

With his hands tucked into his pockets, he strolled off to join the mustached and uniformed man.

"What was that all about?" Katherine asked. She, Christian, and Dinah peered down the fence at Valerie, grinning like Cheshire cats at having overheard their little exchange.

"I have no idea." He'd been enchanted by her, even if he'd been irritatingly confident in breaking the spell. She understood why Mavis had chased after so many men in Ascain. The attention was flattering. "But I enjoyed it."

"So did I," Katherine needled, the four of them falling into a fit of laughter.

"Oh, there's Schubert!" Christian pointed to the tall, black horse with the jockey in green and blue in the saddle. The horse tossed his head against the bridle, nearly trotting in anticipation as he was led out by his groom.

The girls clapped and cheered with the rest of the crowd as the grooms left the jockeys to control the horses at the starting line. The animals snorted and danced in a wide row behind the posts until the gun sounded and they were off, urged on by a chorus of whoops and hollers.

Their Excellencies gripped the fence, pressed in by the crowd as the horses raced past. Bits of grass and mud went flying as the racers crested the hill and bolted out of sight of everyone except the people in the stands with viewing glasses. Over the loudspeakers, the announcer called out the leaders as the horses and riders cleared one hedge and fence and then another. The crowd behind them thinned as people walked out to watch the jumps or set up their shooting sticks to sit and chat until the horses returned to the finish line.

Elm sauntered up to Valerie. "I'm going to watch from out on the field. Care to join me?"

"Isn't that dangerous?" Nothing stood between the people and the charging horses. If an animal tripped and fell or forced the others offtrack, they might trample the spectators.

"I enjoy a little danger." He winked at her and her heart skipped a beat. "It's almost as thrilling as the sheer amount of fun I pack into every night. It's part of my plan to live life to the fullest while I can."

That didn't seem like living but risking the very thing he feared, death. "Thank you, but I have no desire to be crushed and miss my chance to live life to the fullest. Be careful."

"I will be." He set off with many others across the track and the adjoining field. If he gave her another thought after he left she couldn't say. He certainly didn't bother with a second look.

A good reminder, that. Flights of fancy were all well and good, but one needed to keep one's feet on the ground. That'd been Mavis's trouble. She'd believed everything every man had told her, especially Augustus John. The painter had promised the moon and left her with nothing except a baby. Tristan should thank his lucky stars Mavis and Valerie's father had still been married when he'd been born. It'd saved him from being a bastard and completely ruining what was left of his mother's reputation. Believing too many charming smiles and teasing words was a mistake Valerie wasn't about to make.

"Still feeling confident about your bet?" Katherine asked.

Valerie turned to answer, when the sight of a man over Katherine's shoulder made her freeze. *I should have gone with Elm.* It was better than standing here and risk being seen by Mr. Shoedelin. If she sprinted across the track she might catch Elm, but she'd look a sight running over the field, her coat flapping, one hand holding on to her hat.

"What's wrong, Valerie?" Christian asked. "You've gone pale."

"Something in the hamper must not have agreed with you," Katherine suggested. "The egg salad did seem rather off."

"It isn't the egg salad."

Mr. Shoedelin caught her eye before she could duck behind Katherine. He ambled toward her with the same arrogant stride she remembered from when he'd finally deigned to visit her and Father at their last awful lodging in Ascain. He was the single person in the world who knew the true depths of her humiliation in France and the last she ever wanted to see here.

"Miss de Vere Cole, what an unexpected surprise." Mr. Shoedelin raised his pointy chin in that imperious way he'd done when she'd first appeared in his office begging for help.

"What are you doing in England?"

Their Excellencies' eyes went wide at Valerie's brusque question.

"I'm on holiday from my duties in France." Mr. Shoedelin tugged at his houndstooth waistcoat, as irritated by this question as he'd been horrified by the one she'd asked him in France. "I thought to take in a bit of sport. Not much of this to be had in Bayonne, but a great many things are different here than they were there, aren't they?" He narrowed his already small eyes at her and rubbed his thick mustache.

"Yes." Valerie struggled to get the word past her dry tongue. She had to do something besides glare at him. One wrong word from him, and everyone would know how far she'd fallen in France and how unworthy she was to live in No. 10. Unable to think of anything else, she decided on introductions. "Miss Ormsby-Gore, Miss Grant, Miss Brand, allow me to introduce you to Mr. Shoedelin, the British Consul in Bayonne."

The man who'd seen her in the hell of that flea-infested hotel in Ascain and condemned her to the hell of the convent school. The announcer continued to call the race over the loudspeakers while Valerie stood there, not giving Their Excellencies any hint as to her connection to the man.

"I knew Miss de Vere Cole and her father in France." He raised his cap to the girls, who continued to gape at him and Valerie, not sure what to make of this odd encounter. "I saw your picture in the papers. Congratulations on your coming out and being at Number Ten."

He said it as if high society were the last place he expected to find her.

"If you'll excuse us, we're watching the race."

He glanced at the track, having the tact not to point out that it was empty and choosing a dignified retreat instead. "Give my regards to Mr. and Mrs. Chamberlain."

He touched the brim of his cap and wandered off to trouble someone else.

"What was that all about?" Christian grabbed Valerie's arm, keeping her from sagging into the mud.

"Nothing, I'm sorry." She wanted to run to her car, slide in the back, and pull down the shades. Why couldn't Mr. Shoedelin rot away in France like all those other minor diplomats and old army majors? Was he and every nasty person she'd ever known going to pop up in England like an invasion of garden moles?

"It didn't look like nothing," Dinah insisted.

"It's just me being silly."

"Come on, Valerie, out with it," Dinah demanded. "What's wrong?"

"A problem shared is always halved," Christian encouraged.

Not with all Dorothy's warnings rattling around in her head along with her own. She had no idea if Mr. Shoedelin was discreet or as gossipy as some of the ministers in Downing Street, especially Sir John and his crass wife, Lady Simon. She'd heard Their Excellencies carrying on about John Miller's questionable prospects and the horror of dancing with poor solicitors. They'd balk at having her in their circle if they learned from a loose-lipped Consul how close Father had come to going to jail because of his creditors and how near she'd been to starving because there'd been no money for food or stamps to write to Aunt Anne and beg for help. The same searing shame she'd experienced the day she'd met Mr. Shoedelin was something she refused to endure again, but she couldn't put them off. They knew something was wrong and, like terriers, they weren't going to let it go. She had to tell them something.

"There was a misunderstanding between my father and a shop-keeper in Ascain. Mr. Shoedelin stepped in and made it worse, then convinced Father to send me away to that French *école*. It was more a boarding school than a finishing school and perfectly dreadful." It was as much of the truth as she could reveal without giving everything away. She wished she could tell them the whole of it and stop it from weighing on her, to have them say she wasn't the awful person that day had made her, the one Father had never been able to love, but she couldn't.

"No wonder you can't stand him." Dinah clasped Valerie's hands between hers. "Boarding school is dreadful, especially a French one, but you can't let him ruin the day."

"Not with our bet on Schubert. Forget you ever saw him," Christian encouraged.

"I wish I could." It'd be a short Season if Mr. Shoedelin decided to open his mouth to the wrong person and destroy her reputation and whatever chance she had of putting the past behind her. Lady Ashcombe and her ilk would be positively giddy then, and Mavis would crow with triumph. She could stand almost anything except them gloating about her ruin or watching Aunt Anne recoil from her with the same disgust Mr. Shoedelin had flung at her in France.

"You must." Katherine held out a handkerchief to her. "Remember who you are and where you are."

People passed back and forth behind them, tossing curious

glances their way. At any moment she expected Vivien to saunter by and make everything worse. Katherine was right, she couldn't fall to pieces here. She took the handkerchief and dabbed the corners of her eyes. She might be that girl from Ascain but she was also the Prime Minister's niece and everyone expected her to act like it. "I'm sorry. I don't know what came over me."

"It happens to us all at times," Dinah assured. "Especially since we're getting so little sleep and doing so much."

"I'll say." Christian smiled sheepishly. "I cried the other morning when I chipped my manicure. A month ago I wasn't even doing my nails. It's too ridiculous to imagine."

"Is this really what we've become?" Dinah asked.

"Imagine how we'll be by the end of the Season, but we'll manage, won't we?" Katherine added.

"We don't have a choice but to." There was nothing else Valerie could do. It was always chin up, no matter how much effort it took to keep it there.

Overhead, the speakers blared with the announcement that the racers were in sight.

"Your horse is coming in first," Katherine said.

"Is he really?" Their Excellencies cocked their heads to listen to the announcer, the rising excitement of the crowd at the finish line lifting Valerie's spirits. "He is winning."

"We have to cheer him on." Christian grasped Valerie's hand and pulled her to the fence, the rest of Their Excellencies lining up on either side of them.

Overhead, the announcer frantically called the approaching horses. The grueling track had eliminated many, leaving only the fastest and most agile to round the bend. The final three jumps saw two more jockeys thrown from their mounts. Those still seated cussed at the dismounted men and riderless horses to get out of their way, the melee slowing those coming up from behind and giving the four front horses the advantage.

"Schubert's in the lead, with Discretion a distance behind, followed by Mixed Fouresome" came over the loudspeaker to a flurry of whoops and applause. "And it's Schubert for the win!"

"We won, we won!" Christian jumped up and down with Valerie, their screams of victory nearly dislodging her hat before they settled enough to speak, their voices hoarse from cheering. "Ten pounds. Can you believe it? I can finally buy a new pair of gloves."

Finally buy? An odd remark, but Valerie didn't pry. Perhaps Christian's mother wasn't as generous with her allowance as Katherine's. She'd heard more than one girl at a luncheon complaining about her stingy father giving her only a hundred-pound-a-month allowance and fretting over how she'd pay the hairdresser, manicurist, and seamstress.

"How are you going to spend yours?" Christian asked.

"I don't know. I didn't imagine we'd win." She had no intention of spending it. She'd learned the hard way in Ascain what the difference between money and no money meant to a woman.

"Let's collect it and see Schubert in the paddock," Christian said. "I want to thank him for my windfall."

Their Excellencies made for the betting booths to collect Christian's and Valerie's winnings. The thrill of the race had distracted her from Mr. Shoedelin, but the peace didn't last. Mavis wasn't the only bête noir in London she had to contend with, but Valerie couldn't hide and fret either. She must carry on, as Aunt Anne and Uncle Neville encouraged, and enjoy herself for however long this lasted. It was a great deal easier to do with Their Excellencies chattering and laughing beside her.

"MORE LETTERS ABOUT the monarch's dinner?" Valerie sank into the armchair beside the sofa, where Aunt Anne sat with a writing desk perched on her lap. Miss Leaf pored over her calendar, the stack of invitations on her desk having grown in size since this morning's post.

"There's no end to it. I'm certain some military maneuvers have been managed with less discussion than this dinner." With a sigh, she signed the letter and handed it to Miss Leaf before selecting a clean piece of paper. Late afternoon sun filled the White Drawing Room and flickered in the crystals dangling from the chandelier. "How were the races?"

Valerie slid the pin out of her hat and took it off, setting it on the cushion beside her. She might mention Mr. Shoedelin and ask Aunt Anne to have Uncle Neville banish him to some far-flung post, but it would raise questions Valerie didn't wish to answer. "I won ten pounds."

"How delightful." The nib of Aunt Anne's fountain pen scratched over the paper.

Valerie watched her write in fluid curving movements, at complete ease despite the royal frenzy, and entirely trusting Valerie. What she wouldn't give to tell her aunt everything, to lighten the weight of this awful secret, but she couldn't. She'd make her aunt proud, even if it meant burying the past deeper than the ruins of Roman London. "I was wondering if I might have the girls around for tea?"

Aunt Anne took off her glasses and set them on the side table. "I think that's a splendid idea."

"Eunice Kennedy too, if I may. Perhaps it'll improve Anglo-American relations."

"It can't hurt."

"Is it true what they're saying about Ambassador Kennedy? That he thinks we're sunk if we go to war?" There was no limit to the amount of worries swirling today.

"People are quick to criticize anyone in politics, especially during contentious times." Aunt Anne searched her pocket and the sofa cushions for her spectacles.

Valerie slid them off the side table and held them out to her.

Aunt Anne took them and slipped them back on. "You may plan the menu. It's never too early to develop your hosting skills. They'll be useful to you someday, especially if you marry a government man."

"I'm hardly destined to become a political hostess."

"You don't know what you'll become. Never in all my years at West Woodhay House did I think I'd be the Premier's wife, yet here I am. You must prepare for any possibility."

"Including working for a living, like Miss Holmes?" Father had prided himself on being a gentleman. Having tasted true poverty, she wasn't about to fall into that trap and call herself a lady while starving in threadbare clothes.

"I don't think we have to imagine anything quite so drastic."

"It might be good for me to gain more practical skills than planning menus."

"In some instances, planning a menu is a matter of state." She held up the paper with the Buckingham Crest printed on the top, then laid it back on the lap desk. "However, if you wish to develop different talents, the Personal Service League is an excellent place to begin. You'd be well situated if the Crown needs your service, especially if things grow thornier in Europe."

As much as she didn't wish to think of that sort of future, with advertisements in the newspapers calling for women ambulance drivers, it was difficult to ignore. So was her already full schedule. Miss Leaf had shown Valerie her calendar during breakfast, and only the smallest slivers of cream paper beneath the penciled-in engagements had been visible. The thought of cramming something as arduous as volunteering into those slender spaces exhausted her simply by thinking about it. "Perhaps when the Season is over and I have time for it. I'm barely sleeping as it is"

"Quite right. Until then, we'll make you into a fine hostess. Miss Leaf, please review the calendar and we'll select an afternoon for Valerie and her friends to have tea," Aunt Anne instructed when the social secretary returned.

"Yes, Mrs. Chamberlain. You also asked me to remind you about the ship launching?"

"I did. Valerie, the Vickers-Armstrongs shipping company has invited you to launch one of their new cargo ships next week."

"Whatever do they want me for? I'm no one."

"You are not no one, but a member of the Chamberlain family.

Take pride in it. If you don't think well of yourself, I assure you, few others will."

Isn't that the truth? The launch would probably be in the newspapers, and everyone who'd looked down on her would see the high regard others held her in. It might change a great many opinions of her, or at least remind the naysayers who she was related to and to keep their thoughts about her and Father to themselves, or, in Mr. Shoedelin's case, to keep what he knew about her a secret. "Tell them I'll do it."

"Good. Here are invitations I think you should accept."

Valerie flipped through the envelopes, nothing notable about any of them until she reached the last one. She sat up straight. "Vivien Mosley invited me to her coming-out ball? Did she not have enough of trying to insult me and Uncle Neville at the luncheon?"

Aunt Anne shrugged as if the incident, which had spread so fast through the room that it'd reached her table by the salad course, had simply been a mix-up in dates from a florist. "You're a prominent debutante and whatever Vivien might personally think of you, having you at her coming-out ball makes a statement."

"That you and I condone her father's politics."

"That you are capable of mixing with people with whom you do not see eye to eye."

Or trying to scratch each other's eyes out. "Isn't there something else I can attend instead?"

"The Royal Cambridge Home for Soldiers' Widows Ball is that night," Miss Leaf mentioned.

"Good. I'll go there. It'll show people I'm civic-minded and reflect well on you and Uncle Neville."

Miss Leaf looked to Aunt Anne, pencil poised over the calendar.

"Very well," Aunt Anne conceded. "But since she invited you, you must invite her to your dance."

"This is madness."

"This is manners. Social relations are always kept separate from politics. If they weren't, there wouldn't be enough families in England on speaking terms to have the Season."

Given that Uncle Neville, when he was Chancellor of the Exchequer, had rented his London town house to Joachim von Ribbentrop, Hitler's foreign minister, and no one had raised an eyebrow, an invitation to one of the hundreds of coming-out balls wasn't likely to cause much of a stir. Vivien would probably find a reason to decline anyway. "If I must."

"You must, and not all the invitations are bad. Lord and Lady Fallington and their son, Lord Elmswood, have accepted theirs for the royal dinner."

Elm, here, for the King and Queen's dinner. I'm dining with royalty and some of the highest in England and he and his mother will be here to see it. There was an opportunity she never would've dreamed of two years ago, and, like the ship's christening, it would be in the newspapers. It also meant that if Mr. Shoedelin decided to trot her past out through the drawing rooms of London, she'd have a great deal further to fall. She prayed the man had the political savvy to not besmirch the Premier's niece and risk ruining his diplomatic career.

Chapter Eight

MIDNIGHT—the new Paramount picture is due for a
gala charity premiere at the Plaza . . . to be attended by
H. M. Queen Mary.

—the *Sketch*

*H*ow many programs do you have left to sell?" Dinah joined
Valerie from where she'd been stationed near the Plaza
Theatre's entrance. The theater's Italianate lobby, with its dark
wood antiques and black iron trim, was filled with the usual bevy
of diamond- and fur-bedecked matrons, their distinguished husbands, and debutantes in demure evening gowns. Stills from the
movie were posted around the room, the slick pictures a sharp
contrast to the antique oil paintings hanging on the brocade pat-
terned walls.

Valerie counted the large programs with the poster of Claudette Colbert, Don Ameche, and John Barrymore dressed to the

nines for their roles in *Midnight* gracing the front. The organizing committee had invited Valerie and a number of debutantes to sell them for the film premiere to benefit the Princess Beatrice Hospital. Outside, Piccadilly was alight with the Plaza's neon sign announcing the movie, while the press and curious onlookers crowded the pavement. "I have five. I wish it'd hurry up. I could do with an hour or two off my feet." The evening had been frightfully dull despite the whiff of Hollywood glamour.

"We can't start until Queen Mary arrives."

She was the only English royalty scheduled to attend, but not the only royal. "Queen Eugenie of Spain purchased a program from me a short while ago."

"The highlight of the evening, I'm sure, but I suppose it could be worse. We could be with Eunice at the American embassy dinner."

"Or with Aunt Anne at the Danish legation's musical evening. You should've heard my cousin when she found out I was coming without a chaperone. Of course, she wasn't outraged enough to volunteer to accompany me. Thank heavens."

"If selling souvenirs at a charity performance is respectable enough for a Russian princess, it must be respectable enough for you." Dinah motioned to Princess Natasha Bagration standing with another debutante Valerie didn't recognize. The Russian princess was stunning, with dark hair and eyes and a flowered brocade dress with full sleeves and a high neckline. "Poor dear, imagine your country forcing you to flee to Yugoslavia and making it so you can never return home. Beastly Bolsheviks."

Valerie could imagine being banished back to France. It'd been more than a week since the Household Brigade Steeplechase Meeting and not a peep of gossip or a sighting of Mr. Shoedelin. For all she knew, he'd returned to Bayonne. It hadn't stopped her from searching for him at every event, from the Speedway Racing Gala to the Eaton Hall Tennis Tournament. She didn't worry quite so much when Their Excellencies were around to distract her. It was late at night, when she was keyed up after a dance, that her worries proved as exhausting as the Season. "I see Katherine has met her Prince Charming."

Katherine gazed up at Ronnie Howard, who resembled his famous father, Leslie Howard, through the solid line of his chin and his hooded eyes, but his nose was sharper. He wasn't nearly as enthralled with Katherine as she was with him, but he politely listened to whatever she was saying.

"I don't see the appeal," Dinah said.

"Other than his father is one of the most famous British actors alive?" More than one debutante hovered around them, sighing at Ronnie with the same admiration they usually lavished on his father, the dashing star of *The Scarlet Pimpernel*.

"Then far be it from me to quash anyone's aspirations. I leave that to Aunt Nancy."

The venom in Dinah's tone surprised Valerie. "Something wrong at Four St. James's Square?"

"You should've heard Aunt Nancy screaming at Michael at dinner, what an awful row. She ridiculed him for leaving Oxford without a degree and was absolutely furious when he told her he's letting a flat because she's stifling him. She shouldn't have been so nasty, but he shouldn't have been so mean. He's lucky to have his mother, we can't all say that."

No, they couldn't. "What's he going to do in his flat?"

"Paint. He wants to be an artist."

"I thought your aunt enjoyed artists."

"They're all well and good for salons, but have you ever met one really worth his salt?"

"No. They're a self-centered lot." Augustus John and the grief he'd caused her and Father had proved that. "I'm sure Michael won't be so awful, but he'd have some rotten company."

"I'll say. Steady on, you have a customer."

Dr. Cranston threaded his way through the guests crowding the theater lobby. The bright houselights cut across his square jaw and brought out the slight red in his dark brown hair.

"I didn't expect you to be here tonight." If so, she'd have worn a touch of Yardley blush and a more daring shade of lipstick.

"I didn't expect to be here. May I?" He fished a shilling out of his pocket.

"Of course." She handed him the program, her fingertips briefly brushing his and sending a ripple of warmth coursing through her.

Dinah watched with the same amusement as when Christian had spent nearly all of Anne Schuster's cocktail party perched on the staircase with John Miller. "Oh look, there's Katherine. I must have a word with her. If you'll excuse me."

She was off into the crowd with little more than an encouraging wave back.

A few balding gentlemen and their wide-bosomed wives

strolled into the theater behind Dr. Cranston, mumbling about this and that. Valerie expected the doctor to take his leave and follow them, but he lingered, running his thumb and forefinger over the crease in the program. Thank goodness. Better to chat with him than another bespectacled lord ogling her while he made a purchase. "What mother sent you tickets for tonight?"

"My own. She's laid up with a cold, so here I am."

"By yourself?"

"My father wouldn't come without her." He stepped aside for another group of patrons making their way inside. "Anyone of interest arrive yet?"

"Rex Harrison and Diana Wynyard a little while ago, and John Barrymore, who reeked of whiskey. His poor wife was practically holding him up."

"One of his doctors works at St. Thomas's. You should hear his stories about the old thespian."

"Do tell."

"I can't. Patient confidence." He winked at her before leaning closer, the faint smell of iodine mixing with his crisp aftershave. "But a mate of mine works with his London film insurer. He said Mr. Barrymore's penchant for profanity gave the film editor quite a headache. Whiskey loosens the actor's tongue a little too much."

"Alcohol did the same for my father. When he was deep in his cups, he'd tell quite some tales about society matrons and their escapades before the Great War." He stared at her and she tightened her grip on the programs. She'd thoughtlessly made Father sound like a drunken sailor, and in front of a man keener on formality than his chums. Curse her boldness. It wouldn't hurt her to be a bit more reserved. "I assume a doctor used to patient confidences will keep that little remark between us. I should hate to get a reputation."

He flashed a beguiling smile that eased her grip on the programs. "I'm a professional secrets-keeper. Your slip is safe with me."

She had no reason to believe him, but she did. After all, a man so discreet about a famous patient wasn't likely to go around talking about her.

A frenzy of activity at the front entrance drew everyone's notice, while flashes from the cameramen outside illuminated the semidarkness. Queen Mary, resplendent in a sparkling silver silk dress with a matching sable-lined cape entered the lobby. Lord Carisbrooke, President of the Princess Beatrice Hospital, and his wife arranged a number of guests, including Lady Mountbatten, into a receiving line. Queen Mary made her way down it, shaking hands and chatting with various donors, especially Lady Mountbatten, whose black velvet dress and fur-lined cape were a stunning contrast to the Dowager Queen's.

Lady Diana Stuart-Wortley, one of the young marrieds on the fundraising committee, came to collect the unsold programs. "When Her Majesty takes her seat, you may take yours."

She moved on to another group of debutantes, everyone in the lobby stuck there until Queen Mary entered the theater. At least Valerie was standing with Dr. Cranston. At the Royal Opera House opening night reception she'd been caught out with a very dull third son of an earl with a passion for medieval architecture. The King and Queen had been painfully slow about entering the opera house. She wouldn't mind if Queen Mary dawdled in the receiving line tonight.

"Do you enjoy films, Dr. Cranston?"

"Richard, please. I prefer reading. *If I could always read, I should never feel the want of company.*"

"Lord Byron."

"Well done." He eyed her, genuinely impressed. "Books are a welcome rest from dances and my daily rounds."

"I don't know how you do it. I thought I was going to drop off into my eggs this morning. If it hadn't been for my afternoon nap, I'd be falling asleep on my feet." Goodness, how frivolous that made her sound. "Of course, I'm not really expected to do much else except attend balls, am I?"

"That could change if things in Europe get worse. Women did their part in the Great War. They may be called on to do so again."

"I don't know what good I'd be to a war effort. My only skills are speaking French and reciting literary quotes." Drilling the English canon into her was the only aspect of her education Father hadn't neglected, at least in the first few years she'd been with him and Mavis. Once the tart had left, his passion for literature and quotes had faded as fast as his interest in her and everything else.

"You could be a translator in a hospital, entertain the convalescents with your vast knowledge."

"As if the poor dears hadn't suffered enough. I'd much rather be a spy."

"You could throw the enemy off with your charm."

"It does sound rather tempting."

Queen Mary and her entourage approached on their way into the theater. Richard bowed and Valerie dipped a curtsey, her hand brushing Richard's when she rose, his skin without his gloves warm against hers. When the guest of honor was inside, Richard offered her his elbow.

"May I escort you in?"

"Please." The wool of his jacket was soft beneath her palm and barely hid the firm arm underneath. She wondered if the rest of him was as solid as his wide shoulders. It was a devilishly wicked thought but she couldn't help herself. He was no milquetoast, and there was no harm in thinking it. Acting on it the way Mavis had done was the sin, as she'd discovered in France.

Their Excellencies stopped talking when Richard and Valerie reached their row. They looked at her hand on his arm but she didn't snatch it away. There was no point, since they'd already seen it. There'd be no end of ribbing after this.

"I hope you aren't too tired to watch the film." He lowered his arm out from under her hand, and she immediately missed the heat of it.

"I'll stay awake plotting my plans to join the resistance."

"You'll give the Germans a run for their money."

"I hope so."

He clasped his hands in front of him, turning serious. "I'm sure you have more useful skills than you give yourself credit for, ones any charity would be happy to employ."

"Thank you for thinking so."

"Good evening, Miss de Vere Cole."

"Valerie."

"Good evening, Valerie."

She tapped her toes beneath the ruffled skirt of her cream chiffon dress, her name delicious in his deep voice. "Good evening, Richard."

With a nod, he bade her farewell, striding up the aisle to find his seat.

Valerie slid in past Katherine, Christian, and Dinah, their heads turning in unison to follow her. Valerie sat down and fluffed her skirt out around her so it wouldn't be too wrinkled during the film, the stretching quiet proving more than Their Excellencies could stand.

"Well, well, well, collecting a few chaps, are we?" Katherine said.

"Don't snap them all up." Dinah poked her in the ribs before Christian leaned across Katherine.

"Leave a few for the rest of us."

"Come off it. I'm simply being friendly and enjoying myself."

"Don't enjoy yourself too much," Dinah warned. "You don't want to flame out early, not with so much fun left to be had."

Queen Mary sat in the balcony off to the right with her attendants, waiting like everyone for the medieval forest tapestry stage curtain to open. Overhead, the high ceiling, elaborately carved and festooned with crystal chandeliers, gave the vast theater the air of a European palace. Valerie followed the line of it to the seats far up behind her, searching for Richard.

"He's chatting up Princess Natasha Bagration." Dinah turned around like Valerie to look at the audience. The others tittered over Ronnie Howard sliding into the row two down from theirs, his famous father nowhere in sight.

"She's far more glamorous than I am and has important work to do." The Bagration family's diplomacy on behalf of Yugoslavia was well known.

"An impoverished royal with no country. They're a dime a dozen nowadays," Dinah scoffed. "Besides, gentlemen don't look to us for interesting discussion. They want us to be clever but not too clever and show them up or do more than hang on their every word and look pretty. Speaking of which, Richard never took his eyes off you the entire time you were here. We might as well not have even existed, for all he cared."

Dorothy's warning about jealous girlfriends crowded into Valerie's thoughts. "You aren't interested in him, are you?"

"Goodness, no. I like him well enough and he's great fun, but a doctor? My father would have quite a bit to say about that."

She was right. A woman of Dinah's background couldn't possibly marry a mere doctor, no matter whose son he might be. Chaps like that were best left to girls like Valerie. If only thinking that didn't make her sound as desirable as day-old fish. "Who do you want?"

"I haven't decided, but there's plenty of time to think about it."

"Unless war comes."

"What a dreadful subject. What brought that on?"

"Something Richard said. Chaps have real and meaningful work, while we're left to hairdressers and shopping."

"Not all the chaps have work. Michael doesn't, and he desperately wants it, but Aunt Nancy can't see it. I shudder to think how she'll be when I find something to do besides die of boredom in the country when the Season ends."

"What were you thinking of?"

"I don't know, but after Aunt Nancy shrieked at Michael, I don't dare discuss it with her. I love her to bits, but she wants to run everyone's life. I won't let her run mine, not that it matters. If war comes, we might not have a future." Dinah picked at a loose thread on one of the embroidered flowers on her cream organza gown. "I thought I had a lifetime with Mummy when I finally came home, but the pneumonia bitched that up. Everyone expects you to carry on after someone dies, to go about as if it never happened, as if everything you'd hoped for wasn't snatched away, but it was, and it's with you every day. Mummy used to say that about my half brother David after he died. I didn't understand how it weighed on her, but I do now."

"I know." Valerie clasped Dinah's hand before she could undo the flower's delicate stitching. "It's hard to stand in the middle of everyone and act like everything is fine when the past is still bothering you. I feel it every time I wish things about my parents were different, but they aren't, they never can be."

Dinah gripped Valerie's hand tight, a single tear sliding down her cheek. "It's ghastly, isn't it?"

"It is, but you can tell me whenever you like that you aren't happy. I won't expect you to pretend you aren't."

"You promise not to pretend with me too. Agreed?"

"Agreed." The word was barely out of her mouth and it was a lie. She couldn't tell her everything the way she longed to. No one could ever know that much about her, not if she wanted to keep them in her life, but the possibility to share other things, to not feel quite so alone, gave her hope.

"Look at us, acting like a couple of sad sacks when we should be having fun." Dinah tugged a handkerchief out of her purse and dabbed her eyes, careful not to smudge the hint of pink eye shadow.

"I think we have more than our share of reasons to be glum every now and again."

"Over tea where we can have a proper cry and a good chat, but not tonight, when we should be planning something utterly delicious, since our chaperones aren't here. I don't want to see the film, do you?"

"Not at all."

"Then let's do something else." Dinah tugged her out of her seat as the houselights dimmed and the stage curtain began to part.

"Where are you two going?" Christian whispered.

"Somewhere more thrilling than this. Come with us if you like."

"Do sit down and be quiet," an old man in the row behind them spit through his mustache.

Dinah pulled Valerie out of the row and up the aisle, stopping in the quiet lobby, where attendants emptied ashtrays and tidied the room. Footmen laid cloths over long tables and set out trays of food and glasses for the champagne reception after the film.

"What are you two doing here?" Jakie strolled into the lobby with Michael, neither of them skulking in shame at being incredibly late for the showing.

"Shouldn't you be inside watching dear Claudette like good

little debutantes?" Michael was more acidic than charming, the evening row with Lady Astor telling.

"I should chide you both for taking so long to arrive, but not tonight. We want to go to the 400 Club. It's not far from here and you'll take us."

"Yes, ma'am." Jakie snapped a crisp salute. "I'll fetch the car."

"Lady Warrender gave us the evil eye when we left." Christian was nearly out of breath from hurrying out of the theater.

"Where are we going?" Katherine asked.

"Everything all right?" Richard asked before Dinah could answer. "I saw you leave."

Valerie nearly leapt out of her shoes. At this rate the entire theater would be in here wondering what they were up to and they'd be sunk before they'd even begun.

"We're off to the 400 Club if you care to join us." *Do please care.*

"Not what I had in mind for the evening, but why not?"

"Then we'd better go before some old biddy decides to see what we're up to."

Everyone followed Dinah into the street outside the Plaza Theatre. The crowds and cameramen were gone, replaced by a line of parked cars on either side of the street. Liveried chauffeurs mingled about to chat and smoke and crowd into the pub across the way. The Astors' chauffer probably didn't appreciate being pulled away from his leisure to ferry them about, but he brought the car to the curb as instructed.

The group piled into the black Austin 12 saloon, Valerie pinned between Richard and Dinah, his arm resting over the back of the seat behind her, his thigh pressed against hers. If they weren't packed in like a tin of sardines she'd lean deeper into him but she'd endured enough ribbing for one night. She wasn't about to give Their Excellencies fodder for more, no matter how delicious it was to have Richard so close.

"We'll have until midnight." Katherine's shoulders were near her ears at being wedged between Christian and Jakie.

"That doesn't give us much time."

"It's our first taste, but we'll be back." Dinah was practically sitting on Michael's lap.

The car sped down Denman Street toward Leicester Square. Within moments, the marquees of the Odeon and the Leicester Theatre came into view. The square was alight with flashing neon signs and splendidly dressed couples filing into the theaters.

The car pulled to the curb of the nondescript 28 Leicester Square, with its cinema and the side door leading down into what every debutante had been warned was the premier den of iniquity. Michael pushed open the door and in a rush of cool air they spilled out, straightening their wrinkled dresses and jackets. Michael told the chauffer when to return, then faced everyone and clapped his hands. "Are you ready for your first taste of sin?"

"Is it really wicked?" Christian clasped her purse in front of her as if it were a shield.

"Let's find out." He offered her his arm, Dinah joining him on the other side. Jakie escorted Katherine, leaving Valerie to Richard.

He dutifully extended his elbow and she took it, feeling too sophisticated and nervous to notice how close he stood while they descended the stairs to the club to the strains of "Heart and Soul" played by the orchestra.

"Mr. Astor, a pleasure to see you this evening," the dark-coated maître d' greeted, flashing a wide smile beneath his thin mustache.

"A pleasure to be here. Anyone we should be concerned about inside? We have the Premier's niece, Miss Katherine Ormsby-Gore, Miss Dinah Brand, and Miss Christian Grant."

"Michael, don't tell him who we are." Katherine glanced around as if anyone who was mingling nearby might care or notice.

"Don't fret, Mr. Rossi won't tell a soul you've been here."

"If I were so indiscreet we'd be closed in a month," Mr. Rossi assured them. "Not to worry, ladies, no one of concern to any of you is here tonight. Should one arrive, I'll notify you at once. We don't like awkward scenes at the 400 Club."

"How does he know who we should and shouldn't be worried about?" Valerie whispered to Jakie.

"Mr. Rossi knows more about people's lineage than *Debrett's*. Don't worry, you're in capable hands."

"Table forty-eight, John." He handed them off to a young waiter, who led them into the heart of the small and dimly lit club.

Valerie and the girls gaped at the pillars holding up the low ceiling and the dark silk covering the walls. A long string of square tables stood crammed together along the edges of the room, velvet benches on the far side packed with people. Various bottles, glasses, and plates cluttered the tablecloths in front of them.

"What fun." Katherine tossed her purse on the table, tapping her fingers against the chair in time to the music. "Michael, dance with me."

"A lady asking a chap, how daring."

"I feel daring tonight." She took his arm and led him off.

"It's my turn to be bold. Jakie, you can dance with me," Christian insisted.

"I'd be honored, so long as I don't have to do a Highland jig."

"I won't make you jump about. Come on." They crowded onto the already full dance floor, the size of it almost as minuscule as the basement club.

"Are you going to leave me without a partner?" Valerie said to Richard with a saucy shake of her head, making her thick curls bounce around her neck and cheeks.

"I wouldn't dream of it."

"If I'm going to be the odd man out, then you owe me the next dance, and I expect to get it." Dinah leveled one pink-polished finger at him. "While you're gone, I'll order drinks."

She summoned the waiter, while Richard led Valerie to the edge of the dancing crowd. He pulled her into his arms, guiding her as far around the floor as the crush allowed, their steps more of a walk than the jittering jumping of the energetic couples. Valerie could barely see past his crisp white shirt and waistcoat. Not that she minded. His arms around her felt as natural as the chiffon dress against her back.

"What do you think of the club?" He didn't have to raise his voice to be heard. The band played soft enough for everyone to chat.

"Not as scintillating as I expected but I can feel the sin in the air, especially at the tables in the back." A break in the dancers offered a view of the far corners of the club and the couples seated at the shadowed tables. "I'm sure those women aren't their wives."

Their simple clothes gave them away.

"Pretend not to see them and they'll pretend not to see you."

He turned her around, his low laugh rippling through her chest and his.

"Is that how it works?"

"So I've been told."

If all of society adhered to this sort of discretion she wouldn't fret half as much as she did about Mavis or Mr. Shoedelin. She refused to worry about it tonight, enjoying Richard and this naughty adventure. "No skeletons in your closet, then?"

"None except my anatomy one. Elm and I had a ripping time with him during a Thursday to Sunday at Cliveden. We hid the old boy in Lord Beresford's bed. He was over the moon at having a partner and very disappointed when he wasn't as lively as he'd hoped. He chucked my skeleton out the window and if he'd known Elm and I were hiding behind the curtains he'd have thrown us out too. The gardener found it the next morning and if Elm hadn't explained everything before he called the magistrate I'd have lost a perfectly good specimen and been sent down without a degree or the means to pay for my evening clothes and flat." Richard laughed, but it faded fast. He adjusted his hand in hers, the weight of the one on her back lightening. "It isn't easy being raised with all this and then be told it isn't really for you."

"It's like living in Downing Street. I'm in it but not a part of it, at least not the government part. We're both outsiders in our own way, aren't we?"

"Being the fourth son does set one pretty far down the aristocratic pecking order."

"A man is better off with work. It gives him something worthwhile to do besides gad about." It was more than Father and half the aristocrats in society were willing to do, even at their most desperate. After watching her father flail about in debt, more concerned with being a gentleman than being properly fed, clothed, or housed, she couldn't respect a man who refused to help himself.

"You don't think me too serious, then?"

"I think you're divine and your dedication to work dashing."

"You might be the only deb who does."

The number drew to its close and they let go of one another to clap and return to the table. They weren't ten feet from it when Dinah leapt up and rushed at Richard. "It's my turn. Katherine and Christian swapped partners and I'm not going to sit out again."

"Then I'll endeavor to do my duty," Richard assured.

"Don't do it too well, I wouldn't want Valerie to be jealous."

Valerie hoped he couldn't see her blush in the dim light before Dinah tugged him to the dance floor. She sat at the table and picked up the drink, leaving a water ring on the tablecloth in front of her. She sipped it, wincing at the strong liquor in sugary syrup. All around her, women enjoyed their cocktails without blanching, a highball glass in one hand and a cigarette in the other. Valerie wasn't about to take up that habit, but she lounged in the chair, feeling quite chic even while the drink burned the back of her throat.

When she'd had enough sophistication, she took a turn around the club, twisting this way and that through the tables until she came face-to-face with Vivien.

Her eyes went as wide as Valerie's. Apparently she wasn't supposed to be here either. They set their shoulders, bracing for another verbal match. There was nothing holding them back except Mr. Rossi's mandate against awkward moments.

"I see they let nearly anyone in nowadays." Vivien threw down the gauntlet. "Perhaps this club isn't as exclusive as it used to be."

"It isn't if they're letting in fascists. Shouldn't you be at a Black-shirts meeting?"

"We aren't all defined by our fathers."

"Of course we are." There was a bit of honesty they could both suck on. "Best to remember that when chucking words about. We have enough to manage with the family hand we've been dealt to add anything more to it."

She wasn't about to beg Vivien to keep her stupid mouth shut, but a little reminder that neither of them benefited from the other snitching about being here tonight couldn't hurt.

Vivien took Valerie's meaning, nodding and making her gold teardrop earrings swing. "I think it's best if we not mention we saw one another here."

"I agree."

They stalked past each other. What Vivien told her friends when she reached their table she didn't know, but like Christian, Katherine, and Dinah, who were watching from over their partners' shoulders, that group wasn't likely to let anything slip either. None of them needed chaperone troubles or to find their fun curtailed this early in the Season, not with all the other London nightclubs left to visit.

"You and Miss Mosley appeared quite chummy," a familiar voice said.

Valerie whirled around to discover Elm leaning against a chair, not caring that he crushed the fur coat draped over the back of it. He wore the standard white-tie, not filling it out as solidly as Richard, but no slack either. His Jermyn Street tailors had done a fine job of fitting it to his slender frame. "How much of that charming exchange did you hear?"

"Enough. She's a wicked minx, isn't she?"

"I could think of a few other words to describe her, but I don't want to send anyone into a faint."

"I can manage bold words."

"Not from a lady. I'll leave them to your imagination."

She led him to their table and Elm held out her chair. She sat down, shocked by the quick clip of her heartbeat when he sat beside her, the tight quarters pushing his knee against hers.

"Since this is your first time here, you must have the full experience. Waiter!" He snapped his fingers at a passing waiter, who rushed to their table. "A bottle of Veuve Clicquot."

"Yes, Lord Elmswood." The man hustled off, returning a moment later with the uncorked bottle and glasses. He poured, not dribbling so much as a drop on the white tablecloth, set the bottle between them, and then vanished into the crowd as fast as he'd appeared.

Elm raised his glass. "To telling Vivien what's what."

"And friends at the 400 Club." She clinked her glass against his and took a sip. Champagne and a Viscount. The evening was really shaping up. She considered kicking off one shoe and leaving it behind in the hopes he or Richard might bring it home, but didn't dare. That was all fine and dandy in movies, but it didn't happen in real life.

The music ended and Elm set down his glass before taking hers out of her hand and placing it on the table. He never let go of her as he raised her out of her chair and tucked her hand into the crook of his elbow. She barely noticed the people passing them to reach the parquet, not even Dinah and Richard until Elm stopped them.

"Hello, old man. I see they're letting the riffraff in."

Richard laughed. "We'll take over the place in no time if you lot aren't careful."

"Then we'll have as much fun as our few free hours allow. It's back to work for us in the morning. You to the wards, me to the barracks, while the lovely ladies enjoy their beauty rest."

"You're the one who needs the rest," Dinah challenged. "Burning the candle at both ends the way you do."

"Nonsense. The new recruits are better faced half-tight."

"Same with some patients and certain members of society." Richard glanced at Valerie's hand in Elm's and she couldn't read the fleeting expression on his face. He shouldn't mind her dancing with Elm. They were friends having a marvelous time and there was nothing more to it.

He wasn't the only one who noticed. Dinah could barely hold back her smile. "Have fun, you two, but don't have too much fun."

"I wouldn't dream of it." Elm clapped Richard on the back, the two parties continuing on.

Elm swept her into his arms with a smooth practiced flourish, sparing her the rough handling of most of her usual partners. "There won't be any champagne left by the time Richard, Jakie, and Michael are done, but better they drink it than let it go to waste. I never order anything I can't finish in one night."

"How very prudent of you."

"I'm nothing if not prudent."

"Hello, Elm," a cooing voice interrupted. "What a pleasure to see you."

Elm's hand went stiff in hers.

"Miss Digby." He shifted them around to see the Honorable Pamela Digby dancing with the distinguished Fulke Warwick, Earl of Warwick. With dark eyebrows above languid eyes, it was no wonder MGM had placed him under contract. It'd been quite the sensation in the newspapers, a lord in the pictures, and he counted Douglas Fairbanks, Leslie Howard, and the rest of the British film stars as part of his set. He was also a good ten years older than Lord Digby's pudgy redheaded daughter, and a married man.

"How formal you are tonight." Pamela giggled, batting her eyelashes at him, much to Lord Warwick's irritation. "Are you attending Ascot? I'd so like to see you again."

How often had she seen him before?

"I haven't decided." Elm stared over Valerie's shoulder at some spot on the far wall, doing his best to ignore Pamela and end the conversation. Pamela didn't either notice or care, and was about to ask another question when Lord Warwick had the tact to cut her off. "Let's not trouble Lord Elmswood and his partner. We'll sit out the rest of the dance."

"I don't want to." Pamela pouted, her lips a daring shade of red that matched her far too low-cut dress.

"Yes, you do. Lord Elmswood." Lord Warwick offered a terse nod, then tugged the petulant Pamela off to a shadowed table.

"Are you two intimately acquainted?" Valerie asked.

"I'm acquainted with her reputation, and thanks to her current escort, so are you."

Liar. "Are you saying she isn't all innocence?"

"She and some others I could name, but I don't want to shock your delicate sensibilities."

She could tell him a few things that'd turn him a whiter shade of pale but she wasn't about to leave him with a bad impression of her. "But we need something fun to discuss over tea. We wouldn't be proper society ladies if we didn't."

"Then why not talk about me?"

"You aren't nearly so interesting." Even if what she'd learned about him tonight was rather shocking.

"I can be extremely fascinating when I want." He swung her around, making her hair and skirt twirl out before he settled them into a steady sway. "Or so my parents tell me. They think I'm too serious about some things and flippant about others. I'm quite serious about my red Bentley and my rank in the Coldstream Guards, one befitting a viscount and future marquess."

A superficial list, but she wasn't surprised. There wasn't a man with a title who didn't think the way he did. They simply weren't as charming in their self-centeredness as Elm. "Difficult to believe they don't consider those real concerns."

"The nerve of them, especially when they chide me for worrying I won't live long enough to really enjoy them." He peered off into the dim lights beyond the dance floor, his body moving from habit, not intention. "I wish they'd get on with this war instead of leaving us to wonder and wait."

"There won't be a war to get on with. I believe in Uncle Neville's commitment to peace."

"That's comforting, coming from the debutante in Downing Street." He let go of her, stepping back to applaud with the others at the end of the dance, all smiles and charm as he escorted her to the table. "We've returned."

Elm pulled out her chair before taking his place on her left. Richard sat on her right, the two of them leaning across her from time to time to exchange jokes and ribbing. The conversation flowed as fast and easy as the music, everyone crowded around the table, cocktail glasses empty, champagne glasses full. If any of them were the worse for wear, they, like most of their class, hid it well. If there could be more evenings like this, Valerie would gladly sneak out to every nightclub in London. Dorothy might bang on about rules, but there were other, whispered ones she'd follow too and wring more fun out of the Season. Dinah was right, the only way to truly enjoy it was to be a little daring.

"Did you see Pamela Digby?" Dinah whispered to Valerie. "Hard to believe she can wrap men around her pudgy finger the way she does. I heard she and Lord Warwick spent a weekend in Paris together. She tried to play it off as a shopping trip but everyone knows her family doesn't have that sort of money. He's paying her bills."

"If everyone knows, then why is she still here?" According to Dorothy, debs, even ones from last Season, who weren't good girls were immediately shunned.

"Amazing what a family name and a modicum of discretion can do, but it won't last. She isn't that discreet."

There was a bit of hope. If Mr. Shoedelin or Mavis decided to tell tales, as long as they were whispered about and not broadcast across a luncheon ballroom she might come out of this better than she believed. There were no guarantees, especially with Mr. Shoedelin having made himself scarce, but he couldn't speak if he wasn't around. As for Mavis, who knows what mischief she'd decide to make? Until either was decided, Valerie must continue to do everything she could to force people to see her as the Premier's niece and not as her father's daughter.

"Ladies, I hate to be a rotter, but if you have any hope of maintaining your ruse of being good little girls you'd best be on your way." Jakie made a show of checking his watch. Dinah grabbed his arm and read it.

"Oh dear, we must be off."

The women rose, bringing the men to their feet.

"Whatever will you do without us when we scurry back to the theater?" Christian gathered up her purse, her rosy cheeks brighter from the excitement and the champagne.

Elm finished the last of his drink and set it on the table. "The usual. Attend some dance or other until it's time to motor back to Windsor. Richard will keep an eye on me, won't you, old chap?"

"The responsible one as ever," he said with pride as they made their way out of the club. "Friends must watch out for one another. If they don't, few others will."

"I'll say." It was exactly what she and Their Excellencies did.

"Thank you chaps for a lively evening," Dinah said as Jakie's car pulled to the curb. "Far more fun than that boring old film."

Richard held open the door and the girls filed in. "Our pleasure. I look forward to doing it again."

"So do I." Valerie paused, about to say more, when Elm came up behind Richard and clapped a hand on his shoulder. "The Bentley's around the corner. I'll give you a lift. Good night, Valerie."

"Good night, Elm." Her name spoken by him didn't have the same rich ring to it as it did in Richard's voice, but it was quite chic on the lips of a viscount. "Until next time."

"Until then." Richard closed the door behind her and he, Elm, Jakie, and Michael strode off down the street in search of more amusements.

"The chaps have all the fun, free to do what they like, while we have to be proper," Christian complained as the car drove away from the lights of Leicester Square.

"They don't have nearly as much freedom as you think." Dinah rested her feet on the seat between Katherine and Christian. "Richard is practically chained to St. Thomas's, and Aunt Nancy has such a tight thumb on Michael he can barely do anything."

"None of us can, not yet." Katherine kicked off her shoes and wiggled her stockinged toes. "Once we're married we'll be free to do more of what we like."

"I'm not ready to be married or even close to it. What am I to do until then?" Christian challenged.

"Enjoy yourself. This nasty business with Germany might make it so none of us has a say in anything for a long while." Dinah trilled her nails on the edge of the car window, surprisingly serious, until the marquis for the Plaza came into view. "Pull yourself together, ladies. We're almost there."

They powdered their noses and applied fresh swipes of lipstick, checking each other for any telltale signs that they had been any-where but mingling in the lobby of the Plaza.

"Mr. Jackson, drop us here," Dinah instructed the chauffer, who let them out in front of the building beside the theater. "If anyone asks, we were outside getting some fresh air. Are we ready, ladies?"

"We are."

All four of them strolled leisurely up the pavement and into the lobby, quickly blending into the mass of guests milling about. They stayed off to one side where no one noticed them until Christian's and Katherine's mothers came to collect them. They were too busy speaking with friends to ask their daughters what they'd thought of the film.

There was no one to trouble Valerie or Dinah, who stood be-side a large urn filled with a spray of flowers. They waved off a footman's offer of champagne, both having had their fill for the evening.

"If I wasn't mistaken, and I rarely am . . ." Dinah began.

"Spoken like Lady Astor's niece."

Dinah shrugged as if it couldn't be helped. "Richard was none too happy when Elm danced with you, and you were the only thing he talked about when I danced with him."

This made her heart race more than it should. "Come off it. They were only having fun, like Jakie and Michael."

"Those two could do with a little less fun now and again, but not Richard. He needs more of it. You could do worse. His father is a baron from an old line and I'm sure his family wouldn't look askance at having the Prime Minister's niece join their ranks."

"How mercenary you make it sound."

"You have to be a skilled hunter to catch a husband. I'd say you have a nice tiger in your sights."

"I'm not about to pull the trigger on anyone." It was hard to resist the excitement of Elm. When he wasn't dreary, he was the dashing lord who swept her off her feet, but Richard's levelheadedness held a certain appeal. She'd endured enough flighty people like Father to appreciate this quality, but now was no time for matchmaking. "Society is quite enough to contend with, and I want to be myself for a while before I become a wife."

"So do I, but don't rule it out completely. The Great War made a lot of women spinsters. If you get a chance, you'd be smart to take it. It may not come again."

Chapter Nine

W hat's all this?" Valerie entered the breakfast room to find a selection of china laid out on the table, a single place serving with a different pattern at every seat, and all of them far grander than anything the Chamberlains or No. 10 owned.

"It's a sample of Buckingham Palace's collection. I'm to select the set to use for Their Majesties' first dinner with us. What do you think?" Aunt Anne asked.

Valerie studied the various settings emblazoned with coats of arms, lions, and crowns. Some were gaudily floral in the Victorian fashion, while others were more Art Deco sleek with platinum edgings and stylishly intertwined ERs. "The platinum-rimmed one with the Grecian border will complement the candelabras and epergnes nicely."

"I agree. Mr. Watson, the Greek setting, if you please."

"An excellent choice, Mrs. Chamberlain. I'll arrange it at once."

The grave-faced Government Hospitality butler in his immaculate uniform snapped his fingers and a cortege of palace footmen swept in to carefully pack away the samples.

"Thank you, Mr. Watson." Aunt Anne laid her arm around Valerie's shoulder and escorted her from the bustle of the breakfast room to the serenity of the White Drawing Room. "How are we doing, Miss Leaf?"

"Sir Alec sent word that he's consulting the Royal Arms about whether the Marquess of Lothian or the Marquess of Fallington has the oldest title."

"Speaking of the Marquess and his family, with Lord Elmswood there it might be a good opportunity to secure an escort to the Queen Charlotte's Birthday Ball. You don't want to wait and be caught out," Aunt Anne advised Valerie.

"No, I don't." She'd practically have Elm to herself at the royal dinner, the two of them the youngest in attendance. It would be the perfect time to ask him. Imagine what Lady Dunsford and Lady Ashcombe would think when they saw her on the arm of a viscount at the ball. She shouldn't be so petty but she couldn't help herself.

"I have another surprise for you." Aunt Anne slid a red and gold Cartier box off of Miss Leaf's desk and held it out to Valerie. "The Vickers-Armstrongs company sent it as a thank-you for christening their ship."

Valerie gasped when she lifted the lid. A square, cushion-cut diamond dangled from a line of three smaller ones connected to a diamond-encrusted lavaliere, and four smaller diamonds flanked the chain. It was far from outlandish but it was the most impressive piece she'd ever owned. Father had pawned whatever jewelry he'd inherited years ago, and lost his family's signet ring while drunk, the fool. "I didn't think bracing the rain to swing a champagne bottle at a hull was enough to earn this."

"It's common for companies to send gifts. I have quite a collection of jewelry from the Birmingham businessmen I've opened factories for over the years."

"If something like this is going to arrive every time I launch a ship, I'll gladly do it again." She unhooked the lobster clasp and put it on, the platinum warming against her skin. She skipped to the large oval looking glass between the two far windows, turning this way and that to admire the brilliant sparkle. She imagined walking into the King and Queen's dinner wearing this, and what Elm might think of it. No dowager in her family gems would look twice at it, but it drew attention to all her right places.

"It's a touch too ostentatious for a debutante, but we'll find an appropriate place for you to wear it when the Season is over." Aunt Anne held out the open box. "I'll have Mr. Dobson put it in the safe."

Valerie unhooked the necklace and reluctantly laid it in the box, hating to lock it away when it should be worn, but, as always, the rules of the Season made their demands.

"While Miss Leaf and I see to the seating arrangements, you must finish your thank-you notes."

"Must I?" Valerie sighed. Every event she attended required a personal note of thanks to the hostess. What she wouldn't give for preprinted cards. At least Aunt Anne wasn't forcing her to learn flower arranging like Katherine's mother was doing to her daughter. "The social secretaries are the only ones who ever read them."

Miss Leaf kept a list of who'd sent what cards. They were all opened, but Aunt Anne rarely saw them.

"They are tedious but they're good practice for future correspondence." She held up a letter with the Buckingham Palace crest on the top. "Don't forget, you're taking my place at Mrs. Corrigan's dinner tonight."

"Will I get another diamond necklace out of it?"

"No, but you're sure to garner a few good stories to share with your friends." Aunt Anne led Miss Leaf out of the room, leaving Valerie to wonder what exactly was in store for her tonight. What waited for her at present were thank-you notes.

She sat at the Queen Anne writing desk in front of the window with a view of the garden and fingered the fine paper on the blotter and the expensive fountain pen. Her suffering at the convent school would've ended a great deal sooner if she'd had these, and more stamps, but then she wouldn't have garnered so many more glorious secrets to bury inside her.

She uncapped the pen and selected a piece of paper and the list of politely composed sentences of gratitude she kept in the desk drawer. It ensured she never sent the exact two pithy lines to the same hostess. While she wrote, she marveled at her handwriting. Great-Aunt Lillian had helped turn Valerie's once-illegible scrawl into a more refined hand, and had greatly reduced her need for the dictionary. She might not ride to the hounds but she could compose respectable correspondence.

A small cough from the doorway made her turn.

"Good morning, Miss de Vere Cole. I'm sorry to intrude, but I have a note for Mrs. Chamberlain." Miss Holmes handed Valerie the letter. "The Government Office has yet another question about her plans for the King and Queen's dinner."

"They're a difficult lot, aren't they?" Valerie turned the envelope over to reveal the royal coat of arms on the flap. "Makes one wonder why they deign to leave the palace. If we went there it'd save everyone the trouble."

"It's an honor to have the monarchs come to you instead of you going to them, but I agree, it is a bit of a nuisance. Mrs. Stenhouse says it was like this before when they came to dinner with the Baldwins. They have their ways. I suppose we all do."

"I suppose so." Valerie set the letter aside and rose. "Please, sit and chat. I'll only keep you a minute. I'd like to know more about the situation in Europe. I read the morning newspapers, but there's so much to take in, I can hardly make sense of it. I asked Mr. Colville about it when I saw him this morning, but you know how he is. I'm lucky to get more than a quick hello or good day from him."

"He isn't one for conversation, and I shouldn't dally up here either, but I suppose I can stay a moment." She joined Valerie on the sofa, perched on the edge as if she were about to take dictation. "To state it simply, France, Poland, and Russia are squabbling like children over how to stop Germany from overrunning whatever country or territory they fancy next. Most think it'll be Poland. Not even Mr. Chamberlain's negotiations are breaking the impasse or bringing the countries to some agreement. No one knows what'll happen if Germany invades Poland, especially if Britain pledges to defend her."

"It can't be that bad if the King and Queen are carrying on with their American tour in May. They wouldn't leave the country if there was an imminent threat."

"I should think not, but who can say? If there is war, we'll need the Americans' goodwill along with a great many other things. Father is setting aside stores of tinned food in case there are shortages as there were in the Great War. I use what money I can spare from my earnings to help him. Mother thought we were foolish until I told her I'd overheard the ministers discussing plans to send their children to Canada and their wives to the country. They think it'll be safer for them there, especially if Mr. Churchill is right about the Luftwaffe bombing London. If they believe it's prudent to prepare, then so should we, although how does one truly prepare for war? We can't leave London. We have no choice but to stay." She picked at a loose thread on the cuff of her sweater, untangling it from the others, the same worry that'd darkened Elm's eyes at the 400 clouding hers. The Coldstream Guards officers weren't the only ones afraid of war. It touched everyone.

"But of course it won't come to that, will it?"

Miss Holmes smiled brightly, cheerful and optimistic as always. If she could remain hopeful in the face of the growing threat and the few options she possessed to meet it, then so could Valerie. "No, it won't."

Miss Holmes smoothed her skirt over her knees, glancing about the room as if this were her first real chance to see it. "How exciting to think Their Majesties will be here. Merely being in the same building with them will be the closest I've ever come to meeting royalty."

"The staff aren't paying their respects?"

She shook her head. "We've begged Mrs. Stenhouse to put in a word with the secretaries about it, but with everything going on she refuses to bother them."

"You should have the chance, especially with the work you do for His Majesty's government. I'll speak with Uncle Neville on your behalf."

"You can't. What would the Premier or Mrs. Stenhouse say if they heard I'd talked to you about it?"

"I won't say you asked. I'll say it's my idea. I've seen the long hours you work. How many times have you been here when I come home from dinner parties?" She nearly winced at how shallow that made her sound, but it was true. The Garden Room Girls were typing their fingers to the bone while Valerie and Their Excellencies danced. She couldn't change that, after all, the staff had their livings to earn, but for once she could use her position to do more than help herself. Maybe someday she could employ it to the benefit of more people than the No. 10 staff. It wasn't expected of her, and it might not be appreciated, especially if Mr. Colville or Sir John got wind of it, but in this instance she had to try. "You should be allowed to pay your respects to the sovereigns like any proper Englishwoman."

Miss Holmes lit up the way Valerie had during her final court dress fitting. "Mother and Father will be so proud. Of course, my sisters will say I've gotten too big for my britches, but I don't care."

"Nor should you. I'll teach you to curtsey too." She pulled Miss Holmes to her feet, positioning them across from each other in the center of the large rug. "Slide your foot behind you like this, then lower yourself, back straight, head down, yes, like that, then hold it."

They maintained the low curtsey for a brief moment, Valerie steadier in her stance after hours of practice.

"What good shape you must be in from doing this. I might fall."

"You won't. When you think your legs are going to give out, that's when you stand and slide your feet back together."

They went through the motions a few more times, giggling while bobbing down and up to the imaginary monarchs. There wasn't much difference between them but their worlds were utterly separate; Valerie's lineage gave her entrance to this one as much as Miss Holmes's kept her out of it. Aunt Anne had said war might change things. With everyone's place so firmly fixed, it was hard to imagine anything except an utter catastrophe mixing it all up.

"Thank you, Miss de Vere Cole, for that. It was fun, but I must get back to work."

"Call me Valerie, please."

Miss Holmes sobered, lacing her fingers in front of her. "My name is Marian, but we won't call each other that except in private. I don't want to give anyone a shock."

"Especially my cousin."

"Certainly not her." With a wink, Marian left, a little bounce marking her stride.

Valerie took a deep breath. It was time to keep her promise. She slipped through the drawing rooms to Uncle Neville's study, hesitant to bother him, but if she didn't do it today, there might not be another chance. She hoped it didn't mean too much more correspondence between Aunt Anne and the palace. Her poor aunt didn't need more work, but she wasn't about to disappoint Marian. She'd promised that she'd ask for the Garden Room Girls to be presented and she would.

Outside the closed door, she took a deep breath and knocked.

"Come in." Uncle Neville removed his pince-nez and laid them on the desk, his stern expression softening. He sat in his large tufted leather chair on the other side of the wide mahogany desk. The red dispatch box stood in its pride of place on the corner and a neat stack of papers rested before him. "What brings you to my side of Number Ten?"

"I have a favor to ask." There was no point beating around the bush. He preferred directness. "I'd like the Garden Room Girls to be presented to Their Majesties. They work so hard on His Majesty's government's behalf, they deserve to be allowed to pay their respects."

He straightened the papers on the blotter while Valerie waited, hoping her appeal to his patriotism would win the argument. It was difficult to read Uncle Neville sometimes. He kept things close to the vest, barely ruffled by anything except the most outlandish claims or behavior of his party or the opposition. Even in the Commons, while answering hostile and accusing questions, he rarely raised his voice. He was the most levelheaded person she'd ever known, but even a small hint as to what he thought of her request would be appreciated. It would stop Valerie from sitting on the edge of her seat like a nervous Nellie.

He leaned back in his chair, lacing his long fingers over his stomach. He winced in pain, then opened his hands, resting them on the chair's arms, and she braced herself for a Dorothy-like lecture about not being too friendly with the staff. "It's not up to me to make that final decision. Their names must be submitted to Sir Alexander Hardinge, His Majesty's private secretary, for approval for presentation by the King."

That wasn't a refusal or a rebuke. "Surely you have some influence, and it'd mean ever so much to the Garden Room Girls. Miss Holmes has been a dear to me, keeping me abreast of the European situation. I'd hate for her and the others to be overlooked when something so small would mean the world to them and give them something special to hold on to if things turn as dreary as some say. It'd also show people that even when the highest of the high are at Downing Street, the Prime Minister has a care for all Englishmen no matter what their rank."

Uncle Neville smiled beneath his mustache, his tired eyes brightening with amusement. "A little flattery never hurts an argument, and you're right, we all need a bit of cheer during these uncertain times. I'll present your request through the appropriate channels and see if your reasoning sways them as much as it did me. I agree, they have as much right to pay their respects to the King and Queen as anyone with a title."

"Thank you, Uncle Neville." She came around the desk and

hugged him, shocked by how bony he'd grown. He'd never been stout, but he'd never been this thin either.

He patted her hands where they rested on his shoulders, gripping her fingers tight. "You have a kind heart, Valerie, and I'm glad you think so highly of the Garden Room Girls. It's good to care for more than frocks and dances and to not let the Season make you shallow or the past make you hard. Many things could've made you bitter, but they haven't."

"I have you and Aunt Anne to thank for that." They and getting to them had been the single shred of hope that'd kept her going in the convent school. "How are you feeling? You look tired." The way Father had the day they'd parted for good.

"I'm all right." He rubbed his side with his long fingers, working out a stitch. "Too many cabinet meetings and rushing through meals or the line of ambassadors waiting to see me. Some are worried their countries will be crushed by Germany, others are afraid to be embroiled in what they see as a European problem. I worry the most about those. Whatever happens, we'll need their support."

She glanced at the papers on his desk, the War Office address visible at the top. "Will there be war?"

He forced a weak smile, more sad than cheering. "Things are bad, but there's nothing you need to worry about."

Not yet, lingered in the air between them. "Whatever it is, you'll see us through it, I'm sure of it."

"That means a great deal to me." He placed the pince-nez back on his nose. "Now off you go. You have your duties and I have mine."

"I do." She made for the door, pausing to look at him as he leaned forward, engrossed in his papers, worried concern darkening his lean face.

She closed the door behind her. How different her life would've been if he'd been her father, but that wasn't how fate had decided things. Fate had not been in her favor in the past, but that had changed. She hoped fate was more forgiving where Uncle Neville and England were concerned.

Chapter Ten

"M rs. Corrigan didn't really do that, did she?" Christian slowly stirred her whipped cream into her chocolate malt. The whir of ice-cream mixers and the chatter of girls filled Selfridges' brass and wood soda shop. Behind the marble counter, women in light gray smocks and floppy baker's caps scooped ice cream and made other confections beneath the large red Coca-Cola sign.

"She most certainly did." Valerie fished the cherry out of the bottom of her empty glass. "When he told her he was plain Mr. Lancaster and not the Duke of Lancaster she stood up and called down the table to see who was a duke. When the Duke of Wellington raised his hand, Mrs. Corrigan made Mrs. Lancaster change places with her so she could sit beside him."

"What about Mr. and Mrs. Lancaster?" Eunice propped her elbows on either side of her tall glass. "They must've been mortified."

"I'm certain they were, but they didn't show it. The Lancasters and everyone simply carried on as if nothing had happened." They could've crumpled at the snub or stalked out. Instead, they'd kept a stiff upper lip, refusing to be cowed by the American socialite who possessed all the manners of a lorry driver and enough money to make everyone call her eccentric instead of rude. Valerie was determined to develop the Lancasters' tolerance for enduring cuts and thickening the hide she'd been growing since the court presentation.

"I wish something that exciting had happened at the Italian Ambassador's luncheon." Eunice sighed. "The conversation was as dull as listening to my dance partner go on last night about how Harrow will finally beat Eton at cricket this year. Even I know that isn't likely to happen."

"Invite Americans like Mrs. Corrigan and the conversation will be much livelier," Dinah suggested.

"We aren't all so uncouth."

"Speaking of interesting dinner guests, I understand Elm is joining you at Number Ten for the King and Queen's dinner." Dinah turned to Valerie, drawing everyone's attention to her.

"I heard you were rather chummy with him at the 400 Club." Eunice exchanged a conspiratorial glance with Their Excellencies.

"Don't believe a word of what they've told you. They're teasing me."

"So was Elm, and he isn't one to tease," Katherine shot back.

"He isn't as somber as you think."

"He isn't as jovial as you think, except when he's chatting you up."

"Speaking of jovial, your aunt made an interesting comment

about Prince George at Guinevere's coming out. Something about a silver syringe. What did she mean?" Valerie asked, eager to change the topic.

"The prince is a dope fiend," Katherine stated in the same sage tone she answered all their society questions with.

The table went silent. The whir of a mixer filled the quiet before they burst out laughing. Girls at the next table turned to see who was making so much noise before resuming their conversations.

Valerie shook her head at hearing yet another one of those secrets almost everyone knew but didn't dare say too loudly. To her ire, Mavis was right, the money, titles, and lineage did cover up a great deal of coarseness. The more time she spent in society, the more she saw it. If ever the need arose, she hoped it might do the same for her. "That should shock me, but it doesn't, not after what I heard about the Duke of Windsor being a German supporter. Can you believe it?"

"I can after having listened to Sir Arnold Wilson bang on about how grand a leader Herr Hitler is during one of Aunt Nancy's dinners. Imagine being daft enough to still believe in that tinpot dictator."

"This is all news to me." Eunice sat back in a huff. "Why am I always the last to know?"

"Because you're a Yank. You don't hear people whisper the way we do."

"I don't suppose I do." Eunice glanced at her watch. "Oh, look at the time. I must be off to dress for the Guildhall reception. The Queen will be there. Katherine and I are her second guards of honor."

"The first are mothers from Wales who've received help from the National Birthday Trust," Katherine explained. "Shall we?"

"Please. Mother will have a fit if I'm late."

"Christian, care for a lift home?"

"Oh yes, I want to hear what else I don't know before I have to dress for Lady Denedin's Caledonian Ball."

"Will John Miller be there?" Dinah asked in a singsong voice.

"He might be, and we'll dance a Highland reel. Where are you off to tonight?"

"The Lillian Baylis Memorial Ball. How about you, Valerie?"

"The Royal Ballet opening, but first I'm going upstairs to peruse the book section. I'm desperate for something to read while Miss Lang does my hair. Uncle Neville's library is far too dull."

"How very blue stocking of you," Dinah ribbed. "Walk me out so we can chat."

The girls signed their names to the bills, except for Christian, who paid with coins from a small change purse. A twinge of guilt struck Valerie as she charged the food to the account Aunt Anne had opened for her, one of many established at various stores throughout London. She'd spent years agonizing over every franc in France. To simply write her name and have everything taken care of felt too indulgent, but she must get used to it. Poverty was long behind her, at least for the Season. After that, she wasn't going to be left to starve, but she wouldn't have the freedom of Aunt Anne's purse forever. There might be some money from her mother's trust waiting for her, but she wouldn't know how much if any until she and Aunt Anne met with the banker in May.

Katherine, Christian, and Eunice made their way out of the

soda shop in a flurry of clicking heels and conversation, leaving Valerie and Dinah to gather up their things.

"Since I finally have you alone, we must have a serious chat." Dinah slid her arm in Valerie's. They strolled out of the soda shop and through the various departments of the massive store.

"Are you saying Prince George's evening habits aren't a serious topic of discussion?"

"Quite, but I was thinking of a titled lord a little closer to home."

"Elm?"

"The very one."

"Don't tell me he has a silver syringe."

"He has the silver spoon, and he'll be expected to marry a girl with an equally polished one."

That threw a bit of cold water on Valerie's grand plans for Elm and the Queen Charlotte's Birthday Ball, but she couldn't fault Dinah for pointing out the obvious. Aunt Anne might enjoy touting her lineage, but Uncle Neville was no lord, and that held more sway with many toffs than anything else. She was only a near-penniless niece, a detail any potential in-laws would discover in their due diligence. With all the ladies and honorables tossed in his path, the son of a marquess wasn't likely to choose her. However, for someone with higher aspirations he was paying her a lot of attention.

"I simply adore him, but I'd be an awful rat if I didn't warn you to be careful," Dinah continued. "He's a charming chap, but don't be fooled into thinking it's more. He's far too preoccupied with his own concerns to bother with anyone else's."

"What happened to seizing a husband if one comes my way?"

"If you and Elm hit it off, I'll be the first to raise a toast, but unless he falls at your feet declaring his undying feelings, be careful. I'd hate to see you hurt."

Dorothy's warning that her friends may not have her best interest at heart and the possibility that Dinah was warning her off of Elm because she had designs on him drifted through her mind, but the concern in Dinah's eyes crushed it. Dinah wasn't at all like Dorothy believed. "I promise I'll be careful."

"Good, because I expect great things from you, Miss de Vere Cole, a title or a seat in the Commons."

"Heaven forbid. I want nothing to do with politics." Her hide could never be that thick.

They passed the women's dress department and the dummies adorned with ready-made frocks. A mother and daughter debated over which one to purchase for a coming-out dance. Valerie and Dinah continued on, reaching the fragrance department near the entrance and sidestepping the salesgirls with their dubious French accents wielding perfume samples. "Would you ever go back to France?"

"I'd rather swim the Channel naked."

"That's how I feel about Switzerland. It's dreadful how families ship children off to boarding school like unwanted baggage and then forget them. They're selfish, the lot of them. Mine didn't even think to cable me after David died. I read about it in the newspaper at school. The bloody newspaper." She slapped her glove against her palm, making the women in furs waiting at the fragrance counter turn. Dinah lowered her voice as they stepped off to one side, hiding behind the large, glittering bottles of Shalimar catching the light coming in through the massive front windows. "It wasn't an accident, the way David died. He didn't fall out of the window in New York. He jumped."

Valerie clutched her hand to her mouth in horror. Not even on her worst day in France had she ever considered doing anything so awful. "I'm so sorry."

"Mummy was torn up about it but no one cared, all they worried about was what people might think if they learned the truth. You have no idea how awful it is to carry around a secret like that."

"Yes, I do." Valerie's palms went moist beneath her gloves. Dinah had trusted her with this story. Valerie owed it to her to be as open, at least with as much as she could be. "Tristan isn't really my half brother. Augustus John is his father. He and Mavis had an affair, and that's only the tip of the iceberg. You wouldn't believe the rest." Nor did she have the courage to reveal it, especially in Selfridges' fragrance department.

"I would believe it given all the things I've learned about my lot and everyone else's." Dinah shook her head in disbelief. "Are any of us normal?"

"No. There's more scandal and secrets than jewels in society, but everyone pretends they don't exist, like they pretend the servants can't hear everything they talk about."

"That doesn't give us much hope, does it?"

"None at all. We must do better."

"Assuming we have the chance." Two army officers in their drab uniforms strolled by, ignoring the fragrances and cosmetics but taking note of the women. "Of course we will. Perhaps even the opportunity to show them we have more mettle than they do."

Dinah tidied her hair in the mirror on the counter, then faced Valerie, the chipper Dinah not failing to return even while the old pain dampened her smile. "I'm glad I can tell you these sorts of things, it makes such a difference to have someone who understands and listens."

"I know."

"I suspected you would. Now, no more crepe-hanging. We don't want to be droll like that. Off to the books with you. I have a memorial ball to dress for." She gave Valerie a quick hug, then darted off to the revolving door, pushing through it and out into the bright sun.

What she wouldn't give for Dinah's knack for shaking off the dreary. She leaned against the counter, the men and women coming and going from the department store oblivious to her. Uncle Neville had guessed Their Excellencies were carrying awful things too. What he hadn't imagined was them trusting her with their secrets while she held hers back. Loneliness settled over Valerie as it had the night she'd learned of Father's passing and realized no one was coming to fetch her from the convent. She'd spent a lifetime wishing for people like Their Excellencies, but she couldn't tell them everything and risk them turning from her like so many others had.

Time. I must give it time. Eventually she might be free to reveal more, but not today.

Valerie made for the bank of lifts and the women attendants in their dark uniforms and caps standing outside the available ones. She selected the nearest and stepped inside the mirrored and chrome box. "The book department, please."

They stood in silence, facing forward until the doors opened on the fourth floor and Valerie wound her way to the book department. It didn't glisten like the display cases on the ground floor, but the tall windows above the bookshelves illuminated the different-colored covers. She picked up a copy of *Lord Jim* by Joseph Conrad, a novel Father had read many times in the Saint-Jean-de-Luz library. The potted plants on top of the dark wood bookcases reminded her of the English lending library in France. She and Father had spent many mornings there transfixed by the musty smell of old pages and the fine dust covering the desks. It was the single fond memory she had of him, and the only time she'd ever enjoyed his full attention, unless Mavis was with them. He used to ignore Valerie then, trying to improve Mavis through books, but the tart had recoiled from reading with the same fury as Bram Stoker's *Dracula* had from sunlight. It hadn't mattered to Father; as long as Mavis was with him all had been right with the world. Once she'd left, the drinking had consumed him until nothing but wailing about his miserable life had remained. Not even the books, the library, or Valerie had mattered anymore.

She jammed the book back on the shelf and continued browsing, selecting W. Somerset Maugham's *Theatre*. She'd read *Of Human Bondage* and enjoyed it well enough, but she hadn't read many of his other novels. With his brother, the Lord Chancellor, Lord Maugham, regularly visiting No. 10, it was prudent to pick up another of his works.

"Hello, there." Richard stood at the end of the aisle, a book in his hand and the same beguiling smile he'd worn while they'd danced at the 400 Club decorating his face.

"Hello, yourself." She clasped *Theatre* to her chest. "It's been ages since I've seen you at a dance. Are you taking your suppers elsewhere?"

"I've been busy at the hospital, but don't worry, my club is keeping me fed." He motioned to *Theatre*. "Mother wouldn't let my sister read his works. It didn't stop her, of course. She snuck them from me."

"You're a bad influence, then," she teased, cocking her head to the side so her hair fell forward to cover one eye.

He stepped closer, his voice low but strong. "I can be from time to time."

"I hope so. Otherwise life would be very droll." My, she was bold today, and he quite handsome in his dark blue suit. She'd only ever seen him in ties and tails. "Was your sister disappointed to discover Mr. Maugham's books are far less shocking than she was told?"

"Most people find adultery shocking."

"Surprising, since most of society is so intimately acquainted with it. It's practically a conversation at breakfast, usually not between spouses."

Richard cocked his head in disbelief and her sauciness crumbled into embarrassment. Then he threw back his head and laughed, drawing the attention of the pencil-mustached clerk arranging novels on the shelf behind the counter. He scowled at them like a spinster librarian. Richard choked down his laughter but not his smile. "Are you this blunt with everyone?"

"I shouldn't be this blunt at all."

"Don't hold back on my account, I quite enjoy it."

Valerie trilled her fingers on *Theatre*. They were skirting closer to opportunity than she cared to venture and she was enjoying it, far more than she should. She motioned to his selection, eager to change the subject. "What's a poor resident doing spending money on books?"

"I'd rather starve than go without them."

"My father used to say that." Except, for him it'd been cruelly true.

"A man after my own heart. He must've had marvelous stories about his time with Virginia Woolf and her Bloomsbury Set."

"He had stories, but they weren't marvelous. He said they weren't brilliant but a clutch of snobbish, vulgar bores. Virginia's brother Adrian was the only one worth his salt, and even that isn't saying much." Adrian and Father had been great friends since grammar school, but when he'd realized Father was beyond help, even he'd left him to sink.

"I'm sorry to hear that, but not surprised. Many from that time were self-indulgent. They thought the Great War gave them the right to be selfish hedonists."

"What do you think war might do to us?"

"I hope we never find out. *Until then, let us behold joy and gladness, slaying oxen, and killing sheep, eating flesh, and drinking wine: let us eat and drink; for tomorrow we shall die.*"

"Isaiah 22:13."

"You know your verses."

"A year and a half in a convent school will do that to a girl."

"What was a good Church of England girl doing in a convent school?"

Dear heaven, what was she thinking, to slip like that? It was a finishing school to anyone outside the family. She'd nearly given up the game. "There aren't many Anglican schools in France, especially not in the provinces, and it was an excellent way to perfect one's French."

It was the best lie she could think of, and to her relief he bought it, nodding in agreement.

"Then I'll have to see what else you know during our next dance. Until then." He stepped around her, laying his purchase on the sales counter and chatting with the mustached man. With his book in hand, he headed out of the department, pausing to raise it in goodbye. Instead of scurrying behind a shelf and pretending she hadn't been watching him, she waved in return. He strolled off, turning a corner and vanishing from sight.

She tapped *Theatre* against her palm. Maybe she wasn't as rational as she believed, if two men could easily turn her head by simply showing her a touch of attention. He'd also almost lulled her into forgetting herself. In the future she must be more guarded. If she fell for either of them and she revealed too much of her past or they saw the flaw in her that'd driven so many others away, it'd crush her. There were a great many things to endure this Season without the burden of a broken heart.

Chapter Eleven

In honor of Their Majesties

King George IV and Queen Elizabeth
The Prime Minister requests the company of
Miss Valerie de Vere Cole
At a dinner at 10, Downing Street

On Wednesday, 12 April, 1939, at 8:30 P.M.

Thrilling, isn't it?" Marian stood beside Valerie at the library window overlooking Downing Street. Cheers from the crowd gathered along Whitehall signaled Their Majesties' approach. The Lanchester came into view, the car's black paint gleaming beneath the lights of the surrounding buildings and the small royal standard attached to the front fender fluttering.

The bobbies formed a line of linked arms, parting the people to let the car through.

"Very." No. 10 sparkled like the grand houses Valerie had visited for various coming-out dances over the last few weeks. Elegance whispered in every touch, from the silver and gilt table settings to the large vases full of yellow daffodils sent down from the Chequers' hothouse. The anticipation and excitement of the evening had filled the air all day, even putting a spring in sober Mr. Colville's step.

"Me, curtseying to the King and Queen. My sisters were green with envy when they heard." Marian smoothed the skirt of her simple black dress with the white cuffs and collar. "I can't thank you enough for arranging it."

"Do you remember what I taught you?"

"I've been practicing it for days." Marian stepped into the center of the room and with the polish of a debutante dipped into a regal curtsey.

Valerie clapped, the sound muffled by her gloves. "Well done."

The rest of the Garden Room Girls waited with Mrs. Stenhouse in the anteroom at the top of the Grand Staircase outside the White Drawing Room. Their humble frocks were a sharp contrast to the glittering tiaras and flowing evening gowns of the titled guests mingling in the Blue Drawing Room, oblivious to the women gathered a short distance away. Valerie should be in there acting the hostess while her aunt and uncle were downstairs greeting the monarchs, but she'd left that to Dorothy. Marian's excitement was far more appealing than the aristocratic ennui. "I wish you could dine with us, given everything you do."

"This is enough, especially considering the news today."

"What news?" Uncle Neville had been drawn and tense when he'd come to escort Aunt Anne downstairs, the lines of his angled face more pronounced. Valerie had thought it because of the dinner. She hadn't imagined it might be anything worse.

Marian glanced around to make sure no one was listening. "I know you won't repeat this, but the Premier received word that Germany is planning to invade Lithuania. Poland will soon be next. I don't know how he can be so calm tonight with that weighing on him. If Germany invades Poland, we'll be forced to go to war to defend them."

Like that, the glitter of the evening dulled, war casting its awful shadow over everything once again. Valerie refused to lose faith in Uncle Neville. Many had said he'd fail in Munich with Herr Hitler, but he'd succeeded. He would again; he must. She'd endured the ugliness of an uncertain future too much in her life to wish that agony on England.

"They're stepping out of the car." Marian pointed to the street, where the Queen emerged from the back of the Lanchester, the gravity of uncertainty eased by the royal arrival. If everyone was carrying on as if all were well, then perhaps it wasn't as grave as Marian's news suggested.

Her Majesty wore a luminous white dress with a matching white fur wrap, her tiara vibrant even under the dim outside lights. The king was less regal in his plain evening attire, with no medals or gold braiding to fill out the slightness of his chest. Aunt Anne and Uncle Neville came outside to greet them, escorting the monarchs into the house.

"Miss Holmes, it's time to line up." Mrs. Stenhouse waved her in from the passageway.

"Wish me luck. I hope I can get through the curtsey without tripping."

"You'll be grand."

Marian hurried to join the others, all of them dressed in their Sunday best.

Once Valerie was alone, she reached into the bodice of her black velvet gown nipped in at the waist with a tasteful V-neck between two wide chiffon shoulder straps and tugged out the Cartier necklace. She'd asked Mr. Dobson to fetch it from the safe a few hours ago, ready with a good excuse for why she needed it. Deferential as always, he'd never questioned her request. She could ask for a man's head on a platter and she suspected he'd bring it to her with the proper garnish.

Valerie undid the lobster clasp and slipped it around her neck, then joined the official guests in the half circle arranged according to rank in the Blue Drawing Room. Valerie stood at the end of the line beside the bushy-mustached artist Mr. Birley. Elm was near the head with the rest of the viscounts and viscountesses. He glanced down the length of the line of people to her, his gaze flicking to her chest and the necklace. A knowing smile tugged up one corner of his mouth and she smiled back. They hadn't enjoyed so much as a moment together since the whirlwind of introductions and arrivals, but he could wait. It was Marian's turn before the monarchs.

Valerie could just see the Garden Room Girls through the drawing room doors. Marian stood at the end of the line on the landing waiting for her turn. Valerie couldn't hear what Uncle Neville told the King and Queen as he introduced the typists, but he and the royals showed them the same respect as if they were the highest ladies in the land. Each woman dipped a small curtsey, their smiles brighter than the diamonds dripping from the Queen's neck and wrists. None was so bright as Marian's who executed her curtsey with the grace and poise of a debutante. Valerie almost clapped at the triumph but kept her hands at her sides, refusing to commit another faux pas in the presence of the King and Queen.

Her aunt and uncle escorted the King and Queen into the Blue Drawing Room and down the receiving line. The monarchs shook hands with each guest as Aunt Anne presented them. When they reached Valerie, she faced them with stronger nerves than in Buckingham Palace. Everything was different this time. She wasn't before them because the Lord Chancellor had approved her name on the long list submitted for presentation but because she was the Prime Minister's niece, a true member of society.

When I used to read fairy tales, I fancied that kind of thing never happened, and now here I am in the middle of one! The *Alice in Wonderland* quote made her smile as she dropped into her curtsey, wondering if her aunt had noticed the necklace. If she did, she said nothing, carrying on with her hostess duties as His Majesty escorted Aunt Anne into the State Dining Room. Uncle Neville and the Queen followed and everyone fell into line according to precedent.

The King and Aunt Anne sat at one end of the long oval table, while the Queen and Uncle Neville occupied the other. Valerie was escorted in last by Mr. Birley, who trembled more than some of the nervous chaps she'd danced with at balls. His portrait of Aunt Anne in the upcoming Royal Academy Spring Exhibition had won him his place at the table. He paused at the dining room door, unsure what to do or where to go, his face whiter than the painting of Sir Thomas Graves above the Adam sideboard.

"Our places are in the middle." She gently guided the artist to their chairs.

Mr. Birley flashed a broad smile of relief. "Thank you, Miss de Vere Cole. This isn't my usual affair."

"It's my pleasure." She sat down, marveling at the china laid out at each place on lace mats. Aunt Anne had eschewed a tablecloth, allowing the mahogany table to gleam beneath the silver candelabras and reflect the candlelight and the yellow and orange petals of the roses and daffodils. The wood paneling had been polished too and glowed like the white plaster of the vaulted ceiling.

"What a lovely necklace," Elm complimented. Valerie didn't rank high enough to sit above the salt, but by merit of being a woman who evened out the numbers, she enjoyed the privilege of the Viscount on her other side. "A little daring for a debutante, isn't it?"

"If Their Majesties don't deserve our very best, then no one does."

Not everyone thought so. Dorothy's indignation was palpable from across the table. Valerie would catch an earful later, but it was worth it. The dress and the diamonds took the smell of the schoolroom off of her.

The order of conversation required Valerie to speak with

Mr. Birley first. He talked of his artwork, more at ease after a glass of wine and the first course of chilled consommé madrilène. When the signal to turn was finally given, Valerie relished having Elm to herself, but before she could ask him anything, discussion down the table drew everyone's attention.

"Are the plans for increased munitions production progressing?" the King asked Admiral of the Fleet Lord Chatfield. The slender, mustached man appeared grand in his full dress uniform dripping with medals and gold braid. His honors far outranked those of Captain Margesson, who sat across the table from him and between the elegant Lady Fallington and plump Lady Simon.

"It is, Your Majesty. Thanks to Mr. Chamberlain's Munich Agreement, we've had time to implement my plans and we'll be ready should the need arise."

"It might very well arise, if what my diplomatic contacts tell me is true." Lord Maugham, the Lord Chancellor, wiped the corners of his mouth with his napkin.

"They say Herr Hitler is a leashed dog ready to pounce. I say let him attack and discover that Britain is full of men of action, not just words." Lord Fallington rapped his knuckles against the table, making his silverware rattle on the plate. "The men of Britain will do their duty and defend this land to their last breaths."

"Hear, hear." Lord Maugham raised his wineglass. "If Germany invades Poland, we'll stand with her to drive the Huns back."

"We haven't pledged to defend Poland yet, and I say we shouldn't. Leave them to their troubles and us to ours," Lord Chatfield disagreed. "We needn't be dragged into another continental conflict."

"We don't wish to look weak either," Lord Fallington insisted.

"Herr Hitler is still leashed, so we need not dwell on such unpleasant things, not tonight," Lady Fallington diplomatically suggested, stopping a war of words before it could begin. "Mr. Birley, tell us about your portrait of Mrs. Chamberlain. I'm told it's a fine likeness."

People returned to more mundane topics, the air in the room lightening except around Elm.

"My father wants war, but he's not the one who'll have to fight. He didn't serve in the last one. He was too young, but his brothers weren't. They were both killed in France. It's how he came into his grand title, otherwise he'd be an honorable barrister at Temple Bar." He balled his fist before opening his fingers one by one. "More sons of the aristocracy died than anyone else in the Great War. They promised never again, and here they are, twenty years later, sabers rattling, ready to fling us off as cannon fodder." He pushed his half-eaten poussin à la polonaise around his Buckingham Palace china. "But you ladies in your diamonds don't have to worry about that, do you?"

"Of course we do." She touched the necklace, her hackles rising. "We'll be here too if the Germans bomb or invade."

"But you aren't left to wonder if your future is nothing more than the wrong end of a gun barrel."

"You're a fool if you think so, I don't care what your title." She glanced across the table at Dorothy, who practically dipped her bosom into her plate leaning forward to try and listen. Thankfully, Lady Maugham asked her a question, drawing her attention away.

Valerie dropped her voice. "After my father died, I had no idea what was going to become of me, the same way you have no idea what'll become of you. It's awful to feel as if you have no control over your life and future, that everyone besides you is deciding it, and quite self-centered to believe you're the only one suffering. The typists and their families are worried sick about being blown to bits by German bombs and they don't have country houses to flee to. People all over England are afraid. It isn't simply you."

He stared at his plate, and Valerie gripped her napkin in her lap, expecting another self-pitying bout of mocking or a snub to make his mother proud. She shouldn't have been so sharp with him, but she couldn't help it. It was one thing to have troubles. It was another to wallow in them or strike at her because of it. Father used to do that, and she wasn't about to put up with that from anyone, no matter what their title.

"I'm sorry, you're right. We're all living with this awful uncertainty." He rubbed his palms against the tops of his legs and she released her tight grip on the linen in her lap. "What are we going to do about it?"

"There's nothing we can do except wait and enjoy the present. *Let us eat and drink; for tomorrow we shall die.*"

"Dreary Shakespeare. There isn't a tragedy that old hack didn't write some witty verse for."

Valerie didn't correct him about the saying's author. She'd already danced close enough to putting him off, and this was not the night for a tiff with a gentleman. "You can't argue with the drink part."

"I can't." He finished the last of his wine and motioned for a footman to refill it. He traced the stem of the crystal goblet, turning it slowly with his thumb and forefinger. "You're a swell girl, to listen to me carry on, not like all those empty-headed chits at the dances. You really understand a fellow."

"Oh, I have my share of frivolous concerns, for instance who will escort me to the Queen Charlotte's Birthday Ball." She was done being somber and serious.

"Fishing for an invitation?"

"I'm asking outright. Will you escort me to the ball?"

He sat back to allow the footman to take his plate. "I don't much fancy watching debutantes bow to a cake, but for a girl like you, I'll endure it."

"You won't regret it."

"I don't suppose I will."

With the final course cleared away, Aunt Anne gave the signal and the women rose.

"Until we meet again."

"Until then."

Valerie followed the ladies into the Pillared Drawing Room and Lady Bridgeman fell into step beside her. "You and Lord Elmswood are getting along quite well."

"We've seen a great deal of one another at dances."

"How fortuitous."

"Not everyone thinks so."

Dorothy bore down on her with as much fury as she could in the Queen's presence while maintaining a semblance of grace.

"Leave her to me. The men won't be in the dining room long,

and I don't want her to stop you from charming Lady Fallington. Dorothy, what a stunning frock, and how slender you look. Tell me your secret." She linked arms with Dorothy, deftly maneuvering her onto one of the settees to discuss a slimming regime.

Valerie touched the necklace, debating how best to approach Lady Fallington. She stood beside the mantel. The Queen sat with Aunt Anne on the sofa, engaged in conversation with Lady Halifax, the Foreign Secretary Lord Halifax's wife, and Lady Simon. It was a great deal of rug to cross to reach Lady Fallington, but it was now or never.

Valerie approached Lady Fallington, coming to stand beside her. She might as well have been one of the footmen emptying an ashtray, for all the regard the woman paid her. She should've known better, but if there was one thing the Season had taught her, it was to not give up. "Your peacemaking at dinner was admirable, Lady Fallington."

The Marchioness eyed her as if she were a maid who'd dared to speak. "Was it?"

She should've remained across the room. "Yes. Ladies have a unique ability to bring people together, especially during these contentious times."

Lady Fallington's expression didn't thaw in the slightest, especially when she glanced at the diamond necklace. "Not all of us aspire to be so conspicuous with our politics or our lives."

Oh goodness. She glanced at Lady Bridgeman, who winced in sympathy. With things not proceeding well, it was time for a noble retreat. "You're right, of course. If you'll excuse me."

She walked as regally as she could after that belittling to join

Lady Maugham on the love seat. The Lord Chancellor's wife greeted her with more enthusiasm, less interested in discussing her brother-in-law's novels than in sharing Valerie's love of Lewis Carroll. They discussed *Alice in Wonderland* while waiting for the men to appear. It eased the sting of Lady Fallington's cut. Not everyone of high rank believed her beneath them. Why Elm couldn't be the Maughams' son instead of the Fallingtons' was another of those nasty twists of fate that had dogged her entire life.

True to Lady Bridgeman's prediction, the dining room doors swung open after only a quarter of an hour and the men entered the Pillared Drawing Room. Uncle Neville led the King through to the Blue Drawing Room, where he held court, enduring more formal introductions to the male guests.

Valerie wandered to the door, lingering close enough to catch Elm's eye but not so close as to be accused of eavesdropping. He joined her, the two of them huddling together between the rooms. Valerie eyed Lady Fallington, nervous that she might pull them apart, but she was too occupied with the Queen to notice. Lady Simon, however, took quite an interest in them, barely able to concentrate on whatever Lady Halifax said because of it, much to Lady Halifax's irritation.

"What has the gentlemen so enraptured?" Valerie nodded toward the lords jamming cigars and fingers at one another as they spoke.

"Who'll win Royal Ascot?"

"Very important business."

"As important as the Eton-Harrow cricket match. I'm an Eton man myself, so you know where my sympathies lie."

"My father attended Eton. I suppose I must root for them."

"It'd be unsporting of you not to. How was the ladies' conversation? Anything scintillating?"

"Your mother doesn't like me." She wasn't telling him anything he probably didn't already know.

"You're in good company, then. She doesn't like anyone. She barely tolerates me on most occasions."

"Lady Simon is probably inventing some story about us."

"I hope it's a good one. All her others are usually rubbish. There's the signal. It looks as if we'll soon be off."

The King and Queen rose in their separate rooms, bringing the conversation and the evening to an end. With the same solemnity and ceremony with which they'd entered No. 10 they took their leave, the guests following on their heels to climb into the line of cars parked outside.

Valerie, released from the rigors of precedent by the royal departure, walked beside Elm as they descended the stairs behind his parents. At the door, Lord and Lady Fallington stopped to pay their respects to Aunt Anne and Uncle Neville. Valerie stood beside them, garnering a very polite goodbye from Lady Fallington, who was forced to finally take note of who she was and where she was privileged by right of her family connections to stand.

"Thank you for a very pleasant evening, Miss de Vere Cole." Elm drew her off to one side while his parents spoke with her aunt and uncle. "And for tolerating all my moaning. It means a great deal that you don't fob me off or give me any of that stiff upper lip nonsense. You simply listen. It's a rare quality."

"I'm glad to do it. I know what it is to need to air one's thoughts before they become so tangled in your head you don't have a hope of sorting them out."

"I appreciate it, and I await your official invitation to the Queen Charlotte's Birthday Ball." He took her hand and bowed over it. A few strands of his hair fell over his forehead before he straightened and brushed them back, his gaze never leaving hers. She did all she could to maintain her poise and not blush or giggle at his attention, the thrill of his flirting blunted by the sight of Aunt Anne and Lady Bridgeman exchanging a pleased look. Dorothy was too busy with her husband to see it, but not Lady Fallington, who hid her thoughts behind practiced languor as she gathered her fur wrap tighter around her shoulders and walked outside with her husband. With a wink to Valerie, Elm turned on his dress shoe heel and followed his parents to their car.

"I'm so sorry about Lady Fallington," Lady Bridgeman offered. "But you handled it with admirable poise. Well done, and the gentleman was quite pleasant."

And far more understanding of her plight with his mother than she'd expected. She shouldn't hang any hopes on this or expect more from him than a steady dance partner, but it was difficult not to be carried away by the magic of tonight.

When Henry finally closed the black door on the last of the guests, the clock in the entrance hall chimed eleven o'clock. Weeks of preparations, letters, borrowed china and menus, and the royal evening had lasted less than three hours.

"Congratulations, Annie, for a successful dinner." Uncle Neville kissed Aunt Anne on both cheeks. "I couldn't have done it without you."

"We can finally relax, at least until Valerie's coming-out dance. I never thought planning a supper for twenty and a dance for two hundred would be a breeze, but it is compared to a royal visit."

"Enjoy your triumph. I have matters to attend to. No rest for the weary." The same drawn expression he'd flashed during un-guarded moments at dinner pulled at his long face, the intelli-gence Marian said he'd received about Lithuania weighing heavily on him. The pageantry was over, along with the brief respite it'd given him from European concerns. "Good night, Annie, good night, Valerie."

He walked down the long corridor, Mr. Colville joining him from the secretaries' office with a stack of papers. Very soon Val-erie expected to hear the bells from the Garden Room jingle.

"Come along, then," Aunt Anne urged. "We have the luxury of retiring early tonight." They climbed the stairs, the excitement of the dinner giving way to the exhaustion of night after night of events. "You certainly sparkled this evening." Valerie adjusted the necklace, waiting for a telling-off, but Aunt Anne didn't say a word about the diamonds. "You've set your sights quite high with Lord Elmswood."

"I haven't set my sights anywhere." They passed the sitting rooms where the maids and footmen emptied ashtrays and picked up discarded glasses. The Government Hospitality footmen bus-tled about the dining room collecting the china and carrying it downstairs to be washed and packed away. "He's nothing more than a friend who's agreed to be my escort for the Queen Charlotte's Birthday Ball."

"Many great partnerships have blossomed out of friendship." They continued up to the second floor.

"I'm not grand enough for him or his family."

Aunt Anne stopped outside her bedroom door and brushed a strand of hair off Valerie's face. "The world changed after the Great War, and it will again, perhaps in your favor. Either way, enjoy this time. There won't be another like it for you and most others."

Her solemn expression made Valerie's heart stop. She'd never seen her aunt truly worried. If she was concerned about the future, then Elm had a right to be afraid for his, they all did. "Good night."

She made for her room, closed the door behind her, and leaned against it. A fire burned in the grate and her night things had been laid out on the bed by Miss Logan, Aunt Anne's lady's maid. It was all as it should be, and at the same time it wasn't. She wasn't the same person she'd been in March, but if war came, it would pull her new life and those of all her friends down with it. She undid the necklace's lobster clasp and slid it off, laying it over her palm. There was no point giving it to the butler to put away. She might as well keep wearing it. Let people look sideways at her, it didn't matter. None of anything society considered so important might matter for much longer.

Chapter Twelve

A father bringing out his daughter, how gauche," Dorothy mumbled when they left Miss Rosemary Beale-Brown and her widowed father at the head of the receiving line. "I find it hard to believe he couldn't find some female relative or family friend to bring her out. A man knows nothing about these sorts of things, hairdressers and seamstresses and the like. He can't possibly do it properly."

"They seem happy enough and the ball quite up to snuff," Valerie said. Six Stanhope Gate was stuffed to the gills with debutantes, chaperones, and gentlemen. The house was decorated like any other grand home in London, with multiple rooms of fireplaces, elaborate mantels, thick velvet curtains, and antiques, but everything was far less cluttered, leaving the rooms open for guests to comfortably mingle. The house was regularly let for dances, and Valerie and Their Excellencies had been to at least three here since the start of the Season, including Christian and Anne Schuster's joint coming-out ball last week. It'd been a grand evening because she'd known one of the guests of honor, but every dance since had blended into an endless round of exotic flowers, creative decorations, and the same orchestras and dance numbers. How far she'd come since France and her presentation, to be so nonchalant about an evening out.

"Of course you'd say that, you don't know anything about anything."

"*I'm not strange, weird, off, nor crazy, my reality is just different from yours,*" Valerie mumbled, quoting the line from *Alice in Wonderland.*

"What did you say?"

"Nothing." With Aunt Anne in bed with a headache, Dorothy had agreed to chaperone tonight. Valerie had nearly run downstairs to find Marian and ask her to come, but of course that was impossible. As Dorothy was fond of reminding her, there were rules. Valerie might sneak a chat with the typist, but she couldn't bring her to something like this and she wouldn't want to. It'd taken tears and frustration to build up a decent tolerance to aristocratic snubs. She wasn't about to inflict that on someone as nice as Marian.

Thankfully, Dinah rushed up to greet them before Dorothy could offer any more lectures on behaviors. "You're here at last. The chaps are asking about you."

"Who's asking about her?" Dorothy's demand left Dinah, for the first time, without a blunt response.

"My friends and usual dance partners, Viscount Elmswood and Lady Astor's sons." The cow, who did she think Valerie was, a complete social outcast? She'd spent the last few weeks working diligently to make sure she wasn't. "And Dr. Cranston."

"He isn't here," Dinah said. "Work has kept him away."

What a pity.

Dorothy screwed her lips tight together as she weighed the need to fret against Valerie hobnobbing with the sons of aristocrats. "All right, then, but remember yourself and don't think of sneaking off to a club with a gentleman, I don't care what his lineage. They won't be regular partners for long if they think you're easy."

"They won't be regular partners if my sour chaperone hangs about constantly insulting me in front of them."

Dorothy narrowed her eyes at Valerie. "Mind how you address me."

"Mind how you speak to me, especially around others." She squared her shoulders and faced her cousin, tired of her constant belittling and nagging. "I'm not your whipping boy."

"There's a bridge room for chaperones upstairs," Dinah offered, her innocent smile worthy of an acting award.

Dorothy adjusted her gloves, caught between continuing her

undignified rampage and noble surrender. For once, she chose the more honorable option. "I'll be in the bridge room if you need me, but I expect your best behavior."

With that last little nag, she went off to find the card room. Hopefully, one of her friends would be there and keep her out of Valerie's business for an hour or two.

"Bravo, old girl, telling your cousin what's what," Dinah congratulated.

"If I don't murder her before they play 'God Save the King' it'll be a miracle."

"And quite the scandal if you do. Come on, everyone's waiting for you."

They waded through the sea of familiar faces, the same people from last night and the night before dancing or talking in small groups. She guessed if she visited the ladies' loo the same teary wallflowers would be in there too. At least at the Queen Charlotte's Birthday Ball in two weeks there'd be the novelty of a cake to bow to and the intricate procession of debutantes crossing each other in long lines that they'd spent the better part of yesterday afternoon practicing. It would break up the monotony, and Elm would be there to dance with her in front of everyone. It made the hours of practice worth it.

"At last, the debutante in Downing Street deigns to join us," Jakie greeted with a hearty wave, the smoke from the cigarette pinched between his fingers circling his head.

"How are things on the front lines?" Michael asked.

"As you might expect, with the Pact of Steel formalized." Mar-

ian had barely been able to hide her worry this morning when she'd explained the military alliance between Germany and Italy. By afternoon, it'd been in all the newspapers, swelling the crowd outside Downing Street who'd watched her leave for the ball with drawn faces.

"Ghastly news," Elm drawled, languid as always but without the cigarette. He plucked a glass of champagne from a passing footman's tray and handed it to her, his fingers brushing hers before he pulled away. She took a quick drink, heated more from the brief touch than the stifling room.

"At least Japan didn't sign it. We don't need trouble in the East too," Dinah added.

"When are you going to favor a dress uniform over white-tie?" Jakie asked Elm.

"When they tell me I must. I don't need another cleaning bill."

Valerie noticed a number of chaps wearing regimental dress uniforms, the red shell coats standing out among the somber black jackets. "Why the change?"

"More are joining up," Michael explained. "They want to choose their regiments before conscription is enacted and the choice is foisted on them."

"Are you two enlisting?"

"All in good time," Jakie said.

"Enough of this, gentlemen. We're boring the ladies."

Valerie was about to tell Elm she was far from bored when the first chords of "The Chestnut Tree" carried through the room. Couples hurried to form up, ready to wave their arms and clap their hands in time with another of the wildly popular but silly dances. Dinah convinced Jakie to pair with her, while Michael nabbed Katherine.

"I love this dance." Valerie waited for Elm to ask her, but he scowled.

"It's ridiculous, jumping about and pretending to be a tree. It's all right for the plebs but not the better sort."

"Snob."

"I can't help it. It's bred into me, along with permanent boredom. Let's get out of here."

"I can't. My cousin is sure to conduct hourly checks on me."

"There's so many people, she won't notice you're gone, and we'll be back before the end. You don't really want another evening of this, do you?"

People pushed past them in the rush to dance to the same songs in the same evening attire as every other night, Stanhope Gate interchangeable with the Dorchester Hotel or Cadogan Square. There were numerous balls taking place all over London tonight and again tomorrow evening and every week until the Season ended. There was no reason to stay, except fear. The royal dinner had bolstered the social cachet she'd spent the last few weeks building. It'd be foolish to risk tossing it away. "What about the others?"

"It'll be more fun if it's only the two of us."

"I don't want to be mistaken for someone like Pamela Digby."

"You'd have to do more than slip out of a dance to be mistaken for a woman like her. Come on, old girl, live a little."

Elm held out his hand, his smile as bright as the orchestra's brass horns.

She shouldn't go with him, but of all the people in the ballroom, he'd picked her for this escapade. If she turned him down, it'd be another evening dancing with the same round of partners instead of one of daring and true fun. The risks were very real, but so was Elm. She'd avoided walking out with him at the Household Brigade Steeplechase Meeting in deference to propriety and come face-to-face with Mr. Shoedelin. If she stayed here it might be another catfight with Vivien or Dorothy or who knows what ghost from her past. That wouldn't do her any good. "All right, then, but we can't be gone too long."

"I promise, you and your reputation are safe with me." He led her through the crush filling the house, the heat overwhelming until they stepped out the front door.

The pavement was crowded with guests from Stanhope Gate and the Dorchester Hotel across the square, the revelers from the different dances mixing in the cool evening air. Couples strolled on the pavement or crossed the street to take advantage of the dark walks and shadows of Hyde Park.

"Are we going to sneak into whatever dance is being held at the Dorchester?" It'd be one of the most daring things she'd done since leaving the Plaza to go to the 400 Club.

"I have something far more interesting in mind." He led her down the street and around the corner, away from the cluster of guests mingling between the two venues, and raised his arm to hail a taxi.

Valerie froze when the black cab pulled to the curb. There were rules against riding alone with a chap in a taxi. She should turn around and march back to the party, but with Elm motioning her inside she couldn't. In Stanhope Gate there was nothing but more of the same. In the taxi, who knows what she'd discover, and this was the chance to find out. Taking hold of her skirt so it didn't catch on her shoes, she climbed into the backseat with Elm.

She sat crushed up against the far door while trying to appear perfectly at ease, wondering if he was one of those must-touch-flesh types. "Where are we going?"

"You'll see." He didn't make a move for her, resting his arm on the windowsill and proving quite tame for a taxi tiger.

The cab snaked its way through London, passing other grand houses teeming with guests in evening attire, until the more fashionable streets of London gave way to a humble maze of alleys and lanes she didn't recognize. It pulled to a stop along a row of simple fronted shops, all of them dark and locked up for the night except for the slim building with a neon sign above a battered red door that read TANGO CLUB.

They climbed out of the taxi, the moist smell of the Thames lingering in the air along with the jazz music drifting up the club's damp staircase. Elm spoke to the driver and paid him, then shut the door. The taxi sped off, leaving them in the dank alley in who knows what part of London.

"This way." Elm led her down into the dark basement club, past the maître d', who sat at the front desk reading the newspaper. He wasn't as solicitous as Mr. Rossi, merely nodding to Elm before taking his cigarette out from between his lips and knocking the ash into a tin tray.

Moldering brick walls and a deep wood bar manned by a bartender with a great deal less continental suave than the 400 Club waiters dominated the room. A three-piece band played on the small stage in the corner beneath a bare light bulb. The saxophone, cello, and drums emitted a sultrier tempo than anything played at a dance. A postage-sized dance floor separated the band from those sitting at the spindly wood tables in arch-backed chairs. A few couples danced, the women's paste jewelry dull against their off-the-peg dresses.

"What is this place?" The two of them stuck out like sore thumbs in their fine evening attire.

"Somewhere I like to sneak off to from time to time. There's no milording here or debs or any of that nonsense, simply a bloke, his gal, music, and a good stiff drink."

His gal. An interesting choice of words.

He led her to a table near the dance floor. No one rushed to serve them, leaving Elm to order two sidecars from the bar and carry them to her. A few people looked up from their highball glasses but their interest in them didn't last. No one gave a fig for who they were or why they were here and she relaxed against the chair, appreciating the anonymity. "I've forgotten what it's like to simply exist, to not have everything I do, say, and wear scrutinized by my family, society, and the newspapers."

"It's a rare pleasure." Elm withdrew a silver cigarette case from his coat pocket, opened it, and held it out to her. She waved it away, and he selected one, set it between his lips, and struck a match on the underside of the table. The flame light flicked across the angles of his face as he lit the cigarette, then shook out the match. "Don't you wish you could do it every day?"

"Once the Season is over I probably will. No one's likely to be interested in me then."

"Don't bet your future on it." He pointed his cigarette at her. "Once you're in society's sights there's no escaping it or its silly demands."

"I don't suppose there is." Mavis was proof of that. Simply being the widow of a third-rate gentleman had been enough to make that nobody's second marriage newsworthy.

Elm took a deep drag off the cigarette, then exhaled a long, smoke-filled breath. "My entire life is governed by it and my lineage, the past, what's expected of me. I don't have any more say in things than a performing monkey."

"Few of us do." She pushed one melting ice cube deeper into her drink. "Would you give it up if you could?"

"I don't know." He peered across the smoky air, his aristocratic arrogance fading into a lost hopelessness that made her heart wrench. Christian thought the chaps were luckier than the girls, but Valerie wasn't so sure. If war came, death wouldn't hang over England's women the same way it did the fighting men. Afterward, women's lives would go on, while those of Elm and his friends might end in European mud.

"Would you give society up if you could?" His question pulled her out of a sinking mood.

"No." On the dance floor, a dark-haired woman in a red dress stepped and twirled with a slender man in a cheap suit, their cares lost for a moment in the dance. "It's easy to see others, duchesses and the like or even the Garden Room Girls, and think they have it better, but everyone has troubles. Money and station make ours a touch more tolerable."

Having lived as low as anyone of their class could, she had no illusion about what life without money and security was truly like. Society was a mess of hypocrites, secrets, and silly rules, but it was better than any other she'd ever endured. She wasn't about to abandon it for some mythical freedom that didn't exist or tell Elm her reason for clinging to it. He was open-minded enough to come to a place like this but she doubted he was that open-minded.

The steady beat of the drum gave way to a slower, smoother tune. Elm rested the cigarette on the edge of the ashtray, took a drink of his sidecar, and set it down. "Shall we dance?"

He didn't wait for an answer but drew her up from the table and led her out, turning her to face him and pulling her into his arms. She followed his lead with no awkward conversation, alphabet game, or dance cards, simply the two of them. She laid her head on his chest, the wool jacket smooth against her cheek, and breathed in the heady scent of his cologne mingling with the smoke and stale liquor of the club. She closed her eyes, savoring the moment, because it wouldn't last. It was an illusion, like the anonymity here, but she enjoyed the weight of his arms around her and his strong chest beneath her cheek until the music drifted to a close and the clarinet sparked into life with a faster tune. It jarred them apart and they left the dance floor, taking their seats to watch other couples, the girls' dresses flaring out as their partners spun them around before joining in a frenzy of Charleston kicks and waves.

"You enjoy jazz?" Valerie asked, not sure what else to say.

Elm dragged his chair around the table to sit beside her. "My regiment mates have threatened to toss out my records if I keep playing them, but I can't. They were a gift from my mother. She adores jazz."

"Difficult to imagine your mother listening to such earthy music."

"Father hates it, of course, that's probably why she plays it, to torment him, not that he doesn't deserve it." Elm lounged back in his chair, his white waistcoat and bow tie as crisp as when he'd arrived. "If he'd been faithful to her she wouldn't have a reason to torment him. Of course, I didn't know the half of it, holed up at Eton and Oxford, but the tension was thick whenever I came home. My poor sister had to endure it. She blames me for not being there, but what could I do? No one asked me if I wanted to go off to school, and when I was home, Father made sure I understood my place. It's a wonder I can still hear after the dressing-down he gave me when I confronted him about it. The great and powerful Marquess of Fallington won't be questioned, especially by his son."

"I'm sorry, Elm." She laid her hand on his.

"Me too, but that's the way of things, isn't it, and there's nothing we can do to change it. Not a damn thing." He reached for the sidecar, throwing back the rest of it and bringing the glass down on the table with a thud before flashing that charming smile of his. "But let's not be gloomy."

"Let's not."

They enjoyed mundane conversation, him telling her about his regiment and training, her explaining the day-to-day workings of No. 10. There was little of the snobbish or gloomy viscount, but a humbleness she hadn't seen before. This must be the friend Richard knew, the aristocrat without all the airs and graces.

When it came time to leave, the taxi was waiting to ferry them back to Stanhope Gate. They climbed inside and sat close together, his arm around her, her head on his shoulder. They didn't talk, the whir of the tires against the streets reverberating through the cab. He toyed with the strap of her dress, brushing her skin and sending small shivers racing through her. She tilted her head back to peer up at him, the streetlights cutting across the angles of his face. He looked down at her, his fingers stilling. She held her breath, waiting for him to kiss her.

The moment stretched on and she silently urged him to press his lips to hers. She couldn't very well throw herself at him. The last time she'd been too bold with a gentleman still haunted her, but this wasn't France and she was no longer that poor girl.

"We're almost there," he said at last, withdrawing his arm from around her.

She sat up, noticing the faint dusting of face powder on his jacket, but she didn't brush it off, afraid to appear as if she were trying to climb back into his arms. He hadn't kissed her. He'd wanted to, it'd been in his eyes, but he hadn't. Of course not. There were rules and they'd broken enough of them already, but she didn't regret it. Even with the disappointing ending, nothing in Stanhope Gate could have compared to this.

The lights of the Dorchester came into view. The taxi pulled to the curb around the corner from Stanhope Gate. Elm paid the driver, then helped Valerie out, not taking her arm but walking beside her until they joined the cavalcade of people coming and going from Hyde Park, the Dorchester, and 6 Stanhope Gate. They entered the festive house.

"This is where I leave you. Good night, Valerie."

She held out her hand for him to kiss, the most innocent and socially acceptable thing she could think of and the last chance for them to touch flesh, as it were. "Good night."

He took her hand and dropped a low bow over it, but he didn't press his lips to the back of it. He straightened, offering a flash of the serious chap who'd faced her at the club, before he let go and walked off into the crowd.

People pressed in around her, the strings of the violin smooth after the frenzied tempo of the Tango Club. No one had noticed she was missing and no one cared that she'd returned, her head spinning at how different everything had been for a brief time.

"Valerie, where have you been?" Dinah was at her side, her dance card wrinkled about the edges.

She was wrong, people did care. "With Elm."

"You cheeky little devil. I want to hear all about it." Dinah grabbed her by the hand and dragged her to a quiet corner beneath the main staircase where they could chat while people went up and down the stairs. In quick words, Valerie told her about the club, the dance, and the near-kiss. Dinah listened, as enraptured as when Valerie had told them about Diana Mitford and Sir Oswald. "That is serious."

"I'll say. I wish he would've kissed me." Her first kiss from a viscount. That'd really be something for the scrapbook.

"He couldn't. Kiss in a taxi and you might as well consider yourself engaged. You remember what I told you about him?"

"Of course." At least she did now. She'd quite forgotten it when Elm had caressed her shoulder. Her skin still tingled from his touch.

"Speaking of gentlemen, Mr. Chaplin keeps asking about you. Find him and dance with him, and let's write names in your card so your cousin won't be suspicious." Dinah snatched up the card and pencil and began scribbling in names. She tucked the pencil in its elastic holder when she was done and clasped Valerie's hands in hers. "I hope it works out for you and Elm, I sincerely do, but until you're certain, be careful."

"I will be." The fantasy was over, it was time to return to reality. She'd believed in Father's empty promises until his passing had crushed them. She couldn't be fooled by a gentleman's illusions again. Difficult to do with the faint smell of Elm's aftershave still clinging to her dress.

Chapter Thirteen

"Mr. Mason, what does this mean for Valerie's future?" Aunt Anne asked.

They sat in matching leather chairs before the portly Bank of England trustee's mahogany desk. The ring of a telephone and the secretary's voice filtered in through the closed door, and the smell of cigars and wood polish mixed with the heat coming in the open sashes. The unexpected May warmth had made the last week of events, including the Docklands Settlement Ball, stifling affairs, forcing guests outside onto the pavement and balconies of the Savoy and Claridge's. Even Dinah's coming-out ball had been an exercise in patience. Lady Astor's elaborate decorations hadn't been enough to tempt everyone to spend the entire evening inside, as the two thousand guests had crowded 4 St. James's Square's terrace or crossed into the grassy St. James's Square. With any luck the weather would cool before the Queen Charlotte's Birthday Ball next week and her coming-out dance at the end of June.

"The financial difficulties of the last few years haven't been kind to many trusts. Assuming war doesn't interfere with the markets, the value of the trust could recover by the time Miss de Vere Cole comes of age, but I shouldn't count on more than two thousand pounds a year."

"As much as that?" It was far more than Valerie had expected. She tugged a handkerchief out of her purse to dab her forehead. The fleeting thought that Elm and his mother might look at her differently if she had money shamed her. She shouldn't care about Elm, but he was nearly all she'd thought about since the Tango Club. His having been conspicuously absent from recent events hadn't helped.

"Not a substantial amount, but enough to keep her well settled and make her an attractive prospect," Aunt Anne mused.

"You make me sound like a prized horse."

"In the marriage market it never hurts to have a little something in your corner. This could be yours when you're ready. Mr. Mason, can you ensure this information discreetly makes the rounds?"

"I will, although there's still Mrs. Winterbotham's portion of the trust to consider."

Valerie paused in blotting her forehead. "Mrs. Winterbotham?"

"Your mother."

Good heavens!

"She draws an annual income in accordance with the terms of the trust established by her father, Colonel Daley, before he died," Mr. Mason explained. "The divorce court established your right to a share in it when you turn twenty-one. Your father petitioned the court for earlier payments, but the court denied his request, convinced he couldn't correctly manage them on your behalf."

"Did my mother have a say in the court's decision?" Had she, in this small way, shown some concern for her daughter?

Mr. Mason shifted in his chair, glancing uneasily at Aunt Anne before answering. "Mrs. Winterbotham never responded to the inquiries. Mr. Winterbotham objected to his wife corresponding in any manner with her former husband, even through solicitors, and he was quite vocal in matters pertaining to the trust until she divorced him."

"Is she in London?"

"At present. She divides her time between London and Ireland."

"Best to leave that alone," Aunt Anne softly suggested. "Mr. Mason, what are the figures as they currently stand?"

Mr. Mason and Aunt Anne continued to discuss the trust, but Valerie barely heard a word of it. Her mother was here and she must have seen Valerie's pictures in the papers, but there hadn't been so much as a calling card from her. She wasn't entirely surprised, especially with Aunt Anne warning Valerie off of her. The divorce had darkened Father's social standing. It must have made her mother a pariah. For all Mavis's bad behavior, marriage and widowhood had at least given her a thin sheen of respectability. Valerie's mother hadn't enjoyed that luxury.

"Thank you once again, Mr. Mason, for all your help." Aunt Anne shook the banker's hand and allowed him to escort them out of his office.

Valerie walked with her aunt through the Bank of England's seemingly endless marble corridors. Despite the news of the inheritance, all she could think about was her mother and why she hadn't tried to contact her. Given Father's reluctance to leave her with Aunt Anne, he might have forbidden her mother from seeing her, or perhaps Mr. Winterbotham had been the difficult one. Maybe her mother hadn't abandoned her at all but had been too weak to stand up to her second husband, although she'd had the fortitude to leave him. Perhaps she was too ashamed after all this time to approach Valerie, leaving it to Valerie to break the silence.

Don't be a silly child. She'd visited Mavis, and that'd been a disaster. She should listen to Aunt Anne and let it be, but she couldn't. Even if Valerie never did anything with her mother's address, simply having it meant she could reach out to her if she chose. It was more than she could hope to do with Father. If she didn't act today, she'd have to return with the chauffer and everyone would know what she'd been up to.

"I forgot my handkerchief in Mr. Mason's office." Valerie brought them to a halt in the center of one of the numerous hallways. "I'll run back and fetch it."

Aunt Anne studied her with her usual languid expression. Valerie gripped her purse, expecting to be challenged about the lie, but Aunt Anne simply nodded. "Very well. I'll see you at the car."

Aunt Anne carried on, passing various men with files.

She knows what I'm doing. But she couldn't back out and blatantly admit she'd disobeyed her. With quick steps she returned to the office, losing her way twice before a helpful young clerk led her to it.

Mr. Mason's secretary looked up from his work. "What can I do for you, Miss de Vere Cole?"

"I'd like Mrs. Winterbotham's address, please." She was ready with a reason for why she needed it but he never asked. He simply removed a black book from his drawer, flipped it open to the appropriate page, and copied the address on a small slip of paper and handed it to Valerie.

Mrs. Winterbotham, Hotel Meurice, Bury Street, London SW1. Whitehall 6767

All this time she'd been in London and her mother lived only a few streets away. Valerie could've strolled across St. James's Park and met her for tea or walked past her in Fortnum & Mason and she never would've known it. They might have been on different continents, for all the difference it'd made. "Thank you."

She stuffed the paper in her purse and made her way back through the labyrinth of hallways, asking directions three more times before reaching the massive twisting staircase leading to the bank's mausoleum-like lobby. Long lines of tellers standing behind the stretching mahogany counter helped various customers. The tellers didn't wear their usual dark suits but special constable uniforms, all of them trained to help in case of an air raid. It was as ominous a sight as her mother's name and address on the paper inside her purse.

Nodding to the gatekeeper in his salmon coat and red waistcoat, she hurried out of the bank entrance and down the stairs to the waiting car.

"Is everything all right?" Aunt Anne asked when she slid in beside her, flustered from the long walk and her clandestine errand.

"It's a great deal to take in, the trust and all." Never mind her mother. Until today the future had been a hazy image of bouncing from house to house like a spinster aunt supported by others' generosity, always leaving before the hosts tired of her. In one meeting, at least that worry had been relieved.

"It'll make a great difference to your future, give you a touch of security."

It was hard to believe one of her parents had finally offered her that. "What will I do until then or after? I haven't noticed being a lady of leisure has done many in society much good."

"There's still the Personal Service League. I spoke with Lady Bridgeman and she said you could easily join now and take up a position when the Season ends."

She had no idea what she might do to help the Personal Service League, but she longed to make decisions about her own life instead of others doing it for her. This could be her chance. "All right, I'll do it."

"Good. Now I have some news that isn't nearly as pleasant as Mr. Mason's. Prepare to be quite shocked when we visit the Royal Academy of Arts opening."

The Exhibition of the Royal Academy of Arts 1939
The One Hundred and Seventy-First

It was like viewing two trains colliding, and Valerie couldn't look away. Hanging on the wall of the Drawing and Etching Gallery of the Royal Academy of Arts Summer Exhibition was a pencil portrait of Mavis by Augustus John. Mavis lay with one hand be-hind her loose hair, the other off to the side, the rest of her dis-played without a stitch of clothing.

"At least they had the decency not to hang her near your aunt or uncle's portraits," Dinah whispered from beside her, as stunned by Mavis in all her glory as Valerie and Christian. Behind them, two mustached gentlemen waited at a respectable distance for the debutantes to clear off so they could have a crack at the drawing.

"I suppose there's that to be grateful for." Nothing Aunt Anne had told her in the car about the submission, or No. 10's failed ef-fort to have it removed, had prepared her for the reality of it. Aunt Anne was in another gallery with Uncle Neville, refusing to give it any attention. Valerie had been too curious to ignore it.

"Why would your stepmother do such a thing?" Christian asked.

"To teach me a lesson for flaunting my new situation in her face, and having the temerity to demand she behave with some decency." Valerie adjusted the veil on her cocked astrakhan, push-ing it farther up over the high brim but it kept slipping down to tickle her forehead. To see her dressed in the smart pale green Molyneux frock, her hair perfectly curled and arranged, no one might guess she was fuming. "I'm sure she told Augustus John to submit it."

"Poor Valerie, you must be mortified."

"Not as much as I should be." Or would have been in March. For all the awful spectacle, Valerie stood beside friends who weren't ashamed to be seen with her in front of this *masterpiece*, and she had the weight of No. 10 Downing Street behind her. "Mavis thinks she's knocked me down a peg or two, but she's the one who looks dreadful, and I'll show her. I'll face this little stunt of hers with far more dignity than she's ever shown."

"Well done, old girl," Dinah congratulated as they turned away from the lurid drawing, leaving the mustached gentlemen to it. They passed through the interconnected galleries of Burghley House in search of the portraits of her aunt and uncle. "You're learning how it's done."

"I don't have the hide of a rhinoceros yet, but I've gained a few calluses." Aunt Anne had said the Season was about dealing with difficult people and situations with grace and poise, and she hadn't been lying.

"Your stepmother isn't the only one creating a spectacle. It seems the Royal Academy is determined to be saucy this year, hanging the Premier's portrait across from"—Dinah checked her program as they entered Gallery IV and crossed the room to view Uncle Neville's portrait—"*Models for Goddesses* by Sir William Russell Flint. Rather cheeky placement."

"I'll say." Mavis's image couldn't compete with the painting of the three nude women in an artist's studio bending over a draped fabric box. It hung opposite her uncle's portrait and was drawing quite a bit of attention. Any debs who lingered too long in front of it were quickly pulled away to view more respectable works.

Valerie, Dinah, and Christian kept their attention on Uncle Neville's portrait by Sir James Gunn. The likeness of him in his pinstripe suit and wing-collared shirt was good, but the portrait didn't reflect how much more gaunt and drawn he'd become since sitting for it. Ever since the King and Queen's dinner, it'd been nothing but bad news from Europe, and here was the Royal

Academy heaping on more difficulties. They must not be great supporters of Uncle Neville, to be so insulting with their arrangement and submissions. "Uncle Neville and his staff don't need headaches from Mavis or the Royal Academy, not on top of everything else they're facing."

"One of the chaps I danced with last night said he and his friends are all rushing to their Seville Row tailors." Christian's low tones mingled with those of the other guests passing through the Royal Academy's cavernous galleries. "They're afraid of war rationing and think if they don't get their summer whites they'll have to go without."

"One bloke said all the regiments are being fitted for new uniforms," Dinah added.

"I'm not surprised, given the government's pledge to defend Poland. Why do we have to protect them anyway?" Christian asked.

"It's the only way to stop Germany's warmongering, especially now they've ended the Anglo-German Naval Agreement," Valerie said, explaining what Marian had told her while waiting for the car that morning. "Despite everything Uncle Neville is trying to do, things are getting worse."

Although one wouldn't know it from looking around at the people milling about the galleries in their morning suits and day dresses. They carried on murmuring over this artist or that landscape as if nothing were wrong with the world. She wondered how many of them had appointments with their tailors or seamstresses, quietly collecting things that might soon be in short supply. She thought of the ten pounds she'd won at the horse race and wondered what she should buy with it. She hoped Marian and her father were continuing to set aside tinned food.

"What an interesting portrait of an undertaker." Vivien's voice carried over from behind them.

Their Excellencies turned together, standing side by side to face Vivien. She wore a pale pink frock with a rose pattern. It suited her dark hair and eyes and her enviously smooth complexion. One would think a sour disposition was better for the skin than the ladies' magazines suggested.

"Good morning, Vivien, what a pretty dress," Valerie complimented, refusing to take the chit's bait.

Vivien was struck silent by the unexpected compliment. Valerie remained as friendly as she could while inwardly gloating. Despite Dorothy's fears, she could be quite composed when necessary.

"Vivien, introduce me to your friends." Lady Ravensdale, a stately woman of mature years, and the aunt bringing Vivien out, appeared at her niece's side. She wore an expensive mink stole and a Vionnet dress of dove-gray silk with a matching cape held in place by a large diamond broach. A velvet pillbox hat was pinned over gray hair brushed back from her temples. A well-practiced social smile softened the severe lines of her face, but it was full of condescending judgment covered by manners, the same look nearly every titled matron had perfected.

"Lady Ravensdale, may I introduce Miss Valerie de Vere Cole, Miss Christian Grant, and Miss Dinah Brand."

"A pleasure, I'm sure." Lady Ravensdale examined each of them the way the Mother Superior used to do during morning uniform inspections. She was no more impressed by what she saw than the old nun had ever been. They were being judged, and harshly, but it was thinly camouflaged by silk and Joy perfume. "That's a fine likeness of Mr. Chamberlain, Miss de Vere Cole. I had the pleasure of meeting the Prime Minister last summer during a lovely weekend at Cliveden with Lord and Lady Astor. He and Mrs. Chamberlain were quite the charade players, although one was surprised to find him engaged in such trivial activities during a European crisis. I hope he's far more serious this year."

Valerie bristled at the thinly veiled insult but she'd be damned if she'd show it. The Season had taught her that much. "He and Admiral of the Fleet Lord Chatfield discussed rearmament at the King and Queen's dinner. They and Lord Fallington are convinced that Herr Hitler will be checked. Lord Elmswood is quite certain of it too." It wasn't exactly the truth, but it was enough to remind Lady Ravensdale that she was talking to the Prime Minister's niece, a young woman who had dined with the monarchs, not some scullery maid. "He's my escort for the Queen Charlotte's Birthday Ball."

Lady Ravensdale slid Vivien an admonishing look, making her niece's haughty shoulders slump, then she fixed narrow eyes on Valerie. "I didn't realize you were so well acquainted with the Marquess and his son. I was speaking to Lady Fallington a few moments ago. She was quite astonished by the drawing of your stepmother. One imagines a man of Mr. Wheeler's professional standing would be more discreet about the advantages of his new young wife, but I suppose his connection to the Premier's family far outweighs the disadvantages of such a public display. Please give my regards to your uncle and aunt and your beautiful step-mother. Good day, ladies."

Valerie silently seethed as Lady Ravensdale escorted Vivien out of the portrait gallery, not sure who to curse first, Lady Ravensdale for insulting her or Mavis for giving her the perfect means to do so. Lady Ravensdale's cut wasn't even the worst of it. Lady Fallington had seen Mavis's portrait and her connection to Valerie and she'd been horrified. Everything Valerie had accomplished at the monarchs' dinner had been darkened by Mavis, the past once again stronger than anything she might do in the present, but she refused to be bested. Enough of the Season remained for her to prove she was better than Mavis or people like Lady Ravensdale believed.

"What I wouldn't give to be able to make an insult sound enough like a compliment so you almost thank her for it," Christian said, sharing Valerie's indignation.

"The daughter of the Viceroy of India has the right to be haughty even with all the scandals hanging on her." Dinah waved them closer and dropped her voice. "She was Sir Oswald's mistress before her sister became his first wife. Aunt Nancy used to tell stories about how difficult it was to assign bedrooms during house parties at Cliveden because she never knew whose room Sir Oswald's should be closest to."

"Yet someone like her has the audacity to look down on us." Valerie pushed the veil up over her hat, wanting to yank the annoying thing off, but she wasn't about to ruin her polish.

"I'm not surprised." Christian dug her toe into the floor. "A viceroy's daughter can't have a very high opinion of a lowly Scottish baron's daughter paying for her own Season."

"What?" Valerie was more astonished by this than the Lady Ravensdale gossip.

"I thought you knew. Father's will left Mummy practically penniless and with the four of us to raise. It's why we live in Chelsea, it's all we can afford, and why Anne Schuster and I shared our coming-out dance. I have the right sort of lineage but it isn't worth a farthing. If it hadn't been for my dear governess leaving me two hundred pounds I'd be at home reading about you lot instead of enjoying it with you."

"You're brave to admit it."

"Mummy says I shouldn't, but we're not fooling anyone, especially when she sends me to luncheons on public transport." Christian shook her head, making the feathers in her felt homburg flutter. So it wasn't only Dorothy threatening fire and brimstone if debutantes told the truth. "I can only imagine what they're saying about me."

"They don't have the right to say anything, especially when most of them are acting as if they're still flush while selling the family silverware out the back door." Valerie was tired of the ridiculous pretenses, of adulterous viceroys' daughters stuffing skeletons into their antique wardrobes while wagging censorious fingers at Valerie. "As for public transport, ring me when you need a lift, I'd love to have someone to chat with on the way to things instead of sitting stone-faced like a Buckingham Palace guard." It was the least she could do, since she was living on handouts. They were quite fine ones, but it was still charity. However, she'd be an utter heel to complain after the meeting with Mr. Mason. She might be poor, but when she turned twenty-one, she'd have more than Christian was ever likely to get.

"You'll regret that offer. I'm going to call you for everything simply so I can say I arrived in the Prime Minister's car. Won't Mummy swoon when she hears that?" Christian's dreamy look suggested she was the one who'd do most of the swooning.

"Speaking of swooning, there's a chap who'll have Valerie doing it in spades."

Dinah pointed to where Richard stood across the room admiring the portrait of an old woman hung between those of Queen Mary and Marlene Dietrich. Queen Mary appeared stiff as usual, while the actress was stunningly swathed in white, her dark eyes in her tilted face giving the viewer a come-hither look that entranced Ambassador Kennedy. He admired it with as much enthusiasm as the men did *Models for Goddesses*. Mrs. Kennedy wasn't keen on the likeness, standing beside him in her Paris suit of white silk with black-edged lapels.

"Why don't you purchase it and stop making a spectacle of yourself?" the Ambassadress hissed.

Ambassador Kennedy cleaned his glasses with a handkerchief. "Perhaps I will."

"I won't have that woman hanging in the house."

"I'll hang her wherever I like." He perched the glasses on his nose as his wife stalked off.

"Come along, girls."

Eunice threw Their Excellencies a small wave and followed her mother and older sister Kick into the next gallery. Kick wore a dark blue dress lined at the sleeves in white. She was similar in looks to Eunice, but there was something more refined about her features yet with a freshness one couldn't miss.

"Poor Eunice," Valerie said. They'd been ordered to stay with their mother instead of their friends, the matriarch afraid of missing the chance for the three of them to be photographed together. It must be awful to have to constantly trail behind her popular older sister.

"Don't worry, we'll find a way to catch up with her, but first we must see to you. I think there's a doctor in need of a house call." Dinah pushed Valerie toward Richard. "We'll be looking for John Miller. After all, Christian needs a little cheering up too."

"Is he here?" Christian turned this way and that searching for him.

"Let's find out." With a toodle-oo wave at Valerie, she and Christian went in search of the Scotsman.

Valerie adjusted the veil on her hat and debated whether or not to approach Richard. If he was here, there was a good chance he'd seen Mavis's portrait. She didn't relish him looking askance at her before wandering off to less scandalous pastures, but there was only one way to find out if he'd treat her like Their Excellencies or like Lady Ravensdale. She took a bracing breath and strode up to Richard. "The hospital must be keeping you busy for you to have missed so many dances lately."

"Not the hospital but Lady Bridgeman. She's made it her mission to properly stock every hospital in England. She's quite the taskmaster."

"As I'm about to discover. I've joined the Personal Service League. I take up my duties in August."

"Congratulations. I'm sure you'll be splendid in your new position." The admiration lighting up Richard's face was worth more to her than any of her recent social accomplishments, including accepting an umbrella-shaped clock on Uncle Neville's behalf from the British Industries Fair, and it took the sting out of the possible scandal hanging in the other gallery. Either he wasn't aware of the connection between the drawing's subject and her or he had the tact to not admit it. She wasn't about to raise the topic and find out which. "Was it a great shock to receive an invitation to my dance instead of finding it posted on the hospital noticeboard?"

"It was. I've been in Londonderry House, Holland House, Stanhope Gate, Devonshire House, but not Number Ten. I'm looking forward to it."

"I think most people are attending for that reason, not that it matters. I've gone to more than one dance out of curiosity too."

"Richard, you're still here. I thought you'd have made it to the still lifes by now." An older gentleman with a brown waistcoat covering his large stomach approached, accompanied by a short woman in a mink stole.

"I think he's found something more interesting than art." The woman, who resembled Richard in slenderness and the shape of her face, eyed Valerie with more delight than Lady Fallington and her ilk had ever shown.

"Miss de Vere Cole, allow me to present my parents, Lord and Lady Lansdown."

"You're the Premier's niece," Lady Lansdown observed. "Richard has told us a great deal about you."

"Has he?" This made her nearly flutter off the floor. His father's next comment kept her feet firmly planted on the parquet.

"She's that old hoaxer de Vere Cole's daughter, remember him?" Lord Lansdown placed his hands on his round belly and tilted back his head as if considering a great matter. "My mates and I howled it up when he stuck it to those stuffy Cambridge officials by pretending to be the Sultan of Zanzibar. Of course, I was at Oxford, which made it even more delightful."

Delightful. There was a word she'd never associated with Father.

"There's no need to bore the young people with those old stories." Lady Lansdown patted her husband's shoulder. "They want to enjoy the show and so do we. It was a pleasure to meet you, Miss de Vere Cole. Richard, we'll be in the next gallery."

That she pulled her husband away and not her son heartened Valerie. Hopefully, they wouldn't see Mavis and march back in to drag Richard off.

"I apologize for my father."

"No need, he remembers mine fondly. He's one of the few."

"Someday we'll bore our children with the same type of stories. If we get the chance."

If. There it was again, the gloom that'd hung over Elm at the dinner and flashed in Aunt Anne's eyes afterward. A chill raced through Valerie. She was tired of this specter tarnishing everything.

She was about to say so when movement out of the corner of

her eye made her turn. An old man with a Van Dyke beard and a far too jauntily tilted trilby approached. If Valerie could have rolled up her program and beaten him about the shoulders of his three-piece suit she would have, but she couldn't, not here. It simply wasn't done.

"Miss de Vere Cole, I don't know if you remember me. I was a friend of your father's."

"I remember you, Mr. John." Valerie's curt reply drew a curious look from Richard.

Mr. John took off his hat and fingered the brim, having the decency to at least feign embarrassment. It was more than Father or Mavis had ever done. He extended his hand to Richard when Valerie made no move to introduce him. "Augustus John."

"Dr. Cranston. A pleasure to meet you. I'm familiar with your work."

"So am I," Valerie hissed at the Welsh artist. "Tell me, Mr. John, did Mavis ask you to submit that salacious drawing or did you do it on a lark or even realize the trouble it might cause me and my aunt and uncle?"

Richard's eyebrows rose in surprise. Spite made her appear peevish, but she didn't care. She refused to allow Mr. John to leave without facing some grief for his submission.

"It was never my intention to cause you or the Chamberlains distress. I wanted to see Tristan. Mavis said I could if I submitted it." He dabbed his forehead with a paisley handkerchief, one of those annoying affectations artists always adopted for attention. "I apologize if I've harmed you and your family."

Valerie stared at Mr. John, stunned to receive an apology from the man who'd ruined Father's marriage and shoved him deeper into the pit of melancholy.

"Sadly, it was all for naught. Mavis didn't uphold her end of the bargain and the London Museum refuses to give me their address. I simply wish to know if Tristan is well and to do what I can for him." He tucked the handkerchief in his pocket, for the first time in however long she'd known him appearing humble and genuine. Maybe this was why Father had thought him a friend despite the many betrayals. Clearly Mr. John could muster up a show of concern when necessary, except this wasn't a show. His desire to see his son was in his aged blue eyes, Tristan's eyes. As much as she wanted to tell him to sod off, she couldn't be the one to deny Tristan the chance to have at least one parent who cared about him. It'd make her as callous about his welfare as Father and Mrs. Winterbotham had been about hers. "They're at Number Ten Chelsea Embankment. I've seen them and they're both doing well."

Mr. John set his hat on his head, his gratitude more genuine than any other expression he'd ever plied on her or Father. "Thank you, Miss de Vere Cole. It means a great deal to me."

He nodded, then walked off, leaving Valerie and Richard standing in the middle of the gallery.

"I'm sorry you had to see that, I wasn't at my best just then," she said, owing Richard some explanation. "Mr. John and my stepmother were lovers and one of the nudes in the Drawing and Etching Gallery is of her. It's caused me and my aunt and uncle a great deal of grief."

There was no point in hiding the truth now.

"I see." He tapped the program against the palm of his hand. She waited for him to make some excuse about why he should hurry off to find his parents, but he remained beside her, nodding sagely. "And you still gave him his son's address."

"I didn't do it for him but for Tristan. It isn't the boy's fault things happened the way they did, any more than what passed between Father, Mavis, and Mr. John was mine. I was simply caught in the middle of it. Tristan doesn't deserve the same fate."

"That was very kind of you."

"As long as Mr. John doesn't thank me by amusing his patrons with nasty tales of how he cuckolded my father." Heaven knows what pithy words would appear under her newspaper pictures then.

"*Let us not become weary in doing good, for at the proper time we will reap a harvest if we do not give up.*"

"Paul the Apostle."

He smiled, his humor reviving hers. "Someday I'll stump you."

"I'll enjoy you giving it a good try." He'd seen her at her worst and thought the best of her. It touched her more than any manners or adventures in smoky clubs ever had. "Thank you for your view of things. It's hard at times to see past slights to how situations really are."

"It's easier for me. I'm not in the thick of it, but I'm glad I could help. Please let me know if I can do it again."

"You'll be the first I call." Valerie trilled her fingers against her program, the sincerity in his voice stirring. The fleeting thought that she should've asked him to escort her to the Queen Charlotte's Birthday Ball instead of Elm flittered through her mind before she dismissed it. Vivien and her ilk were going to see her at one of the most important social events of the Season on the arm of a viscount.

Across the room, Lord Lansdown pointed to his watch. Richard pushed back his cuff to look at his. "I must get back to the hospital. No rest for the weary. Until the next dance."

"Until then."

He crossed the gallery and at the door offered a wave before he was gone.

"Prince Charming leaving already?" Dinah came to stand beside her, concern in the small frown furrowing her brow.

"He has work to do."

"So do we." She motioned to where Eunice stood alone in front of the Marlene Dietrich portrait. "Eunice, is something wrong?" Dinah asked when they joined her.

She didn't take her blue eyes off the portrait. "My father and Marlene are having an affair."

Good Lord, this place was teeming with secrets, and it was only an art showing. "Are you sure?"

"She was with us on the Riviera last year and he flaunted her around Mother. It was awful. Mother went to Paris to shop, determined to spend as much of his money as she could to make him pay for what he was doing. He didn't care. He never does, not with any of them." Eunice's knuckles went white where she clasped her hands together in front of her. "His immortal soul is in peril, but Daddy won't stop. It makes Mother miserable and she takes it out on us. She thinks we don't know why, that we're too innocent, but we're not stupid."

"I'm so sorry, Eunice." Valerie laid a comforting hand on Eunice's shoulder. "My father and stepmother were the same way."

"Yes, Mother told me about the drawing Mr. John submitted."

Valerie wondered how the pious Ambassadress had come by the connection, but Elm was right. Once a person became visible to society, they and any of their offenses were never forgotten. Mrs. Kennedy might be a devout Catholic, but she enjoyed gossip as much as anyone else. "They're absolutely rubbish, aren't they?"

"Most of society is," Dinah huffed. "It's a trait both of our countries have in common. Perhaps we should send our wives over there and their husbands over here to encourage more cross-country relations."

"It isn't funny." Eunice blotted her cheeks with her handkerchief, trying to remain composed.

"It's perfectly awful, but there's nothing we can do except laugh about it. It makes it so much less nasty."

Eunice blew her nose, eyeing Dinah from over the top of the linen. "I suppose so."

"Of course." She cuffed her on the chin, bringing a weak smile to Eunice's wide face. "Chin up, old girl. Can't fall to pieces here."

"That's what I love about you all, you're so sensible and understanding and discreet. You won't tell anyone what I said, will you? Mother is worried about the press finding out about Father and publishing nasty things."

"We won't say a word." Valerie wasn't about to betray any of them, not after how wonderful they'd been with her.

Two matrons passed by in their fur wraps, eyeing them as if

they'd slipped one of the small portraits under their skirts. The girls smiled back as if they didn't have a care in the world, but it was a lie. Almost everything in society was, and the more time Valerie spent here, the more she saw it, playing her part in maintaining the illusion along with the rest. No one said anything aloud, everyone pretended as if everything were all right, but it wasn't, it never had been, and it might never be, and they could barely talk about it for fear of ridicule, humiliation, or worse. It made her want to stand on the bench in the center of the room and scream for everyone to stop pretending so no one would have to feel alone in their troubles. Even if she did, it wouldn't change anything. Everyone would hiss at her to stop making a fool of herself, too absorbed in their titles, houses, and manners to admit to anything more real. "Maybe war will force everyone to own up to the nastiness instead of pretending it doesn't exist, make people face their awful behavior instead of constantly sweeping it under ancestral rugs."

"I doubt it." Dinah sighed. "The Great War didn't change anything. It simply gave people something else to think about. When it was over, they rushed back to their petty little habits and rituals like curtseying to cakes."

"I'd rather curtsey to a cake than have Joseph and Jack fight and maybe never come home," Eunice said.

"Me too." Dinah nodded. "I can't bear to imagine something dreadful happening to Jakie or Michael."

"None of us want to lose anyone or each other." Fear struck Valerie as hard as it used to every time she'd left Aunt Anne to return to school. Their uncertainty about the future was as obvious as the paintings on the walls, but society continued on as if it would always be like this. She didn't blame them. The tension beneath everything grew stronger each day and it was a comfort to cling to the familiar and believe that everything would be well. "*Begin at once to live and count each separate day as a separate life.*"

"Byron?" Dinah asked.

"Seneca, but I believe someone of great wit and foresight once told me we shouldn't be crepehangers."

"I believe she did, and it's still grand advice. We won't mope about but enjoy ourselves and our Season as if it were the last."

"Hear, hear." Eunice waved the handkerchief like a flag, not caring what old ladies gave them odd looks when they passed.

"We will," Valerie agreed, thinking Dinah might not be too far off the mark.

Chapter Fourteen

*P*oor Vivien." Christian read the newspaper, shaking her head while the butler cleared the dishes from the linen-covered table in the Downing Street garden. A wide lawn stretched across the backs of No. 10 and No. 11. Their Excellencies sat under the large tree enjoying another warm spring day, the many herbs Aunt Anne had planted along the borders filling the air with the scent of thyme and rosemary. Through the small windows of the ground-floor Garden Room, the subtle clacking of typewriters carried out to mingle with the birds' twittering. "How awful to have your own father tell the newspaper he has nothing to do with you and reveal to everyone you're a ward of Chancery, and all because the *Sunday Express* wrote a glowing article about her."

The newspaper had called Vivien *The Perfect Debutante of 1939*, a title Their Excellencies had laughed over during tea at Claridge's a week ago.

"He aired all of her dirty secrets for everyone to read." Christian handed Katherine *Action* so she could read the letter from Sir Oswald Mosley practically condemning his perfect debutante daughter.

"Considering how mean she's been to Valerie and the rest of us, I think she deserves it." Dinah lounged back to catch a bit of sunlight coming through the leaves. "Maybe she won't be so snotty after this."

"I don't like her, but I wouldn't wish that article on anyone." It was a slight comfort to see Mavis wasn't the only one doing all she could to embarrass her debutante relation. Apparently it was quite the trend in society, one Valerie wished she hadn't been dragged into. After the Royal Academy showing there'd been a number of titillating mentions of Mavis's drawing in the newspapers and it'd earned Valerie more than a few odd looks, but nothing as dreadful as Vivien's plight.

"Maybe she's mean because her family is so dreadful," Eunice suggested, charitable as always. "Perhaps if we were nicer to her, she wouldn't be so sour."

"I doubt it. Half my family is nothing to brag about and it hasn't made me a witch," Valerie said.

"Lady Ravensdale took Vivien off to Paris for what she calls social obligations for a few weeks." Katherine folded up *Action* and laid it on the table between her and Valerie. "Leaving for a spell so things can die down is the only way to save face."

"It won't help Pamela Digby. It seems she wasn't as discreet with Lord Warwick as she thought." Dinah leaned in with this bit of delicious gossip. "Aunt Nancy said Lady Simon caught the two of them sneaking back into a house party the morning after a very intimate night out. Lady Simon made sure everyone heard the story."

"Pamela should've known better than to go off alone with him or at least been smart enough to return before breakfast." Katherine shook her head. "Most people never recover from something like that becoming more than whispers. They spend the rest of their lives banished to the country, a social pariah."

"At least she'll have all those Parisian gowns Lord Warwick bought for her to wear to visit the family stables."

The girls laughed and Marian's head popped up in the window of the Garden Room. She waved to Valerie, who waved back before the typist returned to her work. "I think we should be a little quieter. I hate to interrupt the Garden Room Girls' work." Or rub their noses in the fact that Their Excellencies could lounge about in the middle of the day while they had to hunch over typewriters in a rather dingy room.

"I'll need work when the Season is over, something respectable Mummy can't object to, except I have no idea what." Christian swatted at a fly before it flittered off over the wall to the training horses. "I don't know anything except how to curtsey, and no one will pay me for that."

"You could be a professional curtseyer," Dinah suggested. "There's oodles of grand old aristocrats who'd pay to have someone bowing to them every day."

"I'm quite serious. I need to learn something useful so I don't sink into genteel poverty."

"What you want is the Monkey Club," Katherine advised.

"Whatever is that?" Eunice asked.

"Don't let the name put you off. It comes from the see no evil, hear no evil, speak no evil monkeys carved on the front of the building. It's a kind of finishing school. Many of the right sort attend. They teach politics, shorthand, typing, and such. Deborah Mitford was a student for a spell, and Princess Gayatri Devi. She's engaged to the Maharaja of Jaipur."

"I'm not searching for a maharaja, but something more substantial than flower arranging would be smashing."

"Aunt Nancy says I should volunteer somewhere, that us girls will have to do our part if war comes. I haven't told her that Jakie and Michael are teaching me to drive. Her hair would turn white if I did."

"With the way they drive, I'm not surprised." Valerie rested her chin in her hands. "Are you going to join the London Volunteer Ambulance Service?"

"I don't know what I'll do with it, but I figure a woman who can drive will be more useful than one who can't, and it gets Michael out of the house for a few hours when Aunt Nancy is after him."

Valerie wondered what Aunt Anne would think if she asked Mr. May for driving lessons. It wouldn't be a bad thing to learn. "I'm joining the Personal Service League in August."

"Your interest in medicine doesn't have anything to do with a certain doctor, does it?" Dinah teased.

"Maybe it does." She picked up *Action* and tossed it playfully across the table at her friend.

"Miss Ormsby-Gore, your car has arrived," Mr. Dobson announced, ending the afternoon.

"Come along, Excellencies. Your chariot awaits."

Valerie saw out Katherine, Christian, and Eunice, who'd arrived together and left discussing the Monkey Club. Dinah lingered in the entrance hall in no hurry to leave and Valerie in no rush to see her off.

"Funny we should all be so concerned about the future when we didn't give a hang about it a few weeks ago." Dinah climbed the Grand Staircase beside Valerie, leaving the activity on the ground floor for the quiet upper reaches of the house.

"I wish I could ignore it but I can't, not with all the beastly foreign news I hear around here."

"Michael told me that he and Jakie are joining up."

"Hard to imagine either of them knuckling down to military discipline."

"It's their chance to choose the branch they like, as you're doing with the Personal Service League. What brought that about?"

"I need something more than all of this." She waved her hands at the drawing room, the voices of Aunt Anne and whatever politician she was hosting for tea today carrying in from the Blue Drawing Room. They climbed the stairs to the second floor and Valerie's bedroom. "I don't want to end up a self-centered sod like my father, or my mother, for that matter."

"I thought she was gone."

Valerie closed the bedroom door and leaned against it. "She's in London."

"Good heavens!"

Dinah dropped into the chair by the window, listening while Valerie explained about the meeting with Mr. Mason.

"It isn't right. She walks out on you, then lives mere blocks away and can't get off her duff long enough to post you so much as a letter."

"I'm not sure it's her fault. Father could be beastly about Aunt Anne's interest in me. Maybe he kept my mother away and she still thinks she can't contact me." The calls of the Horse Guards forced her to shut the sash. Their training had noticeably increased during the last couple of weeks. "I'm tempted to send her a note and see if there's something there."

"What does your aunt say about it?"

"To leave her be. She must have a reason for it, but she hasn't told it to me. It's always been a rather taboo subject. I don't know what to do."

"Your mother never should have placed you in this rotten position to begin with." Dinah crossed her arms and leaned back in the chair. "They're all awful, aren't they, your parents, Eunice's."

"At least Mrs. Kennedy cares enough about her children to raise them."

"I couldn't endure that sort of scrutiny. Imagine, index cards for every child with their weight and other ridiculous things typed on them. There's being involved with your children, and then there's being involved."

"It would've been nice to have had a parent with at least a passing interest in me."

"I had one of those. It isn't as grand as you think." Dinah flicked the arm of the chair, her lips drawn tight. "They have us, then act as if we aren't worth the bother, shipping us off to boarding school and barely hurting themselves to leave the Riviera once a year to take us to tea for our birthday. The few times Mummy bothered, I begged her not to leave, to take me home with her, but she wouldn't. It didn't matter how hard I cried or what I said. She always left."

"My father was the same way. I begged him to collect me too, but he didn't." Valerie traced the gold trim on the old dispatch box. She shouldn't say more, but there were no saleswomen, theatergoers, or art lovers here, simply the two of them. It wasn't enough to be distracted from the past. She wanted to bring it into the light and let it die so it didn't bother her anymore. If anyone could stand beside her and stare it down, it was Dinah. "Things with him were far worse than I've told anyone."

"How so?" Dinah leaned forward in the chair.

"We weren't in France for Father's health but because he was broke, and even there he ran up debts he couldn't pay. He was too drunk to care, willing to live in squalor rather than work or ask for help. We were on the verge of being evicted and practically starving when I went to Mr. Shoedelin and begged him to do something. He didn't believe me until he saw how dreadful things really were." It'd been Valerie's weakness from the desperation of filth and poverty that'd made him recoil from her, but she didn't say it. Some things could never be shared, not even with her closest friend. "He arranged a place for me at the school, yet it wasn't a finishing school or a boarding school but a convent home for unwanted girls, a miserable, stinking orphanage." Valerie lifted the letters out of the dispatch box, flicking the creased edges with her finger. "I used the few stamps I had to write to Father, begging him to fetch me or send me to Aunt Anne. I didn't have the postage to send a letter to England. When I ran out of stamps, I begged the Mother Superior for more, but she said it was indulgent, that I was there until Father decided to remove me and I should accept it, but I couldn't. I thought he hadn't received the letters, but he had. They found them with his things after he died and they'd all been opened. He'd read every one of them and ignored them. He didn't even write to Aunt Anne but left me to rot like he always did. I was there for months after he died."

"Why didn't your aunt come for you?"

"Because Mr. Shoedelin lied to her when he sent her the rest of Father's things. He told her I was happy and well settled, and with the Anschluss, she couldn't come see for herself. The only reason I'm here and not stuck in that hell is because I snuck into the Mother Superior's office and stole enough stamps to finally write to Aunt Anne with the truth." She flung the letters back in the box and slammed the lid shut. "I thought she'd abandoned me too until the morning she arrived and told the Mother Superior I was returning to England with her. I can't tell you what it was like to see her and have that awful nightmare end."

"That's how it was the day Mummy finally came for me." Dinah rose, tears shimmering in her eyes. "I'm so sorry you had to face it."

"I'm sorry for you too."

Dinah hugged Valerie tight, giving her the comfort she'd sought for years and grasped at with Nanette. Dinah understood some of what Valerie had endured and didn't sneer at her because of it but stood with her, eager to help ease the old pain. It meant the world to her.

Dinah let go of her and wiped the tears from her face with the back of her hands. "We won't be like them when we're parents, will we?"

"I'd rather toss myself in the Thames than be like that." Valerie slid two lavender-scented handkerchiefs out of her dresser drawer and handed one to Dinah.

"Me too. We'll learn from their mistakes and be real mothers, and if we ever forget we'll be sure to remind each other. We'll be better than them."

"We already are." She was no longer the abandoned and ridiculed convent girl. It wasn't because of the dresses and where she lived but because she mattered to people who genuinely cared about her, and she refused to lose this. "We'll marry better men too, ones worth their salt."

"I'll see to it you do, and you'll do the same for me. There's no reason why we should be the same miserable sods as our parents."

"Or make anyone else suffer because of it. We'll stand by each other as we do at the dances, and tell it like it is even when it hurts to say or hear the truth. Promise me we will."

"I promise."

Chapter Fifteen

Ever since 1927, Queen Charlotte's Birthday Ball, in aid of England's largest maternity hospital, has been an immensely important date for debutantes. In fact, to be chosen as a Maid of Honor is almost essential to a young lady's first season success.

The *Tatler*, Wednesday May 24, 1939

This arrived for you, Miss Cole." Miss Leaf handed Valerie the envelope with the Fallington family crest engraved on the flap. "The Marquess's chauffer delivered it."

Aunt Anne paused in drinking her coffee. "A note the morning of the ball can't be good."

No, it couldn't. She tore open the envelope and her heart dropped. "It's from the Marchioness. Elm asked her to write on his behalf to say his leave has been canceled and he can't escort me tonight." *His leave, my eye.* After the Royal Academy of Arts opening and Mavis's ridiculous stunt, she probably thought Valerie wasn't good enough to be seen so publicly with her son. The slight cut deeper than any Lady Fallington could've made in person, especially since Elm had obviously agreed to it. Curse Mavis. She'd wanted to strike at Valerie and she had.

"We can press one of the secretaries into accompanying you, Mr. Colville perhaps."

"I won't spend an evening with that humorless drip." She wasn't that desperate, but she must find someone else in a hurry, one who didn't think the Prime Minister's niece beneath him. They'd soon set off for Grosvenor House and the last round of rehearsals for the entrance and the grand curtsey before the cake. The final run-through had taken up the last three afternoons, the three hundred girls drilled with the precision of the Horse Guards. She wouldn't even come home afterward but remain at Grosvenor House to dress and have one of the hordes of Elizabeth Arden makeup artists employed for the day treat her to a special makeup session. The thought of going through all that to have the glum-faced Mr. Colville for a dance partner made her want to plead a headache and stay home. If she did, Lady de Walden would likely send footmen to drag her out of bed before she'd allow the fluid lines of debutantes to have the smallest of gaps.

"You may not have a choice but to ask Mr. Colville."

"I have another idea. If it doesn't work, we'll go begging downstairs."

This must work. Most of the private secretaries had impressive pedigrees as younger sons of lords, but everyone knew they worked here. No one would be fooled into thinking they were anything but a substitute for Valerie's first choice and that instead of dancing with a viscount she'd been stood up by one. She hurried to the phone in the drawing room, snatched up the receiver, and asked the switchboard operator to put her through to St. Thomas's Hospital. It took a number of connections and informing everyone along the line that there was an urgent call from Downing Street before Richard finally came on the line.

"Dr. Cranston speaking."

"Richard, I'm sorry to trouble you, but I'm in an awful jam. Elm can't get away from his regiment and escort me to the Queen Charlotte's Birthday Ball tonight. Do be a dear and take his place."

"Are you asking your second choice to save your bacon?"

She winced. There wasn't nearly as much humor in that question as she would've liked, but now was no time for coyness. "Yes, and I'm not ashamed to admit it. Desperate times call for desperate measures."

"Hippocrates."

"Pardon me?"

"Hippocrates said it first, well, not those exact words but *for extreme diseases, extreme methods of cure, as to restriction, are most suitable.* I can say Erasmus's version in Latin, if you'd like."

She laughed. There was the humor she adored. "Hippocrates is good enough."

"Then I'll see you tonight at the Dorchester."

"Thank you, Richard. You have no idea how much this means to me."

"I think I do. Until then."

VALERIE AND DINAH processed down the left staircase leading from the balcony to the Grosvenor House ballroom dance floor, two of the four girls in their part of the line. At the bottom, they joined up with the four girls from the opposite staircase, the eight of them falling into formation to walk in long rows down the length of the ballroom. Guests seated at tables on either side looked on: Richard sat with Aunt Anne, Dorothy, and her husband, Stephen, at a table near the front.

Valerie glanced at Richard when she passed, thankful he was here. All afternoon she'd feared the hospital might hold him up and force her to sit out the dances. He threw her a muted wave that she returned, not caring if she broke the line of solemn debutantes preparing to greet a cake as if it were victorious Lord Nelson. They looked ridiculous enough already with these keepsake Schiaparelli hearts hanging around their necks.

Halfway across the ballroom, she and Dinah shifted sideways with the rest of their line, the girls crisscrossing until all three hundred debutantes stood in two columns with an aisle up the center. The procession was seamless, and they watched in their columns as the select group of debutantes, Katherine included, pulled the massive cake on its trolley to the front of the ballroom.

"What a gas," Dinah whispered from beside Valerie. "All of us standing here waiting for a cake."

"We look like a horde of vestal virgins," Valerie whispered, staring straight ahead as Lady de Walden shot them a sharp look from where she stood overseeing everything like a battle-hardened general.

The Elizabeth Arden makeup artists had been heavy-handed with the rouge and Valerie could see Katherine's overdone red cheeks from here. Valerie and Dinah pulled faces at her, trying to make her laugh, but she held it together, executing her duties as the cake's maid of honor with admirable aplomb.

One of the four chefs standing ready to cut the cake handed Princess Helena Victoria a large knife. The direct descendant of Queen Charlotte was playing the role of the dance's namesake tonight, her tiara so heavy it looked as if it were pushing her head into her neck. The Princess raised the knife with both hands and plunged it into the cake.

"Oh, the horror," Dinah choked through giggles as they and the rest of the three hundred debutantes went down for the curtsey.

"Murdered by a member of the royal family." Valerie snorted, wobbling and threatening to tip over as they rose. "It's too much."

The debutantes took four steps back in one massive group, a sweeping movement of white dresses. One by one the lines came forward to receive plates of cake sliced by the chefs who descended on the confection to carve it up like a prized kill.

Valerie and Dinah were up next when Lady de Walden huffed over to them. Her laurel-wreath tiara with the massive yellow sapphire in the center made her look more like Caesar than a baron's wife. "I saw you both snickering and laughing. There's a reason neither of you were chosen to be maids of honor. You wouldn't be here at all if it weren't for your families. Now straighten up. We'll have no more of this tomfoolery."

She marched off in a twinkle of diamonds and her sequined dark blue evening gown. Valerie and Dinah stared wide-eyed at one another before collapsing together in muffled snorts of laughter.

"This is all too much."

"Did you see her face? It was redder than your lipstick."

"Careful, we're up."

They pulled themselves together long enough to collect plates of sliced cake. The debutantes served the hundreds of guests seated at tables along the edges of the ballroom, under the balconies, and high up in the gallery overlooking the room. Chandeliers shaped like upside-down mushrooms illuminated everything, while the band tucked into the corner played softly.

"Well done, Valerie," Aunt Anne complimented when Valerie laid a plate of cake in front of her, the delicate tiara set in her hair catching the light. The large number of duchesses in attendance had warranted the wearing of tiaras and the spectacle didn't disappoint, all the family jewels dusted off for tonight adding to the sparkle.

Valerie smiled her thank-you, then handed plates to Dorothy and Stephen before serving Richard. He watched her, lips pressed tight together. He managed a thankful nod, working as hard as Valerie to hold back his laughter.

"What did Lady de Walden say to you and Miss Brand?" Dorothy demanded, garnering a surprised look from her husband.

"She complimented us on a job well done," she lied, refusing to be lectured like a wayward schoolgirl in front of Richard.

With one last look to Richard, who was thoroughly enjoying this, Valerie returned with Dinah, Christian, and Eunice to continue serving cake.

"I'm glad that's over," Dinah said as she and Valerie fell back into line. "I'm going to chisel off this horrid lipstick as soon as I can."

"I can't wait to take off this ridiculous heart." Valerie adjusted the red ribbon that was pulling at her neck from the weight of the small bottle of perfume tucked inside. She'd give the expensive souvenir to Marian as a thank-you for her hard work.

Serving the cake continued until the guest of honor had been reduced to nothing but crumbs and dirty knives. The chefs carted the carcass away and the bandleader raised his baton to end the ambient music and begin the first dance.

"I suppose it's time to play my part," Richard said when Valerie returned to the table, finally able to take off the hideous necklace and leave it with Aunt Anne.

"You've acted the role of Prince Charming by simply showing up. You don't know how grateful I am." Especially when he took her in his arms for the dance.

"My sister went through it a few years ago. I have an inkling of the importance, but I had no idea it was quite like this."

"You should rent your services every year, place a discreet advertisement in the *Tatler* and see what invitations arrive in your post box."

"I think this is an experience best savored once."

"I'll say." She wasn't likely to be invited to play Queen Charlotte and cut the cake. "Once is definitely enough, but I'm glad I did it."

"This might also be the last time it takes place, at least for some time."

"Not if Lady de Walden has anything to say about it. She'd assassinate Herr Hitler if it meant Germany didn't interfere with her prized event."

"We should be so lucky, but I doubt we will be."

The sea of white dresses and black coats shifted and turned around them, an elegant monochromatic mass of debutantes and gentlemen who might not return if Uncle Neville and peace failed. "*Tout passe, tout lasse, tout casse.*"

"Nothing lasts, everything breaks, everything fades."

She gripped his hand tighter, hanging on to him as he turned them in time to the music. "Are we wrong to fiddle while Rome burns?"

"No. We have to live life as it is at present, no matter what we think might or might not happen in the future."

"*Eat, drink, and be merry, for tomorrow we die,*" they said in unison, raising themselves out of the threatening despair. Difficult to believe that all those quotes Father had drilled into her were coming in handy to impress a gentleman, but they were. People said chaps didn't like clever women, but Richard clearly enjoyed her.

A couple nearby bumped into them and so did another, hampering the smooth motion of his lead. There were too many people, too much heat and wool and silk. "It's a dreadful crush."

"Will your aunt mind if we step out for some fresh air?"

"She won't, but my cousin will, so let's be quick about it so she doesn't notice. She can be such a prudish busybody."

"My grandmother is like that." He took her hand and led her through the throng of debutantes and escorts. "My sister calls her a great Victorian nag."

"Then your grandmother and my cousin would get on splendidly."

Valerie held on tight to him, glancing through the melee to catch sight of Dorothy. Aunt Anne was deep in conversation with one of her old friends, her simple tiara elegantly wispy beside their thicker ones. Dorothy eyed the dancers with the same frantic look of the nurses in St. James's Park watching their young charges. If she knew Valerie intended to walk out with a young man, she'd make a scene. If she asked any of Their Excellencies about her, they'd lie for her. With the sheer number of people milling about, it'd be easy to say she'd been here the entire time.

Valerie kept her head low until they slipped out the Park Lane entrance, climbing the stairs up to the Marble Foyer before stepping out under the Great Room entrance and onto Park Lane.

The pavement was crowded with revelers and she and Richard joined the steady stream of people in evening attire crossing the street to Hyde Park. Most congregated around the large fountain surrounded by a low iron rail, remaining respectably in sight of the street and hotel. A few wandered deeper down the paths in search of shadowy privacy. Valerie waited to see which way Richard led her, disappointed when he let go of her hand but thrilled when he guided them into a ramble down the gravel walk.

"Did your mother enjoy the Season when she brought out your sister?"

"She enjoyed seeing her old friends, but she and my sister were exhausted. She said she hadn't been that tired since taking care of us as children."

"Your mother raised her own children? That's like saying leprechauns are real."

"They are, and she did. She was an only child who spent more years in boarding schools in England than she did with her parents, who were in India. She always said she'd raise her own children, although I think there were days she wanted to hire a nanny, especially when my brothers and I slid down the entrance hall banister, my sister right behind us."

So it was possible to learn from the past, and not everyone in society was a rotter. "Your parents are happy, then?"

"They are."

"Next you'll tell me they're faithful to one another."

"To the day."

"Rare specimens indeed."

"I'm all too aware of that and glad for them. They've found a fulfillment most of their class can't or won't, the same way I have with my work." Across the road, Grosvenor House glowed, and laughter and voices carried around them. Overhead, the stars were visible above the trees, the branches lush with leaves after the bareness of winter. "It took me a long time to come to terms with having to make my own way. If you can believe it, Elm and I were rather wild at Oxford."

"I don't believe it." He was so responsible and levelheaded.

"We were hellions and almost sent down once for our antics.

It straightened me out. I couldn't afford to fail. I didn't have the family pile to fall back on." He leaned against the tree beside her, his profile lit by the moon as he stared up at the sky, hands behind him to protect his tuxedo from the bark. "I used to envy Elm. He's the heir, his future set, or so I thought. One holiday with his family made me realize he didn't have it any easier than I did, none of us do."

She toed a pebble in the grass. "Uncle Neville said something similar once, how people pretend to be fine while hiding the awful things they're facing. I didn't believe him until I saw it this Season."

"It's not society but everyone. There are days when I have to deliver terrible news to patients as gently as I can. They return to their lives with that awful diagnosis hanging over their heads. I want to do more for them than dispense pills or empathy, but often I can't."

She took his hand, clasping it tight, never having thought of what it might be like for him at the hospital. "That can't be easy."

"It never is." He turned his hand in hers to hold it tighter. "But I'm glad it's me they hear it from instead of the more hardened doctors. Everyone deserves compassion no matter what their rank or situation. Offering that to people is worth more to me than all the titles and manors in England."

"I'm sure they appreciate it." She could remember every kindness shown to her over the years, from the boulangerie owner who used to slip her day-old bread to the librarian who'd set aside the new novels for her. "At least you're doing something noble. We can't all say that."

"You will in time."

"You seem so certain of me."

"I've seen enough people face bad news to know who can manage things and who can't. You simply have to get the stardust of all this out of your eyes, like I did, and you will. You're clever, like your uncle." He brushed a curl by her cheek back behind her ear. His skin was warm against hers and the faint light from the hotel glinted in his eyes. She waited for him to touch his mouth to hers, eager to be in his strong arms. There was a calm surety about Richard, a sense that no matter what happened everything would be all right. He was a voice of reason in a sometimes crazy society.

The toll of Big Ben carried across London and over the traffic and parties, sounding twelve times before falling silent. Richard lowered his hand and straightened, regret as potent as the gentlemanly restraint filling his eyes. He was right not to kiss her, no matter how much she longed for it. There were still rules and she didn't rush to break them, eager to maintain his good opinion. "It's time to get you back. I don't want your aunt or cousin barring me from your coming-out dance."

"Neither do I."

He offered her his arm and they walked together through the park, past the other guests, returning to the light, noise, and music of the Grosvenor House Great Room. They arrived in time to join the Lambeth Walk, strutting around the room, arms swinging, before they turned to one another to slap their knees and hands in tune with everyone else, then returning to the circular promenade. The entire dance floor shifted around together, matrons and husbands joining in the long parade of dancers that circled up one staircase, along the balcony, and down the other. Valerie and Richard laughed, carried by the energy and cheer filling the room. It was as it had always been, and it would remain this way for as long as Valerie, Richard, and society could hold on to it.

Chapter Sixteen

Her Majesty's Representative

———————

Lord Hamilton
invites applications for
the Royal Enclosure at the Royal Ascot

———————

Tuesday 13th to Saturday 17th June 1939

The end of May and the beginning of June passed in a whirl of the usual dances, luncheons, and dinners until the Royal Ascot brought a welcome change to the schedule. Valerie and Their Excellencies paraded about the Royal Enclosure in their flower-print dresses with calf-length skirts to keep the hems from dragging through the wet grass. Stylish hats with wide brims were much in vogue, along with the men in their morning suits and gray toppers. The day was clear, with no hint of the rain that had dampened the previous race days, but Valerie's heels sank into the soft turf whenever she stood in one place for too long. Katherine, ever the mad horsewoman, had braved the bad weather with Jakie, Michael, and her brother David, but the rest of Their Excellencies had waited until the sun came out to attend. With the King and Queen still abroad on their North American tour, the royal pageantry was lacking, but there were plenty of the usual titled and privileged about to make a show of things.

"Valerie, you're looking lovely as ever." Elm swooped in around the other chaps to take her hand, the tails of his morning coat cut sharp, the top hat adding to his height. "Did you receive my note?"

"I did." It'd arrived the day after the Queen Charlotte's Birthday Ball full of apologies for missing it but with no request to see her and explain his absence. This was the first time they'd met since the night of the Tango Club. She should be boiling mad at him having chucked her over, but she'd hardly given it much thought. The evening with Richard had kept her in a near-daydream, disappointing her every night when she didn't see him. He'd been as absent from the recent events as Elm, leaving her quite peeved with both men. If Mr. R. M. Chaplin had even one iota of either chaps' charisma, she'd toss them both over for him and spare herself the bother.

"I'm dreadfully sorry to have missed it. We've been swamped with training the mass of new recruits. Hardly any of us can get away. I had to call in a favor to come here."

He hadn't called in any favors for her. "I'm sorry you couldn't make it. Thankfully, Richard stepped in at the last minute."

"He can always be counted on, can't he?"

It wasn't a rousing compliment, but she didn't say so. This wasn't the time to be cross or make a fuss. The etiquette for Ascot was strict, and the wrangling for tickets to the most exclusive event of the Season put everyone on their best behavior. No one wanted to be denied entry next year. It didn't mean she couldn't make her irritation clear. "He's quite reliable, unlike some chaps."

"I deserve that."

"You most definitely do." She good-naturedly poked him in the chest, preferring to have a regular dance partner over a grudge. Men had been rushing to join up and it was possible he hadn't been able to get away. Or his mother had insisted he cry off after Mavis's disgusting display. Even then she couldn't entirely fault him for his filial duty. She'd been far more loyal to Father than he'd ever been to her. She'd had no choice, especially when he'd been nearly all she'd had. "You missed Eunice's coming-out dance too. Mrs. Kennedy was quite irritated by the heat driving guests outside Prince's Gate. She went to some trouble to decorate the embassy."

The building had been well turned out, providing everyone curious about the inside of America in England a chance to see it. She was sorry Richard had missed it, given the impressive collection of buildings he'd already visited.

"Then I'm doubly sorry I've been lax in my social duties. I would've liked to have seen the notorious Ambassador and his wife in the flesh."

"There's nothing remarkable about them."

"Except his reputation."

She didn't ask him to explain, afraid Eunice might approach

and overhear or the conversation might come around to her questionable family connections. The Ambassador and his wife had made a solid showing during Eunice's dance with no hint of the tension from the Royal Academy. Relations between America and Britain, however, were growing more contentious with every curt remark Ambassador Kennedy made about Britain's poor chances of winning a war. "Should I expect you or another note for my coming-out dance?"

"I wouldn't miss it for the world. I owe it to you after my beastly conduct in May. You'll save me the waltz, won't you?"

"Only because no one can dance it the way you do. It's so much more fun when my toes aren't being stepped on."

"Then I'll endeavor to leave your shoes unscuffed." He raised his top hat, then drifted off to speak to Lord and Lady Duff Cooper. For a man seeking forgiveness, he could've stuck around a little longer.

"Elm out of the doghouse with you?" Dinah tilted up her head to see out from beneath the wide-brimmed picture hat dipping down over one side of her face.

"He shouldn't be, but he's too charming to ignore."

"The title helps."

"Even if it annoys me to tears that a little flattery can make me forget what an utter swine the Viscount is."

"A charming swine."

"I should know better than to fall for it, but I can't help it." The moment in the taxi when she thought he might kiss her and the faint possibility that she meant something to him held her interest more than it should, as did his title. She hated how charmed she was by his rank, but with everyone else so concerned with standing, how could she not be? If it weren't for Richard and his very practical take on things, she might be completely fooled by the fantasy of society, one she knew wasn't anything like what it seemed.

"Then enjoy it. It won't last forever."

"I don't suppose it will." Something would change everything between them, war, the end of the Season, his mother, or Richard. Time would decide which one.

No. 10 WAS A frenzy of activity when Valerie returned from Royal Ascot. Men from the BBC in their cheap dark suits carrying cables and equipment added to the usual mix of people milling about the ground floor.

"Dreadful news." Marian shook her head as Valerie joined her behind the ministers and secretaries at the back of the Cabinet Room. The BBC men adjusted the microphone on the table in front of Uncle Neville, turning knobs and fiddling with wires in advance of his radio address. "The Japanese are blockading the port of Tientsin, a British concession in China, and making it so not even food or medicine can make it through."

"They don't mean to cause trouble too, do they?" The situation in Europe was bad enough without the Japanese throwing their hat in the ring.

"If they do, it'll be on Germany's side. The Japanese are desperate to conquer China, they need their oil and resources and believe our concessions are interfering with their success."

"Silence, please," the balding radio operator commanded. "Five, four, three, two, one."

The red light in front of Uncle Neville lit up and he smoothed the papers on his desk, tension choking the room as he began to read.

"The Japanese blockade of the British Concession at Tientsin continues. British subjects are detained and searched and subjected to unspeakable indignities while the entry of perishable foodstuffs and ice into the British Concession has been intentionally delayed. His Majesty's Government is doing all it can to remedy the deficiency, and His Majesty's Ambassador at Tokyo has made it quite clear to the Japanese government that we cannot acquiesce in the blockade. With regard to the local incidents at Tientsin, it is becoming increasingly clear that this is a new attempt at world domination in the Far East by the Japanese, who I hope will be able to restrain their subordinates in Tientsin."

The longer Uncle Neville spoke, the hotter the room grew. Valerie rubbed her neck, afraid she might faint, and she wasn't usually wilting.

"Are you all right?" Marian whispered.

"No, I need to step out." She twisted through the gathered officials and secretaries to make for the freer air of the anteroom off the main corridor. Marian followed her, waiting patiently while Valerie paced the carpet, anxiety making it impossible to stand still.

"Those poor people. Trapped, and with no idea what's going to happen to them." She understood Richard's helplessness with his patients. Here she was in No. 10, and there was little she could do to offer the Englishmen in Tientsin any comfort or hope. "I wish there was something I could do, collect medicine or food to send to them, anything to help see them through this."

"Even if you could, it'd take four weeks to reach them. The British China Station in Hong Kong is preparing ships with aid."

"Will it be enough?"

"I can't say."

Valerie leaned against a secretary's desk and trilled her fingers on the polished edge. "If we could wire them money, they could purchase more food and medicine and other things navy men might not think of, such as food for babies and children."

"Do you have such an amount?"

"I don't, but society does. I'm sure I and my friends can impress on them to be generous." Their Excellencies would do all they could to help her. They couldn't sit back and do nothing any more than she could.

"Even if you can raise money, how will you get it there in time?"

"I don't know." And then it struck her. Valerie stood upright, snapping her fingers. "Katherine's father, Lord Harlech, is in banking. I'm sure she can have him arrange a wire transfer of whatever funds we collect."

"I can contact someone on Admiral Sir Percy Noble's staff to arrange receipt. He's the Commander in Chief of the British China Station. He'll be in charge of sending ships to Tientsin, but I'll need the Premier's permission. That's far above my duties, and you'll have to act quickly. There isn't much time before those ships are dispatched."

"I'll get you the permission you need." Valerie hurried upstairs to the White Drawing Room, where Aunt Anne was arranging the flowers sent down from West Woodhay House in a crystal vase. She paused in fussing with the roses to watch Valerie rush to the desk and remove her list of thank-you-note addresses and stationery from the drawer. One thing about the tedious business was that it'd given her quite an extensive list of people she could contact for donations.

"I've never seen you so eager to write thank-you notes. Was Royal Ascot that exciting?" Aunt Anne asked, leaving the roses to lilt in the vase.

"This is far more important than pithy lines to hostesses." Valerie explained her and Marian's plan to Aunt Anne, who listened with her usual calm, hoping Aunt Anne didn't object to Valerie asking members of society for money.

"I think it's a marvelous idea."

"We'll need Uncle Neville's help too." She explained about the warships and the political red tape.

Aunt Anne brushed a bit of pollen off her skirt. "Leave that to me. Mr. Colville isn't likely to let you interrupt Neville, but he isn't about to stop me."

"Thank you so much." Valerie turned to her list of addresses, ready to begin writing, when Lady Ravensdale's name caught her eye and made her pause. "One more thing."

"Yes."

Valerie turned in her chair, gripping the carved wood back, hesitant to mention it, but the thought, like the plight of the people in Tientsin, nagged at her. "Should we carry on with my coming-out dance in the face of everything? Lady Ravensdale was awful about you and Uncle Neville enjoying yourselves at Cliveden during the Anschluss. What will she and others say about my coming-out ball?" She could practically see the headlines from rotund Lord Castlerosse in his *Londoner's Log* about the Prime Minister dancing with debutantes while the world burned.

"We are not canceling your dance. People look to us to set the tone. If we act as if nothing is wrong, they'll see it and take heart that things are not as dire as the newspapers suggest. If we appear glum, it won't raise anyone's spirits but make them more fearful."

"I hadn't thought of it that way."

"After I speak to Neville, we'll see to the letters and place a call to Lady Bridgeman. A woman so adept at arranging supplies must have a few ideas on how to help the British stranded by the blockade. You'd better ring your friends. You don't have much time." With a determined nod, she strolled out of the room to approach Uncle Neville and secure permission for the donations.

Valerie rushed to the phone and within moments Dinah was on the line.

"What a smashing idea," Dinah breathed after Valerie explained the plan. "I'll be there at once."

"Bring the others. I need time to collect everything here."

"I won't disappoint you, Your Excellency. See you soon!"

Valerie drafted the donation letter and Aunt Anne helped polish it. They perfected it just in time for Their Excellencies to arrive, and in a flurry of excited chatter and gossip they wrote out numerous copies on the No. 10 stationery Aunt Anne provided to lend more gravitas and urgency to their collection efforts. She even enlisted the No. 10 footmen to deliver the letters once they were complete.

By the next morning, more envelopes of donations than invitations arrived with the post, and Miss Leaf helped Valerie organize them. Checks continued to trickle in throughout the day, delivered by footmen from a number of posh London addresses. Even the Princesses Elizabeth and Margaret were kind enough to send money for the benefit of the English children in Tientsin. Valerie wished she had time to collect more, but Marian's announcement that the ships were to set sail in the morning and everything must be sent off at once put paid to that. With Katherine's father's help, the funds were cabled to Hong Kong and all remaining money collected was placed in a special account managed by Lord Harlech to be used as directed by Their Excellencies for future aid projects.

The grandfather clock in the entrance hall chimed nine times as Valerie came downstairs. After all her hard work, Valerie was dead-tired. She could imagine how exhausted the staff and Garden Room Girls must be, and their day was far from over. She'd be sure to have sandwiches sent down to them before she retired. It was the least she could do.

"Here it is." Valerie handed Marian the list of essential supplies to be purchased that she and Lady Bridgeman had drawn up that evening.

"I'll have them cabled to Mr. McBride, Admiral Sir Percy Noble's private secretary, at once. It's four A.M. in Hong Kong."

"Will that give him enough time to collect everything?"

"When I told Mr. McBride it was the Premier's niece organizing this, he assured me he'd personally make sure it was done."

"Please include a note of thanks from me."

"I will. He'll appreciate the sentiment, coming from so eminent a person."

"I'm hardly eminent, just fortunate to be where I am."

"We both are."

Mr. Rucker and Mr. Seyer strolled by, each man looking a bit rough around the edges. Mr. Seyer covered a large yawn with the back of his hand while Mr. Rucker braved the over-roasted coffee Mrs. Bell had brewed to keep them going. "Is there any end in sight for all of you tonight?"

"No." Marian rolled her sagging shoulders and stood up straight. "There's too much to be done and the time difference is making it worse. No rest for the weary."

Marian's tired smile suggested there might never be rest for her. In some ways she enjoyed a great deal more freedom than Valerie, but in others she had very little of it. The typist could no more decide to not work than Valerie could pursue employment. Like all of them, Marian's future, even the next few hours, was dictated by others and events far beyond her control.

"Thank you, for everything," Valerie offered, feeling this was woefully inadequate.

"Thank you for helping, and remember a great many Londoners will need aid too, especially if supplies become scare."

"I won't forget them." She couldn't, not after seeing the concern and worry in Marian's eyes when she'd spoken of her family and what they might face if war came. Yesterday's news pulled them a step closer to it and all the awfulness it would entail. She'd used her position to help fellow Englishmen a world away. She feared it wouldn't be long before she must do it again much closer to home. "This has given me a great deal of practice in how to arrange these types of things."

Chapter Seventeen

The line of cars arriving at Downing Street to deposit their guests stretched all the way down Whitehall. Valerie stood for over an hour at the top of the Grand Staircase at the head of the receiving line with Uncle Neville and Aunt Anne. They shook hands and greeted people until there was little feeling left in her fingers. Nearly every face from the court presentation paraded past her and she didn't shrink in shyness from welcoming them to the prestigious address. These people had been strangers to her a mere three months ago. They'd become a regular part of her life since, some more friendly than others.

Uncle Neville winced as he rubbed his side during a pause in the stream of guests paying their respects. His black evening jacket deepened the dark circles under his eyes. He'd slip off to work once hosting duties were finished, but his being here at all meant the world to her.

"Everything all right, Neville?" Aunt Anne asked in a low voice.

"Indigestion. The fish was very rich, but well made." Before the dance, Aunt Anne had hosted a grand dinner in the large dining room in Valerie's honor. "I'm fine."

He smiled at Aunt Anne, setting her and Valerie at ease before Mr. Dobson called out the next names.

"Lady Fallington and Lord Elmswood."

Valerie clasped her hands tight in front of her, hoping the quick beat of her heart wasn't visible beneath the glittering diamonds of the Cartier necklace. She stood up straight in her white tulle evening gown with the midnight blue lace accents on the wide skirt and a royal blue waist sash. They were here. It meant Mavis's little exhibition hadn't done as much damage as she'd thought.

"Lady Fallington, thank you ever so much for your donation to the Tientsin relief." She'd taken quite a chance sending a request to her and had been equally surprised when she'd received money in return. The woman's patriotism must have outweighed her objections to Valerie and her stepmother.

"I was more than happy to donate." Whatever Lady Fallington's thoughts on Valerie and her various relations, they remained hidden behind her usual aristocratic smile as she greeted her, then moved on to her aunt and uncle.

"Don't forget, you promised me the waltz," Elm reminded, charming as ever.

"I haven't forgotten." She raised her arm with the dance card attached to it and he took it, his grip on her fingers firm while he wrote his name. The moment in the taxi when she thought he might kiss her flashed before her. "Until our dance."

"Until then." She studied him for any hint of feeling about her, but he was the proper Viscount tonight, not the man who'd held her close in the seedy basement club. With his mother hovering nearby, he couldn't be anything but the dutiful son who escorted his mother into the drawing rooms.

"Good evening, Miss de Vere Cole." Mr. Chaplin's greeting brought her firmly back to her hostess duties.

"Mr. Chaplin, you've joined up." His uniform shocked her as much as the high collar of it sharpened the soft line of his jaw.

He hooked his thumbs in his lapels, puffing out his chest. "The Household Cavalry, the last mounted regiment in England."

His pride didn't settle Valerie's unease. He was a nice chap who'd been a regular partner at every dance and she'd learned a great deal about horses because of him. She hated to think what that uniform meant to his future. "You'll be quite distinguished among your fellow servicemen."

"Thank you, Miss de Vere Cole. Might I partner with you for the foxtrot?"

"You may." She held out her dance card, allowing him to sign it before he carried on into the Pillared Drawing Room and Mr. Dobson called out the next names.

"Lady Aschcombe and the Honorable Miss Rosalind Cubitt."

Lady Ashcombe approached with the same imperious look from over her thick cheekbones that she'd pinned Valerie with at the court presentation. Valerie didn't shrink under the scrutinizing glance but faced the Baronette's daughter with the confidence expected of the Premier's niece. She might have a whole parcel of questionable experiences and family members in her past, but so did most of the people passing before her. If they could hold their heads high, then so could she.

"You've truly blossomed, Miss de Vere Cole," Lady Ashcombe complimented. "You're a credit to your aunt and uncle, especially your work on behalf of the Tientsin unfortunates."

That was certainly unexpected. "Your donation to our collection was greatly appreciated, Lady Ashcombe."

"My pleasure, of course."

Rosalind wasn't so conceding, still indifferent to Valerie but a touch more respectful in light of the event and venue. The two of them exchanged stiff greetings before Rosalind followed her mother into the Pillared Drawing Room. It served as the ballroom for tonight, the doors to the adjacent rooms thrown open to accommodate the full house. She had yet to see Richard. He'd assured her he'd be here and she very much looked forward to dancing with him.

It wasn't long before the most surprising guest of the evening stepped in front of her and her aunt and uncle.

"Lady Ravensdale and the Honorable Vivien Mosley." Mr. Dobson's voice carried over the noise.

Lady Ravensdale regarded her with the same polite arrogance she'd lavished on her at the Royal Academy of Art.

What the devil is she doing here? Valerie had avoided Vivien's coming-out dance in favor of the charity ball. She thought Vivien would do the same, especially given her need to retire to Paris for a while. Maybe she was as curious as Richard about No. 10, but for a woman who despised Uncle Neville she didn't think his residence a big enough draw. Perhaps she should suggest Henry inspect her for a bomb or a concealed gun, her motive for coming more revolutionary than respectful.

"Good evening, Miss de Vere Cole," Vivien said with barely concealed distaste, while Lady Ravensdale exchanged a few words with Aunt Anne and Uncle Neville. After the dustup over her and Lord Mosley one would think she'd be a little more humble, but arrogance sometimes hid a lack of confidence. Vivien had arrogance in spades.

"Miss Mosley, thank you ever so much for coming." Whatever her reason for being here, Valerie would avoid her, hoping she wasn't so ill-mannered as to pull something while a guest in the Premier's house. One might expect more from the granddaughter of a viceroy, but, as she discovered, lineage was simply a gilding for coarseness.

"That's almost the end of it," Aunt Anne said with no small measure of relief when Lady Ravensdale and Vivien moved on. The line had dwindled down to a few stragglers.

"The Honorable Dr. Richard Cranston," Mr. Dobson announced. Thank heavens!

"Is there any room left on your dance card for me?"

"I saved the Big Apple especially for you. I hope you don't mind." She couldn't imagine anyone else joining her during the large promenade around the room or kicking and stepping with the same devil-may-care delight he'd shown during the Lambeth Walk at Grosvenor House.

"A rollicking bit of fun." His fingers curled around hers while he wrote, his grip warm and firm, making it quite impossible for her to think of anything but him until he let go. "May I have the pleasure of taking you in?"

She smiled, near-giddy at his request. "You may."

People streamed up and down the Grand Staircase, many making for the cooler air of the lawn that had been strung with paper lanterns to light the walks between the rose beds. Richard led her to the Pillared Drawing Room, taking in everything as he went. In the Pillared Drawing Room, the large Persian rug had been taken up, leaving the parquet floor for dancing. There were no elaborate decorations turning No. 10 into a German beer garden or a Spanish castle. The historic elegance of the house was background enough.

Valerie hoped he appreciated the understated décor. "Is Number Ten everything you expected?"

"Less ostentatious than I'd anticipated but certainly worth the cab fare."

"You make it sound like the Tower of London menagerie."

"Isn't it?" He motioned to the various government and society people mingling through the rooms, bushy mustaches and boutonnieres broken only by the flash of scarlet dress uniforms and silver lamé gowns.

"It's quite the collection of specimens, especially the men in uniform." Her smile faded even while the chaps carried on laughing, drinking, and dancing. "I'm worried about what'll happen to them if war comes. It sounds awfully silly to say aloud, but I'm glad they're here to enjoy this in case it's one of the last. They'll need cheerful memories if things turn ugly." Thoughts of Christmas at Aunt Anne's had comforted Valerie more than once during the darkest times in Ascain. All of them might have to cling to the past like that again.

"Then I'm honored to be a part of it." He laid his hand over hers where she rested it in the crook of his arm. It was the most they could exchange in the crowded room, not without her earning a few sordid lines in *Mrs. Sketch's Diary*. She wished she could walk out with him in the garden as they'd done in Hyde Park, but tonight she couldn't favor one guest over all the rest.

"I believe the waltz is my dance." Elm cut in between Valerie and Richard, breaking the spell. "Nice to see you, old chap."

"They finally let you out of the barracks."

"Only because I've been a good boy."

Richard, unflappable as always, handed Valerie to Elm, who escorted her onto the dance floor. Through the guests, she caught sight of Vivien dancing with Jakie, less impressed to be on the arm of a viscount's younger son than a viscount. Valerie fell into rhythm with Elm, matching his moves step for step. They'd waltzed enough at various balls for her to know his style, the two of them the picture of grace and syncopation, and most of the room turned to watch them.

Elm pretended he didn't notice the sudden rush of attention, but it was there in the regal set of his shoulders. "You're shining this evening."

"I have an accomplished partner." He twirled her and she met his energy, making the skirt of her dress shift and sway. "Do you know, I considered going back to the country after my presentation to avoid all of this? I wasn't sure I could face it."

"Not a confident deb like you."

"It's a bit overwhelming for us girls, all but ignored our entire lives, then suddenly shoved into the limelight and expected to be witty night after night."

"Then you've learned a great deal in a short time. Did the Season live up to your expectations?"

"It exceeded them." Even the less savory moments. The old regrets and worries that used to pile on her in the middle of the night when she was too keyed up from the evening to sleep had been dulled by her friends. Mr. Shoedelin seemed like a distant memory and Mavis had proved to be little more than one of those eccentric relatives English families were famous for, an embarrassment shrugged off with a nervous laugh and a few blushes. In the rare moments when worry did get the best of her, Their Excellencies helped settled her, as did dancing with Elm.

He guided them elegantly around the floor, drawing more attention. During one turn, she caught Richard's eye. He smiled, but it was tense about the corners of his lips. Whatever he thought of her dancing with Elm, it didn't thrill him nearly as much as it did her.

Whatever Lady Fallington thought of them dancing, she didn't know. She couldn't see her. She must be in another room, mixing with more of her sort. At least the Marchioness wasn't hovering around shooing Elm away from Valerie.

After Elm there was a string of other partners but none as dashing as the Viscount. It didn't matter, every one of them was as polite or charming as they could be and the conversation never lagged. She saw to it, employing every trick she'd learned during the last three months to be a splendid hostess.

"You're really turning heads tonight," Richard said from behind her as they promenaded during the Big Apple. Dinah was ahead of them with Johnny Dalkeith, the Earl of Dalkeith's son, while Christian, Katherine, and Eunice promenaded on the opposite side of the circle.

"It's my coming-out dance." They stopped to kick into the circle and back out again with everyone else. Perspiration dotted his forehead, his hair slightly disheveled from the energy of the dance. For all the world she couldn't imagine Elm dancing like this. He was off somewhere, standing out because there were more than enough gentlemen to ensure no girl went without a partner. "I should hope to shine."

"You deserve to collect more memories."

"I am. Hoards of them. Including you."

Around and around they went in the circle, kicking and swinging, wagging fingers in the air with everyone until the dance brought everything to a rousing end. Valerie and Richard came to a stop with the rest of the circle, breathing hard from the dance and the thrill of the night. "Can I take you outside to the garden for some air?"

"I wish I could." Over his shoulder she caught sight of Mr. Chaplin coming to collect her for the foxtrot. "But I don't want to hurt anyone's feelings."

He glanced at Mr. Chaplin, then nodded. "I understand."

She didn't doubt it, what with all the times Elm had cut in between him and Valerie. "Perhaps later?"

"I look forward to it."

He relinquished her to Mr. Chaplin, who talked excitedly about his horse and their new training regimen. She listened to his steady stream of words while silently hoping nothing happened to him. He didn't deserve the awful sorts of things she'd read about in *All Quiet on the Western Front*. None of the chaps she danced with did, but she didn't say so to any of them, eager for everyone to enjoy tonight as much as she did.

She begged off the next dance, needing a breather and a good chat with Their Excellencies. She wove through the guests in the drawing rooms searching for them, squeezing through the crush of young people filling the hallways before making her way down the Grand Staircase. Girls and boys sat on the steps chatting, giving their feet a rest from biting slippers and pinching dress shoes, the string of late nights catching up with many. Downstairs, she turned a corner, surprised to see Lady Ravensdale and Vivien standing alone in the dark passage between the private secretary's office and the Cabinet Room, the only place not filled with people. The few staff not released early ahead of the festivities were upstairs with Uncle Neville.

"They're fools to host this party when Europe is nearly in flames," Lady Ravensdale said to Vivien. "They're a disgrace and not at all capable of leading us through this crisis."

Valerie was about to rush in and defend her uncle, to say he as much as anyone in England deserved a bit of merriment, but curiosity got the better of her and she listened, careful not to catch their notice.

"Why are we even here?" Vivien sulked. "I didn't want to come."

"I wanted to see how far you're failing. Someone like her is capturing the prize and what do you, a Viceroy's granddaughter, have to show for the Season?"

"I might have a better go of it if Father weren't embarrassing me at every turn. Why can't he and Diana disappear? Must they be so obvious?"

"He is what he is and you'd better think on how you'll manage it. Miss de Vere Cole has to contend with that slut Mrs. Wheeler and she's still succeeding. Remember who you are and do better." Lady Ravensdale stormed off, pausing when she caught sight of Valerie. She didn't stop and apologize or sputter about not meaning what she'd said about Uncle Neville. She simply swept past her as if she owned No. 10.

The nerve of the witch.

"I suppose you heard that." Vivien ground her teeth as if chewing on the next thing to say.

"I did." She approached the girl as if Vivien were a snake about to strike. Eunice had said she might be nasty because of what she endured. Maybe it was true. "My father and stepmother aren't exactly an asset to me either. It's perfectly dreadful when relations hinder more than help us."

Relief flashed across Vivien's face and Valerie waited for her to commiserate the way Their Excellencies did during confessions. She didn't want to be pals, but a truce like the one from the 400 Club would be nice. They weren't so different. There was no reason for them to constantly be at each other's throat.

The peace vanished as fast as it'd come and Vivien hit her with a haughty sneer. "Don't insult me with your false sympathy. You're glad to see my family humble me. Jumped-up girls love to see the betters torn down."

She pushed past her, leaving Valerie in the hallway to fume.

Betters. Hah! Not with all the scandals tied to her family like tin cans on a newlywed's car. But in this world it was strike before you were stuck, climb as high as you could by pushing others down. Vivien could bloody well live that way. Valerie wouldn't.

She marched out of the hall, running into Eunice.

"What's wrong?" Eunice asked, noticing the fury on Valerie's face.

"I caught the sharp end of Vivien's bite."

"She can be quite rabid, can't she?"

"She's a right regular bitch."

Eunice clamped her hand over her mouth, her eyes wide with surprise. "I should say a Hail Mary for that, but you're right. I'll confess it on Sunday."

"What are you doing down here?"

"I needed a breather. Kick's dancing with Billy Harrington, and it's the talk of the ballroom. She'll end up married to a duke and I'm simply an afterthought. Never mind that I'm the reason we're here, not that I'm only interested in you because of this but I like you, all of you. You've been so nice to me. You don't care who my father is or that he and Marlene Dietrich are an item. Oh, listen to me going on with all my gloom and doom during your ball. I'm sorry."

"You needn't be. We all need a good cry and complaint now and then."

"So this is where you two have gone off to." Dinah turned the corner, nearly as familiar with No. 10 as Valerie from her many afternoon visits here. "I'm exhausted. I've never danced so much at a ball."

"Come on, I know where we can rest for a while." Valerie led them up the stairs, meeting Katherine and Christian as they came down. "Follow me. I promise you, it's grand."

They slipped past the revelers and upstairs to the family's private floor. Along the quiet corridor they giggled and laughed like thieves about to steal state secrets, especially when Valerie guided them up to the third floor and through the servants' quarters under the attic. Everyone was downstairs serving tonight, leaving the rooms deserted. They reached the last and highest stairway in No. 10 and followed it up to the roof.

London spread out before them, Parliament and Big Ben visible in the distance, the lights of Buckingham Palace glowing behind them. The twinkling was broken by the wide swaths of dark parks dotted here and there, the cars' headlights snaking through the streets.

"It's beautiful," Dinah breathed, leaning against the edge of the rooftop.

"Mary showed it to me once. She said Mr. Asquith's children used to watch the suffragettes parading in front of Downing Street from up here." Valerie leaned against the wall beside her friends, the breeze catching her curls and brushing them against her cheek before she tucked them behind her ear. The putter of cars and the occasional horn off a boat on the Thames drifted across the city, mingling with the music from downstairs and the conversation of people strolling along Downing Street or in the garden.

"Everything looks so peaceful from this high," Eunice said.

Christian sighed. "Don't you wish a night like this could last forever?"

"I do." Valerie traced the line of grout in the brick. "Did you notice all the men in uniform?"

"Hard not to when they're the color of lobsters." Dinah stood beside her, chin in her hand. "Poor dears. Difficult to think they and the city might suffer the way Mr. Churchill keeps warning."

"London's been here since ancient Rome," Katherine said. "It'll endure."

"So will we." Valerie glanced to her friends standing on either side of her, the sleeves of their dresses ruffled by the breeze. "Promise me, whatever happens, we won't forget one another. No matter where we go or end up, we'll face this together."

"Absolutely," Christians said. "I couldn't think to bear it without you."

"Hear, hear," Dinah cheered. "To Your Excellencies."

"To us!"

Chapter Eighteen

The clink of china beneath the soft conversation of women and the notes of the piano dominated Claridge's tearoom. Large curve-topped mirrors encased in chrome ironwork shaped into swags gave them the appearance of French palace windows. They reflected the light from the tall windows with a view of the street across from them. A gorgeous chandelier hung in the center of the vaulted ceiling above a large pink floral arrangement and a pale blue circular leather seat. Servers in white coats moved quietly through the tables, bringing plates of food and new pots of tea for the diners to enjoy.

"Have you decided what you're going to do about your mother?" Dinah asked from across the table. They were taking tea alone today, the rest of Their Excellencies engaged with other commitments. They'd decided to splurge, passing up the cheap sandwiches at Selfridges for something a touch more refined. It'd been a week since Valerie's coming out and the whirl of the Season was beginning to quiet as many left for country estates in anticipation of Sarah Churchill's coming-out ball at Blenheim Palace. Valerie and Aunt Anne would spend the Thursday to Monday at Cliveden with Their Excellencies, Michael, Jakie, Elm, and Richard.

"I haven't." They hadn't discussed Valerie's mother since the tea in Downing Street weeks ago, but there wasn't a time when Valerie opened the red dispatch box and saw the address beside the books and letters that she hadn't thought about it and what to do. There were nights when she'd lie awake imagining a tearful reunion or at the very least a polite conversation. It was all fantasy, but without having met the woman she had nothing else. "What brought that up?"

"Papa came to see me this morning. When I told him Aunt Nancy had already motored to Cliveden he said how much he and Mummy used to enjoy house parties. He hasn't been the same since she passed. The doctors wouldn't let him or us see her when she was sick, they were afraid it'd upset and weaken her. He wishes he'd insisted, but no one, not even the doctors, thought she'd die." She pushed her empty plate away. "If war comes, a great many people could be lost and you might regret not having visited her before things went to pieces."

"I might regret it if I do. I still can't shake the nasty things my stepmother told me about her not wanting me. If that's true, she won't like me showing up on her doorstep." She'd told Dinah about the awful visit during one of her many afternoons at No. 10.

"If you can speak, it might be good to hear her side of things so you aren't left wondering. Then you can put it all behind you, have a clean slate, as it were."

"I suppose." This wasn't about telling her mother to bugger off but finding out why she'd left, and if there could ever be anything between them besides trust payments. Even if it didn't go well, she'd have the truth instead of all this wondering. Good or bad, it'd be a great deal easier to face with friends around and a weekend at Cliveden to distract her from anything distasteful. "I'd have to do it without anyone at Number Ten knowing. Aunt Anne isn't one to lose her temper, but I've never gone behind her back before." She probably shouldn't do it but she had to know. The what-ifs were torturing her. "How will I manage it?"

Dinah leaned forward with that conspiratorial look of hers. "If we put our heads together, we'll think of a way."

VALERIE HANDED THE cabdriver the coins and stepped out of the cab. Bury Street was filled with gentlemen coming and going from nearby Jermyn Street. She saw couples waiting in line outside Quaglino's for a table. At the newsagent's, a placard board beside the newsstand announced PEOPLE DEMAND CHURCHILL RETURN in bold letters. Everyone was agitating for the political exile to have a place in Uncle Neville's cabinet. Uncle Neville had spilled more than a few words during dinners about how little he cared for the seasoned politician.

"Shall I wait for you, luv?" the cabbie asked.

"Please." Her interview with Mavis had been shockingly brief. This one might be too. She adjusted the short-brimmed hat, amazed by how quickly tea with Dinah had turned to a clandestine reunion with her mother. It'd been Dinah's idea for Valerie to hail a cab and leave Mr. May waiting at Claridge's. If Aunt Anne ever got wind of this she'd be disappointed that Valerie had defied her instructions. If she thought she could make her understand why she needed to come here she'd tell her, but she wasn't certain she could. She still wasn't sure what she expected from this visit.

Taking a deep breath, and unwilling to sit in this awful suspense any longer, she walked into the hotel, nodding to the liveried doorman, who tugged open the glass door. Smartly dressed people lingered in the lobby, checking in or conversing with their friends. It was an altogether respectable address a woman with six thousand pounds a year and no children to clothe and feed could afford.

"May I help you, miss?" the man behind the counter asked.

"Miss de Vere Cole to see Mrs. Winterbotham. She isn't expecting me."

He picked up the phone and dialed her room. Valerie glanced at the cab through the hotel's front door. This might end quickly if her mother wasn't home or declined to see her.

"You may go up. Room Twenty-Three. Third floor." He directed her to the lifts.

Valerie shifted from foot to foot in the tight confines of the lift as the slender operator ferried her up.

If the lobby was nothing special, neither was the third floor, and she followed the plain number on each door until she reached 23. With a shaking hand she knocked, waiting for an answer.

It wasn't long before a woman with Valerie's blue eyes and a mop of short, frizzy dark hair tugged open the door. She wore a long wrap in peacock-feather greens and purples tied loosely about her slender waist, a woman with nothing to do and nowhere to go. She didn't seem particularly surprised to see Valerie, eyeing her as if she were a maid bringing up the post.

Valerie stood there, not sure what to do. She hadn't known what to expect but it'd been a touch more emotion than this. It hollowed out her already-aching stomach and left her at a loss for how to greet the woman who'd brought her into this world and then vanished from her life. An embrace didn't feel right, but neither did a smack with her purse. There were questions she wanted to ask, answers she'd longed to hear. An arrest for battery would get her nowhere.

"I'm—"

"I know who you are. Come in." She stepped aside and Valerie entered the room, no more welcome than she'd been at Mavis's. It didn't bode well.

Bags and hatboxes from Harrods and Selfridges lay strewn about the sitting room beside the wrinkled pages of fashion magazines. The furniture, a respectable set of Queen Anne reproductions, was clean enough but ratty about the edges. From somewhere down the hall a maid whistled along to the music from the wireless while she worked.

Mrs. Winterbotham sat down and motioned for Valerie to do the same. She didn't ring for tea. This was going to be a short visit. "You're, what, eighteen now?"

"I'll be nineteen in August."

"Really? I could've sworn it was April, but it was all so long ago. Where are you living these days?"

"With Aunt Anne and Uncle Neville. Aunt Anne is bringing me out from Number Ten. I'm sure you've read about it in the papers."

"I don't read the newspapers. There's nothing in them but gloom and doom." Her words carried an Irish accent softened by a hint of Englishness.

"Then you didn't know I was in London?"

"Mr. Mason told me when I visited him last month after coming over from Ireland." She rose and went to the table near the window, where a selection of decanters and crystal glasses stood beside a chrome ice bucket. She tonged out two cubes and dropped them in a highball glass before filling it with a healthy dose of whiskey and soda. "He thought I might wish to contact you, I don't know why."

"Because you're my mother." *Steady on, girl.*

"An inconvenient side effect of an unfortunate marriage." She snorted into her glass, sloshing some over the side and wiping the rest from the corners of her mouth with the back of her hand. "It's amazing what a little bit of gold around a woman's finger will gain her, and how much more a healthy inheritance attracts. I wasn't about to waste my youth on some old fool and his baby."

"I was your child too."

"I never wanted to be a mother. I wanted my freedom and my inheritance, and marrying that old man was the only way I could wrest both from Chancery Court control. I told Horace so when I married him, but he didn't believe me. He thought we were in love, as if a nineteen-year-old can see anything in a forty-year-old besides freedom, and satisfying a bit of curiosity. If I'd known it would leave me up the duff, I'd have stayed curious. Bedding him was the second greatest mistake I've ever made after marrying him."

"And leaving me? You don't consider that a mistake?"

She shrugged. "You seem to have come through it all right."

The woman's callousness knocked the breath out of her. It wasn't all right, it'd never been, and this woman was part of the reason why. Every day of hunger and depredation Valerie had endured, each lonely night in Cambridge or Ascain when she'd gone to bed without a mother's kiss, washed over her along with the old aching loneliness.

Mrs. Winterbotham finished the drink and set it on the cart. "I know you came here expecting me to wail with regret about having given you up, but I won't. I've had my fun and I'll have more of it before I'm through. I suggest you do the same. You're in a better position to enjoy your freedom than I ever was. Now, if you'll excuse me, I have things to do."

She fluttered off in a cloud of metallic green and purple silk.

Valerie struggled against the regret and anger pulling at her to stand up and leave. She held back the tears in the lift to the lobby, walking with as steady a stride as she could manage out of the hotel and to the cab. "Number Ten Downing Street."

The cabbie turned to gape at her as if she had three heads.

"Number Ten," she snapped. "Please."

It wasn't his fault that he didn't know who she was or where she lived or that her mother had tossed her out of her life for the second time.

Fool. Fool. Fool! She'd insisted on learning the truth, and what had it gotten her? Another slap in the face. She should've listened to Aunt Anne, but her aunt should've told her the truth, that Mavis was right and her mother had never wanted her.

It didn't take long for the cab to reach No. 10. He dropped her off at the corner of Downing Street and Whitehall. She paid him, then stepped out, unrecognized by the crowd until the police moved aside to let her through. The gathered men and women called out questions about Germany and Japan but she ignored them, unable to offer any answers, barely able to see Downing Street through the haze of tears blurring her eyes.

Henry opened the door at her knock, forcing her to smile when he greeted her. There were more people on the ground floor than usual and it took all her strength to walk to the Grand Staircase instead of racing up it. Valerie climbed the seemingly never-ending stairs, past the old prime ministers, the history, everything that made the house what it was. At the top, she instructed Mr. Dobson to send word to Mr. May at Claridge's to return. The butler's eyes widened in surprise but he didn't question her, leaving to do as he was asked.

She hurried down the hall toward the second-floor staircase and paused outside the drawing room. From inside came the clink of teacups and Aunt Anne's soft voice muffled by the closed doors. Her At Home gave Valerie time to have a cry and pull herself together before tonight's dinner party, even if all she wanted was to shove the door aside and hug her aunt. She longed for her to carry her away from this nastiness as she'd taken her from the convent.

She pressed her forehead to the cool drawing room door and ran one finger along the molding.

I'm afraid I can't explain myself, sir. Because I am not myself, you see?

Alice's words from Wonderland drifted through her thoughts. Aunt Anne was so close, but even if she could hug her she couldn't tell her everything or how deep the hidden scars ran. If she did, Aunt Anne might finally see the flaw inside Valerie, the one that'd made her mother and father scorn her. She could face almost anything except losing Aunt Anne.

"Valerie, are you all right?"

Valerie straightened to see Marian coming back from Uncle Neville's office. If she stayed down here much longer she wouldn't be. "I'm fine."

"You don't look it."

"I'm tired, that's all. It's been a long Season." More lies, but she couldn't tell her the truth. Their Excellencies had shared their secrets and she'd revealed some of hers, as many as she'd dared. They hadn't judged or turned away from her, but for all she and Marian had done, it'd never been as personal as this. She wished it could be, and someday it might, but today all she could do was stand there pretending to be strong while crumbling inside. Nothing was wrong. Nothing was ever wrong, it was always chin-up.

Marian studied Valerie, the faint vanilla scent of the Schiaparelli perfume Valerie had given her marking the air. "If there's anything I can do for you, please let me know."

"I will. Thank you for your concern." She appreciated it far more than she could say without bursting into tears.

She climbed the stairs to the second floor, hoping to make it to her room without running into anyone else. She reached the top and came face-to-face with Dorothy.

"Valerie, I'm glad I caught you. There are a few things we must discuss before you leave for Cliveden tomorrow, some things to keep in mind while you're with the Astors."

"Tomorrow morning." After the lovely time she'd spent with her mother she wasn't in the mood for Dorothy. She tried to push past her, but Dorothy stepped in her way.

"No, young lady, this moment. Father is worrying himself sick over Germany. He doesn't need you forgetting yourself in the relaxed atmosphere of the country and causing trouble."

"Causing trouble? When have I ever caused trouble?"

"I know you snuck off to the 400 Club. Lady Simon said Lord Warwick saw you there."

So much for mutual discretion. "Did she tell you he wasn't there with his wife?"

"That isn't the point. You're a representative of the Prime Minister and this family. If you forget yourself, you'll be ruined and become a weight around Father and Mummy's necks, a spinster for them to support. They can't be responsible for you forever. Mummy indulges you too much as it is."

"Spare me your worries. You didn't care about me or what I did when I was in Ascain or with Great-Aunt Lillian, sick from not having eaten enough in France, covered in rashes from that awful coarse uniform they made us wear."

"Stop dwelling on France. It does you and no one else any good, especially when you exaggerate so."

"Exaggerate? Why, you spoiled, narrow-minded cow." Dorothy drew back in openmouthed horror. Valerie should bite her tongue, but she couldn't contain the wave welling inside her. "Aunt Anne and Uncle Neville loved you and gave you everything. You don't know what it's like to be hungry or destitute, to have your father ignore you every day, even while you're starving, and your mother not want you. All you know is how to belittle people, expecting the worst of them at every turn even when they've given you no reason to, and making them miserable. Now get out of my way."

Valerie shoved past her and rushed to her room, slamming the door behind her and turning the key so hard in the lock it almost snapped. She held her breath, listening for Dorothy's heavy steps in the hall, but they never came. She'd catch hell for this later, but she didn't care. Not since the Mother Superior had scowled at her tears when she'd begged to be allowed to write to Aunt Anne had anyone been so heartless, and it struck as deep as her mother's disregard.

It didn't matter what she did or how she behaved, it was never good enough for Dorothy and her ilk, who thought nothing of belittling her or insulting her at every turn. She didn't deserve it. She'd been the dutiful daughter, the proper debutante, and still it wasn't enough. Dorothy, her mother, Mavis, Lady Fallington, all despised her or believed she was rotten to the core. Perhaps she was as bad as Mr. Shoedelin believed, but if so, it wasn't her fault. It was her parents'.

She opened the dispatch box and dug beneath the book to yank out the letters.

Father was the one to blame, but he wasn't here. He never had been. He'd ruined everything and left her to deal with the consequences.

She tore the letters to pieces, each rip releasing a lifetime of frustration and hurt. She flung the scraps in the grate, snatched up the matchbox from the mantel, and lit one after another, flinging them in to burn the horrid begging words and desperation. The fire flared hot and fast before fading, leaving the letters a crumbling mass of black bits at the bottom of the fireplace. Heavy tears rolled down her cheeks. She wanted to crawl into bed and never come out again

"Miss de Vere Cole?" Miss Logan's northern accent carried through the door along with a few small knocks. "It's time to dress for Lady Bridgeman's dinner."

Valerie drew in two long, difficult breaths, trying to force the tremble and tears out of her voice. "In a few minutes, Miss Logan. Please. I need some time alone."

She waited for Miss Logan to insist, her aunt's lady's maid not nearly as deferential as Mr. Dobson but she didn't. "Yes, Miss de Vere Cole. Call me when you're ready."

Miss Logan's footsteps faded down the hallway, probably going to Aunt Anne's room to leave a note that something was amiss. Miss Logan would have to stand in line behind Dorothy, who'd probably barged into the At Home to give her mother an earful. Valerie leaned against the chair and pressed her fists against her forehead. Thank heavens Aunt Anne wasn't likely to tramp up here to demand an explanation.

Valerie wiped her cheeks with the back of her hand and pulled herself off the floor. She couldn't sit here crying and feeling sorry for herself. There were obligations, immutable, unforgiving ones for conversation and smiles and pretending everything was well even when it wasn't. She had no choice but to face it all.

Chapter Nineteen

*V*alerie whacked the tennis ball to Elm. He returned the vol-
ley, sending it sailing over the net and her head to bounce
in front of Dinah. She swung and aimed the ball at Richard, who
wasn't so quick, missing it before it bounced inside the line and
into the grass outside the court.

"Our win!" Dinah twirled her racket in triumph, her pleated
skirt beneath a short-sleeved jumper swaying with her motion.

Behind her, the weathered light brown stone of Cliveden
rose above the green lawn, the floors stacked like three tiers of
a square cake topped with points. A wide patio rimmed with a
balustrade projected off the back of the manor house, a hugging
staircase accented with ivy leading down from it to the sprawling
lawns that stretched out before sloping into the formal gardens
and the forest beyond.

Aunt Anne hadn't ridden up to Cliveden with Valerie. At the
last moment, Uncle Neville had asked her to stay behind. It'd made

the hairs on the back of Valerie's neck rise. Uncle Neville relied on Aunt Anne to unburden himself from everything he faced in the Commons and the Cabinet Room. If he was asking her to delay her trip, it couldn't be good. There hadn't been a chance for Valerie to find out. She'd been packed off alone, spending too much time in the back of the car thinking over everything with her mother, Dorothy, and the past. There hadn't been time to discuss it with Dinah before she'd left or after she'd arrived, the sheer number of guests at the house party pulling the hosts in a thousand different directions.

Try as she might to shake off her mother's nasty spite and Dorothy's cruel dismissal of her suffering, it had all ridden beside her during the drive to Cliveden and haunted her while Dinah had shown everyone around the Italianate house, the opulence of St. James's Square paling in comparison. Even her room was the most elaborate she'd ever slept in, with a canopy of blue and bronze silk set against a wall of yellow paper and wainscoting. The bedroom had a spectacular view of the River Thames snaking through the thick forest, and Valerie had spent too much of last night standing at the window searching for some calm in its beauty.

Dinah tossed the ball in the air and caught it. "Another game?"

"I've been beaten enough for one day." Elm loped off the court to drop down at the table and pour a glass of lemonade.

"Sore loser." Dinah stuck her tongue out at him and he returned the gesture.

"Singles?" Richard suggested to Valerie.

"I see I'm to be left out again." Dinah winked at Valerie and left the court, taking a chair beside Elm, who slouched in the wrought-iron seat, making the front of his white jumper crumple. He appeared as Valerie felt, as if all this joy were a little too much to endure.

Valerie served, she and Richard racing across their sides to send the ball back and forth over the net. The hard breathing and physical activity calmed her more than the cocktails after last night's dinner.

Richard wasn't as agile as Elm but he was solid, hitting the ball with enough force to make Valerie's racket rattle in her hand. He wore a long-sleeved jumper with stripes along the collar, the deep V of it showing off the solid chest beneath. White pants accentuated the length of his legs and the slenderness of his waist. Elm looked like a mannequin in his tennis clothes, while Richard was more a sporting man, his breathing matching the quick darting back and forth as he chased the ball, giving Valerie a good run until his final shot sent the ball over the net and past her racket.

"I win." He held up his arms in victory. "It must've been Elm pulling my game down."

Elm raised his half-empty glass to Richard. "I bring down a great many people in a great many situations. You have only to ask my father to know that."

"We both must've been awful partners, judging by how well they played alone." Dinah poured Valerie a lemonade as she and Richard joined them at the table.

"Father been at you again?" Richard gulped down his drink.

Elm swirled the ice in his glass. "When isn't he?"

"Well, he isn't here to bother you, so cheer up. You don't want to be a right gloomy specter at the ball tonight. I hear the Churchills spared no expense on this little affair."

"A swan song deserves a lofty venue."

"Hardly a swan song," Dinah challenged.

"Mark my words. There won't be another evening like tonight again."

"You haven't even seen it yet and you're already calling the game."

"Anyone who's been paying attention can see it." Elm pushed up straight in the chair and leaned hard on the table toward Dinah. "You think these families can go on with this pointless frippery when the world is about to come crashing down around us? They can't spend in this vulgar manner, not in front of the masses."

"Elm, a man of the people," Richard good-naturedly jeered. "What brought that about? You don't usually bother with the lower orders."

"You make me sound like a callous sod."

"Aren't you?"

"A sod, maybe, but far from callous. I care a great deal about my valet and groom. I couldn't live without either man."

"How magnanimous of you." Richard laughed, but it wasn't his usual deep and throaty one. "What about you girls? How will you dress yourselves when your lady's maids are pressed into war work?"

"I already dress myself most of the time." That garnered Valerie an impressed cock of the head from Richard.

"I suppose I'll have to learn, but I welcome the challenge," Dinah said. "After all, it can't be any harder than learning to drive."

"It's tedious as hell," Elm drawled. "But I suppose it's the smallest of the sacrifices we'll have to make when our valets are killed in battle."

A bird dipped over the tennis court, the calls of it and others back and forth between the trees loud in the long quiet.

"Shall we go in? It's nearly time to dress." Dinah stood and brushed bits of grass off her skirt. "Perhaps I'll do it myself simply to show you I can."

"No need to preen on my account." Elm walked with Dinah back to the house, leaving Richard and Valerie to follow.

"What's wrong with Elm? Too many martinis last night?"

"Too much father before we left. He's always like this after the old man gets at him. I suspect his mother had a word or two with him too."

"About what?"

Richard flicked the racket strings with his finger. "His station and the responsibilities that come with it. She's been quite keen on the subject lately."

"I see." It was the polite way to tell Valerie that Elm's mother had warned him off of her. It shouldn't matter, it was hardly a surprise, but she was tired of yet another person thinking she didn't measure up even when she was doing everything expected of her.

"Congratulations on your efforts on behalf of Tientsin. My mother happily contributed."

"Thank her for her generosity." His compliment meant more to her than the personal note of thanks she'd received from Foreign Secretary Lord Halifax. "How are things at St. Thomas's?"

"Fine for the moment, but I won't be there for much longer. I've joined the Royal Army Medical Corps. I'll probably be assigned to the Queen Alexandra Military Hospital."

"Then you'll stay in London." At least he wouldn't be in danger if fighting began, but eventually he might be, and she'd lose him like she might lose her friends and everything she'd built over the last few months.

"Until I'm needed elsewhere."

"Wherever you go, stay safe." She laid her hand on his arm, stopping them at the foot of the stairs. "You mean a great deal to me."

"Do I?"

"You do." In more ways than she could express.

"No canoodling on the grounds, you two." Dinah leaned over the stone railing at the top of the stairs. "You can do that at Blenheim. Plenty of dark garden walks for that sort of thing."

Valerie wasn't sure whether to giggle or die of embarrassment. This was no time to lose her heart or her head. She let go of Richard and bounded up the stairs. Elm met her at the top, walking beside her as they ambled toward the house.

"Aren't you tired of it all?" Elm shoved his hands deep in his pockets. "The showmanship and trumped-up ideas about what's important and who everyone is supposed to be, when it's lies underneath. It makes me sick. I wish war would come and get me away from it."

"There's a cure far worse than the disease, but I understand what you mean." She was pretending she was fine while suffering from everything her mother had said and all that'd happened in Ascain. "Except we can't leave. This is where we are and what we're supposed to do. People expect certain things of us and we can't disappoint them."

"They don't mind disappointing us."

"No, they don't."

"Then we must find a way out, be more than what they want us to be, marquises or cannon fodder." He grabbed her by the hands and spun her around, making her dizzy. Then he jerked them to a halt, Valerie stumbling before his hands on her upper arms kept her steady. "Promise we'll find a way to live on our own terms in our own way."

"I can't promise that because it isn't possible. The only thing we can do is find something more meaningful than this."

"You sound like Richard."

"He's right."

"He doesn't know half as much as he thinks he does." He stuffed his hands in his pockets and shuffled off toward the enclosed courtyard with the pool.

"Where's he going?" Dinah asked from the doorway.

"To think things through."

"There's been a lot of that lately," Richard said. "Give him time. He'll come around. In the meantime, I believe you ladies must learn to dress without your maids."

"I assure you, the results will be shocking," Dinah teased. The three of them entered the house, winding through it to reach the dark carved-wood main staircase beneath the high ceiling and Renaissance frescoes. They climbed it, passing the medieval figures carved into the banister. At the top of the stairs, Richard turned and headed toward the men's rooms, leaving Dinah and Valerie alone.

"Do you have time to chat before you dress?" Valerie was about to burst with the need to speak to her.

"I've been wondering when you'd ask. You look as ghastly as Elm when you think no one's looking."

"I saw my mother yesterday. I don't have to wonder anymore about why she vanished." Valerie told her about the meeting and the nasty things her mother had said, relieved to finally share it with someone.

"My poor dear." Dinah hugged her tight. "I never should've encouraged you to see her."

"I'm glad you did, because I finally know the truth." Valerie screwed her eyes shut tight against the tears, as tired of crying as she was of hurting from the past. "She's a bitch. I don't know why I thought she wouldn't be."

"Because you're an optimist." She let go of her, holding her at arm's length. "It's one of the things I adore about you. Despite everything, you always carry on. It's more than most do."

"I'm tired of it, of struggling and fighting. I don't want to do it anymore."

Dinah laid a comforting hand on her shoulder. "If you gave up, you'd be no better than your father or mother, and you don't want to be like them."

"No, I don't. Thank you for the reminder."

"I'm simply upholding my part of our pledge. You'd do the same for me."

"I would." No matter how much it beat her down and exhausted her, she had to keep going through all the insults and snubs and the awful defeats, otherwise everyone who'd ever worked against her or thought so little of her would win.

Aunt Anne came down the long hall dressed in a traveling frock of mauve with a row of brass buttons down the front.

"You're here."

"I arrived an hour ago."

"And you haven't changed." It wasn't like Aunt Anne to be improperly dressed.

"Do you have a moment? I need to speak with you."

If Aunt Anne wanted to have a chat, then Dorothy must have told her about their tiff, making her out to be the most wicked person in the world, or Aunt Anne had found out about the visit to her mother and wanted to know why Valerie had defied her. If Valerie hadn't, it would've saved them both a great deal of grief.

"I'll leave you to it, then. No one should bother you in the drawing room. Everyone is too busy upstairs dressing." Dinah pointed to a room just down the hall before heading off to her bedroom.

Aunt Anne guided Valerie into the nearby drawing room lined with bookshelves in a much lighter wood than the entrance hall. The higher ceiling and brighter colors made it far less oppressive than the downstairs. Valerie and Aunt Anne sat on a light cream silk sofa near the tall windows overlooking the woods and sprawling lawns. The matching cream silk drapes framing them cascaded down either side before pooling on the hardwood floor.

"I hate to burden you with this, but you're far more levelheaded and calm than Dorothy." Aunt Anne worried one of the brass buttons on the front of her dress, the constant motion of her fingers as out of place as her traveling frock.

"I don't mind listening." It was the least she could do for the woman who'd done so much for her. "What is it?"

"Probably nothing, and it's silly of me to fret about it before there's a real reason to, but I can't help it." Aunt Anne laced her hands together in her lap to keep from fidgeting, a measure of her usual calm descending over her, but it didn't hide the worry in her eyes. "You know Neville's gout has been troubling him a great deal lately; so has his stomach."

"I do." The few times he'd joined them for dinner he'd hardly eaten anything, and he couldn't bear to grow much thinner.

"He spoke with Dr. Tillerson, who thinks it might be something more serious. They must run tests before they can be certain, but Dr. Tillerson suspects it might be cancer."

Cliveden could've collapsed on top of Valerie and it wouldn't have crushed her as hard as that bit of news. She wanted to rise and pace the room, wear a tread in the floor to shake off the fear, but she forced herself to sit still. Aunt Anne didn't need her to fall to pieces. "Are they sure?"

"I don't know, and we may not find out for some time." Tears filled her blue eyes. "What am I going to do without him?"

"Don't think like that, you can't." Valerie clutched her aunt's hands, unable to still their trembling. "He's been working so hard. Maybe it's only exhaustion. We mustn't give up hope until we know for certain." *Please let it be something else.* She couldn't lose the one man who'd been more of a father to her than her own, who struggled and strived to keep England out of a war and give the country a fighting chance if war came.

"You're such a good girl to listen to me like this." She slid a hand out from beneath Valerie's and laid it on her cheek. Valerie wanted to cry in fear but she forced back the tears. This was no time for her worries or wails. She had to be strong for Aunt Anne and help her face whatever was coming. "Promise me you won't tell anyone about this. The press, society, no one can know. Any show of weakness and the opposition and press will pounce."

"I won't tell."

"I'm sorry to put this on you, especially before Miss Churchill's dance, but I needed to speak to someone."

"I can manage it." Even if the news nearly crushed the breath out of her.

Chapter Twenty

$\mathcal{V}$alerie stepped out of the car with Dinah, Katherine, Eunice, and Christian, joining the others to gasp at Blenheim Palace, the country seat of the Churchill family. Massive floodlights illuminated the Greek-temple entrance, glinting in the massive windows and lightening the faces of the stone statues perched along the top of the Palladian front. Behind them, car after car filled the Great Court, letting out the massive number of guests coming in from family seats all over the countryside.

Elm's red Bentley coupe with the curved and bulging fenders and the bright chrome grille enjoyed a pride of place among the parked cars. The sight of it lightened Valerie's steps. The chaps were already here, Michael, Jakie, David, and Richard having traveled over with Elm. She wanted to rush into the ballroom and grab the first one she saw and dance until she forgot everything about her mother, Dorothy, and Uncle Neville, but there were receiving lines and greetings to manage before she could think about the dance floor.

Lady Astor and Aunt Anne walked a few paces behind Their Excellencies, having ridden over in the Chamberlains' Rolls. Lady Astor's high voice carried over the constant crush of tires on the gravel, her continuous conversation showing no signs of flagging. How Aunt Anne listened so patiently instead of jumping out of her skin with worry, Valerie didn't know. If it hadn't been for the humor and conversation of Their Excellencies on the way here, she might have fretted herself into a fright. Thank heavens for them and the lightness they brought to everything. Her world would be a great deal darker if it weren't for her friends.

"No wonder they call it a palace." Christian whistled as the three of them climbed the front stairs and passed under the high-columned entrance.

"Are you saying Monymusk House isn't this grand?" Dinah craned her neck to take in the six massive eyes painted beneath the classical entrance.

"That old Norman pile is a hovel compared to this."

They passed from the chill and floodlit majesty of the outside into the blinding brightness of the Grand Hall.

"No wonder everyone scrambled for an invitation," Katherine breathed.

The marble walls and carved pillars were nearly as white as the floor with its black inlaid marble diamonds. It glowed as if midday under massive lights that left few shadows, even in the darkest reaches beneath the arches and nooks surrounding the room. Large portraits of past dukes and duchesses of Marlborough hung on the far wall above the main staircase hidden behind a line of aqueduct-like arches. Plinths along the sides of the room supported statues of Greek gods and goddesses. Valerie turned, the massive windows above the entrance offering a view of the illuminated statue atop the apex of the front portico. There was no hotel or private house in London to compare with this.

The Duke and Duchess of Marlborough stood at the front of the room with their daughter to greet their guests. Lady Sarah Spencer-Churchill hadn't been a regular fixture of the Season, having spent the past few months in Paris and leaving her presentation to the last court. At six feet tall with blond hair, Sarah would be hard to miss even if she weren't at the head of the receiving line. A gold lamé Worth dress draped her lithe figure, setting off her blue eyes and blond hair to perfection. Her shorter mother with her dark hair and eyes stood beside her like a queen. Everyone who was anyone, from the highest-ranking peers to every politician of note, was here.

Their Excellencies, followed by Lady Astor and Aunt Anne, paid their respects to their hosts before filtering in among the people filling the Great Hall. The sheer opulence of it was difficult to take in, and Valerie understood Elm's dark prediction that this might be the last of the grand manor house parties. The expense of running the estate and then dressing it up to the nines couldn't last. None of this could.

"Miss de Vere Cole, it's a pleasure to have you here," Mr. Churchill mumbled. He stood with Mr. Eden smoking cigars and discussing who knows what politics, probably plotting their next assault on Uncle Neville. She should snub the old bulldog and the backstabbing Mr. Eden, who'd turned on Uncle Neville after Munich, but, as Aunt Anne had said, one did not mix politics with society. "What do you think of my family's humble home?"

"It's magnificent." This wasn't a lie. The marble stretched to the massive ceiling with its elaborate fresco in an oval gilded medallion.

"Mrs. Chamberlain, you look lovely as always," Mr. Churchill greeted Aunt Anne, as suave as any courtier. There was no animosity between him, Aunt Anne, and Mr. Eden despite the near-floods that passed under all of their bridges daily. It simply wasn't done. Despite the drawn lines of Aunt Anne's face during the long procession through the receiving line, she smiled, conscious of her place as the Premier's wife. Duty forced her to endure polite conversation even when she needed to be alone to absorb the news that had been foisted on her mere hours ago. Valerie felt the strain; it was the same one dogging her as she made her excuses and left to join Their Excellencies.

"What did your aunt want to speak to you about at Cliveden?" Dinah asked, pushing close to her as they pressed through the men and women crowded around the edge of the dance floor, all of them stiff-necked from gaping at the grandness.

"I can't tell you here, but it isn't good." She shouldn't say anything but if she didn't talk to Dinah about the worries filling her, she'd come out of her skin. Dinah would keep her secret, she was sure of it, and she'd understand better than anyone the uncertainties piled on an already shaky future.

"I didn't think it was, but we'll have a good chat about it, I promise." Dinah squeezed her arm in comfort before the approach of John Miller took Christian out of the group. It wasn't long before Katherine, Eunice, and Dinah were snapped up for the dance.

"Are you all right standing out?" Dinah asked when Johnny Dalkeith asked to lead her out, concerned as always about their pledge to one another.

"I am. I need a chance to take it all in." The palace and everything that'd happened beforehand.

"Steady on, old girl," Dinah encouraged before following Johnny onto the dance floor.

For someone who'd spent the entire Season working to not be alone, she very much wanted a touch of solitude tonight, but it wasn't to be had. Like Aunt Anne, she had her role to play, and she must do it well. If she did, then she might forget everything for a while until it was all foisted back on her tomorrow.

"I see you made it to the ball in one piece." Richard's voice came from behind her.

She turned, nearly stumbling to see him dressed in a red shell coat instead of his usual white-tie. "You're in uniform."

"Dashing, don't you think?"

"There's nothing dashing about you dead or wounded on a battlefield." Uniforms were de rigueur tonight, but with him in one the cold grip of war and all the horror and destruction it meant crept closer than ever before.

"I'm not charging into battle just yet."

"But you might someday." *And die.* They all could, including Uncle Neville.

"Not tonight." His soothing voice eased the tension tightening her neck. He held out his hand and she took it, his fingers closing over hers solid and reassuring. She followed his steady steps onto the dance floor and he swung her around to face him for the waltz, his hand on her back a strong support in the midst of so much shifting sand.

"Not ever, I hope." He'd do his duty to England as readily as she'd do hers when the time came to take up her position with the Personal Service League. At present, this was her world and she must embrace it the same way he and Aunt Anne did. "I didn't think the waltz was your dance."

"I had to nab you when I could. With this crowd I don't expect you to be free forever."

"Good, because there's something I must ask you." If anyone could give her hope or knowledge of what to expect, it was him. "What do you know of cancer?"

He jerked back, clearly not expecting this.

"I don't mean to be gloomy, but is it always fatal?" Her voice cracked and he drew her closer, offering what comfort he could in the middle of the ballroom. She longed to lay her head on his chest and wrap her arms around him and cry out her anxiety, but she couldn't. Rules, always the rules.

"Did someone close to you receive a diagnosis?"

She nodded but didn't elaborate. It wasn't necessary, the pity in his eyes told her he'd guessed, but he'd never betrayed her confidences before. He'd keep this secret too.

"Everything depends on how early it's caught. Surgery can remove small tumors, but if it's too far advanced or has metastasized to other areas of the body there isn't much that can be done."

"I see." Limbo was becoming a permanent state in England and her life.

"I'm sorry, Valerie. If there's anything I can do . . ."

"I'll be sure to tell you." It wasn't only Valerie who would lose someone close to her if Uncle Neville passed away. He'd be a loss to all of England. The country he'd worked so hard to serve would be left to others to see it through whatever waited for them, and it was war. With all the men in uniform surrounding them, there was no denying it was coming, it was simply a matter of when. "Will you join your regiment soon?"

"I don't know."

Another limbo. "Until then, *imagination is the only weapon in the war against reality.*"

"Lewis Carroll."

"Yes. Let's find something more imaginative than this."

They left the dance floor, winding their way through numerous rooms to the Long Library, with the massive organ at one end and walls covered in antique books behind decorative screened doors. She wished she could select one and escape from everything troubling her, but the long, rectangular tables covered in candelabras and food stood against the bookshelves, leaving an aisle in the middle for guests to peruse the tarts, sandwiches, and champagne. Black marble pillars supported the short gallery above the entrance, and the arched roof curved above the remaining length of space. The light wasn't as bright in here, with flickering candles giving a warm hue to everything and a soft contrast to the massive floodlights brightening the rest of the palace.

Richard plucked two glasses of champagne off a passing footman's tray and handed her one. She took a sip, wanting to drink it down and have another three or four more until the darkness inside her disappeared, but that was Father's way, not hers. She wasn't about to act like him, even if she understood for the first time why he'd turned to the bottle. It was easier to drift into wine than face difficulties sober. She wished she could fade into the fog for one night, but she couldn't. She had to keep acting the perfect debutante.

"There you two are." Elm slid toward them, his uniform as red as Richard's but the insignia different in ways she didn't understand. That it might become familiar to her very soon made her finish her glass of champagne in one discreet gulp. "You're empty, girl, have another."

He grabbed a glass off a nearby table and pushed it into her hands.

"Trying to make me forget myself?"

"If it works for me, it'll work for you." He clinked his glass against hers and she wondered how many he'd already had. Elm could hold his liquor a well as anyone here, but it didn't mean he couldn't be drunk.

"Slow down, old chap." Richard clapped Elm on the back. "I want to make it home in one piece."

"Then you can drive."

"Letting me behind the wheel of the Bentley. You must be deep in your cups."

"You will be too by the time this ridiculous display is over. My mother is all but fawning over the Duchess, as if I have an interest in that gangly daughter of hers."

"You shouldn't be so nasty." Valerie bristled at his mother's preference for Sarah over Valerie. "She's never done anything to you."

"Except exist, along with her family. If I have to hear one more time from my mother what a dutiful son Sarah's brother is, how devoted he is to the family estate and lineage, I'll be sick. I've done everything asked of me, but it isn't enough. It never is."

"I'll say." Valerie snorted into her champagne. "My cousin sounds a great deal like your mother."

"Dreadful bores, aren't they?" Elm clanked his champagne glass against hers again, making the crystal ring.

"Dr. Cranston, what a pleasure to see you." Sir John Simon approached Richard and vigorously shook his hand. "I wondered if I might trouble you for a moment. That irritation on the back of my hand has been bothering me something dreadful. Would you mind?"

"Of course not." Richard, gracious as always, threw Valerie an apologetic look, then followed Sir John toward the organ, where the light was brighter.

"Richard should tell that old toady to sod off. This isn't St. Thomas's."

"He cares too much about patients to do that." Even the ones who should know better than to ask him about their rashes at a dance.

Elm sipped his champagne before he caught sight of something over the rim of his glass. "Bloody hell. There's my darling mother, no doubt searching for me."

He was off in a flash, leaving Valerie to catch Lady Fallington's eye. She didn't wave or acknowledge her, looking through her as if she were one of the Greek goddess statues. She was probably searching for Elm to make sure he wasn't talking to her or to drag him into conversation with some other debutante she thought far more worthy of him.

"Lord Elmswood bade you adieu already?" Vivien's snide remark carried over the hum of conversation drifting up to the arched ceiling.

Not this cow. She and Priscilla Brett, who was standing beside her, were the last people Valerie wanted to see tonight. That Vivien had managed to wrangle an invitation to this dance spoke more to her aunt's standing than her father's, and proved that politics was indeed kept separate from society. "I don't blame him. Anyone in their right mind wouldn't claim a connection with you."

"Isn't there a Blackshirts rally for you to attend, or doesn't your father want you at those either?" She didn't have the patience to be more subtle with her insults. If this cat wanted a fight, she'd give it to her.

"Girls, please," Priscilla begged, but, hackles up, they both ignored her.

"Don't play the high-and-mighty with me, Miss de Vere Cole, daughter of the impoverished Horace de Vere Cole and that slut Mrs. Wheeler. The Chamberlains may foist you off on everyone, but I know the truth about you."

"Do you?" Valerie crossed her arms over her chest to hide the slight tremble in her fingertips. The chit knew something more about Valerie's family than old hoaxes and crude pencil drawings and she was burning with a fever to tell it.

"While my aunt and I were in France, we met a lovely gentleman at a dinner at the French embassy, a Mr. Shoedelin, the British Consul in Bayonne. I believe you know him."

Valerie didn't answer, silently willing her to shut her stupid mouth before anything vile poured out of it to stoke the panic building inside her.

"He had quite a lot to say to Aunt Irene about how he found you living in squalor, riddled with lice, your father half-drunk and you dressed in rags. He told Aunt Irene how he stepped in to keep the creditors from arresting your father and stashed you away in a convent school because he believed poverty had weakened your morals. The Chamberlains told everyone you were in finishing school in France, but it wasn't that at all. It was an orphanage for unwanted girls."

Valerie stared at her gloating smile, every student in the convent school mixed into that wicked look. Not one of those girls had thought to comfort her, to say they knew what it was to be forgotten or abandoned. Not even the nuns, with all their pretenses to tenderness and mercy, had offered her more than "It's God's will," and other hollow platitudes. It'd taken everything in her not to let them or the depredation of Ascain destroy her, the truth hidden from everyone except Dinah, and here was this witch throwing it in her face.

"Rosalind, Priscilla, and I had a good laugh when we heard your French finishing school was nothing more than a papist orphanage, didn't we?"

"You aren't being nice, Vivien," Priscilla chided, but Vivien scowled at her before turning her fury back on Valerie.

"You should've seen Lady Ashcombe's face when she heard the news, but of course she knew what you really are, she said she recognized it the moment she saw you at court. The Chamberlains are trying to foist you on everyone like those pathetic girls Lady Clancarty sponsors. I'm surprised the Chamberlains aren't insisting we call you honorable, like Lady Dunford does with that lot of hers. Wait until the rest of society discovers it. Between this and that stepmother of yours parading herself in front of everyone, you'll be the talk of every debutante ball for the rest of the Season, assuming the mothers don't rescind their invitations, afraid of tainting their daughters with your cheapness. Better scurry back up north before the Chamberlains decide you aren't worth the bother and send you packing, wouldn't you say?"

No, she wouldn't say a thing. She wouldn't cry or curse or beg Vivien to see reason and keep this to herself. Mr. Shoedelin had opened his stupid mouth, but he hadn't told them everything. Not that it mattered; he'd told them enough. She didn't take her gaze off Vivien, but her ears pricked up for the conversation around them, wondering how many people had heard the tale and learned the truth about her. "Tell whoever you like. It makes no difference to me."

Feigned bravado was all she had. She wasn't about to cry at Blenheim and make this gossip more delicious than the story of the thief who'd snuck into Rosalind Cubitt's coming-out dance and stolen a mass of fur coats. She didn't have the excuse of an eccentric relative this time either. It was Valerie who'd been in France, Valerie Mr. Shoedelin viewed as no better than a fallen woman, adding her story to the already sordid ones circling her.

She turned on her heel and strode away from Vivien and Priscilla, careful not to stumble or try to outrun the tears stinging the corners of her eyes. Sobs squeezed her chest but she kept her head high and her shoulders back.

Curse Father and Mavis. Curse them both to hell. She'd done everything she could to place distance between the Valerie in France and the debutante in Downing Street and it didn't matter. Despite how much she tried to raise or improve herself, there was always someone or something waiting to pull her down.

Valerie pressed between the groups of girls and their chaps chatting together, trying to find a way through the maze of long hallways and old antiques to the garden. She reached the door at last, racing past a group of laughing girls, wondering if they were talking about her. She stopped outside and raked in a deep breath of the cool country air, the voices of the hundreds of guests filling the walks between the illuminated topiaries and fountains mixing with the music from inside. It was magical and gorgeous, like the pictures of Versailles she used to see in Madame Freville's magazines, a fantasy land come true. This was the life she'd longed to live for years and it was finally hers, and it didn't matter. Her past would see her banishment from it, if German bombers didn't swoop down to destroy it first.

No one wants to associate with crass young ladies and they certainly don't want their daughters or sons befriending them either. You'll find yourself quite the outcast if you carry on like this. Dorothy's voice rang out like the laughter from the people near the serpent fountain. She'd overcome her father's foolishness and Mavis's brazenness, but in the end she couldn't escape the realities of France. Once everyone heard about it, they'd know her for the impostor she was and they'd close ranks on her as they had Pamela Digby. No, Their Excellencies would stand by her, unless their families told them not to, the way Elm's had. Wouldn't Mavis gloat then? She'd never done anything to deserve any of this and yet it was being piled on her by everyone and everything.

"Cheeky of you to join me." Elm slid up beside her.

"I needed some fresh air." She fought to keep hold of herself. Richard might tolerate her tears, but she wasn't sure Elm would.

"All the elegance inside stifling you?"

"It's been stifling me since I came to London. No matter what I do or how I behave or follow the rules, it doesn't matter."

"Never were truer words spoken." He handed her his glass of champagne and she took a hearty sip, tasting the rich brandy added to it. "Let's get out of here, go someplace where we can be ourselves."

"That sort of place doesn't exist. You said it yourself, once you're in society there's no escaping it."

"It doesn't mean we can't be free for a few hours." The scent of brandy and champagne on his breath was strong, but not nearly as much as his words. Freedom. She'd sought it from Father and his troubles, from her past, her desperation and loneliness, the convent, all the things haunting her. With him she might enjoy a few heady hours of carelessness, like the brief holidays with Aunt Anne when she'd experienced the comfort of a real home and love and food. Those few weeks had carried her through so many dark times. This was her chance to create a few more precious memories before Vivien's gossip left craters in the life she'd built. "Yes, let's get away."

He took her by the hand and pulled her to one of the paths leading around the side of the house to the Great Court. They dashed from shadow to shadow, startling more than one kissing couple risking respectability to grasp a moment together before war swept them apart. The end of this world was as strong in the air as the scent of the summer flowers.

They sprinted across the Great Court to the Bentley, the lights of Blenheim glinting in the high-gloss paint. Elm pulled open her door and she dropped onto the leather seat, the car fitting her like a fine mink wrap. Elm climbed in behind the wheel and started the engine, the sound throaty and deep compared to the Rolls and Chryslers surrounding them. With a flurry of kicked-up gravel that pinged off nearby cars, he turned the Bentley toward the main drive and wherever he was taking them. Valerie didn't care, relishing the darkness of the country road lightened by the chrome headlamps, little visible in the darkness except what was directly ahead of them.

He guided the sleek car over the winding turns, the windows rolled down to let the wind rush around them with the ever-increasing speed. The faint flash of headlights from somewhere far behind them caught in the small side mirrors mounted on the swooping front fenders, but she didn't care. There was no one here to wag a reprimanding finger at her, only the two of them and the night.

"Shall we go faster?" Elm gripped the black steering wheel with both hands, the wind whipping his hair around his forehead like it did hers.

"As fast as you like." They could take off and fly over England

and she wouldn't care, eager to outrun everything and everyone waiting for them at Blenheim, Cliveden, and No. 10.

He pushed the gas pedal to the floor and the car leapt forward, the engine humming harder and louder. He jerked the wheel right, then left, guiding the car around the sharp bends and corners, the trees caught in the light of the headlamps blurring as they passed. Coming out of one turn, the car's tail slid and Elm jerked the wheel to keep it straight. The near-slide into the field made Valerie's heart race faster. She should tell him to slow down, but she was tired of being careful. There was nothing outside of them but this speed and the road. No demands, no rules, only this glorious freedom.

Elm turned the steering wheel again as they came around another bend, the force of it pushing Valerie against the door. Then a sheep appeared in the headlights, its eyes as wide as Valerie's. Elm steered hard to avoid hitting it. The tires screeched as he stood on the brake, the car spinning in a dizzying circle that sent it twirling off the road. Bits of grass and bushes caught in the headlights, the countryside and night blurring together until a large bang made the metal and wood around them shudder and brought everything to a jolting halt.

Valerie released her tight grip on the door handle, wincing with the pain in her upper arm. The smell of petrol mixed with wet grass filled the car as she struggled to focus on where she was and what was around them. Elm breathed hard beside her, his door crushed in against him, the splintered tree bark the only thing visible outside the mangled window.

"Elm, are you all right?" Valerie reached for him, the pain in her arm tearing through her. Blood slid down from a large cut on her upper arm and stained the top of her elbow-length gloves and the satin dress.

"I don't know." He moved his right arm to open the door and winced. "I think something's broken." He reached around with his left hand and tugged at the handle but nothing happened. He leaned back against his seat, dazed, a trickle of blood seeping from a cut on his forehead. "I can't open it. Can you open yours?"

Valerie bit her lip against the pain in her arm to work the handle until the door swung open with a grating metal squeal. She stumbled out, the wet grass dampening her hands and skirt before she stood, horrified by the sight of the car curved in a mangle of chrome and red paint around the tree. How they hadn't been flung from their seats or made a permanent part of the bark, she didn't know. Reaching in through the passenger side, she helped Elm crawl over the seats and stagger from the wreck.

"Bloody hell." He sank into the grass, his shoulder at an odd angle from his neck. He touched the cut on his forehead, wincing before examining the blood on his glove.

"Are you all right?" Valerie slid the white handkerchief out of his inner coat pocket and pressed it toward his forehead before he stopped her with his good hand.

"You need it more than me." He pushed the square back to cover her wound.

She grimaced at the sting and the stain spreading out to ruin the linen. "What are we going to do?"

They were God knows where in the countryside and they needed help.

"I don't know. I can't move my arm."

She stood, peering into the darkness surrounding them.

"Where are we? What's near here?"

"I don't know." He lay back in the grass, his skin moist with a sheen of sweat.

She peered up one side of the dark road and down the other. There was no sign of a lit window across the fields or even the lights of a nearby village. She could walk, but she might wander for hours until someone found her, and she couldn't leave Elm.

Then, over the rustle of the leaves and grass, came the faint hum of a motor in the distance. "Someone's coming."

She staggered to the road, bruised and sore from the collision. She stood on the pavement as the headlights came into view.

She raised her good arm and flapped the bloody handkerchief. "Help, we need help."

The round headlights of the two cars grew brighter as they approached, the light of the first one blinding Valerie as it pulled to the side of the road. Sir John Simon and his chauffer jumped from the car, looking past her to the smoking and crumpled Bentley. "Good God!"

Lady Simon hurried to Valerie as fast as her hefty steps could carry her. "Miss de Vere Cole, are you all right? Is Mrs. Chamberlain in the car? Is she all right?"

"She's at Blenheim, but Lord Elmswood is badly hurt." She pointed to where he lay in the grass, and Sir John and his chauffer rushed to help him.

Lady Simon glanced back and forth between Valerie and Elm, the light of recognition about what she'd stumbled on dawning across her round face. It was more than an accident. It was a scandal.

The second car pulled to a stop behind Sir John's. Dinah, Katherine, and Richard stepped out, taking in the scene with horror.

"Valerie!" Richard hurried to take hold of her arm and turn it to view in the headlamps. "Are you all right?"

Valerie sank down into the grass, Richard helping ease her to the ground. "Elm needs you more than me."

"Keep the handkerchief pressed tight to the wound," he instructed Dinah and Katherine. "That'll slow the bleeding. I'll be back."

Richard left to examine his friend, Lady Simon following him.

Dinah and Katherine knelt beside her. Dinah took off one of her gloves and pressed it against Valerie's cut and tossed away the soiled linen.

"I suppose this will be good practice if we decide to join the Red Cross," Dinah joked, but not even her usual levity could break the stiff mood.

"What are you doing here?" They were the last people Valerie expected to see.

Dinah and Katherine exchanged a look before Dinah answered. "Priscilla Brett told Richard to find you because you'd had a spat with Vivien and were upset. He went looking for us, thinking we might help, and we saw you leave with Elm. We were worried, so we followed you. Oh, Valerie."

"I know." She was in a larger mess than the car crash.

"His shoulder's broken and Miss de Vere Cole has a laceration that must be seen to. Where's the nearest hospital?" Richard asked Sir John.

"Radcliffe Infirmary in Oxford. We aren't far from there. We can take them in my car, it's larger," Sir John offered.

He, his chauffer, and Richard helped Elm to his feet and guided him to the car. Their Excellencies escorted Valerie to it and eased her inside, Dinah gripping her good hand tight to stop the shaking. She missed the comfort of it when she let go, even if she didn't deserve it. They should leave her and avoid whatever taint their friendship was about to cast on them. If Lady Fallington didn't tell everyone that Valerie had gone off in a car alone with her son once she found out, then Lady Simon surely would. The Chancellor of the Exchequer's wife wasn't known for her discretion. This story would give more weight and delight to whatever nasty ones Vivien decided to spread about Valerie's time in France.

"Can you return to Blenheim and collect Mrs. Chamberlain and Lady Fallington and tell them what's happened and where we are?" Richard asked Dinah.

"I can." With one last concerned glance, Dinah closed the door on Valerie, while the Simons and Richard climbed in around them. Valerie didn't see them leave, she barely heard or saw anything during the silent ride to Oxford. Everything she'd worked so hard to achieve this Season was as mangled as the car against the tree.

Chapter Twenty-One

Valerie sat in the back of the Rolls-Royce in front of Cliveden. The sun had yet to rise over the horizon, and the last of the night darkness was soft against the windows. She wore her wrap around her shoulders, still dressed in her stained evening gown, her arm, head, and heart throbbing in pain. She wanted nothing more than to crawl into bed and sleep. They'd spent the last few hours in Oxford, where a country doctor had stitched and bandaged her wound while marveling that her injuries weren't more severe. Richard had been in another room, attending to Elm's broken collarbone. Valerie hadn't seen him or anyone besides Aunt Anne, who'd ridden back from the hospital with her in silence, only speaking to tell her not to get out at Cliveden. They were returning to London immediately.

Footmen carried their trunks to the car, loading them under Mr. May's direction. Miss Logan had packed their things after a telephone call from Aunt Anne from the infirmary.

Valerie leaned her forehead against the cool glass and looked up at the second floor of the house. Dinah stood at one of the windows watching her. Valerie raised her hand to her friend, who raised hers in return before Lady Astor, still dressed in her diamonds and evening gown, drew Dinah away from the window and yanked the curtain shut.

Valerie leaned back against the seat, Aunt Anne's soft voice as she thanked the Astors' butler and footman cutting through the loneliness and regret. She should've stayed at Blenheim. Instead, she'd gone off with Elm, chasing the folly of freedom that could never be real, and ruining everything because of it. Tears slid down her cheeks, the exhaustion of the night pulling at her until she drifted off, barely hearing Aunt Anne climb in beside her or the car start and set off for London.

"MAY I COME in?" Valerie peered around the door to Aunt Anne's room. The salmon-pink walls seemed darker beneath the lights of her lamps, the Louis XV furniture not sparkling so bright. She sat at her dressing table rubbing cream into her face while Miss Logan picked up her clothes.

It'd been three days since their return from Cliveden. Valerie had spent the better part of them in bed sleeping, reading, and worrying. She barely ate the food Mary brought up, she couldn't, not while wondering what was going to happen to her. Aunt Anne hadn't come to see her and every minute she expected Miss Logan to start packing her things for West Woodhay House or wherever Aunt Anne and Uncle Neville decided to banish her. Everyone must have heard the story by now and realized what her father,

mother, Mavis, and Mr. Shoedelin had, that she was flawed beyond redemption and not worthy of good society or love.

She perched on the edge of the claw-footed bench at the end of
Aunt Anne's bed and rubbed the itching stitches. She picked at a
loose thread on the bench, waiting to hear that she'd finally lost
the one person who'd always stood by her. It was too much like the
months she'd waited for some word from Father, a sign that he'd
heard she was suffering and would do something to help, but he
hadn't. This time she deserved exile.

"That will be all, Miss Logan." Aunt Anne turned on her stool,
drawing her dressing gown tighter around her shoulders. "How
are you feeling this evening?"

"Sore."

"That's to be expected. You're lucky. It could've been worse."

"Could it?" She hadn't heard anything from Their Excellencies
either, not a note or a phone call. She wasn't brave enough to ring
them, unable to bear the static on the silent phone lines or to have
a butler reject her call.

"The Number Ten press secretary and I have spoken with Lord
Beaverbrook and the other newspapermen. They've agreed to
keep the story of your accident out of the newspapers. However,
we can't stop it from spreading through society, and it will, especially since you had the bad luck of having Lady Simon discover
you. Whatever events you attend from here on out, people will
look at you very differently."

"I know." The clock on the mantel ticked loudly. "Perhaps I
should go to your town house in Birmingham. No one will notice
me there."

"Is that what you want?"

No. she wanted things to be the way they were before the accident, dishing delicious gossip over tea or at dances with Their Excellencies, but it'd never be like that again. *It's no use going back to yesterday, because I was a different person then.* She was Alice, except instead of Wonderland she was in hell. "Isn't that what you want me to do? Uncle Neville doesn't need my kind of trouble, and neither do you."

Aunt Anne rested one elbow on her dressing table and studied Valerie, her face, as always, a mask of calmness. Valerie braced herself, certain this would finally be the moment when Aunt Anne became like everyone else and shoved her away. "I won't pretend I'm not disappointed and that there won't be repercussions, but I suspect there's more to this than you've told me. I'll hear it now, if you please."

Valerie drew the dressing gown sash through her fingers, not wanting to tell her everything, but she deserved the truth, all of it. "The day before we left for Cliveden, I paid a call on my mother."

"I suspected as much."

"I wanted to see her, to know why she left."

"And?"

"She said the most vile things to me, that she never wanted me and I was an unfortunate side effect of marriage. How could she? How could anyone be so selfish or coldhearted?"

Aunt Anne twisted the gold wedding band on her finger. "She was young when she had you and I'm sure you're under no illusions about the sort of women Horace preferred. He needed her money and she wanted her freedom."

"But she wasn't free. She was my mother, and she should've loved me, stood by me, and not left."

"She didn't, and that's simply the way of things."

"Another lesson I have to learn from and carry on." She could practically hear Uncle Neville's words in her aunt's.

"I'm afraid so."

"What have I learned? That the one person who should've loved me the most didn't, that there's something ugly in me that drives people away, and it's only a matter of time before more leave, and all the inheritances in the world won't change that." Tears burned her eyes and slid down her cheeks.

Aunt Anne rose and came to sit beside her on the bench. "It's not your fault she left. Don't ever think it was."

"But you don't know who I really am, what I almost did." She twisted the sash tight around her finger, unable to look at her aunt sitting patiently beside her. She was tired of carrying the past and allowing it to determine everything. Aunt Anne might as well know how much Valerie deserved her scorn. Then maybe she'd finally be free of it and the other demons that'd tormented her for far too long. "When things in Ascain were at their worst, I went to see Mr. Shoedelin, hoping he could help. I told him what was wrong, how awful it was, but he didn't believe me. He wasn't going to help, and I didn't know what else to do. We were starving and cold, so I closed the door to his office and I asked him the question I used to hear the women in the alley outside the hotel ask the men at night. I didn't want to do it, but I was desperate, hungry. I thought if I gave him that, he might give me something, anything, in return."

"Did he accept your offer?"

"No." Valerie wiped her face with the sleeve of her wrap, waiting for horror to fill her aunt's face the way it had Mr. Shoedelin's. She should stop before her aunt ordered her from the house, but everything she'd held in for so long, the shame, anger, hurt, heartache, spilled out of her like her tears. "He recoiled from me as if I were the worst person in the world, but I wasn't. I didn't want to stoop so low, but I didn't have a choice, and that's when he finally believed me. He came to Ascain and saw how dreadful it was, the lice, the rats, no proper clothes, heat, or food. He saw what it was really like for us, for Father. He was the one who arranged the place at the convent school. Father didn't want to send me, he said they'd fill my head with all sorts of papist nonsense, but Mr. Shoedelin said I needed proper care before I became a lost cause. He didn't send me there because he wanted to help. He sent me there because he thought I was a fallen woman who deserved to be locked away, but I never did anything like that and I never would've asked him what I had if things hadn't been so bad."

Nothing in her life had made her feel more worthless and bereft of sympathy, love, and affection than that moment. She was an awful person, willing to trade her body for bread. No wonder the people who should've loved her most had scorned her. "What kind of woman does such a thing?"

"One who's in the most vile of circumstances." Aunt Anne wrapped her arms around her and pulled her close. Valerie clung to her, crying out a lifetime of despair, rejection, and pain.

"I'm so sorry, so sorry for all of it."

"It's not your fault. It's mine." She rubbed Valerie's back, her touch comforting and soft. "I should've come for you at once instead of waiting for your letter or believing Mr. Shoedelin that you were happy at school. I should've gone to France and seen things for myself instead of believing Horace or simply sending money. I should have insisted you remain with me and not allowed Horace to take you back after every holiday or when he wanted you in France. I should've told you about your mother years ago, but I thought it was the one ugly truth I could shield you from. I regret not trying harder to protect you from Horace's mistakes. I failed you, and I'm so sorry." Her aunt held her tight, her tears dropping onto Valerie's forehead.

"It's not your fault."

"What happened to you isn't yours. I loved my brother, but he was a weak man, and you paid the price for his mistakes."

Valerie clung to Aunt Anne, relief flooding through her as much as love. Her father and mother might be gone, but Aunt Anne would never leave her, she never had. "I'm so sorry about Cliveden and Elm. After the visit to Mother and what you told me about Uncle Neville, and the nasty way Vivien Mosley threw the convent in my face, I wanted to forget myself for a while, but I went too far and ruined everything."

Aunt Anne gently pushed her back, holding her by the shoulders. "No, you haven't."

"I have. Their Excellencies aren't likely to have anything to do with me, and even if they wanted to, their parents won't, Lady Astor certainly won't."

"There's someone who shouldn't be the first to cast stones. Leave her to me. As for your friends, if you give them a chance, they'll stand by you; not all of them, because that isn't how people are, but some of them. That's all you need, but you'll have to face them to find out."

Or she could leave London, but everyone would label her a coward as well as a tart if she did. She'd never be able to hold her head up again and everyone would believe whatever gossip they heard about her. If she stayed, they'd have to treat her as they did Lady Ravensdale and Lady Mosley and all their sordid affairs, and Valerie might claw back some of the respect she'd lost. It wouldn't be easy, but it was better than running away, and it would define her future more than anything else she'd done this Season. "You said cowardice was an awful trait you refused to instill in me."

"I did."

"Then I won't be a coward. I'll face my mistake and my friends."

VALERIE AND AUNT Anne stepped into the Bvlgari boutique, the cases of rings and necklaces sparkling beneath the showroom lights. Valerie recognized many of the matrons poring over the black trays of jewels offered up by the well-dressed jewelers. She'd been to dances, dinners, or cocktail parties at most of their homes during the Season. They all stopped shopping and stared at her the moment she and Aunt Anne entered.

Lady Windon, Elm's sister, was among them. She scowled at Valerie, her vitriol enough to melt diamonds. The rest were merely curious or frowned with disapproval as they watched Valerie and Aunt Anne approach the main counter. Valerie hadn't felt like running this much since her court presentation, but she kept walking, gaze forward, unwilling to let them cow her.

"Mr. Garrison, how kind of you to help us," Aunt Anne said to the balding man behind the counter.

"It's a pleasure to assist the Premier's wife." He said it a little louder than needed, reminding everyone who Aunt Anne was and that she wouldn't be snubbed, and by extension neither would her niece. That was another lesson Valerie had learned over these last few months. Lineage and position did trump almost everything else. "What can I show you today?"

Aunt Anne turned to Valerie, silently giving her the lead. Valerie swallowed hard, aware that everyone was watching and that Lady Windon had abandoned her shopping in the middle of a purchase to storm out the door. Not everyone would accept Valerie, but soon it wouldn't matter. There was a storm brewing in Europe that would sweep them all up in its furor, and little tiffs like this would pale in importance. Valerie smiled at the jewelry. "I'd like to see a collection of engravable gold charms."

The jeweler fetched a tray of shining gold disks while everyone around them went back to browsing. There were sure to be many more scenes like this in the coming weeks, but she was ready for them. With Aunt Anne behind her, she'd endure it, and hopefully with Their Excellencies by her side.

Chapter Twenty-Two

E unice, you came." Valerie hurried down the corridor to meet her friend. "You don't know how glad I am to see you or what this means to me."

She'd been sitting on pins and needles waiting for Their Excellencies to arrive for tea in the White Drawing Room. The invitations had been sent but she hadn't received a single reply, unless their silence was all the RSVP she was likely to get.

Eunice stood in the entrance hallway, a sailor hat perched on the back of her curled hair, her already wide blue eyes even wider with uncertainty. It slowed Valerie's steps.

"I can't stay. Mother will have a fit if she finds out I'm here. After those incidents with your stepmother and Lord Elmswood, she's dead set against our friendship, but I wanted to make sure you're all right."

"Fit as a fiddle." Her emotions were another matter. If she'd thought spending the Season waiting for war or her past to rise up had left her twisting in anticipation and uncertainty, it was nothing compared to waiting for this tea. It was maddening, but she had no choice. There was no other way to know where she stood with her friends. "How are you?"

"As well as can be expected. Father is making plans for us to return to America. We won't be in England much longer."

"Then it'll be off to university for you. How fun. You must write and tell me all about it."

"I can't."

"Of course." She didn't need to say more. It was in the twisting of her hands in front of her. She'd defy her mother to say farewell but nothing more, it wasn't her way. "I understand." No matter how much it hurt.

"I've enjoyed these last few months, they've been like nothing I've ever done before. You and Your Excellencies were grand." Her broad smile faded and she glanced at the door. "I wish I could stay."

"I know." Valerie slid a small velvet box out of her dress pocket and held it out to Eunice. "To remember us by."

"I can't."

"I insist." She pressed it into Eunice's gloved hands, receiving a gentle squeeze of encouragement in return.

"Thank you. I hope all turns out well for you, I genuinely do."

"It will, one way or another. Goodbye, Eunice, and good luck."

With one last smile, Eunice let go and hurried out to the waiting car before Henry closed the black-lacquered door behind her.

Valerie wrapped her arms around her, the house chilly despite the warm July morning. This didn't bode well for the rest of the day or what little remained of the Season.

"Don't take it personally," Marian said, coming up beside her, a pad and pencil with her as usual. "Ambassador Kennedy is in a right rage about war and in a panic to return to America, like a rat off a sinking ship."

"Are we really sunk?"

"Never. Bruised, maybe, but not defeated."

"No, we're not." Valerie motioned for Marian to walk with her to the Grand Staircase.

"I didn't mean to listen, but I couldn't help but overhear."

"I don't mind you eavesdropping." It was better than Mr. Colville scowling at her. Everyone in No. 10 had heard the story. A few of the puffed-up secretaries made their disapproval known with little tut-tuts here and there but Valerie ignored them. If Lady Mosley and Lady Ravensdale could appear in society after everything they'd done, then so could she. "I hope you don't hold what happened against me."

"How could I, after everything you've done for me?"

"It wasn't enough. I should've had you to tea, at the very least."

"We both know that's not possible."

"It is if we say it is. Will you join me at the soda fountain at Selfridges tomorrow for lunch?"

Marian chewed the end of her pencil, then stuck it behind her ear. "I'd be honored to."

She gave Valerie a quick hug, then hurried off down the stairs leading to the Garden Room.

No matter what happened today, Valerie would come out of this with at least one good friend.

She climbed the Grand Staircase and stepped into the quiet White Drawing Room. The lace on the round table in the center ruffled with the breeze coming in through the windows. The Spode china with the turquoise border from her grandmother's collection was laid out beside silver forks and the impressive silver tea service and plates of sandwiches and cakes.

"Eunice not staying?" Aunt Anne asked, searching the desk.

"No."

"Well, that's to be expected from some."

"Perhaps all."

Aunt Anne turned the cushions over on the sofa. "Don't lose faith quite yet."

Valerie slid her aunt's spectacles off the side table and held them out to her. "What do you know that you aren't telling me?"

"I paid a call on Lady Astor yesterday and we had a nice long chat." She set the spectacles on her nose, tucking the ends behind her ears. "I reminded her that we've all made mistakes in our youth and that we shouldn't be punished for them our entire lives. If we were, she'd still be married to Robert Gould Shaw instead of Lord Astor and a New York society hostess instead of an MP. She couldn't argue with that line of reasoning." With a little wave, she slipped out of the room, leaving hope in her wake.

What she should've left was patience. Valerie paced the White Drawing Room, sure there'd be a furrow in the rug by the time she was finished. She was about to ring for Mr. Dobson to take the food downstairs to the secretaries when Dinah, Katherine, and Christian filed into the room. No one rushed to hug or gush about how glad they were to see each other. Instead, they stood across the table from her, silent as if at a wake. It was preferable to them not coming at all. With the tea growing cold and her so excited that they were here, she wasn't about to let them leave, not yet, not until she'd said her piece.

"All right, Your Excellencies, I've been an awful fool and I'm sorry. I hope you'll stay, but I understand if you leave and never have anything to do with me ever again. Either way, I want you to have these to remember me and our Season by."

She plucked up the three velvet boxes on the table and stuffed them into their gloved hands. They exchanged surprised looks, the cat still holding their tongues until they opened the boxes.

"Good heavens!" Katherine exclaimed.

They each removed the gold charms on their delicate chain to reveal *Their Excellencies* engraved on the front and all of their first names in fine script on the back. Beside it was a small gold fork charm to remind them of the Buckingham Palace ones they'd stolen what seemed like years ago.

"Thank you for everything you've done for me this Season. I was quite alone when I came to London, but you were so friendly when everyone else was nasty and mean. I'll never forget what good friends you were to me, all of you. I'm sorry I bitched it up, and I know your parents and such will have a great deal to say about whether or not you'll have anything further to do with me, but if you could forgive me, if we could carry on as we were, it'd be ever so grand." She clutched the back of the chair in front of her, digging her fingernails into the antique wood while she waited for them to say something, anything.

They looked at one another as if they'd talked a great deal in the car, but none of them was brave enough to repeat it here. Valerie braced for more reasons why the rest of her friends had to fob her off the way Eunice had. She'd done her best. It was up to them now.

Then Dinah broke into a smile that spread across Katherine's and Christian's faces. "We aren't going anywhere, Your Excellency."

They rushed at her, throwing their arms around her in a large hug, all of them crying and laughing as the chain of Dinah's charm snagged Valerie's jumper and Katherine's tangled in Christian's hair. When all the gold was free of hat pins and buttons, the girls slipped them around their necks.

"You didn't really think we were going to abandon you?" Dinah straightened her necklace against her pale pink blouse. "Did you?"

"I didn't know what to think, especially with your aunt drawing the curtains on me."

"Oh, she climbed on her high horse, but your aunt pulled her right off of it."

"Everyone is talking about the wreck." Christian laid the charm over the top of the bow in her front collar. "You're more popular than when you told off Vivien."

"Come off it, I can't be. The matrons at Bvlgari scowled at me."

"No one gives a fig for what they think, not with all the chaps and debs taken with you," Katherine said. "The charms are gorgeous."

"Only the best for you lot." She took Dinah's and Christian's hands, Katherine stepping in to complete the circle. "All the times you listened to me or stood beside me. You have no idea what it's meant to me."

"I think we do, especially when you let us carry on about our troubles and never judged us or made us feel bad," Dinah said. "We need each other as much to face all the ridiculousness of society as whatever is waiting for us at the end of the Season. We'll always be there for one another, won't we, girls?"

Valerie squeezed her and Christian's hands. "We will."

They'd seen her at her worst and still believed the best of her. No matter what happened, they'd be together to face it, to encourage and hold up one another while offering shoulders to cry on. It was more than she ever could've asked or hoped for and she'd never take it for granted or risk losing this again.

Chapter Twenty-Three

September 3, 1939

J am speaking to you from the Cabinet Room at Ten Downing Street. This morning the British Ambassador in Berlin handed the German government a final note stating that unless we heard from them by eleven o'clock that they were prepared at once to withdraw their troops from Poland, a state of war would exist between us. I have to tell you now that no such undertaking has been received, and that consequently this country is at war with Germany."

Muffled tears from the few Garden Room Girls watching in the back of the Cabinet Room were barely audible under Uncle Neville's somber voice. He sat at the end of the long table, a microphone in front of him, the BBC radio men and their equipment off to one side. Aunt Anne stood stoically beside Valerie, discreetly touching her eyes with her handkerchief. Valerie didn't dare look at her for fear of bursting into tears. The horror Uncle Neville had worked so hard to spare them from had finally fallen on England. People looked to them to set the tone and they must be strong for him and the country. She glanced behind her to where Marian watched with the secretaries and ministers, as brokenhearted as Valerie.

"We have done all that any country could do to establish peace," Uncle Neville continued, crushing disappointment undermining his dignified voice. "But the situation in which no word given by Germany's ruler could be trusted, and no people or country could feel itself safe, had become intolerable. And now that we have re-solved to finish it, I know that you will all play your part with calmness and courage."

The light on the table in front of him went out and the room was engulfed in an onerous silence.

They were at war.

Uncle Neville rose. Heads turned to follow him as he walked through the gathered officials and ministers in distinguished de-feat. No one said anything as he left, his slender body silhouetted by the light from the hallway. Mr. Colville, Sir John, and the govern-ment gentlemen studied their feet or exchanged looks laden with shame. They should go after him, support him, give him the cour-age to fight on and face this as he'd inspired them to do since Mu-nich. Instead they left him to walk the hallway carrying this alone.

Valerie rushed out to follow him. "Uncle Neville?"

He turned and faced her, the sadness in his eyes making her halt. "I failed, Valerie, you and England."

"It's not your fault." She threw her arms around his thin waist and held him tight. "You did everything you could."

He raised his arm to embrace her, resting his cheek on her head. "It wasn't enough."

"But you tried. That's more than most others have done." Especially Father, her mother, and all the other disappointing people who'd never been there for her. They no longer mattered. Their selfishness and shortcomings had made her face hers and given her the strength to endure difficulties instead of crumbling beneath them, exactly as Uncle Neville would do.

He held her at arm's length, the fatherly gaze she adored replacing the heavy weight of the world in his eyes. "Your faith means a great deal to me."

As his and Aunt Anne's did to her. It didn't matter what all the rest had done. They'd helped her and forgiven her and it'd made all the difference.

"A GENTLEMAN FROM the War Office is asking for you, Miss de Vere Cole," one of the new secretaries said as Valerie came downstairs. She was on her way to tea with Their Excellencies to celebrate Christian starting work at the Halifax bomber factory in Cricklewood next week. Dinah was training to drive mobile canteens, while Katherine had joined the Red Cross.

"Who is it?" There wasn't anyone there in need of her. It'd been two weeks since the declaration of war, and everyone still held their breath waiting for things to begin. The "Phony War," they were calling it, but no one expected the lull to last. There'd be fighting and destruction and hardship, and all they could do in the meantime was prepare for it.

"I don't know." He hurried off, another of the new staff members who'd flooded into Downing Street over the last week. There were so many, it was difficult to learn their names.

Valerie stepped into the entrance hall, coming up short at the sight of Elm. "What are you doing here?"

She hadn't seen him or Richard since the night of the accident. It'd seemed best to leave all that nasty business behind her, no matter how much she missed their charm and wit.

"I'm working at the War Office and had some letters to deliver. I wonder if you'd walk out with me for a moment." He turned his hat in his hands, his right arm hindered by a sling.

"I'd like that."

They stepped outside, blinking at the bright September sunshine as they strolled along the pavement away from Whitehall where the usual crowd gathered. It wasn't policemen holding them back but soldiers in their drab uniforms. Valerie instructed Mr. May to wait for her. She'd only be a few minutes before she needed him to drive her to Selfridges. Despite weekly lessons with the chauffer, she still wasn't confident enough to manage the hectic London streets alone.

"What are you doing at the War Office?"

"Intelligence work. I had to resign my commission in the Coldstream Guards. I'm not likely to see active service with this injury."

"I'm sorry."

"Don't be, it's my fault. I should've known better that night."

He played with the fraying edge of the sling. "I miss my regiment and regret having to give it up, but I enjoy the work at the War Office and the chance to do my part. They say I could have quite a career there, a future. It's more than I thought I'd have before." He stopped and faced her. "I'm sorry for what happened, all of it. My family has expectations for me. Mother had spoken to Lady Ravensdale before the party, something about you and France. She'd told me before I left for Cliveden that I wasn't to see you again. I was mad at her and the world. I shouldn't have caught you up in it, but dealt with it like a man. If things had been different . . ."

"But they weren't." It stung that he hadn't been willing to fight for her, but in the end it was for the best. Dinah had said he was too involved with himself to care about anyone else, but he'd cared enough for her to not lead her on when he'd known there couldn't be anything between them. Even if his parents hadn't objected, the Season was one of the few things they'd had in common. It wasn't a strong enough bond to have weathered the fury of his parents or the weight of his lineage. She'd enjoyed his company, but it was the title, rank, and attention that had dazzled her the most. Not the stuff of a solid and enduring union.

"The Season feels like a different world." He motioned to the Royal Army men piling sandbags in front of the buildings.

"It does, but I'm glad we had the chance to enjoy it, and to get to know one another. I wish you well, Elm."

"Do you really?"

"Yes."

He pressed a tender kiss to her cheek, then turned and headed back to Whitehall before pausing. "Richard is posted at the Queen Alexandra Military Hospital. He'd love to see you."

He hadn't called or written after the accident; she hadn't expected him to. The disappointment on his face at the Oxford infirmary had said enough, until today. "Do you really think so?"

"I do."

"SOMEONE SAID A woman from the Personal Service League is here to see me," Richard said to the soldier manning the front desk. The man pointed to Valerie and she braced herself, waiting for him to march right back to where he'd come from.

"I hope you don't mind my using my credentials to summon you."

"It wouldn't be the first time, would it?" He approached as cautiously as she did, the two of them meeting in the middle of the airy Victorian entrance hall. His olive-green uniform with the caduceus embroidered on the collars and his short-brimmed cap was far more dashing than the formal one he'd worn the last time she'd seen him. She tucked her hair behind her ear, surprised by the heat flooding through her, and not at all sure how to proceed but unwilling to scurry away like a scared mouse. She'd determined to come here, and whatever his reaction, she'd see it through. "I'm sorry about the night at Blenheim. The days before it weren't easy for me and I quite lost my head."

"If someone I loved had been given a dire diagnosis, I might have lost mine too. How is your uncle?"

"As you might expect, with everything that's happened."

"And the cancer?"

She didn't deny it, confident he'd keep this secret along with the petty few others that'd seemed so important during the Season. "We don't know yet, but the doctors are hopeful."

Limbo again, but it didn't scare her as much as before. There were too many things in the present to cherish to allow worries about yesterday or tomorrow to steal her joy, including Richard not recoiling from her. "Are you enjoying your new posting?"

"The discipline of an army-run hospital takes some getting used to, but it's to be expected. *Discipline is the soul of an army. It makes small numbers formidable; procures success to the weak, and esteem to all.*"

"Napoleon?"

"George Washington." He motioned to her uniform. "I see you've been busy since we last met."

She tugged straight the front of her khaki Personal Service League jacket over the matching skirt. "I help decide what supplies are most urgently needed where, and I'm smashing at it. Hours of writing thank-you notes during the Season gave me the patience of a saint to sit and answer the hundreds of requests we receive from hospitals." If Dorothy ever got over her snit and spoke to her, she'd be sure to tell her and offer that little olive branch. She still couldn't stand her cousin, but for Uncle Neville and Aunt Anne's benefit, she'd find some way to call a truce.

"I'm glad you're doing well there and that you're happy."

"As much as anyone can be at present. Elm paid me a visit today." This faded his smile. "He apologized and told me to come see you. I'm glad he did. I've missed you."

"Have you?"

"No one can imitate a chestnut tree quite like you."

He threw back his head and laughed, drawing a frown from the front desk clerk before he sobered. "One of my many unsung talents."

"Along with helping me to see things differently. It's made a great deal of difference." She fingered the gold fork and disk on her necklace, quite through with all this seriousness. "I've been told an army marches on its stomach. I hate to think of you starving from a lack of dances, therefore you must come to dinner at Number Ten."

"It'd be an honor and a privilege." He took her hand and bowed over it, eyeing her from beneath his cap brim as he pressed his lips to her skin. She drew in a sharp breath, her fingers tightening around his. Then he stood, holding her hand for a moment before he let go. Here was reality, not the fantasy of a title or the Season.

With a wink, he left to return to his duties.

She strolled out of the hospital's white-brick entrance, rubbing her hand in giddy excitement where Richard's lips had touched it. She crossed the small drive, passing the military trucks parked along it to reach the Rolls idling beyond the red-brick wall. Six months, and her entire world had changed. She had no idea what the future held, but whatever waited for her or England, she'd face it with the poise expected of the Prime Minister's debutante niece.

About the author

About the book

Insights,
Interviews
& More . . .

Meet Georgie Blalock

Courtesy of the author

GEORGIE BLALOCK is a history lover and movie buff who enjoys combining her different passions through historical fiction and a healthy dose of period films. When not writing, she can be found prowling the nonfiction history section of the library or the British film listings on Netflix. Georgie writes historical romance under the name Georgie Lee. Please visit georgieblalock.com for more information about Georgie and her writing. ∿

Behind the Book

I was fascinated when I read about
Neville Chamberlain's niece being a
debutante during the last London
Season before World War II. I dove
into my research, ready to discover
more about this young woman at the
heart of politics and society during such
a historic time. What surprised me
was the lack of information on Valerie,
especially her time in No. 10 Downing
Street. Valerie left no published
autobiographies or journals about her
life with her aunt and uncle. After the
Chamberlains left No. 10 in May 1940,
and Neville died of stomach cancer on
November 9, 1940, Valerie faded from
public view, appearing here and there
in newspaper articles over the years
and occasionally in Chamberlain family
correspondence. There is a tantalizingly
brief mention of Valerie's involvement
with an unsuitable gentleman in
a letter between Aunt Anne and
Great-Aunt Lillian but nothing more.
Her relationships in the novel, like
the characters of Richard and Elm,
are fictional, as are many of the novel's
details about her life and Season.
However, British high society was
very intertwined, with everyone
connected to everyone else in one
way or another, so it is possible that
Valerie, Katherine, Dinah, Eunice, ▶

Behind the Book *(continued)*

and Christian might have known one another.

Valerie's stepmother and mother are interesting figures as well. Mavis continued to enjoy notoriety from her connection to Augustus John. The nude drawing of her mentioned in the novel is real, but it was not displayed at the 1939 Royal Academy Summer Exhibit. After she cheated on Mortimer Wheeler, who is also a fascinating and scandalous character, he and Mavis divorced in 1942. In 1954, she was found guilty of shooting her lover Lord Vivian and served time in jail. Lord Vivian survived the attack. Mrs. Winterbotham, Valerie's mother, also faced the court, but it was bankruptcy court. In October 1939, she was before a judge for failing to pay bills because the money from her trust had run out. After that, she, like Valerie, faded from the spotlight.

Katherine, Dinah, Christian, Eunice, and Marian lived long and interesting lives. Katherine married Maurice Macmillan, son of Prime Minister Harold Macmillan. She was heavily involved in politics and became a Dame Commander of the British Empire. Christian went on to write her memoirs of her childhood in Scotland and numerous magazine articles. She cycled across America and married three times, divorcing her first husband, widowed by her second, before meeting her third. Like Valerie, Dinah faded from public view, marrying twice and providing only brief glimpses of her life after 1939 through books about Lady Astor. Eunice became an advocate for disabled children and founded the Special Olympics. She married Sargent Shriver, an Ambassador to France and a vice presidential nominee. Their daughter is Maria Shriver. Marian Holmes began working at Downing Street in 1938, so it is likely that she and Valerie were acquainted. Marian continued on under Winston Churchill, often privy to very private or historic moments during the darkest days of World War II. She remained at No. 10 until her marriage in 1957, and earned the Member of the Order of the British Empire for her work on behalf of prime ministers and Queen Elizabeth.

The debutante Season has a long history stretching back to the 1780s. It faded during World War I before roaring back to life in the 1920s and 1930s. King Edward VIII's brief reign saw the court presentation replaced with a disappointing garden party before King George VI resumed the evening palace presentations. War muted the 1940 debutante Season before the practice was suspended for the duration of the conflict. Although the Season resumed after the war, it would never ▶

be what it had been in the 1930s. Debutante presentations to the monarch officially ended in 1958, but one tradition continued, the Queen Charlotte's Birthday Ball.

The Queen Charlotte's Birthday Ball began in 1780 in honor of King George III's wife, Queen Charlotte. Debutantes curtseyed to the Queen, who stood beside the birthday cake, establishing the association between the Queen and the cake. After 1809, money raised from the ball funded the Queen Charlotte Maternity Hospital, one of the oldest in London and still in existence today as the Queen Charlotte's and Chelsea Hospital. The ball continued, and after Queen Charlotte's death, one of her descendants would serve as the ball's namesake. The ball survived World War II, becoming the unofficial stand-in for court presentations. After World War II, the ball resumed even as the practice of coming out faded away. When court presentations ended in 1958, the Queen Charlotte's Birthday Ball remained as the official coming-out event for debutantes, lasting until 1978. The ball has recently been reinvented with a more modern spin.

For those curious about the history, I altered the timeline of Valerie's stay in Downing Street to fit the needs of the story. She actually lived with the Chamberlains from her father's death in February 1936 until Neville Chamberlain left office in 1940. She was first at No. 11 Downing Street when Neville Chamberlain was Chancellor of the Exchequer, and she moved with her aunt and uncle to No. 10 when Neville became Prime Minister in 1937. The names of the drawing rooms in No. 10 in the story are different from today because those rooms are traditionally named after their wall colors, which were different in 1939. While Neville Chamberlain's declaration of war speech is accurate, his radio address on Tientsin in the novel is a compilation of remarks he made to the House of Commons during the crisis. Thank you for reading the novel and learning more about the debutantes and their last glittering Season. I hope you enjoyed *The Last Debutantes* as much as I enjoyed writing it! ∽

Reading Group Guide

1. A theme running through the novel is to "learn from and carry on." In what ways does Valerie learn and carry on? Keeping a stiff upper lip is considered a classic trait for the people of Great Britain. How do you think this helped and hindered them during the war?

2. Valerie and her friends seem to be dancing in the face of upcoming sorrow. Do you think they behaved well, badly, or that they did what young people of any generation would do?

3. What do you think of the idea of debutantes? Is it something fun, or an antiquated way of sending women out into the world?

4. Did this novel change your viewpoint on Neville Chamberlain? Was he in denial about Hitler's rise, or was he trying desperately to avert another war?

5. Were you surprised at how many of the aristocracy seemed to agree with the rise of fascism, even if they may not have liked the idea of Adolf Hitler?

6. Valerie grows to believe that lineage and position trump everything else. Is she right in her viewpoint? Do you think this remains the way things are? Why or why not?

7. During this time, young women like Valerie, Eunice Kennedy, and Dinah, Lady Astor's niece, were dismissed when they tried to become more involved in politics. Given the roles—albeit some behind the scenes—that their relatives play in politics, why do you think this hypocrisy persisted?

8. Valerie's mother gives her up in a quest for freedom. Is there any part of you that feels sympathy for the situation her mother had in her life?

9. Valerie becomes friendly with one of the secretaries, Marian. Who do you feel has the more fascinating life, and why?

10. Does Valerie learn and grow in significant ways during her Season? Or is her biggest growth yet to come? ⮌